Testimony

Lord of Night

Book One

Joshua King

Dedication

For Derek, who is the light of my life, all my colors, and the most impressive person I've ever known. Thank you your daily battles to convince me that playing pretend can actually be productive.

For Mom and Dad, who won't give up on me, despite my best efforts.
For Jamie and Nick, who've already read this book more than anyone else ever will.
For the Order of the Opal Lion: Alek, Danielle, Dion, Jamie, Noreen, SnowBlueHusky, and Tarah.

Author's Note

This novel contains content that may be triggering to some readers, including:

Terminal illness, bullying, graphic violence and gore, discrimination (including ableism, fictionalized racism, and homophobia), sexual harassment of a minor, substance use, gun violence, war, and hospitalization.

Pronunciation Guide

Characters

Aar'nor	AR-NOHR
Achaera'fra	Uh-HAYR-uh-frah
Aea'trox	AY-uh-TROX
Aur'kura	AR-KOO-ruh
Cah'dal	KUH-DAHL
Calan'riss	CAL-en-riss
E'e	EE-ay
Falax'hebos	FAL-uhx-EE-bos
Fus'ybir	FOOS-ee-BEER
Hah'dran	HUH-DRAHN
Istur'riss	ISS-ter-riss
Jury	JOO-ree
Kah'riss	KAH-riss
Kai'mul	KIE-mool
Kiln'aren	Kil-NAHR-en
Kraer	KRAY-ayr
Mal'karos	MAHL-KAH-rohs
Nadd'ilres	NAD-ILL-ress
Nall'ilres	NAHL-ILL-ress
Ona'var	OH-nuh-VAR
Ons'erak	AHNCE-AYR-ek
Pol	PAHL
Rae'vel	RAY-VELL
Rhoska'khenti	RAHS-kuh-KENT-ee
Sala'hai	SAH-LAH-hai
Sark'riss	SAHRK-riss
Shin'ade	Shih-NAH-day
Sol'taris	SOHL-TAH-riss
Sorna'li	SOHR-nuh-lee

Thurv'riss	THERV-riss
Um'therren	OOM-THAYR-en
Xsoran	SHOHR-uhn

Locations

Aethion	AY-thee-ahn
Aurum	AR-oom
Caraby	KAYR-uh-bee
Chiod	CHEE-ahd
Odaial	OH-DIE-all
Pinto'Neth	PIN-toh-NETH
Rae'gal	RAY-GAL
Sozen	SOH-zen
Ty'gjir	Tie-ZHEER

Testimony

—Table of Contents—

————⟨⟩————

Prologue	1
Recollection I	3
Recollection II	16
Recollection III	36
Recollection IV	67
Recollection V	104
Recollection VI	120
Recollection VII	133
Recollection VIII	156
Recollection IX	200
Recollection X	241
Recollection XI	277
Recollection XII	303
Recollection XIII	319
Acknowledgments	336

Prologue

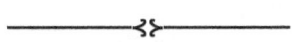

A thread of smoke wandered lazily above his head, the heat drifting away from his lips striking a harsh contrast to the cool of the durasteel against his back. Dangling his boots over the dizzying edge of the utilities tower, he could take in all the city for kilometers around. From the pulsing whine of the busy skylanes to the mechanical hum of the hundreds of meters of machinery below, distraction abounded. The shiver-stick helped. It helped him focus only on what he wanted to, and wasn't too bad for passing the time, either. He took a deep drag and held it in his lungs, allowing the cool tingle spread to his fingertips before he breathed out, coloring the smoggy sky with more glittering smoke. Nothing could happen for hours still and he would be content to spend the time up here, alone.

It was not to be.

Far below, one of the tower doors slid open, sending an automated alert to his communicator. Sitting up, he pulled the rest of the shiver-stick into his mouth and ground the grains between his teeth. The rush of accelerant hit him like a splash of ice-cold water, forcing him to blink, to sharpen his focus. On the tower's ground floor, a small train of hooded figures exited the tower through an alleyway, walking with haste toward a series of unassuming transports waiting on the street beyond. Scanning all possible vantage points of the alley, he made note of every balcony, window, and fire escape, every hovering transport, stopped auto, and sleeping transient. They were almost in the clear. Nothing had tampered with the transports while they were inside, and the drivers opened the doors, ushering them within. Nothing yet.

Movement.

The window of an overlooking apartment cracked open. His eyes narrowed as a metal tube protruded, bit by bit, through the open portal, followed by a hand, an arm, a face. A face he knew very well.

"Shit," he sighed. And, with the shiver rushing through his system, he aimed down the rails of his rifle and pulled the trigger.

I

"No. You are getting ahead of yourself. Let us begin with your earliest memory and go from there."

My earliest memory? Why?

"We want to know you. All about you."

About me? Not about —

"Take your time and, please, be honest. This is part of the evaluation."

Kah'riss reached out tiny hands to search for his father's face. His fingers traced the hard lines scored into it, already weathered and beaten like a man twice his age, and nearly invaded deep-set eyes bounded by sharp cheekbones straining against taut skin and coarse fur. Dignified. Running his hands down the face, Kah felt the powerful jaw muscles which were common among their kind, then trailed to the end of his father's nose and pulled his whiskers, drawing the barest tick of a grin from Sark'riss.

"What're you hoping to find, boy?"

The voice crunched and rasped its way out of his father's throat, its deep rumble vibrating Kah's entire world, masking the dull thuds and hisses which escaped the child's attention. Too young to speak, Kah giggled and grasped the long fangs he discovered when Sark opened his mouth and the older man broke into a toothy smile, pulling his son into his lap and directing his small ears toward the ring.

"Listen, Kah. Hear how they move—how the air shifts around them. Listen for any misstep, any advantage you can find." The rasping voice caught for just a moment. "You'll need it."

Kah heard Sark choke and shake, trying to stifle deep, wracking coughs which Kah, even as an infant, knew to be characteristic of his father. Through the awful sound, he strained to hear his brothers on the other side of the room, the three boys fighting each other in a brutal melee as Kah looked on with wide, unseeing eyes.

He listened—for years, in absolute darkness, for any advantage he could find.

Kah's childhood flowed as a river of shadow, with only the sharpest sensations to break the surface of his memory. An acrid stench of fuel and sweat his father tracked home from the nordium mines. The shout of a peacekeeper, ringing in his ears. Sweltering heat, jostled amongst an education shift of over a hundred young Ty'gjir. Tinny horn music crackling through every loudspeaker in the habitation cells, jubilantly declaring the coronation of Prince Cah'dal as ruler of the Dal Territory. The shriek of Pinto'Neth, the world outside the H-cells, deafening even through the airlocks. Pain.

He learned quickly and well the hollow coldness of an empty stomach, the ache of overused muscles, the sting of overstretched joints, and the impact of his brothers' fists against his body. Equally well, he marked his brothers' innocent softness as they held him while he wept, and while their father observed.

Born and raised on Pinto'Neth, Sark took after his father, and his father's father, and so on, back to the original colonizers. He was a miner of Pinto'Neth's sole precious resource, nordium—a uniquely strong, lightweight, and radiation-resistant metal valued the empire-over for its usefulness in building reactor core shielding and heavy armaments for spacecraft. While valuable, however, its extraction was not without hazard—well attested by Sark's lifelong and rapidly worsening cough, the same shared by most of Pinto'Neth's miners. *Unlike* his father, Sark'riss would not doom his sons to a half-life in the mines. He would get them off-world, but without the means to emigrate, the likeliest path out was through the house fleet of the sector's baron, Mal'karos.

"Listen, boy," Sark roared as Kah sparred with the youngest of his older brothers, Calan. "You have to be sharper than this. No matter how quiet your opponent may be, his feet still impact the ground, his moves still cut the air, his—" He broke off into a bout of wretched coughing, muddying the air with obfuscating noise.

Two quick, hard impacts struck Kah's flanks and he spun around, hoping to catch his brother with a sweeping kick, but there was nothing to catch. An instant later, a low vibration rippled through the warm, blood-slicked floor.

Calan might be able to silence his voice and breathing while they fought, but he couldn't prevent his weight from shaking the floor as he darted around the ring. Kah lunged for the source of the impact, hoping to find Calan before he could cement his balance. Instead, stars exploded in his blind eyes as his brother's knee met his chin—a flash of brilliance before the world returned to darkness.

It was not unheard of for a Pintoth to be born without the ability to see infrared light, that scant radiation emitted by Neth, the namesake of Kah's star system. A thousand generations of colonization on Pinto'Neth had armed the overwhelming majority of Pintoth with infrared sight and, to save on an expense deemed unnecessary, the planetary administrators had forsworn traditional forms of artificial light, leaving those without infrared vision in utter darkness. Specialized eyewear could circumvent the problem, but its prohibitive expense rendered the notion a distant dream for a common mining family.

Besides, it was better to overcome one's weakness than to mask it, Sark'riss often claimed—an encouragement that warped to obsession in the face of Kah's limits.

"Are you okay, Kah?" Blinking awake to familiar darkness, Kah heard Calan's voice from somewhere above him, and ragged breaths deeper in the shadows. Hands grasped either side of his face, gently turning his head left and right. "I'm sorry! I didn't mean to hit you that hard. You almost got me. It surprised me."

Sliding a hand down Kah's arm, Calan grasped Kah by the hand and began to pull him to his feet, until their father cried out, "You have him, boy! Strike!"

Startled to action, Kah extended his claws, digging them into the soft flesh under his brother's fur. Yelping, Calan instinctively pulled his arm away, tearing it out of Kah's grasp even as it dragged him to his feet, still panting and searching about, fear plain on his wide-eyed features.

"Da, he used his claws!" Calan hissed through clenched teeth.

It was enough to provide Kah a fix on his brother's position, listening to the sharp intake of breath and to the gentle tap of blood dropping to the floor. He was too scared to press the attack, however, and he had just broken the rules.

"Do you think the enemies of Mal'karos will care about rules when they're shoving a knife between your ribs or throwing a grenade into your bunk?" Sark shouted, spitting a blood-scented mist across the ring. "You use *every* tool at your disposal to survive. If you run out of ammo, use a knife. If they take away your knife, use your claws. If they lean in while you're bound and defeated, tear out their throats with your teeth! The fight is not over while your enemy is still *breathing*." Sark's voice caught and shattered before Kah sensed a hard impact that he knew well—his father had fallen to his knees, gasping for air.

"Da!"

Kah heard three pairs of paws pounding across the floor to their father. A *pop*, as Thurv opened the cap of a breather, followed by the hiss of aerosolized medicine as Sark's retching subsided. He heard his brothers guiding Sark through slow, deep breaths. He *also* heard the tap of blood from Calan's wound continue to fall to the floor.

He could *smell* it. Clear and fresh over the sweat, and the sulfurous smell his father carried home from the mines, and the sour tang of Sark's medicine. Two meters ahead, off the edge of the ring, slightly to the left—Calan would be just in front of Sark, where six, near simultaneous impacts told him his brothers were all on their knees with their father.

One paw slipping in a warm puddle as he approached, Kah found Calan exactly where he expected him to be. He reached out, running his hand down the damp fur of his older brother's head, to his neck. Calan's tail swayed gently, unwarily, back and forth against Kah's legs. Calm, breathing deeply, he locked his arm around Calan's neck and squeezed, dropping his weight and dragging them both head over heels. Trying to block out everything else, Kah screwed his eyes shut. His brother was flailing desperately, trying to break the stranglehold. Calan would be crying out, but Kah would not allow any air to pass through his throat. He felt other hands trying to pull his arm loose and start striking him about the head and face, but he refused to loosen his grip. The fight was not over.

Something like light burst once again in his empty vision, and everything went quiet.

Kah didn't know how long it took him to wake up. He couldn't hear much above the ringing in his ears. He couldn't see anything, but then, that wasn't new. All he could smell was stale blood. But there was something—a cool, rough hand placing a frigid compress over his brow, saturated thickly with some cold liquid that ran freely down his temples. A shiver woke the rest of his body to the awareness that a great deal of him was covered in similar dressings. When the hand touched his face again, Kah registered calluses as thick as his father's on a hand much smaller, and knew it belonged to his eldest brother, Thurv.

"Welcome back." Kah could tell from the tone that Thurv was frowning—Kah's family often said Thurv could win awards for his frowning—but, as Thurv gingerly daubed his forehead, he reminded himself that the frown was most often born out of concern for Kah himself. "You okay?"

Kah worked his jaw a little before replying, "Yeah, I think I'm fine. What hit me?"

"Da did," Thurv said. "He wants to talk to you. He's—" Tightness throttled whatever words he'd planned to offer Kah to explain what they'd all known was coming for a long time. "He's not doing well. You should go see him as soon as you can walk."

Giving Kah a hesitant pat, Thurv rose to walk out of the room, but Kah snatched his hand.

"Please, help me," Kah pleaded, his throat suddenly dry.

"You just woke up. Are you sure? You really should try to rest." Thurv's voice assumed an admonishing, paternal tone. He'd been using it more and more with his brothers lately. Kah didn't want to think about why. But despite Thurv's warning, Kah began to pull himself to his feet, drawing a resigned sigh from his older brother.

Thurv allowed Kah a single stumble before he lifted his youngest brother into his arms, trying to hold him steady. Still, cool air buffeted against Kah's ears as Thurv carried him through the cold, familiar halls of the H-cell to his father's room. He could hear Sark's wheezing long before they reached the door. Placing a hand on Thurv's arm to stop him, Kah carefully dismounted his brother's arms and adjusted the bandage covering the lump above his eye, wincing at the sharp sting. With a deep breath, he tightened his bandages and knocked on the door.

"Come in," came a weak, haggard reply.

Kah slid the door open and entered. There were three Ty'gjir breathing inside—his father's familiar, crunching rasps, as well as two more who managed only short, halting breaths—his brothers, he was left to assume, as he could neither hear nor smell them clearly enough to be certain. Knowing Sark would be lying in bed, Kah puffed his chest and parted from Thurv on the back of deliberately brave strides. Before he felt his belly bump into the mattress, however, his father's strong hand grasped his own. Encircling his shoulders, Kah felt a smaller arm pull him into a seat beside the bed. He recognized Calan's touch and huddled close to his older brother, still holding his father.

"S-sorry about before, Calan." Kah turned his eyes apologetically toward where he imagined his brother's face might be. Despite his confident, brave entrance, it was altogether more difficult to mask his grief while he spoke.

In answer, Calan merely wrapped his other arm around Kah's shoulders and squeezed him, shushing him. Burying his face against his brother's chest, Kah easily heard the breath catching within. Behind them, Thurv's feet padded across the room before he sat between Istur and Calan, putting a comforting hand on each. Together, the brothers gave their father their complete attention. There were few words left to say.

A short cough and a quick, gasping breath heralded Sark's words. "Istur, there's a box under the bed. Give it to Kah, please."

Istur leapt to attention and crawled under the bed, a small sound of awe preceding his return. Cocking his head, Kah listened, hearing Istur's fingers drag over what sounded like a mostly empty plastic box. Despite the modest auditory footprint, however, Kah's brothers gasped as Istur placed the box in his lap.

"Kah," Sark said. "It's been a long time coming, and here I made you wait even longer, thinking I'd give it to you on your tenth birthday. But I—I don't want to wait anymore."

Kah could tell by his voice that his father wore a rueful smirk, at least until a sudden bout of hacking twisted his face with pain and perfumed the air with blood. Tears sprang to Kah's blind eyes as he gripped the box tightly, desperately. Eventually, Sark's breathing returned to his frail, wracking baseline while his sons waited, silent and helpless. Kah heard his father move his arm off the bed. He felt the shift in the air as he waved his hand twice.

"Come on, boy. We're all eager to see it."

With a swift nod, Kah stroked his fingers over the gift. There was no wrapping paper or ornamentation, just rough, stippled plastic bearing the faintest rise where ink was printed on the box. Unwilling to spoil the surprise, he restrained himself from tracing the lettering of the label and grabbed the latch. A firm tug unsealed the package and Kah quickly dove his hands into the shipping plaster, burrowing through soft, squishy beads to hunt down his quarry.

Something narrow in profile—hard, cold, and metallic on one side, yet soft and cushioned on the other, brushed against his fingers. It bore a recognizable suite of straps and buttons and dials but, whatever the object was, he'd never touched one before. Perhaps impatient, Calan took the thing from his hands and guided it to Kah's face. Something went over his ears and across the back of his head, then the cushioned part of it tightened over his eyes. Soon, all three of his brothers joined in, fiddling with the device on Kah's head. There was a *click,* and Kah was very suddenly acquainted with the concept of brightness.

Hissing in distress, he shut his untrained eyes against the light, but an aggressive, persistent heat still shone through his eyelids, silhouetting blood vessels which webbed under the thin flesh. Little by little, Kah's discomfort lessened until, finally, he grew accustomed to the intruding glow and risked a peek, witnessing shape and light for the first time.

A gentle pulse emanated from somewhere behind his vision and outlined the world around him, allowing for distance and depth, but defining the unforgiving geometry of the room by gradients of heat. What most captured Kah's attention, however, were the white, glowing shapes of his family members, who, until now, had been faceless voices. His huddled brothers shone so brightly that he had to blink away the pain, desperate to see the family he'd always known, but only ever imagined. Then, his eyes drifted down to where his father lay watching him, smiling.

A feline face greeted him, with a wide nose, a powerful muzzle and jaw, and short, round ears trained in his direction. Short fur covered the face, interrupted by patches of bare skin which spread and multiplied down his father's neck and chest. The skin was pulled tight over his bones, and his eyes weren't deep so much as they were sunken. Instead of proud and dignified, he looked . . . *gaunt*. Kah'riss reached out shaking hands to touch his father's face, tracing hard-scored lines to reconcile this visual image with the tactile portrait he had always known. It *was* the same face, not as he had imagined, but as wonderful as he had hoped.

"Not too bad, huh?" Sark chuckled.

Kah *watched* his father's lips form words, revealing the long fangs he had grabbed onto ages ago. Tears fogging the inside of the goggles, he heard a sniff and, finally, *looked* at his brothers.

Almost identical in shape, but not in size, his brothers bore a striking resemblance to their father. As Istur watched him with wide eyes, in fact, Kah imagined Sark would have been nearly identical in his youth. Calan's face was split between a wide grin and shining, wet eyes, but Thurv wore his trademark frown, though it faltered to a smile as Kah reached out to trace his features. He wondered if he looked the same and ran his fingers over his own face, trying to match it to his family. While similar, however, Kah noticed that his own features seemed fuller. He had no lines or pits under his eyes, and very few scars interrupting his fur. Seeing the rest of his family, Kah realized why their faces were different from his.

They're all so tired.

A deep sob erupted from Kah's throat and his older brothers enveloped him, sheltering him in their warmth and light. Unable to join the embrace, their father's hand found Kah's arm and clutched with all the strength he could muster, locking together with his sons in somber joy for as long as they dared, each quiet whimper a solemn reminder that there was little time left to hold one another.

When finally they parted, Sark smiled at his sons, the gaunt face full of pride. He looked to Thurv and, as he spoke, his voice took on a high-pitched, desperate wheeze, forcing the words out of his ruined lungs. "They're in your hands now. You know what to do. You've always known best, just like your mother. Do your job, do it well, and you'll see the task done." A shuddering cough. "Istur, you're soft, and you're too smart to be stuck on this rock. You'll never survive here. But I know you. You're crafty. I'm sure you've already figured out how to get out of here without joining the house fleet of some noble. I know you'll be fine."

At last, with wild eyes, he looked to Calan and Kah and covered their joined hands with his own. "You'll do it. You will. Your enemies will be numerous, and they will want nothing but to *hurt you*. Never play by their rules. Don't fight with honor. Just survive. Honor can come later. Remember; an enemy left behind is nothing but a threat to you later. The fight is *never* over while your enemy remains breathing."

Wheezing harshly, Sark's hand retreated to his mouth as he succumbed to another coughing fit. Afraid to say anything, lest they interrupt the fevered message, the four brothers held each other close.

"That's why you need to know who your enemies are," he panted, falling back onto the pillow. "You may fight.

You may hurt each other. But you will never be enemies. You *cannot*."

"Please—for what I've done to you—for what I've made you do to each other—forgive me." Lifting a hand to grasp for somewhere beyond Kah and his brothers, Sark stared at nothing, his eyes wide with rapture. "She's so proud—so proud of all of you, and *furious* with me. I'm sorry. I did all I could. I gave you a start, and now—now you can be *free*."

Sinking into the bed, their father's chest barely rose again.

"I love you."

II

"So, he died."

Yes.

"When did he die?"

Not long after that.

"Did he say anything else to you?"

He never woke up again.

"And how do you feel about that?"

Sad.

"Is that all?"

Yes.

"No anger, or righteous indignation?"

No.

"No thought for the injustice of your father's death being the unavoidable consequence of the systemic exploitation and abuse of an entire planet's worth of Ty'gjir?"

No.

"You are quite sure?"

In the absence of Sark'riss, Thurv shouldered responsibility for the wellbeing of his brothers, and so did what everyone on Pinto'Neth does when they need money. Shouting down his brothers' protests with the undeniable fact that their family needed the money to survive, he took a job in the mines. He would be fine, he said. It was only for a little while. Only until Istur, Calan, and Kah were safe. The plan hadn't changed—but life had. Their father's parting gift had made sure of that.

With his newfound thermal vision, Kah accompanied his eldest brother everywhere and, on Thurv's commute to work every morning, Kah walked with him through the labyrinthine system of ductways suspended between the massive spires which covered much of Pinto'Neth's surface. Once, it had snaked under the planet's crust, protected from the raging winds. Hunting relentlessly for even the tiniest deposits of nordium, however, ancient miners had stripped the ductways bare, leaving only sparse, tall pinnacles of rock and a city's infrastructure between them, hanging like steel webbing hundreds of meters above the ever-retreating surface. These tube cities, veined with exposed filtration and climate control systems, comprised the entirety of the livable space on the planet.

Hugging his brother tight when they reached the airlock to the world outside, Kah recited, like a ritual, "I love you, Thurv. Please, come home safe."

Thurv, too, had a routine response. He knelt and returned Kah's hug, then patted him behind the ears, whispering, "Love you too, baby brother. Don't get lost on the way home," leaving Kah to watch through the windows as his gondola plummeted into the pits below.

For the first time, Kah was able to see what the world outside looked like—the world Thurv ventured into every day to provide for the family. It was a treacherous place, with its sharp needles of stone sprouting forth from the core and dust-choked winds howling between them at all hours. Even with the thermal goggles, Kah was unable to see the surface below; the temperature grew far too hot as the altitude decreased. He was also unable to see into the skies, though now he knew why he had never seen starlight.

Pinto'Neth had been terraformed enough to have an atmosphere. Unfortunately, it was thick and designed to trap heat, and millennia of excavation had thrust so much dust into the air that, even under the best conditions, vision a few dozen meters beyond the ductways was all but impossible. Still, the hard geometry of the circuitous, life-supporting complex filled Kah with wonder and curiosity, and he was forced to reckon with how few of its tubes he had ever actually visited.

Unbeknownst to Thurv, after seeing his brother off, Kah removed his goggles and tried to navigate home without them. Early on during their daily walks, he had noticed that the clicks and taps of shoes, boots, and even claws on the hard floors of the ductways echoed around him, bouncing distinctly off every obstacle. Using the limited sight granted by the thermal goggles his father had given him, Kah was able to chart these echoes to a visual portrait of the world and, in time, with practice, he learned how different shapes reflected sound.

Initially, he did little more than stand still, tapping his claws on the walls and listening to the reverberations, checking through his thermal goggles to see if he had charted the space correctly. Soon, he learned that with more clicks or other sounds, he could even keep track of the movement of figures as they traveled through the city. Eventually, Kah began to explore the complex using *only* sound after he walked Thurv to work. Kah kept the exercise his secret, however. He didn't want his brothers to worry about him more than they already did. And the best way to accomplish that, he knew, was to overcome his weakness.

After bidding Thurv farewell one day, Kah decided to test himself, to map a part of the city he'd never visited, and wandered through the hanging corridors to one of the spires, into which was built a brace of the city's lifts. Boarding a small personnel elevator, he descended several floors below the safe, familiar level which housed his H-cell and, as the doors to a new world opened before him, he removed his thermal goggles and drew a deep breath, wandering, blind, into the dark.

Click. The noise rippled out from him, uninterrupted for tens of meters down the hall, before striking something short and hard, with several flat faces. A cube. A crate? He proceeded forward, knowing there were neither people nor obstructions between him and his target. In fact, given the lack of the usual hum of the climate control systems and the extraordinarily high temperature, it seemed likely this was one of the city's many abandoned ductways. Perfect.

Click. The crate was only a few steps ahead, followed by a four-way intersection in the hall. The paths branching left and right continued a fair distance without any sort of impediment, and the still air allowed the echoes to bounce a great deal further down here than he was used to. The path ahead, however, echoed back jarringly, without apparent rhyme or reason.

Click. Ah. Kah recognized some familiar shapes in the chaos. A mop and pail, a folding ladder, a few opened boxes. The path ahead was dammed with an assortment of mismatched pieces of equipment and bits of machinery, stacked haphazardly together and barring passage. Instead, he wandered left, striding as far as his echoes had reached.

New sounds found his ears. Barely audible, and unintelligible at the distance, two voices murmured further down the hall. Posing a new challenge to himself, Kah grinned. Could he navigate using only the sound of another Ty'gjir's voice? Laid before him was the perfect opportunity to find out.

Tentatively, he crept forward, trying to make as little noise as possible so as not to interfere with the whispers splashing against the walls. Straining to pick up the fine points of the echoes, Kah found that noises so quiet and muffled seemed to squish indistinctly off surfaces, rather than bounce, abandoning much of their detail. He was so determined to bring his echo portrait into focus that, as he drew closer, he failed to register anything the voices said and, before he knew it, he came to another intersection where he would be visible to the speakers.

Faced with a small conundrum, Kah resolved to try not to look strange or out of place, and walked straight across the mouth of the juncture, aiming to continue mapping before he doubled back.

As he came into view of the speakers, however, he heard one call out, "Hey! It's the wide-eye from class!"

Stopping in place, training his sensitive ears on the speaker, Kah furrowed his brow. He knew the voice from his education shift. He'd never spoken to the person, but knew him to be a boy just one cycle older than himself. Deepening his attention to his other senses, Kah smelled traces of something acrid and sour. It made his nose tingle and his eyes water.

Wrinkling his nose at this strange sensation, he detected footsteps stalking toward him and reached into his pocket to grab his thermal goggles, asking, "What's a wide-eye — hey!"

Before he could put them on, someone snatched the goggles out of his hands and held them away, leaving Kah in darkness. Robbed of his sight, he panicked, floundering desperately in the shadows for any sort of anchor. Two pairs of feet walked around him in a circle, but, as his heart pounded in his ears, he couldn't get a fix on either.

"Look at you — *you're* a wide-eye." The two voices burst into laughter. "And right now, you're a wide-eye without his big brothers around — "

A hand slapped his face. A fist found his stomach. Kah fell to his knees, winded by the sudden assault, but more blows followed, striking him in the back and ribs, pushing him onto his side on the hot floor. As he tried to keep from losing his morning ration, the shoes clicked across the floor in a circle around him.

Why? Why would they hurt him? What did they want? Shouldn't they all be working together? Weren't they all Pintoth?

"Phew! These look expensive, huh? How much d'you think they cost?" one of the voices piped over the laughter. Its owner delivered another sharp kick to Kah's stomach and drove him into a ball, hugging himself for protection from the unseen assailants.

"Dunno. Bet his da saved a *long* time to get them for him. Wonder how much food his family gave up on just so he could see."

"Looking at Calan'riss, they had to've cut their food bar rations in half for years!"

Forced out of his protective curl by a swift kick to the base of his tail, Kah hissed, arching his back against the pain. But it didn't sting as much as the guilt. Was Calan really so thin because of him?

"If their da wasn't so lazy, I bet they'd've had more."

His da wasn't lazy. He was just sick! But—But now that he was gone, they *did* have more food. Was it because Thurv was working instead? *Was* his da a bad worker?

"No," Kah muttered, in answer to his own unspoken question, but the other boys ignored him, except to aim a blow at his back. There were less mouths to feed, and no medicines to buy. His da did the best he could, preparing Kah for whatever might come—preparing him for people who wanted nothing but to *hurt him*.

Tap. A footstep pierced through Kah's thoughts, its echo washing over the area. The hall was crammed full of more tools and equipment, but nothing else, other than his classmates and the pungent scent.

"Can't help some people. Nothing you can do about it. Least he's dead now." The two burst into laughter again. "Bet wide-eye and his brothers are better off!"

Clap. One slapped a hand on the other's shoulder, leaning hard on his companion and leering down at Kah. "What do you think, wide-eye? Are you glad yer daddy's dead?"

Click.

Unsheathing his claws, Kah pounced, burying them in the leg of the assailant on the right and earning a shocked scream as he dragged the boy to his knees. Simultaneously scaling the boy by the hooks in his flesh, Kah crushed his nose in with a knee to silence his cries, before he leapt back and away from the other. Devoid of the good sense to stay quiet, the second ran, panicking, toward the elevator, his shrieks charting a clear map of echoes. Kah was on him in a short breath. Knocking the knees out from under the boy, he twisted his opponent's leg until he felt the bones give way and, at last, released him.

Cocking his head, Kah stared down at his whimpering, sobbing opponent. Why was that so easy? Hadn't their da taught them to fight? Maybe his family was different. Maybe they were the only people who wanted to get off Pinto'Neth. But that couldn't be right. Everyone knew how bad it was. It was no secret. Retrieving the thermal goggles from his fallen foe, Kah began the walk home, wondering how else he and his brothers might be different.

As the years wore on, life improved for all the brothers. They kept up their studies and training, pushing harder than they had before, all feeling a new sense of urgency to get Thurv out of the mines. Kah never again encountered the Pintoth from the abandoned ductway and was never again troubled by a classmate. They were right about one thing, however. With one less mouth to feed and no money being spent on expensive medicines, there were more food bars to go around, as well as more credits for basic luxuries, like restricted holonet access. With this, the brothers were able to see a view, albeit severely limited, of life outside their dark home, and it became their primary source of both information and entertainment.

Watching a holonet news report some two years after the death of their father, Kah and Calan lounged in the H-cell's common room. Holonet access on Pinto'Neth was specially filtered, projected in infrared to better suit the Pintoth population, and appeared to Kah as everything else—in shades of gray. Istur, meanwhile, was hard at work, scribbling away on a pad in the corner, so only seemed to be giving the projection half his attention. Increasingly late to arrive home from the mines, the eldest brother of the Riss family was nowhere to be found.

The grating voice of the holonet commentator overwhelmed any attempt at sound in the otherwise quiet H-cell. *"Princes have, of course, been usurped before, but never by someone so young and with such humble beginnings. Worse still, he's already laid bare his ambition to take even more ground! Can we really trust a cub to rule any territory of the Rae'gal Arm?"*

The voice of another commentator cut him off. *"Perhaps you are forgetting that Prince Cah'dal was only in his twentieth cycle when he was crowned ruler of our own territory. The region has prospered under his wise rule. Prince Sol'taris is not much younger and, perhaps, his worldly experience will be a boon to him and his people. Indeed, if Prince Ona'var couldn't contain an upstart rebellion, perhaps this fall from grace represents the price of incompetence."*

The other commentators all murmured in agreement.

"Regardless, the people of the Dal territory will be safe from any military incursions from the Var terr—er, the Taris territory. The Taris fleet would first have to contend with Prince Kai'mul,

who has a history of strong ties to Prince Cah'dal and maintains the most powerful fleet in the Empire. At least Prince Sol'taris is an Ascend — "

Yawning, Calan tapped a button on his remote, shutting the report off and seizing Istur's attention from his datapad.

"Why'd you turn that off?" Istur snapped.

Indifferent to Istur's cutting tone, Calan yawned again. "It was boring. Besides, I didn't think you were watching."

"It was *boring*? You know this is history in the making, right?"

Calan stretched his full length across the couch, resting his heels in Kah's lap and covering his own face with his hands. "History for the opposite side of the *universe*, maybe. The new prince couldn't be farther away."

Snatching the remote from Calan, Istur tried to revive the report, grumbling the while. "You won't feel that way if he keeps fighting and winning more territory. The whole empire could be drawn into it, and that means us, too."

Before Calan could offer a response, the door to the H-cell slid open, bringing with it the sulfurous smell which marked Thurv as a nordium miner, and cutting off the sound of the holonet, which Istur had managed to bring back to life. Istur and Calan shot waves of greeting toward the door, but Kah pushed Calan's feet off him and rose, trotting to the door to greet his brother. At nineteen cycles-old, Thurv was now larger than their father had ever been and easily swept Kah into his arms, nearly crushing him in a vise-like hug.

"Put me down, Thurv! You stink!" Kah laughed, helpless in the full-grown Ty'gjir's arms.

"You've never complained before, you little jerk." Chuckling, Thurv locked Kah's head dangerously close to his underarm and rubbed his knuckles between the cub's ears, eliciting more giggles and squeals of protest. "Sala, do you think I stink?"

At that, the room fell silent aside from a light, feminine chuckle issuing from somewhere behind Thurv. Stepping into the H-cell was a small, slender Ty'gjir wearing a flowing blouse and a long skirt, as well as sleek, stylish goggles that delicately framed her features. But Kah was still stuck on her clothes. He had never seen anyone outside the holonet wear a skirt. Why was it open on the bottom?

Eventually, Kah managed to tear his eyes away from her clothing to take a look at her face. Her features were unusually slight, with large eyes and a small, sharp muzzle capped with a button nose. She carried a new scent with her as she entered. It was . . . *pleasant*. Like cleaning products are made to smell pleasant. And she didn't have any smell of the mines on her at all.

Examining her closely, Kah guessed she was a Domestic, judging by her fragile-looking build and small teeth. He had never seen one in real life. Istur had told him that very few lived on Pinto'Neth because life here is so harsh and unforgiving, and their little bodies weren't made to endure it.

"Yes, terribly!" Walking around Thurv and into the center of the room, she looked at each of the brothers in turn. "And if you don't fix it soon, perhaps I'll forget all about you and cozy up to" — she pointed a finger, and then another— "Istur'riss. Or Calan'riss. Or even Kah'riss!" At the last name, she spun in place and bent down to look Kah in the goggles. She didn't have to. She wasn't much taller than he was. She also spoke in a strange, lyrical accent that seemed to involve trilling the tongue as often as possible. "That way, I get all the looks without any of the smell!"

Fanning out the rest of her fingers, the Domestic changed her pointing finger into an open hand, waiting to be shaken. Kah took the hand and gripped hard, but loosened when he felt her soft fingers and thin bones. He eyed her suspiciously.

"Guys, this is Sala'hai." Stepping forward, Thurv gestured at the Domestic. "She's the new medical director in our branch of the mines. She's working to improve the health care available to us." None of the brothers said a word. Thurv coughed once, then continued. "She's been living in orbit for a few months, making daily trips to the surface for work, but she needs to move on-world and is hoping to find—well, I offered, if she needed—" His voice trailed off before he scratched his head, frowning.

One brow cocked, Sala'hai gave a short laugh in Thurv's direction and, haltingly, said, "Oh, I see we're doing this right away. Then, please, let me. I was hoping to ask them myself. We were hoping"—she stood up straight and sidled over to Thurv, taking his arm—"that you all would agree to me coming to live with you. May I?"

The couple stood together, arm in arm, under the merciless scrutiny of the three younger brothers, waiting for them to speak, to move, to blink. But nothing came for quite some time. Not until Istur's chair squealed back across the tile floor.

"I need to talk to you, Thurv," he said. "Miss Hai, please excuse us for a moment."

Beckoning to Thurv, who followed without question, Istur descended the four steps into the sublevel and opened the training room. As his oldest brothers entered the chamber, Kah was keenly aware of the smell of sweat and blood which poured out the open door, persistent despite their best attempts to cleanse it. Nervously glancing at Sala'hai, she did not seem to mind. Or, perhaps, to notice. Nor did she notice him staring. She, in turn, crossed her arms and started taking slow, meandering steps into the common room of the H-cell, looking around the room and nodding.

"*Day*, it is *sterile* in here. Thurv told me you kept the place tidy, but this is impressive." She freed one hand from her crossed arms to gesture at the common room at large, beaming at them. "Four brothers, living together in a place like this. What do you do with all the boy ick?"

Kah pointed at the trash chute.

"Miss Hai," Calan blurted, standing stiffly. "May I offer you a beverage?" Without waiting for an answer, he fled to the kitchen.

"No, thank you. I'm quite all right. Thurv and I stopped for drinks on our way here." Sitting in one of the common room chairs, Sala'hai leaned her full weight into it. It was alarming how little the chair cushion sank to accommodate her. Was she made of air?

Despite her reply, Calan produced five glasses from the cupboard and began filling them with water and ice. On the second glass, raised voices from the training room could be heard over the running water, clear and loud, especially to Kah's sensitive ears.

"We're not supposed to get attached here," Istur's high, nasal voice rang out. "We're all supposed to leave and you're practically chaining yourself to the place!"

"We're just trying to live together," Thurv's deep voice soothed. "She could use the place to stay, we could use the credits, and you could all do to see a woman in real life, instead of just on the net." He sounded strained, pleading — the apology of someone who's made a selfish decision for the right reasons. "We're not even married yet."

"Do you hear yourself? You're not married *yet*?" Istur's voice cracked. "You've already signed yourself away! You're giving up!"

Shouting at each other in earnest, the brothers' voices began to overlap. Calan and Sala'hai did their best to pretend they couldn't hear the fighting in the other room, but there was only so much the thin interior walls of the H-cell could do. The Domestic heaved a deep, disappointed sigh.

"What are you doing here?"

The question secured her instant attention and she peered through her goggles at Kah. "I beg your pardon?"

"Thurv said you'd been living in orbit and just arrived on-world. Plus, you're wearing thermal goggles. You're not from Pinto'Neth, and nobody ever comes here." Kah tentatively approached and sat beside her. Even he, he noted, compressed the cushion more than she did. Girls must be light. "Why are you here?"

Sala'hai smiled, exposing her small teeth in her small muzzle, and leaned forward with her small hands clasped together. "Well, I'm a doctor. After I heard lots of Ty'gjir get sick on Pinto'Neth, I came here hoping to make some changes, to help the miners find out earlier if they're sick, and to treat them more effectively if they are."

Kah leered at her. He wasn't sold. "Where are you from, then?"

"I'm from Aurum, it—"

"That's Duke Aur'kura's planet!" Struck with immediate wonder, Kah cut her off. "He's in charge of Baron Mal'karos."

She grinned. "Yes, it is, and he is. It's a beautiful place, with bright skies and wide oceans and lots of big palaces. The wind smells like flowers and fresh water, and—"

"What's a flower?"

Sala'hai tilted her head a little at that. "It's a pretty part of a plant. They're all shapes and colors and sizes—"

"I've never seen a color. What're they like?"

Twisting her face in pain, as if she'd suffered a physical blow, Sala'hai sat back in the seat and thought for a moment, building an answer.

"They're like—Colors are . . . an aspect of how something looks based on the way certain wavelengths of radiation reflect off or emit from it." She grimaced at her own explanation, though Kah nodded knowingly, wisely. Another smile alighting her face, the Domestic leaned forward and took Kah's hands. "Color is also a way the gods let you know how to feel about something. Red things are hot, or dangerous, or full of passion, like the Lady of War—"

"Like a red alert!"

"Yes, like a red alert. And blue things are cool, calm, serene, and knowing—or curious, like the Lord of

Knowledge. Yellow things are bright, happy, and true, like the Lady of Day."

"What color am I?"

Sala sat back and chuckled a little. "I'm afraid I don't know. It's a little too dark for me to tell. If we were on Aurum, I could tell you. If I had to guess, though, I would say bright, bright blue."

She laughed, but the cub's chin dropped, disappointed, and his face assumed a frown to put Thurv to shame. Pulling his hands into his lap, Kah tucked his feet under his chair, grimacing as the angry voices of Thurv and Istur occupied the lapse in conversation. Seeing Kah's face drop even further, Sala placed a gentle, comforting hand on his shoulder.

"Let's make a deal," she said. "If you promise to close your eyes extra tight and cover them with your hands, I'll tell you what color you are. Deal?" Kah had already squeezed his eyes as tight as he could and was nodding along. He heard Sala speak a little louder to Calan. "You have to close your eyes, too, Calan'riss. I would never forgive myself if I blinded you on my very first impression. Ready?"

A moment passed before Kah's eyes filled with brilliance. Even through his closed eyelids, the intensity was so great that he hissed and turned his head away. As quickly as it came, however, it was gone.

Sala spoke, her voice thick with concern. "That's it. All done. How are you?"

Kah cracked open his eyes to the familiar vision of heat and shape and depth, though it was a blurrier world than he remembered. As he blinked clarity back into his sight, however, he grinned. "I'm good. What color am I?"

"Black," she answered. "With darker black rosettes."

Fresh confusion painted Kah's face. "What are rosettes?"

A tired smile spreading across her pretty visage, she paused, bringing a finger to her chin. "They're like spots, which, uh, are little circles of color. Many Ty'gjir have patterns like that in their fur. They're mostly one color but might have spots of another. And rosettes are spots that are shaped like flowers."

Taking in her description, Kah nodded sagely, imagining pretty little plant parts growing among his fur. He held up a finger. "What is black?"

"Black is the color of the dark. It's what you see whenever you take off your goggles," she said, momentarily lifting her own. "Black hides and protects things. People, secrets, the stars—your planet. People are often afraid of black because they don't understand it or the things it conceals."

"So, which god is mine?"

Crossing one leg over the other and resting an elbow on the knee, Sala laughed. "I could be wrong, but I don't think any god belongs to any one person. As far as which god is *like* the color black, I'd say the Lord of Night. He is the great keeper of secrets and the protector of those who dwell where light cannot reach."

Eyes wide with awe, Kah pictured a Ty'gjir made up of the dark space where nobody was looking, dashing out of sight whenever someone turned to see. It seemed like something to be afraid of. But what if it were watching to make sure nobody bad could sneak up? That was probably right. Kah had spent his whole life in darkness and he had never been hurt because of it. Perhaps, he thought, as Istur and Thurv reentered the common room, there *was* something watching out for him.

"I'm sorry for the wait," Istur began. "After some discussion, I think it would be good for all of us, and especially Thurv, if Miss Hai would come live with us for the time being. If she wanted." The strain was audible. He was stiff, formal, uncomfortable.

Thurv, however, beamed widely and looked to the younger brothers. "What do you two think? This is *our* home — *our* family — and, more than anything, I want it to stay that way. So, if you're not comfortable — "

Characteristically restrained, Calan retrieved two glasses of ice water from the kitchen and shoved them into the hands of his older brothers. He sighed and shrugged, but nodded his assent to both Thurv and Sala'hai.

Kah, meanwhile, was already taken with the pretty Domestic, but made a show of circling her, scanning her up and down, inspecting for any ill intent. Apparently satisfied, he turned to his brothers and announced, "I think it's a good idea!"

Passion and necessity spurring them on, it did not take long for Sala and Thurv to be married, and Sala fast became part of the family. Things like that move swiftly on Pinto'Neth. A shorter life than elsewhere in the Ty'gjir Empire left little time for courtship.

In fact, Kah soon learned, the exceptionally high rate of premature mortality among Pintoth was precisely the reason Sala left her comfortable position on the Duke's world. She may have filtered her answer somewhat, but when Kah asked why she had come to Pinto'Neth, she had answered truthfully. Sala aimed to develop protocols for the diagnosis, treatment, and prevention of the often-undiagnosed and untreated work-related conditions from which the miners suffered and died. In this, she and Istur got along famously.

Though it took Kah years to understand, much of Istur's own work as he grew to adulthood was focused on improving the occupational safety measures of Pintoth miners. He made quite a stir among the young miners and the children of miners, all of whom had watched the health of their mothers, fathers, and colleagues decline over their short lives. Employment in the mines trended downward as younger Ty'gjir outright refused to work in the hazardous nordium conditions, joining the limited service industry on Pinto'Neth, inventing other methods of income, or, for the more fortunate, leaving the planet altogether. Unfortunately, the diminished workforce led to lengthened shifts, followed by mandatory labor in the mines for all adult Pintoth, enforced by an ever-increasing population of peacekeepers.

Fleet applications came and went, dismissed by Thurv and ignored by Istur. Thurv had to keep working until the others were out, after all. It might take longer than they thought, he said, but it would be all right. Sala was a doctor. A good one. She could keep him healthy. Besides, once the other brothers were gone, he and Sala would be able to put away so many credits that they could all go into an early retirement on Aurum together. Istur, too, seemed confident life was poised to improve for miners all over Pinto'Neth.

Meanwhile, encouraged by their siblings' high spirits, Kah and Calan kept their sights on their father's plan and, in Kah's fifteenth and Calan's seventeenth cycles, the two were finally prepared to take the exams which would allow or deny them entry to the house fleet of Baron Mal'karos, and a chance at a real future.

III

"You have skipped some details."

Yes.

"Why?"

I didn't think they were important.

"You have very little to say about your brother's activities."

Which brother?

"You know."

I was unaware of most of his activities. I was focused on my studies.

"He never told his trusted brothers anything?"

Sala was more his peer. She was his confidant.

"Fine, then. Let us proceed."

Side by side, Kah and Calan stood staring at the great barrier before them. Behind, Thurv, Istur, and Sala lingered among the other families, bidding final goodbyes and good-lucks to the prospective cadets standing in front of the massive freight elevator which would carry them up the center of one of Pinto'Neth's spires to the spaceport perched on top.

Today was the day the futures of many young Pintoth would be decided—the day of the Mal'karos house fleet entrance examinations. Calan had waited two extra years to undergo assessment, until he felt as confident as possible. Kah, on the other hand, opted to take the exams as soon as he was legally able to do so. Looking over his shoulder at his family, all encouraging gestures and broad smiles, Kah's nerves roiled in his stomach, but he refused to show it. Calan, however, seemed absolutely at ease, his eyes half-lidded, but coolly focused on the door before them.

Groaning an earsplitting protest, the massive steel doors of the freight elevator began to shudder apart. Beyond, the screaming winds of Pinto'Neth could be heard echoing down the freight shaft, carrying the taste of dust to taint the air. Kah took a deep breath, his first of unfiltered air. It was warm, and felt somewhat heavy in his lungs, but he didn't dislike it. He jumped a little when, suddenly, a large hand clapped on his shoulder—Thurv's hand. Turning around with a grin, Kah saw his eldest brother, anxiously bouncing between he and Calan.

Visibly laboring to keep his muzzle from dropping into his characteristic frown, Thurv offered the pair an anxious smile. "Hey. Even if you fail today, I'm proud of you both. I just wanted you to know that. Sala, Istur, and I will be waiting to hear the news when you get back home." He finished up with a tight squeeze that crushed both brothers against his chest. He had never been great with words, but his intentions were pure.

Freed of his eldest brother's arms, Kah steeled himself with another breath as the examinees started walking aboard the elevator. He even took a step to follow, but spun around once more for a final hug, his fingers digging fiercely into Thurv's shoulders, before he swiftly trotted into the lift.

Onboard the elevator, Kah found himself packed among the several hundred bodies of miner's children, looking to escape to a better life. He had seen a few dozen of these Ty'gjir before, but he did not recognize the vast majority of faces. There were many more Ty'gjir here, in fact, than usually took the exams. Kah's ductways produced roughly one hundred applicants annually but, apparently, the restrictions on repeat test takers had been lifted, allowing previously failed aspirants a new attempt.

Kah tried to identify any familiar faces among the crowd, until Calan found his way to him, placing a possessive hand on the back of Kah's neck and steering him toward a wall. From there, they looked back toward their family, but they were already lost in a sea of bodies.

"Kah, look up." Calan's hand tapped him on the shoulder, and he followed the gesture with his eyes. "Do you know what this is?"

Staring up the seemingly unending elevator shaft to the circle of light hundreds of meters overhead, Kah shook his head slowly.

"This is the first time we've stood under open sky."

Gazing skyward, the brothers beamed together. Despite the raging winds and the dust pounding its way down onto their heads, the world felt wide, open, and free. The elevator began to ascend.

It wasn't long before the novelty of staring upward began to fade, however. The lift was slow and stuffed with Ty'gjir. It was hot. Every nervously trembling aspirant smelled of sweat and anxiety. The vast majority—those without eyewear—began to shield their eyes or to crouch down with their eyes closed entirely in order to protect themselves from the whipping particles in the air. Kah and Calan, meanwhile, huddled together, quizzing each other on subjects the exams were set to test. Most of the other examinees started off mingling and meeting others, but by the end of the first hour, nearly everyone had joined them for some last-minute studying.

Eventually, the unwalled elevator breached the surface on top of the pinnacle, and the wind exploded over the Pintoth like wildfire. The heat and the matter in the air made it nearly impossible for Kah to see. Using sound to paint an image of his surroundings revealed only mayhem. The entire group clustered together, turning their backs against the wind and trying to seek shelter in the center of the mass of bodies. Kah covered his ears, the howling gale nearly deafening to his senses, and Calan held him against his chest, shielding him from the noise and dust. Despite his brother's best efforts, however, Kah felt the wind penetrate his fur and rub his face raw. He fully expected to be bloody by the time they got wherever they were going.

As if cued to his thoughts, a cool, female voice cut through the air, artificially enhanced by a microphone. *"Pintoth, please direct your attention to the southeast side of the spaceport. If you proceed in that direction, you will find a ship waiting for you to board. Follow the signs."*

Calm and rehearsed—almost mechanical—it was difficult to tell if the voice was a recording or a Ty'gjir speaking in real time. But that was not important. The voice had provided a way out of the tempest. Slowly, the Pintoth began to shuffle as one throng through the wind to the southeast, following signs, as the voice instructed.

Before long, the boxy, angular hull of what appeared to be a titanic cargo freighter pierced the wind. Under the ship, a lowered gangway came into view, guarded by a soldier wearing full armor, including thermal goggles and a rebreather. Drawing near, the soldier snapped a curt salute and ushered them aboard, into the depths of the cargo bay. With salvation in sight, the pace quickened tremendously, and the entire group was aboard within a few minutes. Once on board the vessel, it became clear that the ship was, indeed, a cargo freighter, though it had been refitted, and its massive bay now played host to rows of flight seats instead of shipping containers.

The same female voice calmly toned through the loudspeakers overhead. *"Examinees, please take a seat. Be sure to move all the way to the center of the rows. Please leave no open seats between you and your neighbors, as there may not be adequate seating for everyone aboard."*

Nudging Kah, Calan led him to the middle of the very front row. Thank goodness, because the first row had much more legroom, and Kah didn't know how long the freighter would take to arrive at the test site. After much muttering and jostling about, every Pintoth found a seat—with plenty to spare—and the gangway closed behind them, abruptly throttling the wind. Standing in the back of the hold, the soldier eyed the assembly, maintaining a silent vigil.

Once again, the voice toned overhead. *"Pintoth, please fasten your seatbelts, secure your belongings, and don the optic shields which can be found under your seats. The lights will be activated in ten . . . nine . . . eight . . . "*

Rushing to heed the warning, every Pintoth reached under their seat and found cheap, lightweight eyewear. Kah removed his own thermal goggles, tucking them in his pocket before he fastened the new, much simpler optic shield over his eyes.

"Two . . . one."

The lights burst to life overhead, drawing hisses, groans, and myriad other sounds of discontent from nearly every Ty'gjir aboard. The shields were basic eye coverings made of a nearly opaque plastic which shut out most of the radiance. Even so, the Pintoth's eyes were so sensitive that it was blinding to them, and none could bear it without complaint.

"Take-off will commence immediately."

True to the word of the mystery voice, the refitted freighter lurched up and forward, churning Kah's belly to instant nausea. It wasn't long after that the feeling of up or down eluded him entirely as the ship broke through the pull of Pinto'Neth's gravity. Considering he hadn't moved from his seat, the sensation was shockingly disorienting. Kah had read about the feeling, but was ill-prepared for it. Slowly opening his eyes, he dared a look at the rest of the bay, and, despite the dark optic shield, was not at all prepared for what the universe looked like *in color*.

The cargo hold, a utilitarian framework of exposed piping, was a smattered selection of beige — the most glorious, vivid hue Kah could have hoped for. Casting his eyes across the other Pintoth, however, Kah was forced to reckon with the limits of his imagination. His people were — were *kaleidoscopic* with color. Colors he had only heard Sala describe, but were now as clear to him as if he'd seen them his whole life. Defying the drab uniformity of his expectations, he found a vast variety among the Pintoth.

He was, as Sala had told him years ago, black, with blacker rosettes. Looking to Calan, he saw a rich gold splashed in pure white across the neck with auburn rosettes throughout. Scanning the rest of the room, he saw white Ty'gjir, and yellow Ty'gjir, and brown Ty'gjir, and silver Ty'gjir, and even some bright red Ty'gjir. There were spots and stripes and rosettes — all sorts of patterns Sala had described for him and more besides. The sheer number of colors was dizzying, the way the patterns flowed with bodies was incredible, and the variation between everyone was shocking.

Every single Pintoth was *spectacularly* beautiful.

"Calan, look at *everything*," Kah said, barely a breath, nudging his brother's arm.

Kah saw Calan's eyes peek open behind his goggles, chancing a quick glance. He watched as Calan's jaw dropped open to welcome a sharp intake of breath. His wonder caught, spread, and built, rippling through the freighter in sobs and soft gasps as, for the first time, the Ty'gjir from the shadow of the dark star shared in the light.

"It's —" His voice hitching, Calan fell silent.

"Yeah," Kah whispered, leaning into his brother's arm. Quiet awe dominated the remainder of the flight. Kah wished there were windows so he could see the stars, but he did not have long to yearn, as the trip was over nearly as soon as it had begun.

The voice shook the Pintoth out of their collective reverie. *"Examinees, prepare to disembark. Do not yet unfasten your seatbelts. Artificial gravity will now engage."* There was a loud sort of gradual ticking sound and the sensation of weight returned to everyone and everything. *"We will be docking with the carrier* Collision of Truth *in a few moments. Please, take all your belongings and wait until docking is complete before unfastening your seatbelts."*

In terms of belongings, Kah had only his thermal goggles and personal datapad, and few Pintoth, if any, had more to their name. So, everyone held tightly and quietly to the kit already in their hands awaited further instructions. They did not wait long. Soon, a loud, mechanical whining shook the room, followed by heavy, resonant thuds, presumably the sound of the landing gear locking into place.

"Examinees, you may now unfasten your seatbelts" — the air filled with clicking as Pintoth unbuckled their seatbelts and looked around, still clutching their datapads — *"and move toward the exit at the rear of the shuttle. Please form four neat and orderly lines and proceed down the gangway with your identification ready for presentation."*

As the loudspeaker voice clicked to silence, the gangway began to open and descend, revealing a markedly brighter outside. Squinting against the light, the examinees did as instructed, forming four neat lines and trying to stay quiet, though the whispering of several hundred Pintoth soon filled the freighter with a dull roar of murmurs.

Because Kah and Calan chose to sit at the front of the bay during the flight, they assumed positions near the very end of one of the lines, Kah standing in front of Calan. Few words passed between them, but Calan kept a hand on his younger brother's shoulder, giving him an occasional squeeze whenever he felt Kah start to fidget. Kah tried to remain calm, but his heart insisted on racing. He had never taken a test like this. He knew what to expect insofar as the subjects of the written examinations, but they were slated to occupy a full ten hours, assessing the examinees' knowledge, of course, but also their ability to maintain focus over protracted, stressful periods. The physical examinations were a mystery, with the specifics left to the discretion of their proctors every year. He could only hope his training over the years had prepared him for them, but the comparatively strong gravity aboard the *Collision of Truth* left him uneasy.

Only taking a few steps forward for every minute that passed, the line moved painfully slowly. The Ty'gjir in front of Kah, a female who was visibly older than both he and Calan, turned to him with a wry smirk, saying, "I should have brought a snack. I didn't expect us to be here until tomorrow."

Smiling politely, his head still full of nerves, Kah tried to calm himself enough to take a good measure of the woman. She was unusual—taller than most Ty'gjir present, still slender, as most Pintoth, but with clear, well-developed musculature. Her muzzle protruded too far and was too narrow. Drooping over at about half their height, her ears seemed unable to tolerate their own weight. Her bushy tail, instead of sinuous and swaying, hung idly behind her. Kah had never seen someone like this before, and studying her helped distract from his anxiety.

"Doesn't talk much, this one." She glanced over Kah's head to Calan, flashing him a broad smile.

Calan shrugged his brows drily and said, "Don't get him going, really." Another comforting squeeze. "The constant yammering is why we're trying to get rid of him."

Barking a protest, Kah turned and gave his brother a playful punch in the gut.

"But the kid can fight, that's for sure," the stranger laughed, clapping Kah on the back. Facing her again, Kah smiled. Confident and passionate, if brash, she reminded him more than a little of Istur. He immediately liked her. She offered a hand, first to Kah, then Calan. Both took it gladly. "I'm Fus."

The brothers pinned their ears a little. She had addressed herself by face name alone, a privilege normally reserved for family. Calan recovered more quickly than Kah.

"Calan'riss," he said, shaking her hand. "This is Kah'riss. It's nice to meet you, Fus. No offense, but you look a little older than most of this crowd. Why are you looking to join up?"

"Well, knowing Pintoth, probably not the same reason as you *kids*." Widening her eyes, Fus stared meaningfully at Kah and his brother, though her smile remained. "My ma served in the fleet when she was young, fighting pirates at the border. That's when she met my da, and they came home here to live happily ever after. They loved our territory, and so do I, even if Pinto'Neth is dark and crumby. And I certainly don't like the idea of some prince from across the galaxy telling us how to live."

Kah nodded. She was right; that *was* a weird reason. A gentle elbow in Kah's ribs told him Calan had somehow read his thoughts, but Fus laughed aloud again.

"It's not so strange to want to serve. Besides, in my current job, all I do is teach Pintoth things they'll mostly forget before they die a miner or go off to war. Feels cowardly to send kids like you when I can fight for home, too."

"It sounds like the baron'd be lucky to have you, Fus," Calan offered with an easy grin.

She had a calming air about her, and her good nature and conversation broke the tension of the long wait. Fus was exactly the kind of Ty'gjir Kah hoped he'd get to fight beside. After some time, she was next in line. Passing the brothers a wink, she flicked on the screen of her datapad and stepped forward to a desk where a uniformed, male Domestic waited for her. He held out his hand without a glance, waiting for her datapad, which she promptly surrendered.

"Stand at attention, please," sighed the Domestic. She was already standing at attention, though he would have to look at her to know as much. Droning, he continued, "Name: Fus, house Ybir. Age: twenty-six cycles. Occupation: primary educator. Species"—he dragged his eyes away from the datapad, gave her a quick once-over, and looked back down, marking something off with a stylus—"Demi."

Stiffening even before the Ty'gjir Kah now knew as Fus'ybir began to bristle, Calan dug his fingers hard into Kah's shoulder.

Startled by the sudden pressure, Kah turned quizzically to his older brother and whispered, "What's a Demi?"

Sharp claw tips pricked Kah's skin as Calan scolded, "Don't say that word. It's . . . bad."

"Excuse me?" Long, slow breaths lifted Fus' shoulders as she stared down the Domestic, her suppressed anger betrayed to Kah's nose by the whiff of aggression in the air and to his ears by the quickening of the heart in her chest.

The little, uniformed male stared up at her through half-lidded eyes, feigning disinterest, but the tiny quirk at the corners of his lips dared her to act out of turn. "Species: Demi. Mother is Ty'gjir. Father is Lupinion. You are a *Demi*. You may return to the freighter."

Breathing deeply, Fus refused to turn away. Kah could see her jaw muscles clenching, even from behind her. Cracking her knuckles, she curled and uncurled a fist. Yet, despite her now-visible anger, she quashed her fury and spun about on her heel, marching past Kah and Calan. "Good luck in their war. I hope *you two* make it, at least."

Confused, Kah watched as Fus stormed up the gangplank and back into the relative darkness of the hold, her thick tail thrashing behind her. Perhaps he stared for too long, because he soon felt Calan pushing him forward by the small of his back. His eyes still full of questions, Kah turned his attention to the Domestic behind the desk.

The Domestic was, perhaps, smaller than he was, though clearly more than twice his age. His uniform was wrinkled and had stains on the cuffs. Compared to the other uniformed figures in the room, the Domestic had fewer stripes on his sleeves. He carried a strange, bitter scent and his eyes were dry and bloodshot. Kah made a note to himself to not be this person.

"Identification." The Domestic shook his hand in the air, impatiently waiting for Kah to present his datapad.

Reluctant to put his datapad into the Ty'gjir's dirty hands, Kah nonetheless relented and stood at attention, waiting patiently. Now that the Domestic had Kah's data in hand, however, he seemed in no rush, allowing time for a new fear to wriggle into Kah's brain. Was his mother a Lupinion? He'd never asked. He'd always assumed she was like his father. Was *he* a Demi? His cool, practiced attention faltered and he began to sweat, but the Domestic didn't seem to notice, now back to his drone.

"Name: Kah, house Riss. Age: fourteen cycles. Occupation: student. Species: Jaguar. Father: Sark, house Riss. Mother: Milta, house Riss. Height: one-point-five-seven meters." He droned off some other details and paused, looking over the information on the datapad, then over Kah. "Do you hereby swear before your lord and all the gods that this information is true and accurate at this time to the best of your knowledge on pain of death?"

"I do."

"You may proceed. Next!" The Domestic tossed Kah's datapad onto a stack in a box next to his desk and waved Kah past. Stopping to wait for Calan, he found himself ushered on by the soldiers posted beside the four lines of examinees.

"You're not going far, kid. Don't worry, and get comfortable," one of the helmeted soldiers whispered, nudging Kah out of the shadow of the cargo freighter and into the light of the docking bay.

The hangar was the largest space Kah had ever seen, extending at least a kilometer ahead and a hundred meters or more to both the right and the left. To the left, the hangar terminated in a great, glowing, blue, translucent wall which extended from floor to ceiling over the mouth of the bay. Kah knew the wall to be an atmospheric shield, designed to allow the passage of ships, but not air. To the right, the room ended in a wall of blast doors and walkways, marking five distinct levels from floor to ceiling. High above, spacecraft hung from the ceiling on rails and great docking hooks, organized by class of craft, holding everything from large cargo shuttles to tiny, one-man interceptors. Beyond, artificial lights buzzed, spilling cold white light over the hangar.

The floor, however, was largely empty, aside from stark, utilitarian tables spread throughout the room, separated from the others by two meters in each direction, and all facing toward the right wall. Seated at each were the examinees who'd preceded Kah, but there were still some unoccupied tables toward the back, so, feeling exposed, he headed in that direction. He looked back to find his brother, but Calan had been ushered a different way, advancing toward the front row.

Arriving at an empty table, Kah pulled out the backless chair with an uncomfortably loud screech, wincing at the noise. Although it seemed to him the only sound in the room, if anybody else noticed, they didn't glance his way. Running his hands over the cold, stainless steel tabletop, he sank into the chair. Alone in the center of the table was a folder doubtlessly containing a datapad which held the written examinations. Waiting only for the signal to begin,

Kah closed his eyes and passed the next several minutes rehearsing his test topics.

Instead of the calm female announcer he expected, however, another voice cut through the silence.

"Hear me, Pintoth!" It was smooth, of middling pitch, and danced on the same lyrical accent with which Sala spoke. It sounded like a noble, Kah thought—although, admittedly, he hadn't heard many nobles speak. Searching for its source, his eyes came to rest on a walkway three floors up. There, a man paced back and forth, imperiously overlooking the examinees.

With tall, tufted ears, facial fur which fell naturally into dignified points below his chin, and a cartoonishly short tail, Kah recognized this Ty'gjir as a Bob. The Bob was dressed in what appeared to be an amalgamation of formal uniform and armor, with a shining plasteel breastplate festooned with numerous ribbons and medals, as well as sharp, red epaulettes, gauntlets, and a long, flowing cape which draped from one shoulder, dramatically fanning with each turn to expose sharply cut black trousers. He appeared to wear no armor over his lower half, and no boots, just finely polished black shoes. His hackles rising, Kah noted that the Baron was heavily bedecked in unbroken blacks and reds—not a speck of yellow or blue on him.

"I am Baron Mal'karos, your liege lord and ruler of your star system and many like it. *You* are my *beloved* people. You stand poised to be granted the privilege of joining the greatest military force this galaxy has ever known—a machine honed to precise and deadly perfection." He paused for effect. "What can you possibly contribute to this perfect machine, you may ask? Fret not, Pintoth, I know all of you—and each and every one of my subjects—has enormous potential, begging to be tapped. Our fleet is the envy of every baron the empire-over. The reason our duke, Aur'kura, and our glorious prince, Cah'dal, look with such favor upon us is because of Ty'gjir like us—those who pull themselves from the mire of mediocrity to serve a greater purpose—the same purpose which brought you all here today."

Benevolently spreading his arms as if to embrace all of his people at once, Baron Mal'karos instead clutched the rail with one hand and jabbed at the air with the other. "The danger is real, Pintoth! Do not be deceived. The forces of our enemies, the traitor princes, Aea'trox, Aar'nor, Hah'dran, and the self-styled Emperor Sol'taris are indeed great. But they do not have our experience or our leadership. They do not have the blessed patronage of our prince, Cah'dal, or our allies, the princes Kai'mul and Rae'vel, and they certainly do not have the spirit of our sector!"

Thrusting both hands into the air, the baron paused, perhaps waiting for applause. The Pintoth, however, seemed uncertain as to whether they were allowed to respond, and silence reigned for an uncomfortable moment before the baron carried on. "It is that danger which requires us to be so discerning in our choice of who may join this glorious machine and who would be safer at home, supporting us in different, quieter ways. Hence, the stringent examinations you are all about to undergo. Know that I am eager to grant you this opportunity and wish all of you great success! Good luck, Pintoth!"

With a dramatic twirl of his cape, Mal'karos swept through a blast door and out of the bay. Except for a few, lonely coughs, the room was pleasantly quiet for an instant.

"Examinees" — Abruptly, the calm voice of the female guide burst from unseen speakers and filled the bay — *"in the folders before you are your written examinations, contained on a single, secure datapad. They will encompass the topics of engineering, history, life science, mathematics, medicine, physical science, programming, and rhetoric. You may take the examinations in any order you wish. You will have ten hours to complete the examinations. There will be no breaks, and questions are not permitted. If you speak, stand, exhibit inappropriate posture, or leave the examination room for any reason, your scores will be uniformly penalized to a degree commensurate to your infraction. If you complete your examinations early, you must remain seated until the final examinee has completed their examinations. You may now begin."*

The slapping of plastic against steel filled the hangar as the Pintoth opened their folders and slid datapads no larger than Kah's hand onto the tabletops. Finally, it was time. More concerned about finishing within the time limit than he was about scoring poorly, Kah began at once. He had a firm grasp of the subjects, he thought, but knew that he tended to be thorough and complete and to give every question extensive thought, often at the expense of sensible haste. Flicking on his datapad, he saw an unassuming list of the eight test topics. For simplicity, he had already decided to take the tests from top to bottom.

At the top of the list was Ty'gjir history, Kah's favorite subject. History played out in his head like an unending story, with larger-than-life heroes and villains and great discoveries and the triumph of ingenuity over implacable hostile environments. The test was fairly basic, however, covering the acquisition of faster-than-light technology from Replid travelers and the subsequent expansion of Ty'gjir space under Prince Rae'gal from a few colonized worlds to the entire slice of the galaxy now known as the Rae'gal Arm, the home of the Ty'gjir Empire. This was ancient history, occurring thousands of years before the Replid Conquests.

The test proceeded chronologically, past the establishment of the Council of Princes and the formal founding of the Ty'gjir Empire to the Replid Conquests themselves, a thirteen-year war which united the galaxy, if briefly, against the Replids, and shaped much of the modern galaxy. When the smoke cleared, with the Replids defeated, the Ty'gjir Empire established itself as the most stable power in the galaxy. Aside from the typical House wars, the empire experienced a measure of peace until the Lupinions had their War of Unification, won, of course, with imperial assistance. The final section of the test covered the lives of Prince Cah'dal, Duke Aur'kura, and Baron Mal'karos, bringing the content to the present year, 121 AC. There was no mention, however, of the ongoing civil war which had led to the present recruiting surge.

Kah checked the time. One hour had elapsed, right on schedule. Opening the programming exam, he found that it was less concerned with Kah's ability to write new program than it was with his ability to interpret and manipulate existing code in a variety of languages. Curious. Not necessarily more or less difficult than he was prepared for, but certainly different than he was led to expect, and, ultimately, much longer than he hoped. But, keeping to the plan, he moved on to engineering.

The engineering examination was almost entirely concerned with the construction and maintenance of weapons, a variety of vehicles, and various robotics. This was likely a strong point for most Pintoth, as it was not uncommon for a miner to bring home complex tools for repair, and most of them made sure their children would be able to do the same if need be. Some miners left the maintenance and repair of the H-cells entirely to their children. Some, like Thurv, nurtured this interest and developed schematics and fully fleshed-out blueprints for devices designed to make the miners' lives easier, though such plans were rarely given the opportunity to bear fruit.

About forty minutes. Not bad.

Next came life science, followed by medicine. In his education shift, Kah had struggled more with these topics than with any others. That is, until Sala came to live with them. A passionate font of information on the subjects, his sister was both an exceptional tutor and an invaluable resource. The life sciences test was broad, general knowledge, covering fundamentals, but also various biological theories, including suspected sources of galactic life, and specific keystone lifeforms found in Ty'gjir space. The medical exam, however, was predictably focused almost exclusively on field triage and emergency care. No surprise, given the likelihood that these would be the cases most frequently seen by the house fleet medical corps.

Fifty minutes apiece. Back on schedule. For the first time since the examinations began, Kah chanced a look around the docking bay. There were some empty tables now, and he saw a few Ty'gjir returning to their seats from somewhere. Kah assumed these applicants had succumbed to the lure of the bathrooms, hoping their scores could survive the resulting penalties. He didn't want to think about the need to relieve himself. He *didn't* need to relieve himself. As long as his adrenaline was pumping, biology could wait.

Physical science. Kah's next examination tested fundamentals of astrophysics, as well as geology, meteorology, terraforming, and everything in-between. There was also a significant portion of the examination devoted to forming a mock hypothesis and designing experiments to test it in order to demonstrate knowledge of proper scientific procedure. Had this examination gone into greater detail on any of its subjects, it would likely have been the most difficult, but, instead, it wanted merely fundamentals. Despite its relative ease, the physical science assessment was far and away the greatest in volume, and Kah watched two hours slip away while he sped through it.

He checked the time, chewing his lip and bouncing his knee nervously. Two and a half hours remained with two tests still to go. It was fine. At least, that's what he tried to believe.

Rhetoric — Istur's specialty, but decidedly not Kah's. Istur was an impassioned speaker himself, and always taught his brothers to look for the intentions hidden in the words they heard. Kah, however, tended to be swept up by the passions of others, and, in practice, found himself agreeing with whatever Istur said, even when he was arguing two opposite sides of the same issue. The entire examination took the form of inspecting a scripted argument, identifying its biases, and refuting it and its positions in an essay. Unfortunately, he found the argument quite compelling, and spent a great deal of time trying to dissect it for bias before furiously scribbling out an essay.

He knew he didn't have the time to waste checking the timer after the test, but a glance around the room told him that many more people had left their seats since he had last looked. Shaking his head, he got back to it.

The final test covered mathematics, his least favorite subject. He wasn't bad at it. Like Calan, he simply thought math was boring. Practical math, like in physics or biology, was fine. Theoretical math — math for math's sake — not so much. Recalling numerous such complaints he'd offered his brothers over the years, he remembered their advice on the topic, the same they always gave. Suck it up. And he did, but it didn't make math less boring . . . Or keep his eyes from starting to drift closed in the middle of a particularly long proof, nor his stylus from sliding off the surface of the datapad and screeching hideously against the table.

Fortunately, the sudden shriek shocked him to fevered wakefulness and he realized, somewhat impressed with himself, that his posture hadn't slackened at all. With new adrenaline coursing through him, he blazed through the remainder of mathematics examination, declared the exams complete, signed his name, and slid the datapad back into its folder.

He checked the time. Ten minutes to spare. Heaving a huge sigh of relief, Kah looked around the room. Most of the other aspirants, it seemed, were finished, and sat rigidly in their seats as they waited for the final examinee to conclude. Watching another Pintoth turn her wrists in small circles, Kah realized that his were sore as well, as was his jaw, which he realized had been clenched tight for what felt like the entirety of the last ten hours. Trying to mask the effort behind his most appropriate posture, Kah slowly rubbed his wrists and worked his jaw for the next several minutes until, as expected, a klaxon sounded overhead, signaling the end of the written exams.

The guide's voice toned from above. *"Examinees, congratulations on finishing your written examinations. Your access to the tests has been closed. If you have not already done so, please sign your name on your datapad and return it to its designated folder. Your physical examinations will begin shortly. You will be guided through them by the staff of the* Collision of Truth. *Pintoth, you may remove your optic shields, as your eyes should now be adjusted to the light. You may now stand, stretch, and visit the restroom. You will no longer be penalized for these activities."*

The invitation incited a stampede. Hundreds of Pintoth stood as one and rushed for the corners of the hangar, where ashen faced soldiers held signs directing the crowd to the lavatory. Kah, stretching his back in a dramatic arch as he rose, searched for Calan, but could not find him among the examinees. He must have gotten to the toilets first. As the lines spilling out the restroom doors were already well established, Kah felt no particular hurry and meandered toward the nearest queue, rolling his neck, wrists, and shoulders. He made a conscious effort to look calm and relaxed, but he could still feel the buzz of adrenaline coursing his veins and it was all he could do to resist jogging in place, rather than standing in line.

The loudest noises were the flush of toilets, the running of water in the basins, and the squeak of soles as shoes took single steps forward in line. Nobody seemed interested in speaking, Kah noticed, likely because everyone knew that many of the other applicants would be summarily removed from the group if their written scores were found wanting. He didn't mind. The quiet gave him time to think.

He wondered what the physical exams would be and, as he glanced around himself, if they would be competitive. Sizing up the other Ty'gjir in line with him, Kah saw that nearly every examinee, male and female, was larger than himself. He should be among the youngest here, certainly, but he'd never before appreciated quite how short he was for a Jaguar, leaving him looking up at all his potential adversaries. But he had been fighting people bigger than him his whole life. It was no problem. He hoped.

After the examinees finished relieving themselves, they congregated back in the hangar, obediently awaiting for further instructions. Kah still could not find Calan in the crowd but, as he looked around, noticed that the herd of Pintoth had thinned considerably. He also heard more than a small amount of noise coming from the direction of the cargo freighter which had transported them all here. Craning his neck to find a view of his brother, Kah started as another voice rang out, this one deep, gruff.

"Fall in!"

Sensing the palpable authority in the command, the Pintoth stopped what they were doing and formed rows, spines straight and eyes forward. There, at the front of the assembly, stood a large, burly Ty'gjir with short, tan fur and black stripes on his muzzle — a Puma. Hands folded behind his back, the Puma leered at the examinees. He wore gray combat pants tucked into black boots on his lower half, but only a plain, white, sleeveless shirt on his upper half. He gave a snort at the company of aspirants before he began to walk down the length of the front row, standing very close to each examinee, inspecting them with a penetrating, unblinking stare.

"I am Chief of Recruits, Gunnery Sergeant Falax'hebos! I will be overseeing your physical examinations!" His voice carried an accent altogether different from any Kah had heard before. Its vowels were lengthened, with a great deal of wind forced into the consonants, sending a large amount of saliva spraying from his mouth as he shouted across the examinees — volume unenhanced, but more than sufficiently loud. "You may have noticed that there are fewer of you now than there were before. Those who were unable to finish their written examinations within the time limit were removed and will be returned to Pinto'Neth to live out their days in the mines."

"The remainder of you will be subjected to a set of physical examinations which myself and Sergeants Kiln'aren, Shin'ade, and Um'therren will directly supervise. You will be split into four companies, with each accompanying an officer to a different test. When that company has concluded the first test, they will rotate to the second and so on. The order in which you perform these tests will not be taken into account during scoring. If, gods forbid, any of you slip through the cracks and manage to join the fleet, you will never know how or when your enemies will attack. *Flexibility* and *adaptability* are essential."

The three other officers to whom Falax'hebos had gestured began moving among the crowd, separating examinees into four distinct groups. Kah still failed to find Calan during this time but did notice that the officers passed him several times without giving him even a passing glance. His pride stinging, Kah felt like he was being ignored, but also realized he didn't know if there were some criteria by which the examinees around him were selected.

"If any of you outright fail any of the physical examinations for any reason, or if you do not meet the acceptable minimums for that exam, you will be removed and returned to the freighter." Relishing the threat, Falax'hebos allowed his warning to hang over the Pintoth as the herding went on. "We will not tolerate failure for any reason. Rest assured, there is the possibility that *none* of you succeed today. In that event, you will all go home to live short, meaningless lives in the mines, and we will recruit from a more deserving system. Do you understand me?"

A chorus of affirmatives burst out, and a dark grin cracked the sergeant's face. "Slow and stupid, but at least you Pintoth know how to listen. Now, move out!"

Taking charge of their companies, the three other officers marched to blast doors spaced well apart throughout the hangar, leaving the fifty or so remaining recruits with the gunnery sergeant. The remaining recruits naturally fell into line before him, waiting for him to lead them somewhere. He, however, did not yet seem interested in leaving, staring down the Pintoth as they fell into rank, before he turned and walked to a wide crate set against the wall, drawing a vacuum-sealed packet from it and throwing it to the first person in line.

As he threw another to the second, he yelled out, "Inside these packages, you will find pants, shirts, and undergarments. You might find the fabric nicer than back home. Consider yourselves lucky. These are your training uniforms. You will wear them during your examinations and during much of your formal training after being inducted to the fleet. And, in the likely event you fail your examinations, you may keep them as a souvenir, such is the generosity of our baron. As you receive your uniform, open it and begin changing at once. It should fit."

At that, the first several Pintoth hesitated, shuffling their feet. On Pinto'Neth, there was no opportunity for casual nudity of any sort. The only time a Pintoth is naked is in the shower or during mating. At least, that was Kah's understanding. Noting also that he was at the far-right end of the line, Kah realized he would receive his uniform last.

How many people would be finished and would watch him changing?

As the echoes of the gunnery sergeant's voice died out, a deafening silence came over the room. Perking up, Kah's sensitive ears caught the dry swallowing of numerous Ty'gjir throats and his nose detected a sudden glut of sweat in the air. The conspicuous absence of the sounds of doffing and donning was not lost on Falax'hebos, who rounded on those holding unopened uniforms, his eyes wild.

"I said at once!" he roared, spurring the applicants to action, the first in line tearing the packets open with their teeth while the remainder stripped out of their clothing.

Modestly turning his head away, Kah tried to give his fellow Pintoth some privacy, but something smacked the side of his head and he reflexively opened his hands to catch it, staring down at one of the sergeant's packages, a clear imprint of his face in the wrap.

"Pay attention, cub!" The thunder of Falax'hebos' marching tore Kah's attention away from the plastic-wrapped clothing in his hands. "What? That the only clean pair of skivvies you've ever seen? Spend a lot of time shitting yourself, boy? Or maybe you're just so repulsed by your fellow Pintoth that you can't bear to look? Can't say I blame you, kitten, but there's nothing so pretty as flowers on the *Collision* and there's no room in this fleet for a cadet who can't keep his pants clean!"

Gaping at the gunnery sergeant, Kah tried — and failed — to keep pace with his roars. "Wh-what?"

"Are you going to let the traitor princes shoot you in the face because you can't keep your eyes off the flowers, kitten?!"

"N-no, sir," Kah stammered, his ears burning hot with humiliation. Up close, the Puma was even larger than Thurv, and bent over at the waist to look Kah in the face, his strange accent spraying spit into Kah's wincing eyes.

"Speak up, cub! Maybe at home they think it's cute that you're so puny and pathetic, but I'm not impressed. You look like you should still be holding daddy's hand, boy! You here alone, or did your parents bring you? No, no, no, I know the story — mommy and daddy died of the rock lung and now a gun is your only way off your shithole planet. You may have survived this long off charity and guilt because the other Pintoth think you're a cute, sweet, quiet, li'l guy, but that won't work here. I don't think you're a *cute li'l guy*. I know what you are. You're a *liability*. And whether or not you're *cute* or *li'l*, a liability is the same. A cute li'l liability breaks formation at the first volley. A cute li'l liability is too weak to drag his comrade back to the bunker when his leg's been blown off. A cute li'l liability can't climb the mountain and drags the whole team to their deaths! A cute li'l liability bears his brothers' coffins because they spent so much time shouldering his weight that they couldn't carry their own!"

Kah could only watch in amazement as the sergeant worked himself into a frothing rage. The Jaguar couldn't help but let his eyes stray to the vein pulsing in Falax'hebos' forehead, the sweat beading on his brow, and the red rushing to fill his eyes. Kah had never in his life seen someone so angry, and he hadn't even *done* anything to him. He simply stared, wide-eyed.

"Nothing to say, cub? Maybe that's how they like them on Pinto'Neth — small, quiet, and coy. I don't see the appeal, but I've never been *satisfied* by a Pintoth — maybe I just need some convincing! What do you all think? Can the li'l liability convince me?" Spreading his massive arms wide, Falax'hebos threw the question to the rest of the Pintoth, meekly changing their clothes and averting their eyes. Hearing no response, he leered back down at Kah and folded his arms across his chest. "Go on. *Convince me.*"

Shrinking before the furious, intimidating creature, his mouth slightly agape, Kah did not know what the thing wanted. He knew only that he was ashamed, and felt the cold heat of it rush to his face.

"You're not wearing your uniform, kitten."

Reminded of the package in his hands, Kah's eyes drifted down across the uniform, and across his own body. He looked up at the gunnery sergeant, at his mocking eyes above his sneering, fanged smile, at his confident, unconcerned posture, and at the swipe of his tongue as the Puma licked his own fangs.

In that moment, Kah learned what it was to feel pure, red, burning hatred. He now knew the difference between opponents and enemies, and he would not be defeated, not while his enemy still breathed.

Narrowing his eyes at the sergeant, Kah curled his lip into a snarl. Without breaking eye contact, he threw the packet to the floor and removed all his clothes, standing defiantly nude for a moment before he cut the package open with a claw and pulled on his training uniform. He donned it so quickly that he didn't even register what it looked like, just that, when he was done, Falax'hebos looked disappointed and decidedly less amused.

"*Satisfied*, sir?" The words hissed viciously between clenched teeth as Kah stood as tall as he could manage, puffing his thin chest. A long moment passed as the two locked eyes, both refusing to give ground.

Finally, Falax'hebos pointed at Kah's shirt and growled, "The number goes on the back," before he stomped away.

With the gunnery sergeant's back turned, Kah felt safe to exhale, and withdrew his head and arms into the shirt. Turning the garment around his body, he savored the instant of privacy within the confines of the fabric. Righted, and with the free time to examine himself, he saw that the training uniforms matched the sergeant's, except all the examinees had numbers on the backs of their sleeveless, white shirts. Kah himself bore the number fifty-six, in large, blocky lettering. Checking to see if the uniform numbers proceeded in order, Kah noticed that the nearest examinee had taken a large step away, physically distancing himself from the Jaguar.

At the head of the company, Falax'hebos swiped a card through a panel on the wall, opening the blast doors behind him, and snarled, "Follow me."

Immediately, the group broke ranks and jogged forward to follow along, greeted beyond the blast doors by a strange sight. A constructed pit of sand occupied most of the secondary bay, and inside the pit was a long series of obstacles, extending from one end of the room all the way to the other. Scanning the course, Kah began to formulate a plan of attack for each obstacle. Would he need to complete each obstacle in a certain way, or was he simply expected to get through it? They would certainly be timed, that much was certain. What was walking on sand like? It looked soft, with some give to it. How much would that affect his footing?

"Welcome to the obstacle course," Falax'hebos said. "The first part of your physical examination. You must complete each obstacle as demonstrated, or you will fail this test. You must complete each obstacle within three attempts, or you will fail this test. You must complete the course in under three minutes, or you will fail this test. I will now demonstrate how each obstacle is to be completed."

Stepping off the metal flooring, the gunnery sergeant hopped into the sand pit. Kah attempted to take note of how much the loose sand shifted under him as his heavy boots thudded into it—five, maybe six centimeters. It was deep. Falax'hebos then demonstrated the entirety of the course, forward and backward, instructing them to run back to the starting line after completing it, at which time their score would be recorded.

As much as Kah didn't like him, the sergeant completed each obstacle with impressive ease. Coolly shouting instructions for each obstacle while simultaneously performing those instructions, his bulging muscles strained the bounds of his shirt, but his face betrayed no effort. Given how much the large Puma must weigh, and the enhanced gravity aboard the ship, the gunnery sergeant must be *incredibly* strong.

"Now, get ready." Falax'hebos dusted his hands off as he finished explaining the course, before turning away from the group to look up to an overhead walkway, where two soldiers holding stopwatches waved down to him, giving him the go-ahead. His back still turned toward the examinees, the gunnery sergeant shouted, "Any volunteers?"

But before waiting for a response, however, he pressed on. "*I know*! How about"—he turned around, seeing Kah, hand raised, and his mocking smile fell to a glare—"the kitten."

IV

"Let us pause there for a moment."

Very well.

"You seem confident in your abilities."

I am.

"At the expense of your prudence."

How so?

"Was it your intent to antagonize your superior officer?"

Falax'hebos was not my superior officer. I was not a member of the house fleet.

"Semantics. Do you often find yourself resentful of authority?"

No.

"Resentful of *abuse*, then?"

Perhaps.

"Better. It is all right to let down your guard. You are with friends."

I'm trying. It's hard.

"You are doing well, so far. Continue, please."

———————❧———————

Kah burst off the starting line in a frenzied sprint. The spaces between structures would be the easiest share of the course, and he had to cross them as swiftly as he could to give himself more time on the obstacles themselves. The first obstacle approached in just a few steps. It was a waist-high, horizontal hurdle blocking his path. Simple, easy, meant to chip away at stamina. Refusing to surrender his sprint, Kah leapt out with his hands before him, planting them on the crossbeam with his body fully extended behind, and pushed off, hard.

Perhaps designed to provide the opportunity for a running start, there was a short distance between the hurdle and the next obstacle, a high bar, but Kah figured he could cross that distance without touching the ground. Still horizontal in the air, he realized he was right, as the high bar came up sooner than he anticipated, and grabbed it at the last moment, swinging himself under, around, and over it. The bar was surprisingly smooth, however, and on his release, he unintentionally launched himself hard into the sand, the bottoms of his feet aching from the sudden impact. Worth the time saved. Probably.

He soon recovered and dashed forward to the next obstacle, a series of tilted platforms separated by a few meters and arranged in a staggered, ascending path. Kah didn't break stride, hopping back and forth between the platforms and up to where a pair of downward-sloping parallel bars waited for him. He landed hard on the last platform, then bent his knees and launched up with a snarl, grabbing a bar in each hand, before swinging back and forth, using the momentum to bring his legs up and over each bar. Gracelessly scooting down the sloped bars until they ended, high in the air, in front of a narrow balancing beam built on the same angle, Kah lifted himself up to a standing position and rushed down the beam, more letting gravity take him than actually running.

A series of five high hurdles waited, each at the height of his head, and a much greater challenge than the previous variety. Leaping toward the first, he became very conscious of his diminutive height, grappling and swinging over the hurdle in a short barrel roll. Required to vault over each of these beams individually — no skipping — it was *exhausting*. The increased gravity had started to wear on him.

Rising from the sand beyond the high hurdles, a tall, flat wall waited. Kah intended to jump up and pull himself over the wall. No problem. Sprinting on the approach, however, he realized how tall the wall was and, as he leapt, did not come close to reaching the top. The impact against the plastic freed the wind from his chest and he slid down the wall, confused, a low chuckle sounding from the starting line. Without looking back, Kah bared his teeth and leapt at the wall again, rising to the same height. On the second attempt, however, he extended his claws and dug them into the plastic, climbing the rest of the height and mantling over top. Kah was tired, but still breathing.

A pair of high, upward-sloping parallel bars stood between him and the final obstacle, a rope climb. Unlike the previous parallel bars, however, the goal was to grip a steel pipe which rested atop the bars and, using his weight and momentum, slide himself up the slope without falling before reaching the end. Even with the increased gravity, Kah's arms were strong and his weight was light, making this particular obstacle likely less challenging for him than for many of the other examinees. Reaching the end of the bars, he dropped the two meters to the sand and, nearly sprinting, pounced for the rope. Slapping a buzzer at the top, Kah dropped to the ground and ran around the course to the starting line, where Gunnery Sergeant Falax'hebos stood waiting with his arms folded across his chest.

"Time!" The Puma looked up to the soldiers on the walkway, who checked their watches.

"One minute, twenty-two seconds!"

The Puma glared down at Kah, not budging from his position as Kah planted his hands on his knees, panting and bending in half. "An exceptional time, kitten," he said lowly. He turned to the remainder of the group, his voice a shout again. "An exceptional time! That's how it's done! Let's hope the rest of you can put on such a show!"

Still bent over, catching his breath, Kah heard a growl at his ear.

"Now, do it in the dark."

Still struggling for breath, Kah shot a glare at Falax'hebos and straightened up, assuming position at the starting line. Almost reflexively, he reached for his pocket and retrieved his thermal goggles, pulling them up toward his face, until a massive hand grabbed his wrist.

"What do you think you're doing?" Falax'hebos, gripping Kah by the arm, lifted him up and off his feet and took the goggles from him with his free hand. He inspected them for a moment before abruptly dropping Kah and spinning around to the company, holding the goggles high.

"A Pintoth who can't see in the dark? Well, that may just be the saddest thing I've ever heard! How in blazes have you survived all this time, kitten?" He threw the goggles into Kah's chest, and leaned in close, snarling and spitting in Kah's face. "Pintoth are only good for one, gods-damned thing, and you can't even do that? But you thought I would allow you to cheat on my course?" A smile started to split the Puma's face. "I guess that means you fail, huh, kitten?"

The hatred boiling inside him again, Kah glared into his enemy's contemptuous face. He bared his teeth and felt his claws extend unwittingly. Again, to his credit, Falax'hebos did not miss the subtle movement and traced it down to Kah's claws, then back up to his snarling face.

"What are you going to do?" The sneering smile never left him. "Try me."

"I don't need them," Kah hissed through his teeth.

"Oh, really? This should be good." Falax'hebos gave a tiny jerk of his head and roared, "Lights!"

Shadows fell over the course, bathing Kah in darkness. He heard the snap of elastic, then felt a heavy blow across his face that sent him to his knees. Blood welled from his lip and, running his tongue over his teeth, felt one wiggle slightly. He spat a little blood into the sand, before rising, straight and defiant.

He felt the heat of the Puma leaning close again. "Are you lying to me, kitten? Or do you just enjoy being smacked around?"

Kah fixed his eyes on where he knew Falax'hebos' face to be. "I don't need them."

Turning his back on the sergeant, Kah assumed his position at the starting line. He stomped one foot in the sand, hard, trying to produce some vibration to feel where the obstacles were. However, the loose sand made detection by feel impossible. Working his sore jaw and chewing on the dilemma before him, Kah snapped his teeth. Then again. And again. With the soundwaves of each click, he painted a brief portrait of the room. This time, Kah's face found a smile. "Ready."

A moment passed and a buzzer blared overhead. Once again, Kah flew off the line, now giving a tiny click of his teeth with each exhalation. Spurred on by the excitement of applying the new tactic, Kah took nearly the entire course at full speed. This time, he didn't pause at the wall climb, his strategy already established, and mounted it on his first attempt.

After dropping from the rope and hurtling back to the starting line, he heard the gunnery sergeant declare, "Time!" and the lights returned to life overhead.

One of the soldiers looked down from the walkway, holding his watch out. "One minute, thirty-three seconds!"

Looking past Falax'hebos to his fellow Pintoth, Kah saw a wall of pride and encouragement. He felt the same pride, proving to the sergeant and himself that Pintoth are good for more than one, gods-damned thing.

Kah straightened up, still out of breath, and looked the Puma in the eye. "Satisfied, sir?" He didn't attempt to mask his grin.

Falax'hebos looked down at him, his lip curling over a fang. "Take a break and drink some water, kitten. You've passed the first of your physical exams."

Finished first, Kah nestled against a wall and watched the remainder of his company run the obstacle course. In general, the group performed very well, with no one disqualified due to failure to complete an obstacle and only three examinees disqualified after failing to complete the course in under three minutes. Privately, Kah felt no small amount of pride that nobody ran the course faster than his lights-on time. Three or four *did* beat his lights-off time, but he could forgive himself his blindness.

Shortly after the last examinee ran the course, Falax'hebos received a hail on his communicator and, after a brief exchange through it, faced the company.

"Well done, Pintoth! Most of you have survived! The failures can now return to the freighter with the rest of the dead weight." He pointed at the three examinees who were separated from the rest, leaning against the wall, dejected, and they began to shuffle back through the blast door to the main hangar. "The rest of you will now accompany me to your next examination, the tolerance exam."

Still bristling at Falax'hebos' brazen cruelty toward the dismissed examinees, Kah nonetheless breathed a small sigh of relief. A *tolerance* exam sounded significantly less taxing than the obstacle course. While exiting the course's sub-hangar, his company passed another on the way in. It had dwindled significantly, appearing to have lost more than half its Pintoth. The remainder looked beaten, sick, and defeated. Shooting a wary glance at the sub-hangar the poor souls had just left, the Jaguar chewed a hole through the inside of his cheek.

Catching a distant glimpse of the remaining two companies as they rotated exam rooms, Kah strained his eyes, searching for Calan. One group looked entirely unfazed, the other like they had just been through a nightmare. His own was headed toward the nightmare exam room. Kah suppressed his dread with rationalization.

He would have a better chance to overcome a difficult test when he was relatively fresh, anyway. That's what he tried to believe.

The group walked in silence. There was no shouting from the chief of recruits and no conversation among the examinees. In a space so large, such quiet was eerie. The walk was happily short, however, and before too long, they had arrived at the tolerance exam room.

Entering the room alongside the other Pintoth, Kah saw something whose purpose he could not even attempt to guess. Dominating the space were four devices, roughly spherical in shape, made up of a pulsating wire mesh which seemed to cause the air around them to tremble. Humming ominously with the promise of action, each sphere was set about twenty meters apart from its neighbors. Set directly in front of each device was a seat with numerous safety straps attached, eagerly awaiting an occupant. Kah did not want to be in that seat.

Breaking Kah's examination, Falax'hebos shouted out, ringing the space with his deep barking. "Welcome to the tolerance examination, Pintoth. During this exam, we will test your ability to tolerate increased gravitational load and extreme speed. You will need to be able to endure such effects if you expect to engage in piloted combat, if you expect to drop in on the many planets of the Rae'gal Arm, and if you ever expect to leave those worlds."

The gunnery sergeant leered down at his audience. "*Most* Ty'gjir have an instinct for this sort of thing. *Most* Ty'gjir don't live underground, so you Pintoth must be tested. This device" — he patted one of the spheres — "is a 360-degree centrifuge. Using this, you will be subjected to forces you have likely never felt before. Your objective during this examination is to maintain consciousness, and to not vomit."

The Puma looked down at Kah, his smile broadening. "Number fifty-six, you've had plenty of time to rest and relax. You can be among the first!"

Clenching his jaw, Kah dutifully stepped forward while three soldiers randomly selected Pintoth from the group. Falax'hebos was right. He had never experienced anything like this before. Even on the ship departing the surface of Pinto'Neth, the takeoff and ascent were smooth and gradual, with minimal force exerted on the occupants, likely due to its function as a cargo freighter, Kah imagined. He was sure some cargo was fragile enough that sudden acceleration and high gravity would damage it. Hoping he was made of sturdier stuff, Kah ran his tongue over the hole in his cheek, tasting iron as it began to well.

Far too soon, Falax'hebos' hands were on him, strapping Kah's arms, legs, and neck against the cushions of the apparatus, perhaps too tightly. Kah's tail, too, was pulled around his front and secured by two straps into his lap. As the Puma secured the tail restraints, however, his fingers wrapped around Kah's thin, trapped legs and crept up his thighs. Trying to suppress a shiver, Kah earned a predatory chuckle from Falax'hebos, but the Puma said nothing before his hands retreated to finish strapping Kah to the centrifuge. He hated that his enemy was simply allowed to restrain him like this, a fact not lost on Falax'hebos, who patted Kah's cheek, letting his fingers linger too long on the Jaguar's smooth fur.

"Don't be nervous, kitten. It'll all be over soon." The gunnery sergeant growled, descending the steps from the centrifuge as he pulled his datapad out of its holster.

With no other choice left to him, Kah stared out over the other Pintoth. They looked horrified, with wide eyes and slack jaws, like they were being made to bear witness to an unjust execution. Gritting his teeth, Kah forced a nervous swallow past the strap securing his throat, trying to look brave. He saw Falax'hebos nod to the three other soldiers, themselves holding datapads, and, all at once, pressed something on them, activating the spheres.

With a gentle whirring hum, Kah's seat pulled back hard, knocked against the sphere, and came to rest scant centimeters from its surface. Slowly, the seat began to travel horizontally around the centrifuge. As it did, Kah saw the steps to the sphere begin to sink into the floor, and the sphere itself begin to rise into the air. His eyes darted down as the seat changed orientation, facing him in the direction of his movement, and his heart quickened. Apparently, the sphere took the cue, because, without further warning, its speed massively increased. The world beyond his seat blurring to indistinction, Kah clenched his jaw, blinking rapidly to try to focus on anything at all. As he did, however, he noticed with some alarm that color had begun to flee the world, slipping back to a vision of gray, somewhat like that which he saw through his thermal goggles.

The speed increased, the change in vision worsened, and familiar blackness began to creep in from the edges of his sight, his head going faint. Sala had told him while tutoring him for his medical exams that such a phenomenon could occur when blood flow to the eyes and brain was reduced, so he tried to reverse the trend. Clenching his jaw shut tight, Kah tensed his abdominal muscles and diaphragm hard, willing the blood back to his head. Slowly forcing the black, bit by bit, from his vision, the next minutes became a direct contest.

Then, the challenge changed drastically. The seat slowly turned around, without altering its movement around the sphere, and Kah felt blood rush forward in his head to his eyes, returning his vision to normal. He stopped bearing down to fill his head with blood and attempted to relax. Soon, though, his vision became tinted with red as, he presumed, too much blood flowed to his eyes. He had no idea what to do about this, but at least he didn't feel like he was going to faint anymore. As best he could, Kah scooted forward in the seat, but kept his head back against the rest and tilted his chin up. He didn't know if this would help to relieve the pressure, but it gave him something to focus on over the next two minutes until the seat gradually slowed to a stop.

Breathing heavily as the centrifuge came to rest, Kah shook his head and blinked, trying to return everything in his body to its rightful place. Though the sphere had stopped, some force insisted on dragging his head forward, and he struggled to keep it against the headrest. At least, at any moment, the sphere would descend and his test would be done. Instead, with a teasing hum, he began to travel vertically. Kah heaved a groan of dread as he realized he wasn't done yet.

"No . . ." he moaned, but closed his eyes and prepared to go again. A minute later, he and the centrifuge had stopped moving, and the seat deposited him where he started. The stairs ascended, and with them came Falax'hebos, wearing his condescending, predatory grin.

As he unstrapped Kah from the seat, he chortled — a deep, rumbling sound that originated somewhere in his muscular chest. Hardly able to think, Kah was in no mood to exchange pleasantries with the Puma and waited impatiently to be freed. Quickly rising from his seat, he just as quickly fell back into it. He hadn't realized he was dizzy until he stood up, his brain insisting that down was somewhere behind him.

Lifting Kah bodily out of the chair, Falax'hebos pushed him forward, forcing him down the stairs with one massive hand. "Tough little bastard, aren't you?" he snorted. "I think I'm starting to like you, kitten."

Kah could not say the same.

Locating a nice, stationary spot against the wall, Kah planted himself, waiting for his equilibrium to return. He watched as, over the next hour, the rest of the Pintoth were tested in the centrifuges. From the ground, it was decidedly easier to keep track of what was going on while the centrifuges hurled Ty'gjir around at high speeds.

A few groups after his, a Leopard was being tested when, suddenly, her head dropped and she went completely limp in the seat, her head and hands offering no resistance to the force of the centrifuge. The soldier monitoring the sphere brought it to a stop and quickly removed her from her straps. Throughout the process, the Leopard repeatedly regained consciousness for a few seconds at a time before fainting again, but the soldier exhibited little concern as he hoisted her over his shoulder, carried her off the platform, and flopped her unceremoniously onto the floor. She was only the first of many Pintoth who spent the remainder of the exam lying on the ground with their legs elevated, sipping water.

As the last group slowed to a stop, Kah tallied the number of Pintoth remaining in his company. Thirty-four were left standing, while nineteen lay on the floor in recovery. As he mused, an older, male Bob came down from his test and sat beside Kah against the wall, holding his head and blinking.

After a few moments, he looked over at Kah, with wide eyes and a wider smile. "Definitely don't have anything like that in the mines. Almost makes a guy want to head back underground, where it's safe—almost. I'm Jov'nors."

Kah cracked a nominal smile and extended his hand, which the Bob shook overenthusiastically. "I'm Kah'riss, and. . . I think that might be part of the plan."

"What? Getting us to run back home?" Jov'nors' smile took on a skeptical shade. "That's just bluster. All the drill sergeants are like that. But you won't run, huh?" the Bob said, digging a friendly elbow into Kah's ribs. "Not until you're *satisfied*."

The reference to Kah's malicious subordination conjured only a polite quirk of Kah's muzzle. "It feels like they want us to fail and—and too many of us are already gone," he said. "How is the fleet going to recruit enough Ty'gjir to fight a war if they slash our numbers so badly?" He gestured broadly over the recovering, failed examinees.

"I guess the Baron wants to make sure he only gets the best of the best, to lead, and inspire," Jov'nors said, shrugging. "He wouldn't want the common people to get hurt."

It was Kah's turn to shrug. That sounded believable, he supposed, but with his pounding head and churning stomach, it didn't *feel* believable. He wondered how Calan and his group were doing. Hopefully, better than his own. Pulled from his thoughts by the crackle of the communicator on Falax'hebos' belt, Kah glanced to the Puma. Ending a brief exchange, the gunnery sergeant stood at ease in front of the group.

"Pintoth, your break time is over," the big Puma roared. "Stand at attention, say goodbye to the failures, and prepare to move out to the marksmanship exam!"

With some residual shakiness, the examinees stood up, helping each other to their feet as needed, and straightened to attention. The *failures*, as Falax'hebos had called them, were led out of the room ahead of the rest of the company, the remaining Pintoth staring in silent mourning at their fallen comrades. Kah didn't want anyone to fail. He knew as well as any Pintoth what these Ty'gjir were working toward and knew that they wanted it as badly as he did. And, as far as he knew, this was not a competition, so there was as much an opportunity for all of them to be accepted as there was none of them. Thus, whenever any Pintoth was removed from the group, the company winced with sympathetic pangs, knowing that the Ty'gjir would soon return home to their dark, sad, little world.

The gunnery sergeant marched the group out of the sub-hangar and into the massive, main docking bay. It was less a march than it was a stagger, Kah thought, and, looking to the other groups, saw they were in similar shape. Each company had dwindled significantly, but the two groups behind his own were decidedly the smallest. Whatever the last test was, it was going to be rough.

Ahead of the company, Falax'hebos opened a set of blast doors leading to yet another sub-hangar, where the marksmanship test awaited new examinees. Stepping through the blast doors, Kah saw that space had been converted to a makeshift gun range, with eight lanes and three weapons set at each lane. He also saw that, in addition to soldiers overhead, there were numerous soldiers on the ground, walking the lanes and inspecting weapons. At least two of the Ty'gjir bore white bands on their right arms, marking them as medical staff. Shuffling into the room, the Pintoth stood well back from the lanes, awaiting instructions.

Falax'hebos, on the other hand, marched directly to one of the lanes and lifted a pistol, ensuring it was unloaded before he turned back to the group. "Welcome to the marksmanship examination," he said. "Unlike the rest of your assessments today, you are not expected to excel here. However, your baseline abilities with a firearm, as well as your ability to heed and apply instructions, must be assessed. If you were planning to goof off during any of your tests today, do not make it this one. Buffoonery in this room will get you killed."

Pointing up to the conspicuously armed and vigilant soldiers on the walkways, Falax'hebos looked solemnly to the company, locking eyes with each examinee. There was no mockery, no bluster. He was deadly serious, and it left no doubt as to the gravity of the situation.

"Now, have any of you used a firearm before?" he asked. A few hands went up. Less than a quarter of the group, Kah estimated. His own hand was half-heartedly among them. The gunnery sergeant just nodded as he tallied the number. "More than expected, given your homeworld. Regardless, you are all expected to listen well to these instructions. . ."

He then launched into a well-rehearsed presentation on firearm safety, outlining first the true fundamentals of handling a firearm, followed by the make and model of each of the three weapons at the lane, the structure of the weapons, the locations of their safety switches and major toggles, how to load and unload them, how to handle each for the best results, and, finally, how to fire each and what to expect from firing them.

Actively demonstrating each point of the presentation, Falax'hebos concluded by firing each type of weapon down the lane into a waiting target. Slapping a button on the side of the lane, a holographic image of the target appeared before him, displaying exactly the points at which his shots struck the target, with numbered labels marking the order in which they struck. His aim was impressive, with a very close gathering of marks right in the center of the vague Ty'gjir silhouette which comprised the target.

"The exam will be split into six parts. When the klaxon sounds, you will load your weapon and hit the buzzer, recording the time it took you to load it. One of the other supervisors or myself will come to check your loaded firearm. When everyone has completed this portion, another will sound, and you will have ten warm-up shots to acclimate to the weapon, after which your lane will automatically display your successful shots on the target, if any. Finally, you will have five shots with the weapon which will be used to determine your score. You will repeat this process once for each firearm, after which your marksmanship exam will be complete, and a new group of examinees will rotate in."

He looked down his nose at the nearest examinees.

"If anything goes wrong with your weapon, or you *suspect* something has gone wrong with your weapon, place it on the table in your booth with the barrel facing down range and immediately contact me or one of the other supervisors for assistance." He gestured to the many soldiers walking the lanes. "You will not be penalized for this."

The Pintoth nodded along, trying to absorb everything the sergeant said, before he selected a group of eight examinees and directed them to their lanes. Kah watched from the back as each of the eight aspirants nervously walked forward into their lane. More than a few knees were shaking. Violence was generally uncommon on Pinto'Neth, and firearms even less so. The integrity of the H-cells and ductways was of paramount importance, and no activities were permitted which might endanger them.

As the buzzer sounded, Kah watched most of the novice marksmen fumble through loading their first weapons, then double- and triple-check that the batteries were safely seated before sounding their buzzers. These examinees met with success. One in the first group rushed to load the weapon as fast as possible and rang his buzzer long before the others. When one of the proctors checked the firearm, however, he unloaded and reloaded the weapon, taking note of that applicant's number.

Shortly thereafter, the room was filled with the staggered ripping sound of laser-based weaponry flashing instantaneous, searing heat down lane. Kah tried to learn all he could by watching, but there were far more mistakes to be avoided than there were enviable models. He did his best, however, and never took his eyes off the others throughout the exam. During the warm-up rounds, Falax'hebos and the other soldiers moved from Pintoth to Pintoth, offering advice and instruction on how to correct their aim or otherwise improve their results. Most were able to improve their groupings, at least to a minor degree, before the scored rounds. The process repeated over the next half-hour or so, at which time Kah was, at last, selected to step up for his exam.

Directed to the booth on the far right of the range, Kah stood beyond the eyes of the waiting and finished examinees. He preferred it this way. Nerves rendering his fingers clumsy, an audience was not something he particularly desired. As he stepped into the booth, Kah looked down at the first weapon and rehearsed the information Falax'hebos had shared about it, nervously mumbling to the unassuming bit of metal and plastic on the table.

"Inix-class laser pistol, model II. Fires beams of pure heat energy, effective at a range of fifty meters before catastrophic dispersal. A standard firearm battery in this weapon is good for twenty shots before it requires a reload. Reliable, resistant to weather and wear, and simple to use. Just point and pull. Easy."

Chewing on his lip, Kah fussed. Simple to use, perhaps, but different from what he was used to. At home, his father had made them practice with a stun thrower, which hurled pods of highly conductive gelatin charged with non-lethal, incapacitating electricity. The difference in projectile alone made the weapons difficult to compare. He—

The siren sounded.

Kah snatched the pistol off the table. It was heavier than he expected. Gripping it in his right hand, his thumb depressed a small switch located near the top of the grip and, with his left hand, he pulled back the slide on top. With a hiss and a burst of steam, the previous battery was discharged, flying off somewhere to Kah's right. Grabbing one of the unused batteries from the table, he inserted it into place on top of the weapon before releasing the button under his thumb, allowing the slide to snap back to its previous position and sealing the battery. Everything went well. No reason to double check. But, remembering the prior examinees, he did anyway. His buzzer sounded—the first of the group.

The nearest soldier, helmeted, with yellow fur and black spots—a Cheetah—trotted to his lane to inspect the firearm. Kah reversed his grip on the weapon, holding it by the barrel and out to the soldier, grip-first, as had been demonstrated. Wordlessly, the Cheetah took the pistol, shifted the slide back and forth twice with no release of steam, and handed it back to Kah.

"No problems. Well done, number fifty-six." The soldier walked away, leaving Kah to wait for the others to finish.

Feeling a tingle in his fingers, Kah noticed his leg shaking. Why was his adrenaline pumping? He needed to calm down. Such pent-up energy would only make him less accurate. Making a conscious effort to slow his breathing, he closed his eyes. Relax. *Relax.*

The buzzer sounded again, shocking Kah to attention. There was no rush. Kah assumed the stance Falax'hebos had shown the group. Right hand around the grip, left hand supporting at the base of the handle. He shifted his legs so that the left led the right, his torso slightly canted to parallel his feet. He aimed down the sight of the pistol at the target, a Ty'gjir-shaped silhouette twenty-five meters away. No rush. Kah pulled the trigger, watching the beam blink in and out of existence, a few centimeters over the head of the target. Right. Unlike his arc pistol, he did not have to account for a dropping projectile. Just point and pull.

So, he did, the beam striking the target in the region of the right shoulder. He grinned to himself, firing off a few more shots, some hitting the target, some not. He noted the minimal recoil, which seemed to be a product of the excess heat being released uniformly around the barrel. On his last warm-up shots, he took his time, getting comfortable as he lined up his shots, breathed out, and pulled the trigger.

Although he was among the last to finish his warmup shots, Kah felt confident about the scored portion to come. When the klaxon blared again, he was prepared, calmly bringing up the pistol, getting comfortable, and firing off five beams in relatively rapid succession. The first struck at hip level, the next at about the navel, the solar plexus, the center of the chest, the neck. His target results automatically flashed to life in front of him and he looked at the pattern he had produced: five evenly spaced marks from the hip to the neck at the midline of the target. He would have preferred a tight grouping at the center of mass but was content with the result.

The pistol scoring finished very quickly, and, without any ceremony, the next section began. The Ioneth-class beam rifle, model I, was good for significantly more shots at greater range than the pistol, and was loaded by means of a port built into the grip of the weapon. The rifle was easier to load than the pistol, Kah found, as the discharged battery fired out of the bottom of the grip and the next battery only needed to be inserted up into the same port, clicking into place. Everyone seemed to finish the exercise without error.

When the buzzer sounded again, Kah lifted the rifle and planted the stock against his shoulder, holding the firearm at its two, tilted grips. The rifle was awkward and heavy against him, and the grip felt unnatural. He fired off a test shot, which went very wide on the right. Kah cocked his head. That couldn't be correct. He attempted to compensate and fired again, sending a beam far to the left of the target.

He swore under his breath. Something about the weight and length of the barrel made it difficult to keep on target. A few more shots, a few more misses. Growling in frustration, he resolved to start over, placing the rifle back on the table before he picked it up and reassumed the position the gunnery sergeant had demonstrated. But it didn't feel any different. Kah reminded himself to breathe, stretching his shoulders and neck, and once again raised the rifle to fire.

A hit! Barely clipping the side of the target's head, sure, but a hit nonetheless! With the near absence of recoil on the rifle, which appeared to have an even better balance of heat vents, Kah adjusted his aim and fired again, putting a beam into the target's left shoulder. Then the right shoulder, the chest, the head, and the chest again. The path of the beam of this rifle seemed less consistent than the pistol, with an uncomfortable degree of randomness. With eighty shots per battery, it seemed the manufacturer favored quantity over precision, but there was nothing Kah could do about it except aim and hope.

It seemed he was the last to finish his warm-up shots and when he turned, giving a soldier a thumbs-up, the soldier quickly relayed the message to Falax'hebos, who initiated the scored section. Rounding on his target, Kah brought the rifle to his shoulder and took five slow shots aimed at the center of the target's chest. When the results flashed in front of him, there were three scattered hits, but no other marks on the target at all. Kah ground his teeth and slapped the rifle onto the table, perhaps a little harder than was appropriate. He did not like rifles. Kah was angry with himself, tired from the weight of the weapon, and ashamed that he would likely fail this part of the exam. Standing in his booth, hands planted on the table as he tried to relax, Kah heard a voice behind him.

"Too big for you, kitten?" Falax'hebos had ducked inside, the same mocking smile plastered on his face. "This can't be the first time you've had that problem."

The big Puma closed the distance between them in a stride and Kah turned back to his table of firearms, trying to ignore the looming presence that rendered the small space suddenly claustrophobic. Pointedly looking down at his hands on the table and the much larger pair flanking his, Kah felt the Puma's chest press against his back.

"Get away from me," Kah hissed under his breath, but the Falax'hebos ignored him.

"We can work on that together, you know. Get you used to *larger weapons.*"

As he whispered the final words, Falax'hebos lowered his mouth right next to Kah's ear, and brought his arms closer together, squeezing Kah between them. He was so close that Kah could hear the Puma's tongue hitting his teeth, enunciating each hard consonant in his strange accent. Instinctively wrapping his tail around his own legs, Kah's teeth began to chatter and he pulled his arms tighter against himself, trying to escape the massive Ty'gjir by becoming as small as possible. Any witness would see he was uncomfortable, but, in the booth, the only Ty'gjir who *could* see were Falax'hebos and himself.

They were alone . . . *Alone.*

Where nobody else could see.

Urged by the quiet realization and by the pressure against him, Kah's fingers slid across the table, moving away from the hands of the gunnery sergeant, and gently stroked the grip of the laser pistol. Then, he felt a different part of Falax'hebos press into his back, and Kah reacted without thinking. Abandoning the pistol with a feral hiss, Kah spun around in the Puma's arms, aiming to rake his claws across Falax'hebos' face, but the gunnery sergeant caught his wrist and snarled, raising his fist to strike Kah just as a soldier poked her head into the booth.

"Sir?"

Both Kah and Falax'hebos, snarling and glaring wildly at one another, froze at the intrusion, snapping their eyes toward the soldier. The soldier coughed uncomfortably, but continued.

"The other examinees are waiting, sir. They've all finished this portion of the test." Ducking her head out the door, her hurried footsteps beat a swift retreat.

Straightening up, Falax'hebos thrust Kah's hand away, his expression returning to neutral. "Consider yourself lucky, number fifty-six." The gunnery sergeant looked down at Kah, whose fangs and claws were still dangerously bare. "You're doing well. Keep up your performance here and there will be plenty of time for private lessons later."

He ducked from the booth, leaving Kah breathing heavily, his heart pounding. The Jaguar barely had time to recover before the klaxon sounded once more. The final weapon on the table, a Xsoran anti-materiel rifle, was one of few conventional projectile weapons still in military service, at least by Ty'gjir forces. Covered in sharp angles and points, the weapon was clearly designed with malevolence in mind, with a long barrel flanked by hooked plates and vents, an integral scope, and a stock to comfortably fit around the user's shoulder.

Hefting an empty magazine from the table, Kah began loading huge, heavy, metal rounds of ammunition down into it against a strong spring. The magazine accommodated only ten rounds, but the slugs were each about a half-kilogram in weight, making the process laborious, but simple in execution. With the magazine primed to deliver death, he slapped it into the under-fed receiver and drew back the bolt, loading a round into the chamber. Falax'hebos had said this was an ancient, effective design which had only been improved upon since its inception. To Kah, it just felt correct.

He rang his buzzer and the female soldier from moments before came into the booth to check his work. She looked guilty, he thought, but said nothing, keeping her eyes downcast and her mouth closed. When she offered Kah a pithy thumbs-up and fled, however, he realized she hadn't been surprised when she walked in before. She was merely uncomfortable she had been the one to see it. If she wasn't surprised, she knew to expect it from Falax'hebos. She had seen it before. Exactly how many times she had seen it, Kah didn't know, but, by his estimation, even once was too many.

As the klaxon sounded again, Kah seethed with anger, wondering how many Ty'gjir Falax'hebos had attacked this way, how much more he had been able to do to his other victims, and if anything was ever done about it. Heaving the fifteen-kilogram rifle from its table and onto the counter, he unfolded the bipod under the barrel and took a seat behind the stock. With the stock planted in his shoulder, still shaking with rage, Kah aimed down the scope to the target, one thousand meters away, and pulled the trigger.

An explosion like a ten-ton hammer crushing ore pelted a round down the range. But Kah never saw where it struck. The stock of the rifle punched back into his shoulder, momentarily knocking the wind out of him as the entire booth shook from the venting of the rifle's shot. Eyes wide and mouth agape, Kah let the aftershock of the rifle's concussive force echo through him, relishing the raw, primitive power he held in his hands. Pulling back the bolt to discharge a smoking shell casing, a smile came to his face, and, almost laughing, he slid the bolt back into place, priming another round. Rage blown out of him by the awe-inspiring force he controlled, Kah was left with a cool, calm eagerness to squeeze the trigger again. This time, he slowed down, aiming properly, and pictured the featureless silhouette as the body of his enemy, Falax'hebos.

Nine practice and five scored shots later, his holographic target appeared in front of him. It bore only one large mark, right in the center of the chest, but had several labels, numbered one through five, all indicating the same point. Kah grinned and rose from his seat, fondly running his fingers over the rifle, before he turned and exited the booth. Planting himself at a wall beside Jov'nors, Kah about to ask how the Bob's test went when the gunnery sergeant marched past them, scanning the next group of examinees. Hugging his knees, Kah abruptly closed his mouth and pulled his feet in.

"What's wrong?" Jov'nors asked, nudging Kah to catch his attention.

"Nothing." Kah shook his head as he continued to hug his legs. "I'm fine."

Whether to comfort Kah or to free himself of the Jaguar's reticence, Jov'nors quickly attracted a small crowd of Pintoth who surrounded them, chatting about their favorite and least favorite weapons, about how similar or different they were to what they were used to, about how they might have performed differently given another opportunity. Kah had no idea how most of the group had performed. For the most part, the energy in the air was full of excitement.

However, as the klaxon sounded for the final time and the last group of examinees left their booths — Falax'hebos and the other soldiers huddling together in discussion — the scent of the air became much more apprehensive.

The examinees sitting against the wall looked up at their proctors with near-pleading eyes as the soldiers wove through the company. Selecting different Pintoth and taking them aside for hushed conversations, the soldiers sent them on their way with no more than a sympathetic pat, and the failed applicants left through the blast doors, presumably bound for the freighter. Thankfully, Kah escaped this number, and he breathed a long sigh of relief as Falax'hebos once again addressed the group.

"Pintoth! There are only twenty-two of you left. More than half of you have failed after only three physical tests, and the most difficult is yet to come." Falax'hebos idly scratched at the right side of his face, where Kah's claws had almost reached him, and Kah noticed that, as the gunnery sergeant's eyes slid over the group, they pointedly avoided meeting his own. He smiled. "We will now proceed to the threshold test, commonly acknowledged to be the most difficult examination. If you are not suited to service in this fleet, it will break you. You will not slip by on good luck. Follow me."

Without further ado, Falax'hebos turned and exited the gun range through the blast doors, back into the main hangar. As the other companies rotated, Kah estimated that they, too, had each lost more than half of their number. But, finally, with a chest-clearing gasp of relief, Kah found Calan among the group ahead of his own. He clutched his left ribs and carried a look of grim determination on his face, but he was leading the company, doggedly putting one foot in front of the other on the way to the final test. Kah chewed his lip nervously as he examined them. There were only eleven left. The entire company looked terrible, with most limping or favoring certain limbs, or even helping each other to walk, but Calan had passed the most difficult test. That's what was most important.

Proceeding through the set of blast doors which Calan's had just exited, Kah saw a setup very similar to the room they had just left. It was clearly constructed to be a range, but this one had only five, very narrow lanes, and the entire length of each was separated from the others by translucent plasteel barriers. Manning four of the five lanes were soldiers in full armor, bearing strange weapons. Mostly framework, the weapons had a familiar, rifle-like shape, but the receiver of each firearm was a sort of bulbous pod of white material, stretched and sculpted to form a funnel-like barrel that terminated in a tiny mouth. Seeing the weapons, the group of Pintoth eyed the soldiers warily and put their backs to the wall, most with their arms crossed and their heads down.

When the group was fully assembled, Falax'hebos stood at ease at the head of the company, his legs shoulder-width apart and his hands clasped behind his back. "Welcome to the threshold exam, Pintoth. You are about to be shot with these security force concussion rifles." Nearly every Pintoth furrowed their brow, inspecting the gunnery sergeant closely, trying to judge if he was serious. "They are considered less than lethal, but, rest assured, they strike with all the force of a conventional projectile weapon, just none of the penetration."

While the Pintoth did not look reassured, the gunnery sergeant went to the empty lane and shouldered an unattended concussion rifle, gesturing down the lane with the barrel. "Your objective in this exam is to run the 250 meters from the far end of the lane to the line in front of your shooter. During this time, *we* will attempt to stop you. Each shooter will have one battery's worth of rounds to bring you down, and you must reach this end of the lane within two minutes. If you fall unconscious, give up, or do not reach the line within two minutes, you fail this examination."

Kah looked around at the other examinees. They all wore the same, confused expression, wondering what purpose such a test could possibly serve. He knew his own expression did not match. Instead, he glared openly at Falax'hebos as the Puma continued.

"In the Karos house fleet, we cannot have soldiers who will surrender at the first sign of difficulty. We need to know that our comrades will fight through the pain to reach their objective! If you know your brothers in arms will stop fighting because they're looking down a barrel, how could you trust them during a charge? This test will reveal which of you will fight on, no matter the odds, and which of you should stay home."

As he finished, the four other soldiers approached the group of examinees and grabbed apparently random Pintoth, shoving them toward the lanes. These soldiers were decidedly less sympathetic toward the applicants, with none of the congeniality or support of previous supervising soldiers. Kah imagined Falax'hebos had personally selected these Ty'gjir, finding those most like himself to execute the absurd test.

The selected Pintoth walked hesitantly to the ends of their lanes, where armored helmets waited for them. Kah could see their shoulders shaking as they walked the distance, taking their time and steeling themselves for the task ahead. The sour, metallic smell of fear was thick in the air. As much as he had prepared for these exams, and he was sure everyone else had, as well, he was certain that none of the Pintoth in the room had ever been shot. The best they could do was imagine the pain and hope they'd helt worse. The seventeen Pintoth outside the lanes looked on, fists clenched and jaws tight, wishing their comrades the best. From against the wall, Kah had a clear view of all five lanes, as well as the examinees in them, preparing themselves.

Nearly simultaneously, each examinee hit a buzzer at the far end of the lane, marking the beginning of their time, and leapt forward. A split second later, five impossibly loud *cracks* split the air as the soldiers pulled their triggers. There was a barely visible disturbance in the air as the concussions flew down lane, each striking its target. One examinee was knocked backwards, mid-stride, as the concussion punched into his chest. Prone on his back, the examinee clutched at himself, gasping for air, his legs kicking wildly. Another examinee dropped as the concussion struck her helmet, bringing her to the ground. She did not move again.

The other three persisted for several meters more, taking a number of concussion rounds, before two slumped against the walls of their lanes, raising a hand as a show of surrender. The large Lioness in Falax'hebos' lane was the least fortunate. The gunnery sergeant did not pause after shots, pounding round after round into her midsection. She made it about one hundred meters before he brought her to her knees, yielding as she coughed a fine spray of blood out of the helmet.

Not one of the first five made it to the end of the lane.

Covering his ears after the first shot, Kah tried to protect the sensitive organs within from the loud, concussive *cracks* filling the air. The entire ordeal lasted, perhaps, eight seconds, after which there was only silence, accompanied by the gasps of agony from the five unfortunate Pintoth in the lanes. Some of the remaining examinees looked on in horror, while others couldn't watch, turning their heads away and trying to pretend they might escape the same.

Five medical staff rushed down the lanes of the defeated Ty'gjir and removed their helmets, leaving them where they lay, and dragged the Ty'gjir out of the lanes to safety. The firing line, meanwhile, rounded on the Pintoth and selected more to shoot, pushing them down the lanes to their fate.

More buzzers. More *cracks* as the rifles sounded. Kah covered his ears again to protect himself, and felt an arm wrap around his shoulders and pull him close. He looked to the left, to the source, and saw Jov'nors looking out with grim determination as the shots of the firing line rang wild. Kah's eyes scanned the rest of the twelve Pintoth against the wall. Nearly all were holding each other, trying to watch as their comrades were brought low. Kah wouldn't dishonor his people by looking away from their suffering, so resisted the urge to avert his eyes and trained them instead on a large male Tiger with a gaunt face and long limbs, rising from his knees.

The soldier overseeing the Tiger's lane punched another round into the Tiger's chest as he stood, forcing him back a step, but he did not fall again. With great, heaving breaths, the Tiger strode forward, taking shot after shot to the chest, then broke into a run. The soldier at the lane fired three more shots, each striking the Tiger without apparent effect. Finally, his rifle produced only weak wheezes as its battery was exhausted. The Tiger did not slow his charge toward the line, racing for all he was worth at the Ty'gjir who had just shot him so many times. The Pintoth against the wall rose to their feet, shouting cheers and encouragement as the Tiger crossed the line, marking the first success.

The soldiers, however, merely turned back to the other Ty'gjir to find more victims. As one grabbed Kah by his shirt, he heard Falax'hebos call out, "Not fifty-six. He's last, and he's mine."

Shrugging, the soldier released him, freeing Kah to look over at the Puma, once again sneering with smug delight, knowing his revenge for Kah's claws was soon to come.

Spurred on by the Tiger's success, the next group refused to stay down. Though each was brought to the ground more than once, they all kept standing, hurtling madly toward success against the *crack* of the concussion rifles. Now, every conscious Pintoth and the medics, too, cheered each new examinee across the line, defying their tormentors. Scanning the company, Kah watched some Pintoth weep with joy at their brethren's victory, only to be thrust into the lanes themselves.

This batch, too, continued the rebellion, sprinting down the lanes and refusing to drop, crossing the lines to the sounds of pained, enthusiastic cheers. Passing by the frustrated soldiers, each victorious Pintoth fell into the waiting arms of their applauding kin, who helped them over to the medical staff. Kah was beside them, shouldering the weight of Ty'gjir much larger than himself in order to get them relief as quickly as possible.

Now, only two remained. Jov'nors tried for a brave smirk farewell as Falax'hebos stalked over to them and grabbed the Bob, shoving him bodily into firing lane. All eyes were fixed on the massive Puma and the slim Bob. Falax'hebos brought the rifle to his shoulder and aimed down sights, waiting for the examinee to start his time. Kah watched Jov'nors' eyes narrow as he assumed a running position, his hand resting on the buzzer. Silence hung over the sub-hangar. Each Pintoth held their breath, waiting for the test to begin.

The buzzer sounded and, before even springing off the line, Jov'nors ducked his head, dodging a concussion round which cracked into the wall behind him. The Bob managed a few steps before he took his first hit to the shoulder, spinning him mid-stride and knocking him prone. Looking up from the floor, he thrust himself to his feet, meeting another round from the Puma's rifle and tumbling backwards. But he wouldn't stay down and, once again, rose, taking yet another round to the head. The feeling of triumph lingering in the air wore thin as, time and again, Falax'hebos knocked his victim to the ground, keeping him from taking even a few steps at a time. Eventually,

Falax'hebos' rifle began to wheeze, but the Bob was already face down in the middle of the lane. Silence, once again.

"Stand up!" Kah couldn't stop the words tearing from his lips, and realized he'd carved bloody furrows into his own palms with his claws. "You can make it!"

In the middle of the lane, Jov'nors' head lifted slightly, and, mustering his strength, he began to crawl toward Falax'hebos. As the Ty'gjir began to put on a final show of rebellion, the remaining aspirants shouted out to him, low at first, but rising into a frenzy as the slim, abused Bob kept crawling nearer and nearer the end. Reloading his rifle, Falax'hebos set it against the wall of the lane before stepping forward and sitting on his haunches at the finish line. The Pintoth were berserk, screaming and cheering and crying as their downed kin pulled himself inexorably to the line, finally thrusting a hand across it and collapsing where he lay.

The cheers only increased, until Falax'hebos leaned down to the prone Ty'gjir, smiled, and stated plainly, "Two minutes, eleven seconds."

Somehow, this broke through the clamor and the applause died, replaced by low, shocked gasps, then a uniform, deep growling. The gunnery sergeant straightened up and looked back to Kah, beckoning him over to the lane. "Let's see if you can do so well, kitten."

Kah didn't bother trying to prevent his lips curling into a bare-fanged snarl, storming to the lane as the medical staff removed the protective equipment and lifted Jov'nors onto a stretcher. Taking the offered helm from one of the medics, Kah felt a thin hand grasp his arm and he looked down, finding the Bob's wide eyes locked with his own, his bloody lips trembling to form words, and Kah leaned close to hear him.

"S-satisfied . . . sir?" he croaked.

Kah withdrew his head and looked down at the Bob with a furrowed brow. Attempting a weak smile, Jov'nors gave Kah's arm a final, fierce squeeze, before his eyes rolled back in his head, abandoning consciousness. Growling lowly, Kah shot a snarl at Falax'hebos and thrust the helmet over his head. It was dark and cramped inside, the plates of the armor flexing to accommodate the shape and size of the Jaguar's head. It stank of blood and sweat, fueling Kah with ever more hatred for the Puma behind him. He practically stomped his way down the lane, feeling every eye in the room boring into his back. Rounding on the starting line, Kah narrowed his eyes at the foe, watching as Falax'hebos crooked a small smile and tapped his cheek, shouldering his weapon.

No warning. Kah punched the buzzer, dashing forward before giving the Puma a chance to properly aim. Then, his left leg went out from under him, bringing him to a knee. He didn't feel any pain, but he was certain he'd put the foot elsewhere. As he kneeled, one foot still planted on the ground, another round pounded into the knee of the uninjured leg, followed by a round to his right shoulder, spinning him in place. Still on his knees, but now facing backwards, Kah felt a series of blunt punches strike his back, shoulders, and helmet.

Now it hurt. Now *everything* hurt. A few shots struck the backs of his thighs and, instinctually, he curled his legs forward under him, assuming the fetal position on the floor of the lane. But the shots kept coming, pounding into every part of his exposed body, denying him any chance to recover. It felt like minutes passed as the *cracks* rang out, followed by dull thuds into his body. Then, he heard Falax'hebos' rifle wheeze, its battery spent.

He was fine. He could make it. Stumbling shakily to his feet and focused on the line, Kah sprang forward desperately, not giving Falax'hebos a glance. Then he heard the hiss of a discharged battery and felt another punch to his chest, taking the wind out of him. The Puma, a smile on his face, held a reloaded rifle to his shoulder. Another *crack*, and Kah watched the disturbance in the air speed toward him. He leapt aside, not breaking his sprint, but took another round to the chest. And another.

Watching Falax'hebos' eyes and his trigger finger, Kah dove aside, ducking, dodging, his shoulders knocking hard into the walls of the narrow lane as the Puma's subtle movements telegraphed his shots. Twenty meters. Kah took a round to the chest and opened his mouth, unleashing a bestial roar. Ten meters. A shot glanced off his helmet, cocking it slightly into his vision. Five meters. He watched as Falax'hebos began to panic, firing blindly, not bothering to aim, and missing nearly every shot.

Kah leapt into the waiting arms of his people, pain forgotten in the moment of triumph. A chorus of praise greeting him, he ripped off the helmet and hurled it back toward the lane, toward Falax'hebos, a wild grin on his face as he shouted, "Time!"

Veins pulsed on the gunnery sergeant's forehead as he checked the results, barely containing a snarl as he looked back to Kah. "One minute, fifty-six seconds."

Without missing a beat, Kah narrowed his eyes derisively at the Puma and called out, "Satisfied, sir?"

V

"How vivid!"

That was the first time I struck a blow against an enemy. It stood out.

"There is that word again."

Which?

"Enemy. Your use of it to describe an allied officer is troubling."

I had hoped my reasons was clear.

"Regardless of Falax'hebos' predations, his status as an officer of the United Fleet of the Dal Territory should have demanded your deference, if not your respect."

A Ty'gjir like that should never have been accepted into the fleet in the first place.

"That line of thought is petulant and futile. He was and was your superior officer. You jeopardized your success for the sake of your childish pride. Do you make a habit of this?"

I suppose I should have lifted my tail to him so he would like me?

"Do not twist our words. You could have handled the situation very differently. Less confrontationally."

But I didn't. That line of thought is petulant and futile.

"You are being difficult."

If I had done anything differently, I would not be here now.

"That remains to be seen. There is more to your being here than simply passing a few tests."

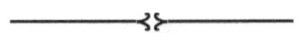

For the next several minutes, Kah found himself overwhelmed amidst a sea of congratulatory hugs, cheering, clasped hands, and ginger claps on the back. All the Pintoth were eventually medically cleared, and the ten who had not passed the exam were dismissed back to the freighter, yet carried with them a rebellious glare as they went. Afterward, Falax'hebos led Kah's group back out into the main hangar, where they saw that the Pintoth who had been relegated to the freighter over the course of the tests had now returned, forming a large semicircle near the middle of the hangar.

Looking for the other companies, Kah found each group reduced to about ten members. He was excited to see that not a single member of Calan's had failed the obstacle course but, despite their success, all the remaining examinees were led toward the semicircle, looking somewhat confused. As they approached, Kah was able to see that, in the middle of the crowd, a makeshift combat ring had been constructed during the last exam. He sighed heavily, his pain back and worse than ever. He thought the threshold exam was the last he would have to face.

The four supervising officers met in the middle and ordered the approximately forty remaining examinees to stand at attention, facing toward the walkway from which

Baron Mal'karos had addressed them nearly sixteen hours earlier. As the four groups met and mingled, Kah shifted his way through the crowd until he could stand at attention beside Calan.

His older brother looked down at him and cracked a warm smile. "You look like shit, Kah."

"And you're the picture of health." Kah grinned, giving Calan a gentle nudge in the ribs he had been holding earlier. Calan's wince elicited a taunting chuckle from Kah, but it didn't last long, the smile dying on his lips as he looked about at the remaining Pintoth and the compulsory audience of failed examinees behind them. "There are so few of us left, Calan."

His older brother shrugged, passing a glance backwards. "Just means this last test will be over sooner and we can get out of here."

"But all of these people *want* to defend their homes. Why doesn't the Baron let them fight?"

Calan shook his head, scanning the assembled Ty'gjir with his hooded gaze and, for an instant, Kah thought he saw fury in his brother's usually-tranquil eyes. "There have to be Pintoth to mine the nordium, Kah." In an instant, however, the look was gone, and Calan examined the fresh sand raked across the combat ring before them. "Looks like the last test will be hand-to-hand combat. You should be excited about that—it's always been your favorite."

Kah recognized the abrupt change in conversation for what it was, but nonetheless chuckled, "Not always. Not being able to see made it kind of a pain for a while." Watching as the four supervising officers walked into the middle of the ring and directed their attention to the walkway, he nudged Calan and whispered, "Which one was yours?"

"Sergeant Shin'ade, the Lynx on the left." Calan inclined his head toward the officer, indicating a short, stocky female Lynx with thick limbs and thick fur which ballooned out from her sleeveless shirt. From this angle, Kah couldn't see her face, but he remembered that she looked particularly severe.

Perhaps sensing Kah's train of thought, Calan continued, "She was nice enough, considering the circumstances. Seemed to want us to succeed. Yours?"

Kah growled, muttering under his breath, "Falax'hebos. Guy was a complete—"

"HA-TTEN-SHUN!" Falax'hebos yelled out, bringing all conversation to an end. "Baron on deck!"

A blast door had just opened above and, through it, swirled Baron Mal'karos, flourishing his cape as he approached the handrail, looking down on the examinees with a fond, paternal grin. Behind him walked three officers whose rank Kah couldn't identify from this distance, but they certainly looked important.

The Baron gave the rail a gentle pat before crying out in his amplified, musical voice, "Pintoth! I am proud to see how many of you are left standing. Your efforts have paid off and you have earned the praise of all the Ty'gjir of our proud sector. A round of applause, please, everyone!"

The baron waved his hand over the congregation and everyone began to applaud. The officers applauded stiffly and formally, but the Pintoth who had not made it so far cheered loudly, congratulating their brethren who, at last, would be able to leave Pinto'Neth.

"Well done, all. You have but one test left ahead of you until you are able to join the glorious cause — to defend your home against the pretender emperor! I will personally oversee this examination and expect you all to give it your best. No slacking!" He punctuated this last point with a flamboyant wag of his index finger. "Chief of Recruits, please outline the final test for our brave Pintoth!"

The baron waved his hand again and, as he did so, someone produced a drink and a cushy chair from which he could watch the final examination in comfort.

Saluting to the baron, a gesture of tapping the right hand on the left shoulder, Falax'hebos turned 180 degrees to face the haggard examinees standing at attention, before he yelled, "Examinees! Your final physical examination will be a test of hand-to-hand combat."

Calan nudged Kah.

"This exam will serve a dual purpose. First, your combat skills must be assessed. After a hard day of action, you will still need to be prepared for combat. The traitor princes and pretender emperor will not stay an invasion just because you've had a long day!" The Puma began pacing up and down the line of Pintoth, standing close and spraying them with saliva as he continued to shout. "Second, you must demonstrate to your baron that you are willing to put worldly loyalties aside. If you are inducted into the house fleet, Pinto'Neth will no longer be your home! The *sector* will be your home, and you must be willing to fight for it, regardless of who your enemies may be."

He stopped, stomping a boot and kicking up a wave of sand. "The exam will be split into four tournament-style brackets, with your bracket being made up of the remaining examinees from the company you've tested with throughout the day. The winner of each bracket will be guaranteed admission into the house fleet. The others will be assessed based on their individual performance in each round of the tournament. Some losers will be admitted, others will not. Each match will continue until submission or knockout. You may use any means at your disposal to win. However, boots will not be worn during bouts, and lethal intent will not be tolerated. Sergeant Kiln'aren, your company will fight first, followed by the examinees of Sergeant Shin'ade, then those of Sergeant Um'therren, and finally my own. Sergeant Kiln'aren, the floor is yours."

Falax'hebos stepped back as Kiln'aren, a slim, long-limbed feline with large ears and hypnotizingly complex fur patterns—a Serval—stepped forth. Unholstering his datapad, Kiln'aren shouted out to the assembly, "Company number one, fall in!"

Nine Pintoth stepped forward and stood at attention while the rest were allowed to sit back and watch. Kiln'aren ran over the rules again, input each of his nine examinees into his datapad, constructing a bracket, Kah assumed, and indicated two of the group, who walked to opposite ends of the sand pit.

Without waiting more than a moment, Kiln'aren shouted, "Begin!"

The two looked more than a little uncertain as they stared each other down, neither making the first move for several moments. One brought his hands up and started to edge forward, slowly crossing the ten-meter expanse. The other mirrored the first, creeping across the sand. Even when they were within striking distance of each other, however, the two combatants seemed reluctant to fight.

Seeing this, Kiln'aren strode forward, shouting, "Fight for your lord!" and struck one across the back of the head with his datapad.

Spurred by pain, the combatants lunged forward, both taking a few, half-hearted strikes before they wrestled each other to the ground, throwing wild strikes and attempting to grapple each other into submission.

Kah and Calan sat together, scrutinizing each and every move by the combatants, strategizing. It was clear these two had not trained much in close quarters combat, but growing desperation lent a furious, frenzied strength to their attacks and cast the sour reek of fear thickly around the ring. Looking around, most of the Pintoth in the room had averted their eyes, refusing to watch their brethren fight for the amusement of some noble. Eventually, one combatant twisted the other's leg in a way he could not tolerate, and he submitted. There was token applause, and the two limped out of the ring.

Looking above to gauge the baron's reaction, Kah saw that he did not appear impressed, or even pleased by the display. And yet, he wore a small, contemptuous smile on his muzzle as he sipped some darkly-colored drink from a delicate glass. Kah wondered how the baron himself would perform in combat. Or, rather, if the baron would ever have to.

The other combatants from the first group were very similar, except for one female Jaguar, clearly an adept striker, who, over three rounds of combat, knocked out each of her opponents before Baron Mal'karos, radiating benevolence, declared her the winner of the bracket and the first examinee to secure her position in the house fleet. At this, the Pintoth broke into raucous applause and the Jaguar fell to her knees, wiping tears from her eyes before she was escorted to a seat from which she could watch the remaining combat in relative comfort.

Falax'hebos gestured to Shin'ade, and the Lynx stepped into the ring. "Company number two, fall in!" Her eyes scanned the gathered Pintoth, picking out her aspirants and summoning them with a look.

Calan rose to his feet, dusting his pants off, and tousled Kah's head fur, holding a fist out for him to bump. "Wish me luck, brother."

Kah looked up, smiling, and touched knuckles with his older brother. He knew that if the rest of the examinees fought like the first group, Calan would be fine.

He was right. It was a slaughter. Over four rounds of combat, Calan, without hesitation, decimated each of his opponents, forcing submission within ten seconds in each round. Characteristically cool and collected, as he was announced the victor, Calan looked over to Kah with his half-lidded eyes and flashed a simple, happy grin. Kah wished he could embrace his brother, could run over to congratulate him on achieving his dream, but the fanfare was done. Calan was simply escorted to the winners' seats and placed beside the female Jaguar, watching the rest of the combat play out while the two shared quiet conversation. But as the baron squeaked out adulations from above, Kah noticed, Calan didn't even glance in his direction.

It was hard to believe that, just like that, something Calan had worked toward for his entire life was accomplished. Kah was impossibly proud of him. He wondered what their father would have said. He, like Calan himself, would probably have downplayed the whole thing, telling him not to get a big head or bowing with mock reverence before the new admiral of the baron's fleet. Remembering Sark fondly, Kah hoped he, too, would make his father proud.

He was so intent on his reverie that he missed nearly the entire third bracket, lost in thought. However, the last match was rather impressive, with two capable fighters matching each other blow for blow. Their fighting focused almost entirely on punches and strikes with the elbows. It was a style of boxing which was especially well-suited to large Ty'gjir, like the Tiger and Lion currently in the ring. Eventually, the Lion got around the Tiger's guard and scored a massive hook to the left side of the Tiger's head. The Tiger staggered back limply but remained standing. His arms, however, fell to his sides as he momentarily lost consciousness, and the Lion pressed the attack, striking the Tiger full force in the muzzle with a closed fist, which dropped the Tiger in a dramatic knockout.

Against their better nature, most of the Pintoth in the audience had succumbed to the excitement of the fighting, and they applauded loudly for the victorious Lion. The baron was significantly more enthusiastic than the Pintoth, however, bouncing on the edge of his seat and spilling his dark drink while squeaking out cheers of delight. Saluting the baron, the Lion raised his hands in a tired show of triumph before taking his seat with the other winners.

Finally, it was Kah's turn.

Before Falax'hebos said anything, the final group had risen and began to assemble. Cut from fifty-six to twelve by the hated Ty'gjir before them, they all wore unhidden malice for the gunnery sergeant, who mirrored them with a remarkably similar expression. Despite the shared animosity, the final group of Pintoth stood to attention, waiting for their fate to be decided as Falax'hebos constructed the bracket. Having completed that, he pointed at two Pintoth and dismissed the others.

One of the two, a female Cheetah, made an impressive showing. She was clearly well trained and made an effort to quickly bring her opponent to the ground, forcing him to submit with elaborate grapples and holds, keeping full control of the action the entire bout as they wrestled in the sand. After her opponent submitted, she rose, straight and proud, and returned to sit among the others.

Next, the large, male Tiger who had first passed the threshold exam took to the ring against a Leopard. The Tiger employed the same techniques as the large combatants from the final round of the previous group, wasting no time in delivering crushing, heavy blows against his opponent, resulting in a knockout within one minute. He smirked as he was declared the winner, but reverently carried his defeated opponent out of the ring, presenting the limp form to the medics before he returned to his seat.

"Fifty-six! Thirty! You're next."

Kah jumped to his feet when he heard his number called and calmly walked into the ring. He didn't know the other examinees by their number designations and didn't look to see his opponent until he was situated in his corner of the ring. It was a male Caracal, distinct for his golden coat, sharp features, and the exceptionally long black tufts protruding from the tips of his ears. Kah recognized him as one of the few who had surpassed his lights-off time on the obstacle course. Over the Caracal's shoulder, Kah could see Calan, chewing on his nerves — a habit shared by their entire House. Kah tried for a reassuring smile and assumed a fighting stance, elbows up high, wrists level with his eyes, body skewed slightly to the left, and left knee loosely bent.

The Caracal, clearly thinking the smile was for him, returned the smile and nodded at Kah, mouthing, "*Good luck,*" before he assumed an identical stance.

"Begin!"

Both combatants advanced to the center of the ring, keeping an arm's length between them. The Caracal struck first with a forward jab to test Kah's defenses, but he blocked it easily enough with as little movement as possible, refusing to compromise his defense for a weak punch. In a flash, however, the Caracal whipped his right leg out for a kick to Kah's side, forcing him to raise his left knee to block it. A strong right uppercut, nearly breaking Kah's guard through force alone. The Caracal was stronger than him, that was certain. Eventually, Kah would be unlucky, a serious blow would land, and that would be it. He couldn't allow that.

While Kah formed a plan, the Caracal struck out with a high kick, forcing Kah to drop his left elbow to block the blow, then tried a forward kick, again forcing Kah to lift his leg to intercept the strike. Trying for a counterattack as his opponent recovered, Kah delivered two quick hooks which the Caracal dodged with surprising speed. Not risking another opening, the Caracal darted forward, pummeling Kah's defense with strong punches and fast, low kicks. Stuck on the defensive, Kah couldn't find any chance to retaliate. His growl of frustration was cut short as the Caracal slipped past his guard, delivering a punishing punch to Kah's abdomen and knocking the wind out of him. Staggering back, Kah tried to collect himself, refusing to fall. He was used to being on his guard, but not against so relentless an opponent.

The Caracal barely looked winded as he edged closer. Kah knew he was making a poor showing, and pure defense clearly wasn't winning this fight. He needed to change tactics. As the Caracal took a final step in, Kah flashed forward, viciously pummeling his guard, trying to bait an opening. The Caracal seemed extremely capable on defense, as well, but Kah wouldn't let up until his foe attempted a cross-jab to force Kah back. Seeing an opportunity, Kah struck out, swinging a hooking blow at the left side of the Caracal's head, but he lifted his left hand to block and ducked his head to the right, closing his eyes for a fraction of a second. That's all Kah needed.

With vicious speed, Kah brought his left leg up to meet the Caracal's ducking head, the top of his foot catching the right side of the Caracal's face with a resounding *crack*, and dropped the Caracal to the ground, out cold.

"The victor is number fifty-six!"

Heaving an agonized sigh of relief, Kah grinned at Calan, who pumped a fist in triumph, eyes wide. Gingerly rubbing his aching arms, he exited the ring and sat on the floor, wiping the sand from the padded soles of his feet.

This was the first time he had had a serious fight with anyone outside his family. It was more difficult than he thought it would be. He had had years to learn his brothers' technique, he supposed, but anyone else could be a mystery.

He wondered what the baron thought of the display and glanced up, a surge of pride soothing his pain as he saw Mal'karos practically kicking his feet in glee, sipping from his drink. Behind him, the three officers took notes on datapads. One, a female Caracal, looked particularly interested. Mentally racking up points, Kah smiled.

The next combatants were a Tigress and a lanky female Serval. As far as Kah knew, both had middling performances on the other tests, but always came through. He had no real sense of their abilities, beyond the fact that both were in very good shape. Looking at their eyes as they stepped into their corners, Kah sensed some animosity between the two, but wasn't privy to the cause.

Stepping forward, Falax'hebos cut his hand through the air, shouting, "Begin!"

The Serval stood stone-still in her corner, unmoving as the Tigress raised her fists into a boxing stance and advanced. The larger combatant bearing down on her, the Serval made no move to defend herself. It was a trap. As soon as the Tigress came within reach, the Serval pounced and her right leg shot up like a piston, catching the Tigress in the chin and dropping her in one blow.

Kah's eyes widened. "Whoa."

Not even six seconds. Running over the brackets in his head, Kah grimaced. If he won his next match, he would then have to fight her. Trying to formulate a strategy, he glanced to Calan, also chewing his lip as he grappled with the same frustration. The Serval had revealed so little information about how she fought. Drawn by a squeaking from above, Kah looked to the baron, his head turned, excitedly chattering to the female Caracal officer. Maintaining a grave, dour expression, her left hand near her chin in thought, she silenced him with a quick twist of her wrist.

Kah cocked his head. Who was she, to treat a baron that way?

The second round of matches began, and the female Cheetah and male Tiger had bouts almost identical to their first. Kah gained no new information on them, except perhaps that they each knew only the one martial art they had exhibited so far, and both were very good at their chosen style. Minimally helpful, but still something.

"Number one! Number fifty-six! You're up!"

Kah bounced to his feet again, the pain of the earlier bout and the concussion shots dulled by the adrenaline pumping through his veins. His opponent, a male Lynx, stepped into the ring—yet another combatant he had yet to see. Unwilling to go into the fight blind, Kah walked slowly to his corner of the ring, watching his opponent for any tells. With each step, the Lynx bore down through the sand, anchoring himself. As Kah assumed his previous fighting stance, the Lynx spread his legs wide and low, holding his arms away from his face and his hands open. A grappler.

"Begin!"

The Lynx charged him, closing the distance as fast as possible. Kah knew speed, distance, and strikes would be his best allies in the duel and, trying to maintain all three, he bounced around the Lynx in a large circle. When the Lynx got too close, Kah delivered a low, chopping kick to the side of his foe's left knee, but he largely shrugged it off and pressed forward. Darting away, Kah delivered two quick jabs to the Lynx's exposed side, a process which repeated numerous times over the next minute or so. Kah tried to make sure his single strikes were impactful whenever the Lynx attempted to close the gap, but still, his opponent refused to go down.

It could not last. Backed to the edge of the ring, Kah's footing slipped and the Lynx had him, both hands gripping his shoulders like a vise. Kah tried to seize control of the grapple, turning his arms over the Lynx's, but the Lynx would not relinquish his hold. Frustrated, growling, Kah lifted his knee into the Lynx's solar plexus, forcing a lung-emptying gasp from his opponent but, still, he wouldn't let go. Kicking at the Jaguar's legs, the Lynx attempted to sweep Kah's feet from beneath him in order to bring him to the ground. Kah would not let that happen. Instead, planting his feet hard, Kah thrust his arms up and under his opponent's, gripping his chest and using the leverage to deliver swift, punishing blows to the Lynx's face with his elbows. One blow connected as Kah had hoped, striking the Lynx squarely on his short muzzle, and he finally gave up the hold, staggering backward from the panting Jaguar.

Without warning, the Lynx dove forward, catching Kah by the right leg and trying desperately to bring him to the floor, but Kah's feet were still planted, allowing him to strike down at the face and head of frantic opponent. Suddenly, Kah felt sharp, horrid pain and trickling warmth where the Lynx had seized him. Looking down, Kah saw the Lynx's claws extended, cutting through his pants and digging deeply into his leg. Clearly, their fathers were kindred spirits.

He couldn't endure it any longer. Determined to drive him off, Kah slammed a fist hard into the Lynx's head, causing his neck to snap back, and pounded blow after punishing blow into the Lynx's exposed throat, feeling unknown structures within give and crack under the force of his fists. While the Lynx's grip loosened, however, his claws remained fixed in Kah's leg, drawing an exasperated, pained snarl from the Jaguar. At last, after a pitiless barrage, the light started to go out of the Lynx's eyes, and Kah wrapped his fingers around his opponent's throat, extending his claws and letting their tips dig into the soft, beaten flesh.

Leaning down, eyes wild and deadly serious, Kah hissed through clenched teeth, "*Submit.*"

Whether it was Kah's tone, the hooks in his flesh, or simply his body giving in, the Lynx released his hold, jaw slack and eyes swollen shut, and limply patted the sand twice, signaling his surrender.

"The victor is number fifty-six!"

There were no cheers this time—no applause as Kah limped off the sand, leaving a red-stained trail in his wake. There was only the trilling, vicious laughter of the baron, high above. By far the longest and most brutal bout, it didn't feel like a test anymore. This was combat, and it was far from amusing.

VI

"Stop."

Why?

"Would you have killed that Ty'gjir?"

No.

"It seems like you might have."

That would have been against the rules.

"And even with fang and claw bared, like an animal, you cared about the rules? . . . Answer the question."

I suppose not.

"What, in that moment, did you care about?"

Victory.

"At what cost?"

At any cost.

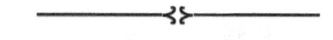

Momentarily safe at his spot on the floor, Kah laid down and curled into a ball, hissing with pain as the movement aggravated the clawed muscles of his leg. He didn't want to watch the fights anymore. He didn't want to see Calan's concerned face, or the baron's mirth, or the mystery officer's cold analysis. There would be no further unknown opponents. In so small a bracket, Kah had had the chance to see each of his future opponents fight at least once. Now, he wanted to rest.

He closed his eyes and listened to the dull thuds of flesh striking flesh, the sickening crack of bone on bone, and the hisses and moans of pain and exertion over the next two bouts. The air of levity did not return. The audience was still and silent, allowing the sound of combat to reverberate, quivering, through the eerie silence of the *Collision of Truth*.

"Number fifty-six! Number twenty-nine! Step into the ring for your semifinal match!"

Opening his eyes, Kah saw the male Tiger carry the female Cheetah out of the ring and to the medical staff. He was slightly relieved. He did not want to fight another grappler. Instead, if Kah defeated his next opponent, he would have the massive Tiger to contend with, gods help him. But first, he was faced with a Ty'gjir perhaps even more dangerous.

The female Serval arrived in her position, fresh and unfazed, long before he painfully rose to his feet and limped into the ring. Whatever was going to happen here, it was going to happen quickly. Kah couldn't risk her kicks. He didn't have the strength to block them. Not anymore. One was bound to strike home. Warily eyeing him as Kah took his place in the ring, the Serval looked . . . nervous?

This time, Kah did not assume any particular stance, merely nodding to Falax'hebos, who brought his hand down and shouted, "Begin!"

Standing their ground, both combatants lay still, staring down the other and waiting for any sign as to the other's intentions. Thirty seconds passed without movement. Feeling the warm trickle of blood running down his right leg, Kah glanced down to where it had pooled, seeping slowly into the sand. As he looked up, he saw the Serval take her final step toward him, jump, and aim a spinning kick at the left side of his head.

It was a trap. Launching up as the Serval's second foot left the sand, Kah twisted his body to the left and caught her leg across his chest with a painful *snap*. In the same motion, he delivered an identical kick just under her ear and hooked his foot behind her head, dragging her to the ground as his body completed its rotation. Desperation lending speed to his limbs, Kah twisted her arm behind her back and dropped a knee on her spine, pinning her to the sand. He knew he had won. He just needed to hear her surrender. After a tense moment, however, it became clear she had been knocked unconscious by the initial blow and was lying completely limp under him.

"The victor is number fifty-six," Falax'hebos said, surprise and more than a small amount of fury coloring the declaration.

Leaving his opponent face-down in the sand, the Jaguar blearily looked toward the walkway, finding the baron wearing a petulant pout. He couldn't contain a sneer, indignant that the baron would be disappointed in his victory. His snort of anger choked by a hiss of pain, Kah gently palpated his ribs, gasping as a few shifted under his fingers. That would make the final fight much more difficult, but it would not shake his resolve. Resigned to discomfort, Kah returned to his corner, waiting for the gunnery sergeant to summon the male Tiger, number twelve, back to the ring. Afterwards, no matter what happened, Kah could rest.

Just one minute later, the Serval was in the hands of the medical staff, replaced by the looming form of number twelve, across the sand. The Tiger was a striker and, at more than twice Kah's size, he was a very big striker. He wasn't particularly fast, but, so far, it didn't seem like he needed to be. His blows were crushingly strong, rendering blocking a futile effort. He needed to be dodged, but Kah knew he couldn't dodge for long. He was wounded and weary, and only more exhausted the longer he stayed on his feet.

Panting in his corner, Kah looked down at the sand he had painted crimson, a trail of blood leading to Falax'hebos on the sidelines, sizing up the two combatants and looking pleased with the matchup fate had produced. The Tiger, for his part, wore worry openly on his face. He appeared to be about Istur's age. Maybe he had younger brothers of his own and felt some sympathy for the diminutive, injured Kah. Maybe he was just concerned about the amount of blood pooling under Kah's feet.

Looking past the Tiger, Kah found Calan on the edge of his seat beside the other winners, clutching his knees with bare claws. Kah blinked. His eyelids felt strangely heavy. Calan was worried. He was going to hurt himself if he kept worrying like that. Kah had to stop him worrying, and soon.

"Begin!"

Kah tore forward, without defensive posture or martial stance. He wasn't going to have the strength to beat the Tiger for much longer, and he needed to bait a thoughtless move out of him. Shocked by the sudden burst of movement from the wounded little Jaguar, the Tiger gave him exactly what he wanted, swinging a wild right haymaker. Just before impact, Kah ducked left under the blow and punched up into the Tiger's armpit. Dropping his arm, the Tiger caught Kah in place, but had no further time to act.

Using his trapped hand as an anchor, Kah vaulted the arm and swung his legs up to catch the Tiger's neck in the crook of one knee, locked in place by the other. Wrapping his arms tight around the Tiger's right elbow, Kah wrestled away every attempt to free his opponent's throat and, with his newly established leverage, heaved with all his remaining strength, producing a hiss, then a scream of agony as, with a sickening *pop*, Kah dislocated the arm.

Falling to his knees, the Tiger roared in pain, trying to free himself from the death-grip Kah had around his now-useless right arm, but the Jaguar continued to twist and pull the limb until, ultimately, the Tiger surrendered with two great splashes of sand. At last, Kah released him and dropped the remaining meter to the ground, lying flat on his back, limbs splayed out in the sand. Unable to hear even his own frenzied breaths past the ringing in his ears, Kah watched the Tiger fiercely clutching his right arm, face twisted in agony.

The audience was still, until one brave voice dared break the silence. "Holy shit."

Kah heard Falax'hebos begrudgingly pronounce him the winner through clenched teeth, and, victorious at last, he closed his eyes.

Above, crying out with unmasked glee, the baron gripped the rail. "A magnificent showing, number fifty-six!

Chief of Recruits, you should be proud of the crop of Pintoth you have cultivated! The resolve! The *perseverance!*"

Kah groaned his way to a vertical position and looked up at the baron. Nominally tapping his left shoulder, he staggered out of the ring and toward the other winners.

"Number fifty-six, you have secured your position in my house fleet, and we are proud to have you among our ranks! Well done!"

However, just before Kah could reach his brother, waiting to receive him, he heard the strange, hard accent of Falax'hebos disturb the air.

"My lord?"

"Yes, Falax'hebos?" The baron seemed somewhat taken aback at being addressed in this moment of triumph.

"As we now have recruits who have confirmed their place in the fleet, who've stood above the rest in martial skill, perhaps we can demonstrate to all these Pintoth what they can expect to learn during their formal combat training?" Hearing the Puma's grin stretch across his features through the suggestion, Kah already knew what the bastard was planning.

"What a splendid idea," the baron said, giddy at the prospect of more amusement at the expense of the Pintoth. "What do you propose?"

"Four more bouts of combat, between our victorious examinees and their respective supervisors. Simply to illustrate how much these exceptional fighters will grow during their time in the fleet." Falax'hebos walked in a slow circle around the ring, finishing his proposition in front of the winners and just behind Kah, who still hadn't turned to look.

The sound of tiny, rapid clapping filled the hangar as the baron gaily applauded the idea. The three officers behind him said nothing, continuing to observe the action below. "Wonderful! A wonderful plan! Perhaps we shall proceed in the same order the winners secured their victories." There was a squish and some squeaking as the baron planted himself back in his chair, scooting forward to watch this new round of action. "That way, poor number fifty-six has a moment to catch his breath."

"An excellent suggestion, my lord." Falax'hebos turned around to his officers, pointing to them and their respective winners. "Kiln'aren, you will be first up, showing number two-twenty-two what she can expect to learn under your command."

Taking a seat next to Calan, Kah looked back into the ring, watching as Sergeant Kiln'aren entered the ring. He looked decidedly displeased at the turn of events but was no less willing to oblige. Next to Kah, the female Jaguar, number two-twenty-two, leapt up from her seat, fresh and ready for action. Facing down Kiln'aren, she offered him a smart salute. He returned it before assuming an unorthodox boxing stance. Perhaps another dedicated striker. He was the shorter of the two, but appeared to have the longer reach, and seemed extremely confident in his ability to win this bout.

Again, Falax'hebos cut the air, barking out, "Begin!"

All at once, Kiln'aren was inside two-twenty-two's guard, delivering a flurry of impossibly fast blows to her midsection. She dropped her hands to guard her punished midsection and, in the same beat, Kiln'aren began assaulting her face, pushing her back with unforgiving blows before knocking her out of the ring entirely.

"The victor is Kiln'aren!"

Two-twenty-two looked as surprised as everyone else as she lay on her back, gasping for air. The rest of the room was silent, other than some faint clapping from above. Kiln'aren stepped out of the ring and offered a hand to the Jaguar, helping her to her feet and dusting her off, before wordlessly returning to his spot among the other supervisors.

"Next, Shin'ade and number one-forty!"

Calan turned, offering Kah a bleak look and a gentle squeeze on the shoulder as he stood from his seat, entering the ring. He followed two-twenty-two's example and offered Shin'ade a salute, which she politely returned before she assumed a grappling stance. As Falax'hebos gave the signal to begin, Kah wondered idly if Lynxes were uniquely well suited to grappling styles of combat.

As he'd seen Kah do, and as they'd both been trained to do, Calan kept his grappling opponent at a distance and punished her with strikes whenever she came too close. However, unlike Kah's foe, Shin'ade was clearly well-practiced in blocking and countering strikes, and she dealt out more than a few punishments of her own, drawing some frustrated hissing from Calan as, over the next minutes, he was unable to land any decisive blows and instead tired himself out dodging around the arena. In the end, he seemed to resign himself to grappling with her, and tackled her to the ground in a burst of sand and snarls. The pair rolled back and forth, breaking and reversing grips until, inevitably, Shin'ade leveraged her superior experience and forced Calan into an arm bar, demanding submission.

When the two rolled apart, clearly winded, Kah swelled with pride that his brother had put up such a fierce fight. Calan didn't seem terribly put out by the loss, either, and offered Shin'ade a respectful salute before he returned to his seat. Falax'hebos, meanwhile, summoned Um'therren and number sixty-three, the big Lion who had won his bracket, and the two set to combat.

As Calan arrived at his seat, Kah gave him a supportive pat and another fist bump as Calan rubbed his injured shoulder. "Good job, Calan. You were great!"

Through hooded eyes and a rueful smile, Calan muttered, "Hard to feel great when I just got my ass kicked. Now I know how it feels to be you." He ended with a lighthearted chuckle, but received no response from his brother.

Instead, Kah locked eyes with Falax'hebos, who gave him an evil, predatory smirk as he watched Kah comfort his defeated brother. Calan followed Kah's line of sight to the Puma, read his expression, and leaned in close to Kah's ear.

"Throw the fight."

Confused, Kah looked over at Calan. "What?"

Calan locked eyes with his younger brother, gravely serious. "You need to throw the fight, Kah. You're already in. You won't win anything by fighting him." Kah opened his mouth to protest, but Calan silenced him. "You're already in terrible shape, and he wants to *hurt* you. You can tell just by looking at him. *Day*, you can tell by this whole, ridiculous display. He wants to hurt you—maybe cripple you. Throw the fight."

Kah's eyes drifted slowly away from his brother and into his own lap. Seeping through the right leg of his pants, the spreading crimson stain attested to Calan's words. The welts from the multitude of gunshots were rising and were sorer than before. His eyes were heavy, and he had lost a lot of blood. But his enemy was right there, laughing at him. Mocking him.

And he was still breathing.

As Um'therren was pronounced the winner of the third bout, Kah slowly shook his head. Looking up, Kah saw Falax'hebos beckon him as he had done during the threshold test. Kah stood, swaying slightly on his feet, and felt Calan grab his arm.

"Kah—" The brothers locked eyes again, and, after a moment, Calan understood. "Good luck."

The young Jaguar staggered into the sand pit, worse now that he was on his feet, and glared at his enemy across the ring.

Smirking, Falax'hebos patted the cheek Kah had tried to claw, licking his lips. "You've earned this, kitten. Let's just call this the first of our many, many private sessions."

Assuming his previous stance, Kah said nothing. His rage and hatred for the Puma had focused into a cold, calculating, liberating malice, the same he had felt when he pulled the trigger of the anti-materiel rifle. If he had to lose here, he would be sure to make his enemy suffer for it.

As Kah focused on his foe, however, an unfamiliar voice rang out over the hangar. It was older, female, with the gentle rasp of time. "Gunnery Sergeant Falax'hebos. Number fifty-six. Are you ready?"

The female Caracal officer stood at the rail, eclipsing the baron and looking down at the combatants with keen interest. In answer, both dipped a nod. Raising her hand, she authoritatively raked her claws through the air. "You may begin!"

Neither Kah nor Falax'hebos made any effort to close the distance. Each stared at the other, Kah with cold malice in his gaze and Falax'hebos with sneering surety.

The Puma raised his arms and gave a mock jab into the air. "Come on, *kitten*. Not scared, are you? You have your chance. Now take it!"

Starting forward, ever on guard, Kah matched the Puma's advance until they were only a few meters apart. As Kah made to close the gap, Falax'hebos spit into the sand between them and chuckled, cracking his neck twice. Growling, Kah lashed out with a low, chopping kick to the Puma's knee, but he was entirely unaffected, laughing off the blow as he lunged forward with a high boot. Trying to block the attack, Kah caught the kick across both arms and found himself hurled back by the tremendous force. Arching his back as his rear hit the sand, Kah landed awkwardly on his tail, and hissed with pain before springing back to his feet, ready for another assault.

But Falax'hebos didn't seem interested in pressing the attack. He wanted Kah upright. He wanted the fight.

He would regret it.

Kah struggled to his feet — *was it always this hard?* — and retook his stance, darting forward to chop the Puma's knee with another low kick.

"Again? Give me something better!" Falax'hebos laughed. Repeating his counterattack, he lunged at Kah with another forward kick from his left leg.

Kah was ready. Ducking under the boot, Kah darted into the sergeant's guard and leapt up, catching the underside of the Puma's knee atop his shoulder. Knocked off balance, Falax'hebos struck down between his legs—too slow to save his groin from Kah's flying knee.

Sudden, debilitating pain put Falax'hebos on his ass. Unlike the Puma, however, Kah *did* press the attack, and dropped an elbow into the soldier's privates, beating back his attempts at defense with relentless, pitiless strikes. Again and again Kah dropped his elbow into Falax'hebos' most tender area, punctuating each blow with a furious, desperate shout, his voice cracking.

"Are—you—satisfied—sir?!"

Kah had no idea how many times he pounded punishment into his tormentor's crotch. He just knew it wasn't enough, and he deserved worse. What felt like minutes passed by before he'd rendered the gunnery sergeant down to a quivering mess. He was dimly aware, at one point, of the Puma turning and vomiting into the sand, but Kah did not let up. He would make sure that this creature would never treat another Ty'gjir the way he had treated Kah.

Eventually, multiple pairs of hands pulled him, struggling, off the prone form of the massive, muscular Puma, now writhing pathetically in his own sick, and the mystery officer's voice rang out again, tinged with distinct mirth. "The victor is number fifty-six—Kah, house Riss!"

Kah looked up to see the officer smiling down at him over the railing, then felt Calan's familiar arms pull him safely against his chest. Amidst the deafening cheers of the hundreds of Pintoth in the audience, Kah clutched to his proud older brother and smiled weakly before, overcome with fatigue and injury, the last vestiges of Kah's consciousness slipped away with the breath on his lips.

"I won."

VII

"You must have been terribly proud of your victory."

I was too tired to be proud. I just wanted to win.

"But you had already won. Surely, what you wanted was to hurt your *enemy*."

And to not be hurt. But yes, I did want to hurt him.

"Do you think you fought better because you wished him harm?"

Did I win because I hated him? No.

"But it helped?"

I suppose.

"Do you perform better when you hate your enemies?"

I've harmed plenty of people for whom I felt nothing at all.

"Please answer the question."

I always perform to the best of my abilities in the circumstances given to me.

"Is it so hard to give a straight answer?"

Sometimes.

"We would remind you that honesty is of paramount importance to achieve a positive outcome here."

I am being honest.

"Perhaps we need to be more rigorous, more thorough, in our questioning. Would you be amenable to that?"

I don't feel like I have much of a choice.
"Good instincts. Now, go on."

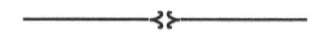

Kah woke up, feeling his eyelids drag, with great reluctance, over tired eyes. Only blackness awaited him. He groaned, and, reflexively, tried to reach out to his bedside table, where his thermal goggles should be waiting for him. But to his alarm, his arms wouldn't move. Neither would his legs. He started to panic slightly, clicking his teeth together to assess his surroundings and, from his echo picture, found with some relief that he was in his bed, back in the family H-cell.

There were some new additions to the room, however. Next to his bed was a thin pole on wheels with a screen, a small sac hanging from it, and a tube running from the bag to somewhere under Kah's blankets. Hanging from the foot of his bed was another, larger bag, with another tube running up under his blankets. Almost escaping his notice, there was some kind of disc resting atop his chest of drawers, but he couldn't discern any more than that.

Opening his mouth, Kah attempted to call his brother's name, but produced only a rasping croak. How long had he been lying here? He was not used to being laid up. It had been a long time since he was last bedridden.

He cleared his throat a few times before calling out weakly, "Thurv! Istur!"

There was no verbal response but, somewhere in the H-cell, someone started to move toward his room. Light, padding steps on the tile floors. None of his brothers walked like that, he knew. Instead, through the door came the pleasant, perfumed, cleaning-product scent of Sala.

"Look who's awake!"

He could hear the broad smile in her voice but would much prefer to see her. Giving a weak smile in her direction, he tried, once again, to sit up, but couldn't.

"Sala, why can't I move?" he croaked, still clearing his throat.

Walking closer to the bed, she checked some things on the screen of the thin pole, and started to fidget with Kah's face, eyes, neck. "It's nothing to be worried about. You're just strapped down because you wouldn't stop squirming. You could probably get loose if you were at a hundred percent, but I'm sure you're still weak after your tests. First of all, let's get you your goggles."

In an instant, Kah's head was lifted off his pillow and the straps of his thermal goggles snapped behind his head. There was a click and, his eyes filling with sudden light, Kah squinted and grimaced. While blinking his vision back into focus, Sala continued to bustle around Kah's room, fiddling with things he couldn't see. She wasn't gentle in her ministrations. Pinto'Neth ground that quality out of her through years of enduring irritable miners for patients. Better, it seemed, to get the work done quickly, rather than delicately.

"Can you undo my restraints? I want to sit up."

"A few more things first. We wouldn't want you to pull anything out," Sala chimed in her sing-song accent. It *almost* made the implications less alarming.

"To pull anything out? What's *in*?" Kah tried to examine himself, to feel what was in his body, but couldn't shake the restraints. He could feel himself starting to panic as nascent claustrophobia set in.

"Now, see? This is why you're tied down. You need to relax. The worst thing you can do for yourself right now is panic."

Sala yanked Kah's blankets off, revealing his body on the bed. He was nude. That was bad enough in front of his sister-in-law, even if she was a doctor, and he felt heat rush to his face. Then he got a better look at himself. He was indeed secured to his bed with cushioned restraints at the upper arms, wrists, thighs, and ankles. His right thigh was bandaged, and Kah could see some sutures poking out. That was good. The bag hanging from the pole was an IV of some clear fluid and the tube ran into his right forearm. Fine, that wasn't so bad. The bag at the end of the bed was also filled with a warmer, darker fluid. His eyes followed the tube up from the bag, snaking up his right leg before it ran into his—

"Sala, what is that?!" Kah pulled at his wrist restraints, trying to get at himself to purge the invader.

"Don't be a baby. It's just a urinary catheter." She looked down at him with a gloved hand on her hip, looking less than impressed. "As much as I love you, I didn't want to clean up your wet sheets every day, and the boys were too scared they were going to do something wrong to help with any of this. Now hold still while I deflate the balloon, and you won't have to worry about it anymore."

Every day? He'd been stuck here for *days*? Wait, a balloon? What was she talking about?

Sala produced a basin and held it under the trespassing tube, then did . . . something, and clear fluid began rushing out of a secondary spigot of the tube and into the basin. Kah felt a sensation of sudden relief and sighed contentedly.

"One, two—"

"Wait, what?"

Without further warning, Sala pulled hard and deliberately on the tube, sliding it clear of his abused male parts, eliciting more than a small yelp from Kah and leaving him panting and nauseated on the bed.

"See? All done. That wasn't so bad, was it?" she chimed.

"We—" Kah glared at the smiling Domestic, wishing horrible, horrible things upon her and her parents and her children and . . . and everyone with a name that sounded like hers. "We are *not* family anymore."

"No? Maybe I'll just pop that back in for one of your *brothers* to take out." Sala brandished the tube in a tiny, gloved hand, wagging it threateningly back and forth.

Kah snorted in frustration and ducked his head to the side, glaring at a wall instead, but he soon had a new focus—a light tapping at the door, followed by Thurv's muffled, but unmistakable voice.

"Is it safe to come in?" He sounded both excited and guilty. Kah was sure he knew of this torture all along and had allowed it. The traitor.

Sala continued to wag the tube, glaring with mock severity at Kah's prone form as she slightly turned her head toward the door and shouted, "Yes, but be careful. The little soldier's grumpy tonight."

Without another word, she set about unfastening his restraints and massaging blood back into his limbs. The door to the room slid open and Kah saw Thurv and Istur poke their heads in, both with big grins plastered to their faces. They hurried over to the bed, Istur retrieving the disc from the top of the chest of drawers as he did so. Thurv sat down on the bed next to Kah, helping Sala undo the last of his restraints, never losing his grin.

"How you feeling, Kah?"

"Sore. And tired. And hungry." Now free, Kah reached down and pulled the blankets up to cover himself, before flopping his head back on the pillow, eyes closed.

"Tired? You're not allowed to be tired. You've been asleep for four days." Stepping closer, Istur leaned against the headboard and looked down at Kah. Kah was still aware of the disc in Istur's hand, resting on his hip, but was distracted by what his brother had just said.

"Four days? Ugh, no wonder I'm so hungry." Kah rubbed his thin belly, drawing a growl in reply. "Where's Calan?"

"Calan had to go already," Thurv said, with a slight tone of guilt. "He passed the exams, got his orders, and headed out yesterday. He was assigned to the orbital defense platform above the planet and is there now" — Thurv pointed up at the ceiling for emphasis — "getting settled in, starting his formal training, and watching over us."

Istur chimed in, sounding equally guilty. "He waited as long as he could. He wanted to be here when you woke up. He talked to you for a while anyway before he went. You were probably a better listener than you usually are."

Kah smiled and gave Istur a weak smack in the arm. Gods, was he sore. But he wouldn't let the pain or lack of a goodbye spoil the good news. "Well, good. I knew he would pass. You should have seen his combat tests."

Sala sat down opposite Thurv on the bed and offered Kah an earnest smile. "From what he said, *you* put on quite a show. And you have the injuries to prove it." She gestured at all of him. "He carried you all the way back home from the spaceport. He was so proud of you, Kah. He said" — she squeezed Kah's hand tightly — "that you passed, too."

Kah grinned broadly and nodded, prompting a storm of congratulatory cheers from his family. Sala squeezed his hands while Thurv jostled him by the shoulders and Istur painfully clapped him on the back. Eventually, they let go of him and Kah once again fell back on his pillow. Even sitting up to talk was tiring.

"Thank you. I wouldn't have been able to do it without all of you. But it was a lot harder than I expected." Kah cast his eyes down for a moment, remembering Falax'hebos.

"We knew you'd be fine." Thurv said, tousling Kah's head fur. "You and Calan worked your asses off for this. And you'd make terrible miners, so what else were you going to do?"

"Aren't you going to ask about your orders?" Solemnly offering the disc to Kah, Istur wasn't doing a good job containing his excitement. "We've been waiting for you before we opened it. Figured it was only fair."

Taking the disc from Istur, Kah swallowed, turning it over in his hands. It was simple, smooth. Almost perfect, except for a small slot on one side, begging to be pulled. He looked around at his family, all of them smiles and nervous excitement. This would be the start of the rest of his life. He could be stationed on the orbital defense platform with Calan, or he could be headed to the galactic east to defend the border from opportunistic Lupinion raiders, or he could head to the frontlines in the galactic north, on the border between the Dal and the Dran territories. He didn't know how or by whom his orders had been decided, but it was done. The only thing left for him to do was to open and listen.

Kah pulled at the slot on the side of the disc, extending a small tray from the disc, out of which beamed an infrared image of the Caracal officer who oversaw the hand-to-hand combat test. She looked out calmly, seeming to lock eyes with Kah, regardless of the angle at which he viewed her. Holding a datapad in her hand as if to read off it, the officer didn't give the pad a single glance. Then she spoke, filling the room with her cool, deep, gently rasping tone.

"This is a message for Kah, house Riss. If you are not Kah'riss, it is your duty as a citizen of the Dal territories to stop watching this message at once and to turn it over to a keeper of the peace, that it may be directed to Kah'riss." She paused, apparently giving any unintended bearer the time to switch the message off. *"My name is Admiral Achaera'fra. I am second-in-command of the United Fleet of the Dal Territory, and the head of the house fleet of Duke Aur'kura. You, Kah'riss, have been selected to serve with a special operations task force aboard my vessel, the* Litany of Ash. *The specifics of your assignment will be conveyed to you upon your arrival. You are expected to take a long-range shuttle from Pinto'Neth to Aurum, where the* Litany of Ash *is currently in orbit. Passage has been arranged and paid for. You merely need to present this disc and valid identification to the authorities at your local spaceport. From the time this message completes, you will have five standard days to arrive aboard the* Litany of Ash *before you are considered AWOL and*

a warrant will be issued for your arrest for dereliction of duty. I'll see you aboard."

The image blinked out, leaving the room in silence. A long moment passed before Thurv spoke.

"Huh. A lot less fanfare with yours than with Calan's. But wow, Kah! An *admiral* selected you? You must have made quite an impression!" Thurv laughed and gave Kah a quick squeeze. "You've gotta be thrilled!"

Shooting Thurv a nominal smile in reply, Kah nodded, staring at the disc in his hands, and breathed a heavy sigh of relief. He had worked hard and achieved his goals. He was free of Pinto'Neth. He had done his father proud. A massive weight was lifted from his shoulders and, for the first time in years, he felt he could relax.

But what now? He had been so focused on becoming a soldier that he hadn't thought at all about *being* a soldier. What would he have to do? Would he fly fighters in space? Would he carry a rifle and charge enemy lines? Would he kill his enemies from kilometers away with a sniper rifle? Would he be captured? Tortured? Killed?

He looked up with full, shining eyes at his family. Thurv grinned proudly at him, a huge miner's hand planted firmly on his shoulder. Sala smiled as well, but her eyes were sad, and her arms crossed. Istur wasn't smiling anymore. His lips were tightly pursed and his posture was rigid. His hand, on Kah's arm, twitched, trying not to grasp Kah too hard, to cling, to keep him home. Kah wondered what Sala and Istur were thinking, but had a feeling they were thinking the same things he was.

People would always be worrying about him. He had to be brave, for all of them. Lifting his goggles, Kah wiped his eyes, sniffing once, and smiled broadly at his family. "Yeah, I'm thrilled! The admiral watched the combat exams with the baron. I think I like her more than I like him . . ."

Kah launched into a long-winded tale of his experience at the tests, telling his family about the written exam and how they could fail if they got up to pee or slouched over, about the obstacle course which he had to run blindly, about the different guns they got to shoot, and about being shot.

He didn't mention Falax'hebos at all. He may as well be dead. Kah would never see him again. He was not a problem.

Even though he was certain Calan had already told them everything, Kah's brothers and sister-in-law listened with keen, eager attention. Eventually, Istur prepared a late dinner, which they took in Kah's room, eating around his bed and sharing in his joyful, irresistible enthusiasm. The future looked bright for him. He just had to keep going. Before long, however, Kah finished his food bars, an effort in itself, and tired out. After Thurv helped him to the washroom and Kah showered, he returned to bed, aiming to fall asleep early and to rise to start packing whatever he might need for his future.

Kah's sleep was not restful. He dreamt of war. He dreamt of killing hundreds of Ty'gjir made up of thousands of colors, each splashing into a different color and a new shape. There were more than his pistol could handle, more than his claws, or his teeth. Eventually, the colors swarmed him, covered him, and drowned him. He dreamt he was captured and tied, naked, to a bed, but when he called for help, it wasn't Sala who came to him, but Falax'hebos, who licked his fangs and looked down at Kah's exposed body with his sneering, mocking grin. Suddenly, he had far too many hands, and they were everywhere. Kah fought and bit and scratched but couldn't get free and couldn't make Falax'hebos leave. The Puma's mouth was on him, around him—everywhere—snapping closed and leaving Kah in the dark.

Kah opened his eyes and tore off his blankets. No restraints and no tubes. That was a relief. But he was a sweaty mess. He took a deep breath, feeling a rattle clear itself from his chest, and shook his head.

"Waste of a perfectly good shower," he grumbled.

Kicking his legs off the side of the bed, Kah rose, with much groaning and stiffness, to his feet. He did feel much better this morning than he had the night prior and could even perform some stretches without much more pain than the soreness following a good workout. In four days, he should be back to normal. For now, he just needed to rest and pack. Slipping on a pair of short pants, Kah hobbled stiffly to the bathroom—closing the bedroom door in his wake—to brush his sharp teeth and, once again, shower himself clean.

One cold wash and a vigorous blow-dry later, Kah shuffled back to his room, but found the door open. Inside, Sala bustled about the room, gathering up medical equipment.

She turned to him with a friendly grin. "Look at you, walking around all on your own!"

Kah gave her a wry smile and jogged a couple times in place. "Turns out all I needed was a shower. Some doctor you are." Closing his eyes, he stuck his tongue out at her, but left himself wide open to the pillow that struck and swallowed his face.

"I'll remember that the next time one of the boys drags your bleeding hide to me." The pillow fell away, revealing Sala's accusing finger and severe expression, but a friendly twinkle in her eye. Sala had told Kah ages ago that she had always wanted a little brother, and she took to the role of big sister very naturally. He didn't mind the arrangement, either.

Lifting his hands in surrender, Kah pleaded, "Just don't throw the pee bag at me! I just washed up!"

Her pretty face split into a smile and the two shared a laugh before she helped Kah set about packing his things. If he had to be at Aurum in four days, he would probably need to leave tomorrow. Hyperspace travel, while fast, could still take a number of days to cross the broad expanses of the empire, and long-range shuttles, while reliable, were not known for their speed.

Luckily, Kah didn't have much in the way of belongings to bring with him to the next chapter of his life. A few outfits, mostly very practical and comfortable, as well as his training uniform, which someone had cleaned for him, his personal datapad, a few trinkets and odds and ends. The entirety of his property could fit into a single, modest duffle bag.

When he finished, he brought his bag out to the common room, where the rest of the family was occupied, and placed the bag against the wall near the exit of the H-cell. Thurv was cleaning up the kitchen — they must have left the dishes from the night before — and Istur and Sala were both reading and writing on their datapads while the news played idly in the background. The speaker was some impassioned noble Kah had never seen before, shouting from a podium to a cheering crowd.

"With the fall this week of Prince Gal'mora's territory to the pretender's forces, the enemy now controls more than half of the Rae'gal Arm. The self-proclaimed Emperor Sol'taris must feel that he is close to achieving his goal of sole sovereignty of the empire. However, our northern border continues to hold strong against Hah'dran, and Prince Kai'mul's forces are pushing harder than ever against the enemy, making deeper and deeper forays into enemy territory and taking back as much space as our fallen allies have lost. In addition, our agents report that Prince Cah'dal has plans in progress to not only put a permanent end to northern aggression, but also to counterattack — to punish our foes for trespasses into territory which has stood proudly as part of our Dal heritage for untold generations! Under our most beloved prince's leadership, we will resist this tide, and come out stronger than before! No matter the numbers of our foes, we will prevail!"

Kah heard Istur snort derisively before he switched off the holonet, looking up at him. "Morning, Kah. Did you hear all that?"

"Just the end, I think." Kah walked to the kitchen to help Thurv clean up while Istur spoke to him over the back of the couch.

"Do you know how Sol'taris toppled Gal'mora's territory?" Istur sat up on his knees, raising his voice to be heard over the running water of the sink.

Kah thought he sounded excited, eager, but just shook his head, shrugging, as he continued to scrub dishes. "Did he promise to bring order, finally?"

It was common knowledge that the Mora territory was chaotic, in a near-constant state of civil war, and, as a result, its forces were perpetually stretched too thin to be of any use to anyone. Prince Gal'mora was something of a joke among most Ty'gjir, but, as an Ascendant, he carried a touch of divinity and, thus, the right to rule, even if he did it poorly.

Istur shook his head, smiling. "He didn't just *promise* to bring order—he did it! First, he showered the people with information about the way his subjects live in his territories. Then, the Moras rose up and seized government properties, demanding effective governance. The Mora forces apparently didn't even know what to do until Sol'taris' fleet swept in. He cast down the nobles who had sat on their hands for so long and appointed new ones from the locals to take their place."

Kah wiped some tableware dry, his expression impassive, and asked without looking at Istur, "How many Ty'gjir died during the rebellions?"

Now Thurv cut in.

"And how many of those people were killed by the soldiers who signed up to protect them?" He frowned and looked meaningfully back and forth between his brothers.

The wind fled Istur's sails. Pausing for a moment, he threw himself across the couch, calling out, "I don't know. The numbers aren't out yet."

Handing the last, dry dish to Thurv to be put away, Kah stood at the sink, looking down at both his hands on the counter, and muttered, "Hopefully it was worth it."

He lost himself to curiosity, considering what life would be like for the people of the Mora territory now. Was it everything they'd hoped? Would they have some peace?

He was still lost in thought when two much larger hands planted themselves next to his, a chest pressed against his back, and a chin rested on top of his head, startling Kah from his thoughts. Hissing, he spun around — claws out and teeth bared — and shoved the assailant away, only to see Thurv, taken aback and wearing a mask of hurt.

"Whoa, sorry! I was just gonna thank you for helping me," Thurv apologized, his voice shocked, hands raised, and eyes wide.

Kah glared up at his brother, his chest fluttering with short, shallow breaths, before he managed to control himself. "S-sorry, Thurv. You surprised me." Squeezing his brother in a short, contrite, unrequited hug, Kah withdrew, his paws already headed back toward his room. "I'm going to finish packing, I think, then maybe nap. I'm still — still tired."

Shuffling off, Kah left the family to exchange concerned looks.

Later that evening, after a few, fitful naps, Kah lay on his bed, staring up at the bare ceiling. Guilt plagued him after shoving Thurv. He and his brothers had always shared embraces and physical signs of affection. After spending so much time fighting each other, they had become very comfortable with physical contact, and didn't feel anything in the way of embarrassment for expressing themselves with it. He didn't want his relationship with his brothers to change, especially not because he'd just been startled.

But why would that startle him?

Kah chewed his lip and reran the situation in his mind, until it occurred to him. Thurv's size and nearness had reminded him of Falax'hebos. Nausea seizing his gut, Kah mentally admonished himself. Thurv was *nothing* like the Falax'hebos. Thurv was his brother, one of the few people who was truly safe. He had nothing to fear from him, not like—

Why was Kah still afraid of him? Is this what his da had meant when he said the fight wasn't over while his enemy still drew breath?

Cursing his restless mind, Kah clapped his face a few times, shaking the thoughts from his head and pulling his shorts back on before he headed for the door. There was no reason he had to feel guilty *and* had to pee. He could at least take care of one of those problems. The relief of an empty bladder and the splash of cold water helped clear his head. He still had time. He could explain himself to Thurv and apologize later, or tomorrow, before he left. It's not like Thurv was suddenly going to hate him because he'd pushed him. That'd be stupid.

He froze as he rounded the corner back to his room. His door was open again. Kah was certain he'd closed it behind him, which meant someone was in there, waiting to speak with him. He was definitely not ready for conversation yet, but squared his shoulders and steeled his nerves, striding into the room to find Istur sitting at his desk, waiting. He looked especially grave this evening. Kah threw a smile and a wave his way, then retrieved the shirt he'd discarded before his naps, pulling it down over his head.

"Evening, Kah." Istur's voice matched his face. Something had him in a very grim mood, and Kah didn't want to find out what, though his brotherly duties obligated him to try.

"Evening. What's up?" Kah sat down on the edge of the bed, facing towards his brother.

"Honestly, I was hoping you could tell me." Steepling his fingers before his face, Istur leaned closer to Kah.

Kah cocked his head, confused. Everything was perfect. Everything.

But Istur didn't blink as he stared at his little brother. Looking into his brother's eyes, Kah idly wondered what color they were. Or what color his own were, for that matter. Istur's face carried no hint of anger or accusation. If anything, it was somewhat sad. Kah couldn't imagine why he would feel sad. He was up and about and walking without trouble, and nothing that bad could have happened in the time since he'd left. Besides, Istur had been in such a good mood after the holonet report, so what had ruined it?

Receiving no response, Istur continued, "You're not as subtle as you think you are. Even if you insist to yourself that nothing's wrong, we can tell. We're your family." Istur scooted his chair slightly forward, still looking intently at Kah. "Besides, Calan told us about the beatdown you put on that officer. That's not like you. You don't like to hurt people. You fight to win. So, you must have really hated that guy."

Istur blinked, for the first time since Kah walked into the room.

"What'd he do?"

Kah looked down and grumbled something about being very subtle. Istur was just extremely perceptive. It's one of the reasons he was so good with people.

"Come on, Kah," Istur said. "You can tell me. It'll feel good to get it off your chest." There was a slight pleading tone to Istur's voice. Kah looked up at his brother. He was worried—really worried. But Kah could tell Istur already suspected what was upsetting him.

Pulling his arms close to his sides and his knees together, Kah folded his hands in his lap. "I don't know," he said. "He was just . . . a jerk, I guess." Istur's expression told him that wasn't enough. "He yelled at me, and made fun of me, and embarrassed me. He said I would be a liability to everyone. I hadn't even had the chance to do anything yet. I didn't deserve it."

Istur slid his chair a bit closer, halving the short distance between them. "No, you didn't. That, or anything else." His voice was so genuine it hurt, and Kah could tell he was angry, and still waiting.

Staring down into his lap, Kah tried again. "He—" He didn't know how to say this part. Nothing really happened, so had Falax'hebos even done anything wrong? "He made me undress in front of everyone. And the way he looked at me was—I don't know."

At this, Istur stood up from the chair and sat beside Kah on the bed, allowing a few centimeters of space between them. "What did you do?"

"I don't know. I mouthed off, or something. And that made him angrier. He would have made me go first on the obstacle course if I hadn't volunteered. Then, when I did it, he laugh at me for not being able to see in the dark. He said it was the only thing Pintoth are good for, and he hit me." Kah looked to his big brother, his eyes swimming with dreadful curiosity. "Do people hate us?"

It was Istur's turn to look away, and he chewed his lip, trying to think of an answer. "Not good people, no. The Ty'gjir who even know Pinto'Neth exists generally don't think of the people who live here at all. We're just where nordium comes from. And, since we're just a place where a rock comes from, we're not people. So, when you show that you're as good as, or better, than someone who thinks that way, they hate you for it." Istur clasped Kah's hand. "It's not your fault. It's theirs."

"But, if he hated me and didn't think of me as a person, why would he want to—" Kah cut himself off, not ready to truly admit to himself what Falax'hebos wanted to do.

Istur's hand gently, warmly squeezed his own. "Why would he want to what, Kah?"

Quiet stretching nearly to minutes, Kah wrestled with his head, trying to come up with an answer.

"He came into my booth between marksmanship tests, where no one could see. And, at first, he just taunted me again. Then, he—he surrounded me. And he wanted to—to mate with me. I could *smell* it. I could *feel* it when he touched my back. It scared me, and I tried to scratch his face, and then someone came in." Kah was shaking now, his teeth chattering as he tried to get the words out, tight fists balled on his thighs. "But she *knew*. She knew what was happening and all she did was tell him that we were ready for the next test."

Kah felt a hand rest on his shoulder—a soft, warm anchor to the present—and heard Istur ask, "Is it all right if I hug you?"

Kah nodded, still shaking, and felt Istur wrap his arms tightly around him in a comforting embrace. He didn't need to say anything. Just his touch, safe and without expectation, was enough to steady his breathing and slow his shaking to a stop.

Eventually, Istur spoke again. "He didn't want to mate with you, Kah. The actions might be similar, but the intent couldn't be more different." Kah heard Istur breathe deeply and steel himself for what he said next. "What he wanted was to *rape* you—to use sex to hurt you."

"But isn't—" In that moment, before the next words even left his mouth, Kah realized just how much of a child he still was. "Isn't sex for people who care about each other?"

He felt his face flush with embarrassment. Sex wasn't something he should talk about with his brother, especially not when it involved Kah himself. Bracing himself, he *knew* Istur would make fun of him. Instead, however, he heard his brother sniff and take a deep breath, trying to keep his voice collected and even. It may be harder for Istur to talk about it, Kah decided, than it was for him.

"Sometimes, Kah. Only sometimes. For Ma and Da, it was. For Thurv and Sala, it is."

"Ick." Kah wrinkled his nose, drawing a brief smile from Istur.

"For some people, it's just a way of having fun. For others, it's a way of exerting power over people." He gritted his teeth before continuing. "That's the case with your officer. He'd use it to cement control over you, to harm you, and to keep you frightened of him—too frightened to retaliate, or report it, or complain. It's an evil, evil thing to do. You were right to be scared and justified in hurting him—humiliating him during your fight. He's probably never had someone really fight back before."

Istur took a shuddering breath. His voice sounded tight. "I've talked to some other Ty'gjir who failed the exams and came back to Pinto'Neth. They said similar things happened to them. It's why I first decided not to take the exams myself. Then, I told Calan about it. That's why he waited to take the tests until he could take them with you. But we didn't expect you two to be split up. We thought we would be able to protect you, Kah, but we were *wrong*. I'm just—I'm so glad you could protect yourself."

Holding Kah tightly against him, Istur broke into tears. Kah was more than a little shocked. He hadn't seen Istur cry since their father died.

Patting his older brother's back, confused as to how he became the one doing the consoling, he said, "I'm okay, Istur. I'm fine! You all taught me to protect myself, so nothing happened."

"Enough happened!" Through his tears, Istur's anger screamed more fiercely than the winds outside the H-cell. "They tried it with you because you're small, but they would have done it to someone else if you weren't there. They know they can get away with it—that there won't be any consequences, because they've done it for years. Any

Pintoth who might object are too scared to speak up because the ones who complain are silenced. That's how they keep us in our place and them in theirs, and they'll keep doing it long after we're gone!"

His face pressed to his brother's chest, Kah's eyes widened with fear. "Who is 'they,' Istur?"

"These people, Kah. The planetary administrators, the nobles — the people who decide what happens to us, to our planet — they're all predators and parasites, sapping us at home, separating us, making us vulnerable, waiting to pounce — to sink their teeth in! The ones too scared to kill just watch from the sidelines, hoping not to get caught. And I'm just as guilty! I knew, and I sent you right to them."

Kah felt tears running off his brother's face onto the top of his head and he squeezed Istur softly.

"I failed you, Kah! I'm so sorry . . . "

Years of guilt and rage pouring out of him in deep, wracking sobs, Istur clutched Kah against himself, his tears shaking them both. Kah's brothers had known this might happen. Even with what little they had, they had taken steps to protect him. Night only knows what other steps they took behind the scenes while he prepared for his examinations. But no matter what they had done, the people in charge maneuvered everything to make it as easy as possible to slip around the protections and carry out their sins. Maybe they didn't get what they wanted this time, but they had before, and would again.

Some Pintoth knew, but, if Pintoth weren't people, who would believe their complaints? Who would they complain to — the baron? He oversaw the exams himself, so he most likely had some knowledge of his fleet's wrongdoings. He also ruled Kah's planet and knew the difficulties its people faced. If he cared at all, it didn't show. As long as the nordium kept flowing, there was no problem.

Istur was right. They were parasites.

But Kah wouldn't be serving under them. Kah would serve under the admiral, someone who reported directly to the duke and the prince—someone more powerful than the baron. He could make her know, and she could make them listen. Until now, Kah's goal was only to get into the baron's fleet. He had done better. He had been admitted to the *prince's* fleet. And what now? *Now* he could help his family, his people.

He was resolved. He would serve Admiral Achaera'fra better than anyone ever had. He would gain her ear, and the ear of the duke, and the ear of the prince. The prince would listen and would fix things on Pinto'Neth. He had to. Kah would make sure that, by working so hard to save his own children, Sark had saved all Pintoth, whether they knew it or not.

VIII

"Are you not worried about revealing such . . . seditious thoughts?"

No.

"Why not?"

My goal wasn't rebellion. My goal was to improve life for my people.

"By circumventing your baron."

By serving my prince.

"And what if the prince was already aware of your troubles?"

It seems more likely that the prince didn't know. He had thousands of worlds to govern. The plight of Pinto'Neth probably never occurred to him.

"Like Istur said."

Like Istur said.

"And what if, made aware of the plight of Pinto'Neth, the prince did not care about your people?"

I would make him care about me.

"Surely, you are not so compelling a person that a prince would carry out your whims?"

I would have to be.

"We see your thoughts on the matter have not matured overmuch. You may continue."

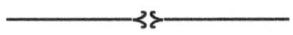

Before long, Kah and Istur's tears had dried. They had shared their sorrow, and, as Istur had said, it felt good to get it off their chests, even if there was little to be done about it in the present. The remainder of the evening was spent in overdue celebration. Thurv fried their nightly food bars — Kah's favorite way to prepare them — and the family ate until they could eat no more. It was a special occasion, after all. Besides, they could afford it; food would go further with just Sala, Istur, and Thurv living in the H-cell. Afterwards, Kah and his family played simple games Sala taught them and laughed away the night, relishing what remaining time they had together before Kah set out the next day.

The next morning, the family slept in. They had the time, and their festivities lasted well into the early morning, so the extra rest was well-appreciated. However, in waking so late, there was little time to spend together before Kah had to be off. So, in a healthy rush, the Riss family prepared and shoveled food into their mouths before taking Kah back to the same elevator shaft he had taken up to his exams. This time, however, he would ride the small personnel elevator the long distance up to the spaceport.

He stared, his finger hovering a centimeter from the button which would summon the lift to them, working up the courage to take the next step. He couldn't afford to question his resolve. Not now. There was too much at stake.

The button depressed with a satisfying click and lit up, indicating the elevator was on the way.

"Ready, Kah?" Thurv's hand clapped on his shoulder. This time, Kah didn't jump, or start, or push his brother away. He turned back and faced him with a look of fixed determination, nodding.

"Thank you," Kah said to his brother and Sala, "I know we were all supposed to get off Pinto'Neth together, but you sacrificed that for yourselves so the rest of us could. Words aren't—"

"C'mon," Thurv cut in, scratching his head. "No rehearsed speeches. I wanted to get you all out of here. Now, Sala and I can have a little more privacy." He grinned from ear to ear and batted his eyes at his wife, who rolled hers in response. "And you'll come back to visit. It's not like this is the last time we'll ever see each other. And hey, if you don't make it back soon, you can come visit us at our retirement home on Aurum!"

He took a step forward and hugged Kah, squeezing him tightly, before whispering in his ear, "Promise this isn't the last time we see each other."

Kah squeezed his eldest brother, refusing to part from him for a minute before he held him at arm's length and smiled. "I promise."

Next, it was Istur's turn. He stepped up and grinned. "Hey, who knows? Maybe the next time you visit Pinto'Neth, it'll be a much better place than when you left."

He reached out to hug Kah, but his little brother looked at him gravely.

"Please, Istur, don't get into too much trouble while I'm gone. Please."

Istur just scoffed and smirked down at him. "You'll be getting into much more trouble, I'm sure. You have to tell us all about the planets you visit while you're gone. Send pictures and stuff!"

Kah watched his brother's eyes dart away for a moment, betraying a concealed intent. But he hugged his brother anyway, and chuckled, "So, now that I'm out in the great big galaxy, you expect me to start getting you stuff? What have you done to deserve it?"

Istur gave him a playful smack in the arm but clutched him close. There was a great deal of desperation in Istur's embrace, and Kah held him just as tightly, before finally parting.

"I'll be fine, Istur. I promise. I'm ready. *You've* made sure I'm ready."

Istur nodded to hide his tears as Sala rushed up, sweeping Kah up into tight hug with strength that belied her size. She rocked back and forth, still holding Kah, before she placed him back on the floor.

"I have something for you." She began rummaging through her pockets to retrieve something. "We are going to miss you dreadfully when you're gone, and I figured you'd miss us even more, so we made this for you."

She held out something hanging by a thin chain. It was about the size of a military service tag, but thicker. Kah took the tiny thing in his hand. He could feel delicate engravings on the steel surface but didn't see anything especially remarkable about it. He did feel some lettering but couldn't quite make it out.

"Thanks, Sala," he said, Kah grinning at her, still trying to figure out what it was. "This means a lot."

"Oh, does it? What is it, then, liar?" She put her hands on her hips and looked at him sternly.

"It's—well, of course, it's jewelry? A necklace. I don't own any jewelry, so it's, um, it's special!" He continued to feverishly inspect the thing, trying to uncover its mysteries.

"Well, yes, I suppose it is jewelry. But it's also a locket, you dolt! It opens and you put something precious to you inside it."

Demonstrating, she pressed down on the loop which connected the locket to the chain, and the face of the locket popped open. Looking inside, however, he couldn't see anything, and continued to stare quizzically.

"You won't be able to see anything down here, but look again when the lights in the shuttle come on. Then, it'll mean something to you. I hope you like it." Sala took Kah by the shoulders and crushed him in another tight, desperate hug.

"Thanks, Sala. I'm sure I'll love it." He smiled through the intense embrace and held her by the shoulders. "Take care of them for me, please."

She sniffed a couple times and nodded, lifting her goggles to wipe her eyes just as the lift's doors slid open behind Kah. He glanced back at the open elevator and picked up his bag, looking back at his family, holding each other as they bid farewell to the youngest among them, sending him off to war. He smiled bravely as he held his hand over the threshold, keeping the automatic doors open.

"Tell Calan I said goodbye. Thank you for—for everything. I love you."

After a moment's hesitation, he stepped inside, chancing one last look back. They were all holding their tears. Kah had to be strong. They were counting on him. Everyone was counting on him. He pressed the button for the spaceport with another satisfying click.

Thurv spoke up as they all waved goodbye, trying to match Kah's smile. "Love you, too, baby brother. Don't get lost on the way home."

The doors slid shut, leaving Kah alone in the small, stark space. He looked up. No open sky above him this time. Just more blank, stainless steel, two meters up. The elevator started to move, lurching upward with surprising speed. He had anticipated a long journey to the top but, unlike the freight elevator, this one rose very rapidly. What had been an uncomfortable, hours-long slog with two hundred other Pintoth became a brief, quiet meditation for Kah as the personnel elevator raced for the peak of the spire, slowing to a stop at its destination in only a few minutes, arriving at the launchpad of Kah's future with an underwhelming, low-pitched ding.

He stepped out into what appeared to be a very large, empty waiting room. He had never been here before, but the rows of chairs arranged back to back in the octagonal space made its purpose unmistakable. At the opposite end of the room was a desk behind a glass wall, at which sat an incredibly bored-looking Lioness, chewing on a stylus. At the sound of the ding, she glanced up toward Kah, then sat rod-straight and waited for him to approach. He didn't make her wait long. Swallowing his nerves, Kah squished his way across the carpeted floor. That in itself was an oddity on Pinto'Neth. Kah supposed they had to have a comfortable welcome for . . . who? Visitors?

A dry chuckle brought him to the Lioness and her desk. Kah couldn't help but note that, despite the howling winds he knew to be outside, the room was utterly silent except for the gentle squish of his shoes on the carpet, followed by a squeak as the Lioness shifted her chair to meet him at the glass.

"Hello, sweetheart. What can I do for you?" The Lioness gave him a friendly, if slightly condescending smile, and leaned forward. She was very pretty. Kah imagined she would be a welcome sight for anyone arriving at this spaceport.

Holding high the admiral's disc, he tried to sound authoritative and official, but his anxiety peeked through unbidden. "My name is Kah'riss. I'm supposed to take a shuttle to Aurum. Am I in the right place?"

"You're the soldier we're waiting for? You're a little younger than I was expecting." With a suspicious look, she checked something on her datapad. After a few moments, however, she clicked her tongue and raised her brows. "All right. I guess there's no mistake. Do you see that gate over there?"

She pointed over Kah's head to a corner on the far wall of the room, just past the central lift he had left moments before. He nodded.

"Through that gate is the bridge to your shuttle. The pilot should be waiting for you. I don't think there's anyone else aboard."

He nodded again and smiled at her. "Thank you for your help." Eager to be on his way, Kah crossed to the gate. Now that he had said goodbye, the journey couldn't come soon enough.

"Good luck, little soldier," the Lioness called across the room. He glanced back in her direction with a wave, and saw she was chewing on her stylus again, looking concerned.

He had to be strong.

Approaching the gate, he scanned his datapad at a small reader, producing a ding which matched the elevator's, and the glass doors of the gate slid open, beckoning him inside. Another deep breath. He walked down a long, slightly declined, winding bridge until he found himself at the burnished door of a shuttle. There was no handle, and nowhere to scan his datapad. Instead, he gave a few tentative taps on the door with his claws. There was the sound of a small scuffle from within, like someone tripping, and the door hissed and opened outward, flooding the bridge with blinding light.

Kah grimaced and closed his eyes against the unwelcome light, unable to see any further into the shuttle and unwilling to step into the unknown.

A voice came through the light. It was tired-sounding, but smooth and fast, of middling pitch. It sounded a bit like Sala's accent, but had a slight, teasing timbre to it. "Huh. Just a little guy, aren't you?"

Removing his goggles, Kah cracked open his eyes just slightly, trying to see, but it was far too bright for him.

"Oh. Right, sorry. I'll turn the lights down a tick."

At that, the light from within the shuttle dimmed and Kah was able to slowly open his eyes. Standing just inside the door, offering passage, was a tall, deep copper Ty'gjir with very long limbs. Kah had never seen anyone like him before. He supposed he should get used to that.

Still squinting, Kah held up the disc. "My name is Kah'riss. I'm supposed to take a shuttle to Aurum."

"Climb aboard then, kiddo. You're in the right place. Though you took your sweet time getting here, didn't you?"

While he blinked and squinted, Kah felt the Ty'gjir take his bag and heard him walk further into the shuttle. Kah did his best to follow, still proceeding largely by feel as his eyes adjusted.

"Sorry about that—I only recovered a couple days ago and spent the last two packing and saying goodbye." Kah found a chair to sit in and planted himself, waiting until he was entirely accustomed to the dim light before moving around more. It smelled very nice in the shuttle, like a mix between charcoal smoke and Sala's perfume.

"Nah, don't apologize. Makes sense. Must be tough to leave home so young. I've been enjoying the time off anyway. Catching up on my reading, you know. But recovered? They must have put you through the ringer, eh? Can't imagine they took it easy on you just 'cause you're a cub."

The Ty'gjir rattled off his words so quickly that Kah found it difficult to keep up, but he caught the last part and bristled a bit.

"On Pinto'Neth, I'm a young *adult*. And I was selected by *Admiral Achaera'fra* based on my performance in the exams. She didn't care about my age, and neither should you."

He sat up tall in his chair, looking around for the Ty'gjir. Somehow, he had lost track of his movements, but his eyes were just about acclimated to the light now. When he faced forward again, he found the pilot standing directly in front of him, his arms crossed and foot tapping silently as he looked down at Kah.

"Leave it to me to decide what I should care about, kid. We'll get along a lot better that way. I'm E'e, by the way." The pilot started out his statement very severely, but, by the end, wore a big smile across his features and offered his hand.

Kah firmly grasped the hand. He was a soldier now. No more delicate handshakes. "E'e?" he asked. "I've never heard a name like that before."

Getting a better look at him now, Kah saw that his initial assessment was not inaccurate. E'e was quite tall, though not as tall as Thurv, and most of the length was in his exceptionally long limbs. He was fairly thin. Kah decided his own build would look somewhat similar if someone stretched him out by his arms and legs. He wore a gray and gold uniform without adornment, which was charmingly disheveled. His fur was a coppery red-gold, but he had white patterns splashed across the fur of his face, surrounding his large, yellow eyes and stretching up almost to his tiny ears. His muzzle was small, like Sala's, but he had powerful jaw muscles, like his own.

Kah had no idea what sort of Ty'gjir he was.

"Back home, all the names are like mine. Short. Sweet. Old. Lots of repeats. Must have been six E'e's on my street alone. None of the others were this handsome." E'e gave Kah a wink and lifted the Jaguar out of his chair by the same hand he had just shaken. "Come on. Let's get you to your quarters. It'll be a couple days through hyperspace. Wouldn't want our newest recruit to be uncomfortable."

With no shortage of haste, E'e began dragging Kah toward what he imagined was the aft of the ship and into a larger space.

Looking around the room, Kah's initial impression was that everything looked . . . soft. There was carpeting on the floor and cushions on the seats. On one side of the room stood a bar, its top covered with fabric and lined with bottles. Coloring the entire room primarily in violet and gold were heavy cloth curtains hanging over the walls, tempting Kah to drag his fingers across as he walked by. The fibers tickled a little. Kah didn't know what violet meant, but it felt like a mix of blue and red, and it looked very nice.

E'e glanced back, seeing Kah touch the curtains, and chuckled. "Fancy, eh? Velvet. No expense spared, I'm sure. Been nice to fly around in style, for once."

He led Kah down a narrow hall which extended from the back of the room, surely to the crew quarters. Kah, however, was distracted by the walls. They were odd. Dark red-brown, rich-looking, and seemingly molded to be very elaborate and pleasing to look at. But the material was strange. It felt like plastic, but was warmer, and had loose, stretched out shapes in it.

"Wood." Appearing at his side, E'e stared at the wall with Kah.

"Would what?" Kah pulled his eyes from the hypnotizing shapes in the wall and looked quizzically at the taller Ty'gjir.

The teasing tone was gone from E'e's voice, and he touched the wall alongside Kah. "The walls. They're made of wood, which is what trees are made of. Trees are big plants that grow as tall as buildings. Most habitable planets have them. Yours doesn't."

"I've read about trees, but never seen wood up close. It's very pretty. I like it." Kah smiled and traced one of the shapes with a finger.

"You'll see it a lot in fancy places and on fancy things. It's too soft and fragile to be used for much beyond luxury, but there are some planets with so much of it that the Ty'gjir there use it for just about everything." The teasing tone came back into his voice as he clapped Kah on the shoulder. "Now, come on. I've gotta get you to your room so we can get outta Pinto'whatever."

Kah wrinkled his nose in slight indignation at E'e's disrespect for his home, but the strange feline didn't seem to mean anything by it. Leading Kah the rest of the way to his quarters, E'e opened the door, revealing more opulence within. The bed, centered on the right wall, was huge, with soft-looking blankets and *more than one pillow*. Wooden, with golden trim, the walls in Kah's quarters were draped in curtains of the same tickly fabric — velvet, E'e called it.

His quarters had their *own* bathroom. It was located just past the bed on the right wall, but, from this angle, he could barely see inside. There was some kind of large tub in it — presumably, the biggest toilet Kah had ever seen. Finally, directly opposite the bed was what appeared to be a window to a remarkably similar room. Kah could only guess at its purpose.

E'e waved an arm into the open door, gesturing for Kah to enter. "I'll let you get comfortable. Just give me a holler when you're ready to take off and we can go."

Handing off Kah's bag, E'e retreated toward the bow of the ship, leaving Kah to explore his quarters.

Wasting no time, Kah stepped inside, tucked the admiral's disc in his bag, and placed it on the floor beside the door. Every other surface in the room looked like it might reject the tawdry duffle bag. He started to walk across the room to investigate the big tub in the bathroom, but nearly jumped out of his skin when another Ty'gjir appeared to his left, standing in the room on the other side of the window. He chuckled to calm his racing heart, embarrassed, and glanced back up at the other person. He looked like he had just had a fright, as well. Standing straight and snapping a wave, Kah saw the other Ty'gjir reply in kind and realized, with some shame, that he was looking at an image of himself. It was a *superbly* clear image, too. Was it possible that the screen was itself a camera? Kah had never heard of something like that.

He stood back a bit and scratched his chin, watching himself do the same, and excitedly realized that, for the first time, he had a chance to see himself as others did. Conspiratorially glancing to the entrance of the room, Kah scurried over, shut, and locked it, before returning and staring at himself. He waved and smiled as the him on screen did, too. Then, he hopped in place once. As he moved and his purple-black fur spread and bunched with his lithe, lean muscles, he could see the faintest traces of gold rippling underneath, accentuating his rosettes, and he thought it looked rather fetching. Then, he frowned. He tried to make his frown look like Thurv's, but he couldn't force the corners of his mouth to drop low enough without furrowing his brow, too. Instead, he just looked angry.

Well, that wasn't good. People must have thought he was crazy every time he intended to look sad.

Kah smiled exaggeratedly at himself, exposing his fangs in a huge, broad grin. He had nice teeth! Then, locking eyes with himself and walking up close, he opened his eyes wide and leaned in, nearly touching the screen with his face. He had bright green eyes, with a corona of gold surrounding his pupils, and blue bordering his sclera. He blinked and took a step back, grinning. He had hoped his eyes were pretty, and he was not disappointed.

A knock came at the door, followed by E'e's light, brusque tones. "Hey. I know I said to get comfortable, but we are on a timeline here. So, you know, stop admiring yourself in the mirror or whatever and get out here. You'll probably want to see the view when we take off."

Kah felt heat rush to his face and ears as he stepped back from the . . . *mirror*, not screen. He trotted to the door, calling, "Coming!"

"Gross," called E'e's voice, matching Kah's tone, more distant than before.

Kah didn't understand. E'e was a very strange Ty'gjir.

Opening the door, Kah started making his way to the bow, padding along the carpeted floor until he reached the threshold of the cockpit, decidedly shut. E'e was already inside, presumably running through pre-flight checks. Kah knocked hesitantly, but, instead of a vocal response, a speaker near the door crackled to life, through which E'e spoke.

"Nope. Sorry, kid. I'm the pilot and you're the passenger. You stay back there, in the passenger seating. The cockpit is my domain."

"Oh, sorry. Okay," Kah mumbled, embarrassed again. He had a lot to learn—like whether or not E'e could even hear his response. He turned to head back to the passenger area, alone, as the speaker crackled to life again.

"Maybe when we're underway, I'll show you around the cockpit. For now, open the curtains, take a seat, and strap in. We'll be off in a couple minutes."

Kah nodded—stupidly, he thought. E'e might not be able to hear him, but he almost certainly couldn't see him. Nonetheless, he returned to the room which greeted him on his entry to the shuttle and drew back the tickly fabric curtains, revealing a large, floor-to-ceiling window to the outside. Though he didn't expect to see anything in the dark of Pinto'Neth, it was especially difficult to see past his own reflection, a phenomenon he'd only read about until today. He looked for a way to dim the lights further, but there was apparently no need, as the engines of the ship burst to life with a muted roar and the lights dimmed to near darkness, possibly automatically. Glancing around, Kah opened the curtains on the opposite side of the room before selecting a central seat with a good view of both windows, and secured his safety belt.

A few seconds later, E'e's voice sounded from a speaker overhead. "Hope you're ready, 'cause we're taking off now."

True to his word, the shuttle lurched upward and off the spaceport platform. Outside, Kah could barely detect movement in the dark, but nothing showed clearly. With ominous rumbling and the frantic drumming of matter striking the exterior of the shuttle, the craft shakily ascended upward through the atmosphere. It seemed the shuttle had its localized artificial gravity already toggled on, however, because Kah felt none of the discomfort of ascent that he had experienced during the tolerance exam. Maybe that was reserved for smaller crafts, those without artificial gravity. Despite the darkness outside, Kah kept his eyes trained on the window, hoping for a glimpse of his world, to no avail. Slowly, over a matter of minutes, the chaos outside began to thin until it stilled entirely.

Then, like the shuttle's door opening and spilling the light within, Kah saw *stars*.

Free of the dust-choked atmosphere of Pinto'Neth, the depths of space became visible, colored by the light of *countless* stars. There were more than Kah had imagined. Some sat alone, shining dimly out into the void, but others clung together in great, light-speckled smears of brilliance across the dark, forming rivers of light to carve up the sky. There must have been millions that Kah could see from this window alone, which meant there were innumerable more in all other directions and beyond, beyond the reach of his eyes.

He grinned at the possibility—the potential of everything else, everything *new*, until E'e's voice crackled over the speakers. "All right. We're free of the planet's atmosphere, so you're good to walk about the cabin. If you're hoping to see it, look out a portside window now."

Unstrapping himself from the seat and rushing to the large, port window, Kah looked for his home. Instead, he simply stared, confused. There was nothing. No lights, no stars. Nothing but utter darkness. Maybe they'd moved so quickly, he thought, that the planet was out of sight already. Maybe E'e was mistaken, and meant the starboard windows. But, slowly, stars began to emerge, yet only around the borders of the window. More and more crept into sight, eventually outlining a huge circle of complete blackness against the sea of stars. Realizing what was before him, Kah recognized this great nothing as his home, his family's home — the site of his hopes, his dreams, his memories.

As the shuttle pulled further away from Pinto'Neth, Kah caught a glimpse of another strange sight. This one, however, he knew immediately, if by reputation alone. From behind the silhouette of utter dark that was his home, a different sphere edged into view. Instead of nothing, this one was a bruised, dull, reddish color, whose surface roiled and swirled with thick clouds of black. Barely any light survived the black clouds, and that light which did manage to escape appeared to scatter before it reached Pinto'Neth. The bleak, dying light belonged to Neth, a star too weak to share its glow, and the black clouds were thick layers of cosmic dust which completely enshrouded the star.

In Kah's school, he learned that there were once multiple planets in the Neth system, but they had collided eons ago, obliterating themselves on impact and, in their ashes, leaving one small, dark, dusty planet. The heat and force of the impact had formed the nordium for which Pinto'Neth was so valued, but the dust which had once been worlds surrounded the planet and the star, choking them off from each other and leaving Kah's people in the dark.

"Everything you'd hoped for, kiddo?" E'e's voice brought Kah out of his thoughts as it crackled overhead. "Good. We'll make one orbit around your planet, then enter hyperspace, where we'll stay for the next two days. Then, the trip is boring 'til we arrive."

Kah nodded and decided to take up position at the starboard window to stare at the stars. He wondered which of them he would visit, which were friendly, and which were hostile. There was *so much* he had yet to see. For an instant, he allowed himself to be completely carefree as he considered the opportunities before him—but then he remembered his mission. He had to earn the admiral's ear and plead the case of the Pintoth. There had to be something she could do for his people. He had only a vague idea about what could be done, but he was sure someone with her influence and experience would know more.

He enjoyed the astral view for only a few minutes or so as the shuttle made its orbit, before, once again, E'e chimed from overhead. "We're about to enter hyperspace, Kah'riss. It's worth seeing."

Kah looked from one window to another, trying to decide which would provide the best view, but, as if in answer to his unspoken question, E'e barked out, "You'll get a good view from anywhere with a window, kiddo."

Maybe E'e *was* able to see him, after all. Kah didn't like that. He couldn't see any cameras in this part of the ship, and, if he couldn't find the cameras, how would he know if his quarters had any privacy? He could ask E'e later. For now, though, he might as well enjoy the sights. And, without further fanfare, he was treated to a most bizarre sight indeed.

The ship seemed to stop dead in its orbit around Pinto'Neth. The pinpricks of starlight all halted, as well, and, one at a time, seemed to stretch out from a point directly ahead of the ship to somewhere far behind. Eventually, so many stars had stretched into blue-white lines of light around the ship that none of the blackness of space was visible, leaving the shuttle in a corridor of starlight.

Kah braced himself and waited, imagining the lines of starlight were elastic, stretching back around the ship, preparing to launch it with devastating speed through space. But nothing came. Once the starlight corridor had completely formed, the shuttle seemed to sit still.

Abruptly, the cockpit door opened and E'e stepped out into the common room, yawning and stretching. Kah, still braced at the window, suddenly felt a bit silly and tried to look at ease, but his eyes latched to E'e for cues. Without giving Kah a glance, however, E'e approached the bar and grabbed a pair of glasses and a bottle, pouring some translucent, amber-colored liquid into one. Then, he looked to Kah with a bored, but questioning expression, holding out the empty glass.

"Wanna drink, Kah'riss?"

"Oh," Kah said. E'e must be done piloting for now. The boring part of the trip had begun.

Kah *was* thirsty, and if the drinks were as fancy as the rest of the stuff on the shuttle, they had to be good. He nodded, watching as E'e filled the other glass. Kah noticed that the older Ty'gjir gave him a decidedly smaller portion and was momentarily indignant, but didn't want to seem rude, so he took the barely filled glass and thanked E'e anyway. He swirled the amber fluid around the glass once. It smelled sharp and burned the inside of his nose. It wasn't like any flavor he could identify, nor did it smell like water.

He had smelled something like it very rarely and faintly after Thurv came home late from work, but he had never asked about it.

"Well? Don't tell me they don't have sapser on Pinto'Neth?" E'e was watching Kah closely now. The carefree charm in the copper Ty'gjir's eyes had been replaced by an unforgiving scrutiny.

"No, yeah, sure," came Kah's answer. Not exactly a revelation.

Kah swigged the little sapser in his glass and instantly regretted it. The liquid burned its way down his throat and left his mouth feeling somehow drier than before. It took a monumental effort for Kah to not let his extraordinary discomfort show, but he must have done a good job, because E'e grinned again and clapped him on the back.

"Yeah, this can't be your first shot! You took that like a champ! But I bet this is a lot better than anything you got back home, huh?" E'e grabbed the glass out of Kah's hand and filled it. This time, he poured a portion equal to the one he had given himself.

Kah nodded, passing E'e a reassuring smile, and tried to sound mature. "I've taken plenty of shots before now, and this is definitely the least painful," he said, not quite lying, as E'e thrust the glass back into his hand.

"Well, then, drink up, kiddo! This'll be the best you get for a good long while." E'e laughed and clapped Kah on the back again, forcing Kah's gaze into the harsh beverage. Kah stared into the glass. He liked the strange Ty'gjir, even if his drinks tasted like poison. If they didn't have water on the shuttle, he would have to remain hydrated with *sapser*, he'd called it. He steeled himself before taking a more moderate sip.

Nope. No better in small amounts.

"Well, Kah'riss, we've got lots of time ahead of us before we arrive on the *Litany of Ash*," E'e said. "Why don't you tell me a bit about yourself? What makes a young cub with his whole life ahead of him sign up with the military?"

Grabbing a few bottles, E'e placed them on the bar before taking a seat at a tall chair set beside it and patted the chair next to his to beckon Kah over. Kah climbed into the seat, resting his feet on a rung halfway up the legs of the chair, as he certainly couldn't reach the ground. Taking another sip from his glass, he turned toward E'e, smiling and ready to make a friend.

"There's not a lot to tell. Most people who live on Pinto'Neth would rather not, and the military is a good way of getting off world. At least, that's what my da told me."

E'e nodded but seemed less than satisfied. "And how did your da prepare you for the military? Say what you will, you're still a kid, and that's a hard life to be pushed into."

Kah felt at ease with the funny, red pilot, and was feeling more at ease by the minute, so he was happy to tell him just about anything he wanted to know. Over the next several hours, well into the evening, Kah did exactly that. Despite his fast-talking, blunt mannerisms, E'e seemed to be a very good listener, and organically drew new questions from every answer Kah gave him. Kah told him all about his family and his life growing up, and about school and the mines, and Sala and her work, and about how sheltered he had realized he was on his little, dark planet. E'e seemed genuinely interested in everything he had to say. As a pilot, Kah reasoned, he must collect interesting stories from all his passengers, and must have a pretty good idea of what life was like on lots of planets.

"What about friends? You've talked plenty about your brothers, but haven't mentioned ever having a friend, or a girlfriend. What about those?" E'e smirked and cast Kah a sidelong glance as, once again, he filled the Jaguar's glass.

Kah shook his head from side to side, finding, with some amusement, that the motion made his head swim, so he continued it long after the gesture had stopped being appropriate. He knew what friends were, sure. He'd read books and had been told stories of friends, but there was never much time or opportunity for friendship for him. His education shift was a quiet affair. There were other Ty'gjir in his classes, but there was no opportunity to casually speak with them or to play any games. Thurv had friends, but he had a job. That's how he met Sala, after all. But he didn't see why he should have a different word for *girl*friends.

Why girlfriend and not just friend? Or girl friend? Or friend girl? Frirl. Grend.

Kah wasn't conscious of saying any of that aloud, but E'e laughed nonetheless, giving Kah a friendly shove which spun the stool on its bearings. "No, no! Not a friend that's a girl! A girlfriend! A sweetheart! Like what's-her-face was to your brother before they got married."

Kah furrowed his brow and squinted at the two or three pilots, trying to decide what they meant, or how to answer.

E'e, seeing this, threw his hands in the air in exasperation. "There's your problem! You don't have anyone who makes your heart race. Someone who you can't stop thinking about, who you want to be with all the time. That's why you don't have any problem leaving home, you poor little bastard!"

E'e grabbed Kah's head and hugged him uncomfortably against his chest. Kah was suddenly keenly conscious of the fact that E'e's scent was suspiciously similar to that of the sapser.

"Don't you worry your little head, kiddo. When we get to the *Litany*, I'll introduce you to the prettiest lady in the galaxy. She's the reason I keep going back, despite my poor, rambling soul. If she doesn't get your blood pumping, I will officially declare you a lost cause, and you will have my permission to live out your days as a good, little, fleet-owned killing machine."

Kah tried to nod his head, excited at the new challenge, but he was held tight. Despite this, his head felt like it kept moving anyway, mostly toward the ground, and he dropped his empty glass. The cushioned *thump* of the glass striking the carpeted floor seemed to echo inside his skull, getting louder and louder, until the only thing he could hear was the thunderous pounding.

"Kiddo? Kah'riss?"

Kah's face was cold. And wet. He started to open his eyes, but unwelcome light peeked through, eliciting a petulant groan and forcing them closed. Everything smelled bad. His head hurt. Someone was snoring *very* loudly nearby. He clicked his teeth to get a picture of whatever room he was in, but everything seemed covered in fluff and he couldn't make out any detail. This meant he had to open his eyes.

"No . . ."

The grumble sounded impossibly loud, considering Kah had barely summoned the strength to push it out of his lungs. Regardless, he cracked his eyes open again, squinting against the intrusion of the harsh, white light. His face was mashed sloppily against a toilet seat in a puddle of his own drool. That explained the wet. At least the rest of him was warm and dry. He sat up, rubbing the heel of his hand across his face, and looked around.

The blanket from the bed of his quarters was thrown loosely over him and across the warm tile floor. It really was soft, but, honestly, that didn't make him feel much better right now. Looking to the right, Kah found his face in intimate proximity to a foot, hanging from the edge of the basin in the bathroom. Huh. He tracked the leg affixed to the foot up and over the edge of the tub, finding it attached to the pilot, E'e, who was sound asleep in the basin, snoring up a storm.

How did he get here?

It didn't matter. He was still tired, and a bed would be nicer to sleep on than the floor. Rising on unsteady legs, Kah wrapped the blanket around himself, suddenly very cold. He shivered once, shaking from his toes to the tips of his ears, and took one step toward the door before he was overcome by nausea, driving him back to his knees and his face back into the toilet, retching violently before, once again, Kah lost consciousness.

"Kah'riss? Kah'riss . . . Wake up, wake up, wake up!"

Kah opened his eyes, looking directly into a larger, yellower pair. They pulled back, revealing E'e's smiling face. He was irritatingly chipper. Kah supposed he would look happy, too, if he had succeeded in poisoning a mark. The bastard.

"Come to mock me while I die?" Kah's voice was a weak, gravelly shade of its former glory.

E'e laughed his rich, rapid laugh while he did something to Kah just out of sight. "Don't be so dramatic, soldier! I'm just trying to make sure you're still alive in here! You need food and water. And a bath. You *don't* need to sleep any longer."

Kah looked about. He had found his way to the bed, somehow, and was curled around a large pillow, now also covered in drool. *Ugh.* Kah didn't usually drool. Being murdered was embarrassing.

"I am beginning to suspect, little killing machine, that you've never had a drink, after all." E'e stood back from the bed with his hands on his hips, looking down at Kah, but the smile never left his face. "We'll get along better if you don't lie to me, kiddo."

Kah glared at the grinning assassin. "I've had plenty of drinks. And I've been shot, too! I've just never had a drink laced with poison!"

E'e snorted and tossed a pillow at Kah's glaring face. "Poison? That was liquor, Kah'riss. It's not poison, but it'll fuck you right up if you drink too much of it, and it looks to me like you drank more than you could handle." He clapped his hands sharply. "Hence, the hangover."

Kah flopped back on the bed, hiding his sensitive ears under the pillow E'e had thrown. Why would E'e do this to

Kah? Why would he do it to himself? It wasn't worth it. It was his fault. He wanted Kah to suffer. Laying the blame for his discomfort firmly at E'e's feet, Kah resolved to never drink liquor again.

"Now, come on, kid. Get out of bed. I've got some water and medicine for you and I drew you a nice, hot bath. By the time you're done with the bath, I'll have some food ready, and you should feel plenty improved. But you don't get to eat if you don't bathe first, 'cause you kinda stink." E'e's footsteps padded away across the room, and the door to the room slid shut as he exited.

Tossing the pillow away and kicking off his blankets, Kah staring at the ceiling. This is what dying felt like, he decided. Admittedly, however, the prospect of food was welcome after he'd emptied his stomach so many times. Thinking about it, his stomach growled furiously. Thank goodness he wasn't nauseated anymore. Slithering off the bed, Kah caught his reflection in the mirror. He looked about as terrible as he felt. He was still wearing the shirt he'd arrived in but had lost his pants somewhere. He'd find them later. The him in the mirror sniffed and sneered at him, then gave him a rude gesture before he dragged himself to the bathroom.

Inside, there was a sweating glass of water resting on the counter next to two pills, as E'e had promised, and the large basin Kah had initially thought was a huge toilet was filled with water that smelled like Sala. Set on shelves beside the tub were plastic bottles full of what Kah assumed was soap. He didn't care enough to search for labels. He was sure he'd smell nice enough after soaking in the perfumed water. But first, a real drink. Kah picked up the cold glass of water and drank deeply, washing away some of the fluff sensation in his mouth.

Why hadn't E'e told him there was water to drink? He could have avoided this whole situation. Jerk.

Finishing off the glass of water, he poured himself more from the sink, taking the pills with a few mouthfuls. Even this water was cold, and it didn't have any ice. Kah placed the glass within arm's reach of the tub and pulled his shirt off over his head but paused when he felt something fall against his chest. Casting his shirt to the side, Kah investigated the object around his neck, discovering, with a quiet smile, the small, circular locket Sala had given him before he left. He hadn't checked to see what was inside yet, but there was no time like the present.

Lifting the chain from around his neck, Kah examined the small, silver pendant closely. It was simple in shape — a circle of silver no larger than the pad of his thumb, but covering its surface were numerous sharp, swirling etchings, which left a floral impression, even if the shapes were pure abstraction. He clicked open the locket as Sala had shown him and looked inside. On the left side of the locket, the back of the faceplate, was inscribed the image of a nine-pointed star, surrounded by a thick ring. This was the symbol of the Lord of Night, who conceals all secrets and separates the realm of the nine gods from the realm of mortals. Under it was inscribed a short prayer which Kah mumbled to himself.

"Oh Lord of Veils and Keeper of Secrets, cloak me in darkness. Hide me from the eyes of mine foes, that I may return home unscathed and unafraid."

Kah smiled as he read the prayer. Sala had been raised with a close relationship to and deep reverence for the gods. She was herself a devoted adherent of the Lady of Life, but had told Kah about all the gods and their works. He was glad she did, too, because the only other mention made of the gods on Pinto'Neth usually involved a disagreement or a stubbed toe. Despite the poignant prayer on the left side of the locket, however, it was the other face that truly caught Kah's attention.

On the other side of the locket was an image of his family. Not a projected image, but a static, colored one, brightly lit and somehow captured perfectly on the inside of the silver piece of jewelry.

It was clear the picture was Sala's idea.

She stood on one side of the image, bright-eyed and smiling, without any goggles. For the first time, Kah was able to see her clearly. She had pink-gray fur and bright blue eyes that complemented her well. Her arm was looped through Thurv's, who stood next to her. His eyes were squinted against the light which had been used to take the picture, but his smile was genuine. He was colored like Calan, with golden fur and dark brown rosettes, as well as white fur which ran from his chin down his neck and under his clothes. His eyes matched Sala's, bright blue and shining.

Standing with his hand on Thurv's shoulder was Istur, who had one eye closed against the light. He, too, had fur which matched Kah's other brothers, but had green eyes like Kah's. Sitting in front of them was Calan, bandaged and injured, with both eyes shut tight, but wearing a great, broad smile to bely his condition. Given Calan's state, the picture must have been taken shortly after the exams, while Kah was still unconscious. His family looked happy, if uncomfortable, but they had braved the light to take the picture for him.

Looking down at the memento of his brothers and sister, he didn't feel quite so awful, and his hangover seemed much less important. He clicked the locket shut and held it against his chest for a moment, then placed it carefully on the counter and prepared for his bath, removing the remainder of his clothes, as well as the bandages around his right leg. The wounds the Lynx's claws had left in his thigh were healing nicely, and the stitches had nearly all dissolved. He would have some scars, certainly, but they would just serve as a reminder of his victory. Gingerly, he stepped into the tub and sank down into the hot water.

"Oh, wow." Kah instantly saw the appeal. He had never been submerged in water before—not that he could remember, anyway—and the heat of the water instantly took the tension out of his muscles and the ache out of his head. He picked up the washing comb to start scrubbing soap into his fur, but, after a moment, decided there was no rush. There was plenty of time left to relax before E'e would be finished preparing food.

Plenty of time . . .

Quite a while later, Kah left the bathroom, comfortable and refreshed, with a nice, plush towel wrapped around his waist. Looking in the mirror, he saw a him that looked decidedly less poisoned, a him that he could see in a crisp military uniform standing beside an admiral. He smiled at himself and popped a quick salute. Then, unable to resist, he flexed both arms and grinned. Maybe not as big as Thurv's, but by the gods, those were the arms of a soldier! So, maybe mirrors weren't completely useless, after all.

After getting dressed, Kah returned to the common room to look for E'e, but he wasn't there. The strange, otherworldly sight of the starlight corridor was completely unobstructed, however, and Kah found himself seized by the bizarre view. Before too long, he managed to tear himself free and made his way to the cockpit, knocking on the door once more, but there was no answer. This was, as far as Kah was concerned, a mandate to explore the shuttle. E'e could be in danger somewhere, after all.

With juvenile excitement, Kah trotted toward the aft of the shuttle. There was a door directly across the narrow hall from his own which Kah reasoned was most likely another set of quarters. He gave the door a tap, not expecting any answer, and was not disappointed. Further down the hall was another door Kah had yet to explore, so he padded across the carpet toward it, not knocking this time before trying the handle.

The door opened and, from it, issued a heavenly scent. It was definitely pleasant, but not like cleaning products or perfume. It was somewhat similar to food bars frying, but there was no burning rubber smell to it. Instead, it was rich and smokey — savory — with a gentle sharpness and the faintest scent of blood. The smell seemed to coat the inside of Kah's nose and mouth, and instantly made him salivate. This time, Kah didn't have liquor to blame it on, and he wiped the back of his hand across his muzzle in an effort to maintain some dignity. With that under control, he could give his attention to what was actually behind the door — a carpeted stairway leading down into parts unknown.

Kah padded down the stairs to an abrupt intersection, with paths leading left and right. The smell seemed to come from both equally, so he chose left and proceeded that way, finding that it would not have made a difference, as both paths rounded back on the stairway, leading to a large, open room, more extravagant even than the common room upstairs. This one had a long, shining, beautiful table down its center with equally beautiful wooden chairs set beside it. It was designed to seat ten, by the look of it, but only two places were set at the far end. Over the table hung an elaborate sculpture made of droplets of dangling glass prisms, capturing light which shone from within the fixture and splashing it across the room in a kaleidoscope of flickering light.

Beyond the table stood a set of closed, wide doors from which the smell drifted. Kah could hear sizzling from the far room, as well as light-hearted humming. He grinned. Kah loved music, but it was rare to hear it except in the background of holonet reports, and he found himself drawn to the closed doors. Peeking through, he saw a large, shining steel kitchen, as well as E'e, with his back turned, wearing civilian clothes and an apron, bouncing back and forth in front of a large, steaming stove.

Kah watched him for a few moments, wondering why he was moving that way. Maybe he had to relieve himself, but the cooking demanded his attention until it was done. Soon, Kah realized that E'e's bouncing was synced nicely with his humming, and, amused by the display, Kah found himself tapping a foot along with the show.

As the click of Kah's toe claws sounded against the wood floor, E'e looked back over his shoulder and grinned, pulling something off the stovetop and sliding it onto a platter in an appealing, twirling motion. Without breaking rhythm, he retrieved a bowl from inside the oven and spun over to the door, which Kah opened for him, swept up in the show. Continuing the twirl, E'e made his way to the table and set both platter and bowl down between the two place-settings, ending the spin in a flourishing bow.

"Dinner is served!"

Not quite knowing what else he should do, Kah clapped enthusiastically, drawing a broad grin from the pilot, who untied his apron and hung it over the back of a chair before taking a seat in front of one of the plates, patting the vacant chair beside him.

"Thanks, kiddo, but I'm not sure I'm so good a cook that I deserve applause." E'e winked at Kah, a gesture, Kah realized, that was characteristic of the funny, copper Ty'gjir.

Nonetheless, Kah sat down next to E'e and, before looking at what he had prepared that smelled so magnificent, Kah clasped his hands together and closed his eyes, declaring, "Thank you for the food."

E'e chuckled as he served himself. "No problem, really. I'm supposed to keep you alive during the trip, and I like to cook, so it's not a big deal." Glancing at Kah, who was slavering over the food E'e had just served himself, E'e pointed a fork at him. "But this is mine. There's enough for you, too, but you keep those paws off my plate."

Kah nodded and wiped his mouth, embarrassed, before mimicking E'e's actions and grabbing a slab of some juicy, soft, red, dense material from the platter and a spoonful of fluffy, yellow-white stuff from the bowl. Both smelled delicious, but it was the slab that really drew him in. Looking down at them, however, he wasn't quite sure how to proceed, and sneaked subtle glances at E'e to watch how he ate.

E'e, however, seemed intent on waiting for Kah to make the first move and, after a long, awkward moment of neither moving and Kah staring at his food, E'e pointed the fork at him again. "What's wrong? Not good enough for you?" Kah could hear by E'e's tone that he was mostly joking, but there was genuine concern, as well, and he tried to assume a disarming smile.

"No, no! It's not that! It's just . . . what is it?" Kah's smile faltered a little and he glanced back down at his plate.

E'e scoffed, laying an arm across the back of his chair as he raised his brows. "Well, I'm kind of a meat and potatoes guy, so, I present to you—meat and potatoes."

Kah was dubious. He'd never heard of potatoes, so that checked out, but neither substance on his plate looked like meat. One looked like a cross-section of muscle and the other was fluffy, not at all like the moldable, pink-gray paste he had grown up with.

E'e sighed and picked up his knife, cutting a small cube off the muscle slab, before popping it into his mouth and looking meaningfully at Kah.

"Meat," he said. Then, scooping a small amount of the fluff onto his fork, he deposited that into his occupied maw, as well. "And potatoes." He watched Kah for a moment as the Jaguar waited for him to swallow, then narrowed his eyes. "I'm not going to feed you, kid."

"Right. Sorry." Kah picked up his fork and knife and began cutting the meat into little cubes. There was no denying that it smelled wonderful, but it looked like it just came off something alive. Eventually, with some last-minute hesitation, he placed a cube into his mouth.

Kah practically melted in his seat.

The meat was salty, sweet, savory, and rich, with some occasional, surprising tartness from whatever E'e had cooked into it. This was, without a doubt, the source of the aroma that coated the inside of his nose. There was a minor taste of blood, but it was so infused with the flavor of the dish that it struck Kah more as meat juice than anything else. The potatoes were thick and buttery and absorbed the juice from the meat well, combining into a flavor all its own—a flavor which Kah had never even imagined. This was what all food should always taste like.

Some moments later, Kah became conscious of E'e staring at him and looked back at the pilot, swallowing.

"Good?" asked E'e. His eyes were wide and there was no hint of a smile or sarcasm on his face. There was only awe.

Nodding excitedly, Kah returned to his plate for another forkful, but discovered, with crushing disappointment, that his plate was now bare, with only tiny streaks of brown and red to serve as evidence that it had ever been home to food. The profound sadness must have shown on his face, because E'e quickly pushed the bowl containing the remaining potatoes toward him.

"Come up for air this time. You'll enjoy it more." E'e's smile had returned as he continued to eat. Judging from his plate, he had only eaten a few more cuts of meat in the time it had taken Kah to empty his plate. Kah felt heat rush to his ears and ducked his head, a little ashamed of his lack of manners.

"That explains why you're so small, at least. They must not have fed you in weeks. You won't have to worry about that on the *Litany*. Three meals a day, though none quite so glamorous as this." E'e chuckled to himself as he spooned a large helping of potatoes onto Kah's plate, inviting him to eat more. "I gotta say, though, I've never seen anyone put away my cooking quite like that. What do they feed you at home?"

With his mouth still full of potatoes, Kah made a rectangle with his fingers and said, "Food bars. Well, nutrient bars, but everyone at home just called them food bars."

E'e shrugged as he continued to eat delicate mouthfuls of meat and potatoes. "Never heard of 'em. What are they like?"

"They're kind of heavy and dense, but you don't really have to chew them. They sort of disintegrate in your mouth. You can also mush them up and drink them. The taste is a little bit rubbery, but they have everything you need to stay fit and healthy." Kah grinned, remembering the taste of home.

E'e gave him a level stare. "Well, that sounds plain awful. What else did you eat?"

Kah cocked his head, looking quizzically at E'e and provoking a pained grimace in response.

"Have you ever eaten anything but—but food bars?"

Kah shook his head. "Why would I need to eat anything else?"

E'e groaned and cast his head to the left and right, as if looking for someone to blame.

"Fuck. Me." He slapped his hands on the table. "Your whole life, you've only eaten mushy, rubber bars of nutrients? How have you not gone insane? You know, for most people, eating is something to enjoy, not just a necessity. In fact, some people like eating so much that they're addicted to it! There are so many different kinds of things to eat and different ways to prepare them that, if you started right now, you'd need a thousand lifetimes to try them all! Lords and Ladies, Kah'riss, you are a depressing little weirdo."

Concluding thusly, E'e exasperatedly slid his plate across the table to Kah and made an inviting hand gesture. "You have a lot of missed meals to catch up on. Might as well start now."

"Well, uh, thank you," Kah said, momentarily offended, but he could see that E'e wasn't trying to insult him; he was genuinely lamenting Kah's lack of worldly experience. Regardless, Kah wasn't going to refuse more meat.

"Okay! It's decided!" Pushing his chair back with his legs, E'e sprang from the table and strode over to a small table with a set of glasses and a bottle of what looked like more sapser. He brought the bottle and a glass to the table and filled it to the brim, taking a quick draught.

"You, my sheltered little friend, need to learn what life is. You need to see that everything isn't pod-cities and darkness and dust and — and fuckin' food bars. Your job is protecting lives now, and that way of life is not worth protecting." He sat down and scooted his chair closer to Kah. "Ask me anything you want to know about me, or about people at large. If, 'what is food?' isn't too stupid or basic a question, nothing is."

Kah nodded along, excited at the prospect of learning something new, regardless of the disparaging remarks about his home. He had a million questions, but he supposed he should start with the basics.

"I guess . . . Where are you from?" Kah kept his eyes fixed on E'e, even as he shoveled more food into his mouth.

E'e assumed his characteristic grin again, which put Kah more at ease, and launched into a description of his home.

"My homeworld is Sozen, one of the very first planets to be colonized in the Dal territory. It's big — much bigger than Pinto'Neth — and is mostly plains and shallow seas. The whole world was apparently a shallow sea, once. Now, it's dominated by grazelands. Everyone on the planet is a Bay, like me" — he gestured to himself — "and we're really good with livestock. That's sort of our thing. All kinds of livestock for all kinds of climates. We supply the meat for our entire sector, like that sholo steak you're munching on. Since our products are in such high demand, most of the planet is fairly well-off, with a very low poverty rate, and even the poorest Ty'gjir have all that they need, and don't have to eat food bars to get by. My family is big. Lots of brothers and sisters and cousins, and everyone in the family is involved in leatherworking."

"What's that?" Kah cut in.

"Leather is animal skin that's treated for use as clothing or upholstery, mostly, but also has a lot of other uses."

Kah looked appalled. "It's . . . skin?"

"Yeah, yeah. Back home, we try to use every part of every animal. So, when the livestock goes to the slaughterhouse, the leather goes to us and the rest goes elsewhere, mostly to butchers." E'e sat back in his chair and took another draught of his sapser.

"But, why would you dress in skin?"

"I'd rather use it than let it rot in the sun." E'e shrugged. "But it's sort of a luxury thing. Rich people love to cover their things in stuff that used to be alive. Like that couch." He gestured at a long, cushioned seat next to the side table from which he had retrieved his drink. It was covered in a red-brown, smooth, shiny material. It didn't look terribly soft or comfortable to Kah.

He would have to investigate later.

E'e looked like he was about to continue, but Kah held up a hand to ask another question, drawing a dry look from E'e.

"The sun?"

"You know, like" — E'e made a vague gesture of something falling from above, with his fingers spread apart. "Or . . . I guess you wouldn't know. It's like a general term for whatever star shines on your planet. Its light is sunlight. That kind of thing."

Kah nodded, mentally taking notes, and asked, "So, if your family is made up of leatherworkers, why are you a pilot?"

"Eh. I got bored of the same sights, sounds, and smells every day. So, I joined up with the military. Nobody from Sozen joins the military." E'e tipped his head and glass toward Kah to emphasize this point.

"You're in the military?"

"What? Yeah, of course! Did you think I was just a transport pilot or something?"

Kah glanced off to the side, a bit sheepish. "Maybe a little." Seeing E'e look less than pleased by this answer, Kah quickly continued, "So, what do you do in the military?"

"Well, right now I fly weird, little Jaguars around and tell them stories so they don't look stupid when they run into Ty'gjir who aren't as nice as me." E'e straightened up in his seat, looking very indignant as he glared at Kah through large, narrowed eyes.

"Sorry . . . " Kah swallowed. Talking to new people was hard. "Do you . . . have a girlfriend back home?"

E'e smiled again with a somewhat wistful look in his eyes. He could change his whole demeanor in the blink of an eye, and whatever expression he wore, it was contagious. "I had plenty of girlfriends on Sozen, yeah."

Kah's eyes widened and he tried to apply some of his new knowledge. "Wow! How many wives do you have?"

E'e look at Kah for a long moment, his smile widening, as if he were trying to decide if Kah was serious, before answering, "None."

"Oh, I'm sorry," Kah said, his heart aching for his new friend. "How did they die?"

At this, E'e laughed aloud, his rich, rapid laugh breaking what Kah had perceived as tension. Kah, however, was too confused to laugh along.

"I've never been married, kid! Is that — is that how life goes on Pinto'Neth? You meet a girl and, just 'cause you get along, you decide you should get married and start popping out cubs before you kick off? And the only reason — the *only* reason you wouldn't get married is 'cause one of you died?" E'e wiped at his eyes as he continued to laugh at Kah's question.

Finished with the remaining food on both plates, Kah folded his hands in his lap, shooting occasional glances at the laughing Bay before responding, "I—I think so, yeah."

This brought E'e's laughter to an abrupt end and he eyed Kah, trying to decide if Kah was naïve or if that was, truly, how courting proceeded on Pinto'Neth.

Carefully, slowly, he said, "In most places, as far as I know, men have more than one girlfriend before they decide to marry one, and women, more than one boyfriend. Even then, it might not work out and the married couple might separate, and then both people might get married again, to two other people."

"But how do you decide which to marry?" Kah asked.

"I dunno, really. I guess that's why people go through multiple partners before they decide who fits best." He paused for a moment. "Though most don't like it when you try out more than one at the same time!" E'e guffawed at his own joke.

Kah didn't get it.

When E'e's laughter petered out, he continued, "But then, most people aren't after a girlfriend or a boyfriend because they're looking to get married. Most of the time, especially at your age, they're just looking for fun, and having someone close to you with a shared romance is pretty fun."

"Why?"

E'e spluttered and coughed on some of his drink, sitting up straight in his chair as he tried to compose himself, then managed to respond exasperatedly, "You're killing me, Kah'riss! It—ah, well, if you like someone that much, you want to be with them. And doing the things you usually find fun with someone you like so much can only make those things more fun, right?"

Kah's expression was stoic as he catalogued the new information, but E'e looked uncomfortable. Wrestling with the thoughts in his head, staring into Kah's blank expression, E'e hesitated for a long moment before he blurted, "Plus, sex rules. And a girlfriend or boyfriend means a convenient, reliable source of sex."

Kah's expression did not change as E'e made this declaration, and E'e finished off another glass of sapser before looking toward the young Jaguar.

"Do they — they do sex on — Don't ask me what sex is."

Now it was Kah's turn to scoff, without an ounce of shame, "I know all about sex!"

"Oh, thank the gods. That means we can change the subject, kiddo." Visibly relieved, E he poured himself another drink.

Apparently oblivious to the older Bay's awkwardness, Kah continued his questioning. "So, other than sex, what did you do for fun at home?"

This, E'e could answer, and with minimal discomfort. He described to Kah games he had played as a child, hiding in the grasses of his homeworld as a friend would try to find him, or pretending they were soldiers and waging make-believe wars. He described his school experience, which revolved around large buildings which housed thousands of students separated into intimate classes, focused, not just on their academic preparation for the future, but also on socialization with other Ty'gjir.

He talked about sports, particularly one called yannik, which was apparently originally a Replid game, but had been largely adopted into Ty'gjir culture and was played and celebrated throughout the Rae'gal Arm. E'e and most of his closest friends played competitive yannik during their schooldays. Kah had never heard of the sport or seen *any* televised sporting events, so he was very interested, and E'e was only too happy to explain the game in detail.

According to E'e, a game of yannik is played between three teams in a circular arena which is itself separated into concentric rings. The teams are spread out, with players starting intermingled among players from other teams on the outermost ring. When the game begins, the players rush to the innermost circle and attempt to move a large metal hoop from player to player from the innermost circle to the outermost in an unbroken line. Points are awarded according to how far the hoop reaches before it is intercepted by another team.

There were other intricacies which escaped Kah, but it sounded like big, organized fighting, and he liked fighting. Seeing that Kah's interest was piqued, E'e was happy to continue his edification and, after cleaning up their dinner, the two returned to the common room, where they spent the remainder of the day and night watching recordings of notable yannik matches from the Dal territory leagues and eating quickly-made snacks which seemed to have no value other than being delicious and easy to eat.

As one of the games concluded in a rousing, come-from-behind victory, E'e grinned, gesturing at the projection, and said, "When you get to be my age, Kah'riss, this is mostly what you do for fun. You grab a friend, you grab a drink, and you watch the game."

Kah smiled, enjoying the yannik games, but happier that E'e had called him a friend. Then, a thought occurred to him and he cocked his head, asking, "How old are you?"

Without turning to look at him, E'e grabbed a handful of snacks and casually answered, "Coming up on forty-nine cycles now."

Kah's jaw dropped. Forty-nine cycles was impossibly old by Pintoth standards. Forty was about as old as Pintoth reached — maybe forty-two, if they were in exceptional health. And E'e appeared *young*. He didn't seem at all slowed down by his advanced age, and certainly didn't seem concerned about his impending mortality.

He wanted to ask how many cycles E'e expected to reach, but couldn't decide on a tactful way to do so, so blurted out, "How old are you going to be when you die?"

Casting Kah a sidelong glance and a bemused smile as he munched on his snacks, E'e chortled around the food in his mouth, "Well, if family history is anything to go by, I'll be sitting on the fat side of a hundred when I decide to kick off."

Kah's wonder only grew. He only nominally watched the remainder of the yannik games, distracted by the prospect that anything could be as old as E'e and still be so healthy. How long would he remain this spry? Eighty cycles? Ninety? One hundred cycles was simply so much time. A person could learn so much — could accomplish so much with a lifespan that long. He wondered what he would have to do to live that long. Was it too late to make the necessary changes, or did he still have a chance of getting there?

After the pair finished watching their games and bid each other goodnight, Kah curled up in the glorious, comfortable bed in his quarters, eventually eschewing the disconcerting softness of the blankets for a thin sheet, and reflected on everything he had learned during the flight with E'e. If E'e had lived a *normal* life, it sounded like everyone else in the Dal territory had so much more experience than Kah did. More than *any* Pintoth did. Kah had already accomplished firsts about which most Pintoth could only dream, and he was, despite his posturing, still a cub.

Had his da really lived his whole life without seeing the stars? Why should starlight be reserved for everyone but the people of Pinto'Neth?

IX

"It sounds like you had a great deal of admiration for E'e."

I did.

"Even when he was merely a pilot to you."

That is correct.

"What exactly did he do to earn your respect?"

He was straightforward. And kind.

"But he concealed the nature of your relationship. Did that not bother you?"

I assumed he had his reasons. We all have secrets.

"So, you are still able to trust someone who conceals information from you?"

I don't trust anyone.

"You are able to respect and rely upon someone without trusting them?"

I rely on people to repeat their established patterns of behavior and to apply them reasonably to new circumstances. Trust is an assumption that someone can be relied upon to have my best interests at heart. It's arrogant.

"At last, we draw something meaningful out of you! You are making progress."

. . . Thank you.

"Thank *you*, Kah. This is all to help you, after all. We are glad to see you taking that to heart. Tell us more, please."

"You ready? We're about to come out of hyperspace."

In answer to E'e's question, Kah nodded excitedly from the copilot's seat. They were almost there, at last. The last two days had gone in an instant, though he enjoyed the time he had spent aboard the shuttle with E'e.

After Kah woke up, E'e had invited him into the cockpit to show him around and to give him a crash-course in deep space flight. Kah felt he had a good grasp on it, theoretically, but had yet to put his hands on the flight controls. Regardless, every little bit learned was an advantage for when his formal training began, and he was grateful for everything E'e had taught him during their short time together. He was going to miss the funny Bay when the flight was over, but at least Kah had made a friend.

As E'e made some last-minute calculations and adjustments, the whole shuttle began to shake violently. Alarmed, Kah instinctively anchored his claws in the arms of the chair. E'e, however, was unconcerned.

"Don't worry," he said. "That's just us passing through the interdiction field surrounding Aurum. Most of the Dal worlds have them right now, what with the war and all. But we have the clearance tags to get through without much more than the wobbles. Otherwise, well, we'd be yanked out of hyperspace the instant we touched the field and maybe we'd both die." He shrugged and gestured broadly at the ship around him as the shaking slowed to a stop. "Now welcome, little killing machine, to Aurum."

E'e pulled hard on the slip throttle and the starlight corridor faded into distinct lines of light which compressed into individual gleaming pinpricks marking distant stars. Without the light tube around them, the blackness of space opened wide, revealing a much brighter star system than Kah had expected.

Off the shuttle's bow was a titanic, blue planet. At least, the blue was what first caught Kah's eye. He hadn't seen much blue yet, but the concentration of such vibrancy in one place felt unnatural. On closer inspection, however, the planet simply had massive, blue . . . oceans, Sala had called them, circumscribed by great green and gray landmasses. Toward the northern and southern poles of the world, green terrain made way for frosty white, and over all of it were great spirals of pale fluff, drifting slowly across the atmosphere.

"This, Kah'riss, is what habitable planets that *aren't* awful look like. Pretty nice, right?" E'e watched Kah with his trademark grin as the young Jaguar leaned far forward in his seat, taking in as much of the planet as he could. "But a proper introduction will have to wait. That's not our destination."

E'e took hold of the flight controls and began to accelerate the shuttle, hooking it into a clockwise orbit around the planet. His eyes scanned screens and information read-outs, checking for things Kah couldn't identify and making adjustments accordingly. With a clear view outside the ship for the first time since boarding, Kah was able to get an idea of how quickly the shuttle moved around the planet. Kah knew the specs of many ships quite well on paper, but seeing what those numbers represented in concrete reality was an entirely different animal. Despite the size of the planet relative to the ship, the tiny craft crossed its enormous landmasses in the blink of an eye, hungrily devouring degrees of rotation around Aurum. After orbiting approximately ninety degrees around the planet, a shining object hanging in orbit came into sight, which grew larger and larger as they approached.

E'e pointed to the object as he steered towards it and began to engage retrograde thrusters. "*That* is our destination—your new home, the *Litany of Ash*."

Kah's eyes were glued to the shining shape as they drew closer. From this angle of approach, they had a good profile view of the ship, and he was quick to take in as much of it as he could. He estimated the ship measured ten kilometers from stem to stern, and its exterior was festooned in violet and gold. Kah imagined, based on the colors matching the interior of the shuttle, that these were the house colors of Prince Cah'dal. He was sure any doubt would be dispelled as soon as they entered the ship.

The vessel appeared roughly cylindrical in shape, but, as they drew closer, more details became apparent, with a great bladed scoop adorning the bow, which Kah could only imagine was a ram, as well as staggered plates of overlapping armor stacked across its flanks. In the crevices between these plates were deep trenches lined with innumerable lights and docking bays, easily identifiable by the blue atmospheric shields over their entrances. These shielded trenches had the effect of etching the vessel's surface with great, ghostly rivers of light, which lent the looming craft an intimidating, pulsing glow. From his position, Kah couldn't clearly make out any of the ship's major armaments but knew that, lurking beneath the bow and the armored broadsides of the vessel were colossal railguns, waiting to be deployed.

While Kah was distracted by his assessment of the *Litany*, E'e pressed a button above his head, hailing the larger craft with an insistent chime. Shortly, the chiming stopped and a calm, male voice crackled to life from the control panel between the pilot and copilot seats.

"This is the Litany of Ash. *We have received your hail, shuttle* Grace and Fanfare. *State your purpose."*

E'e adopted an officious tone, very unlike the casual, conversational cadence Kah had grown to know, as he responded, "This is Captain E'e of the United Fleet of the Dal Territory, currently pilot of the shuttle *Grace and Fanfare*, requesting docking permissions in one of the forward docking bays."

"Captain E'e, your security clearance is confirmed and you are clear for docking in forward bay twenty-one. Welcome home, Captain."

Kah shot a questioning glance to E'e as the Bay clicked the same button above his head, closing the line of communication, and muttered, "*Captain* E'e?"

"Yeah, what? Wanna fight about it?" E'e gave Kah a momentary severe glare, which broke into his characteristic grin and wink combination.

"Why didn't you tell me you were my ranking officer?" Kah was confused. Everything he'd learned about the military painted a picture of a place of rigid, inflexible decorum and order. E'e's casual, even convivial conduct flew in the face of that order.

E'e shrugged as he maneuvered the shuttle along the length of the *Litany*. "What? Did you want me yelling at you and ordering you around, or telling you to make my dinner or shine my boots or something? Seems kind of mean to me."

"I didn't want you to be mean to me, no. I guess I just— I would have expected it from my superior officer." Kah ducked his head a little, feeling foolish.

Now it was E'e's turn to look confused, but he recovered quickly and cast Kah an amused look, with the majority of his focus still on flying the shuttle.

"Listen, kid," he said. "I've never earned a thing through cruelty, but I've gained an awful lot by being nice. Sure, it's selfish, but it's the kind of selfish you can feel good about. People might even like you for it." With a wink, E'e clapped Kah on the shoulder, widened his eyes, and grimaced in mock alarm, drawing a twitch of a grin from Kah. "Besides, if I chose to be a dick to you, it would have made the past couple days pretty awkward."

"I guess that makes sense, *Captain*." Kah replied, earning a comfortable smile from E'e, who shifted his focus fully to flying the shuttle.

At this distance from the *Litany*, Kah noted, all he could see out the frontal viewport was the broadside of the larger vessel and, even by craning his neck, could not see the dorsal or ventral surfaces of the ship. Before long, however, the shuttle slowed to an apparent stop and descended straight down into one of the trenches between the armor plates, through a blue atmospheric shield, and into a wide hangar occupied by numerous and varied shuttles.

E'e pointed at a toggle on the control panel and nudged Kah. "Here, you can take care of the final and most important part of our trip — the landing. Flip that switch and the landing gear will descend, and then, once we touch down, we'll be all done."

Kah instantly did as he was bid. Admittedly, the new knowledge of E'e's rank may have played a role in his urgency, but he was excited to contribute, nonetheless. The toggle clicked into its alternate position and, with some low-pitched, mechanical whining, the shuttle's landing gear moved into place, followed seconds later by the almost-imperceptible impact of E'e's landing.

The Bay flipped a few more switches, powered down the control panel, and turned to Kah with a quick salute. "All right, kiddo, grab your stuff. We'll be heading out immediately. I'll meet you at the exit. Hop to."

Kah jumped up from his seat and rushed back through the common room to his quarters, where he had all his belongings already packed and his room tidied up. He gave the room a final sweep to make sure he had all his property, clutched the locket around his neck to be sure it was where it belonged, and headed back out to meet E'e, who stood calmly next to the door through which Kah had originally entered the shuttle, picking something out of his teeth. E'e didn't appear to be carrying any bags or other belongings, aside from a somewhat bulky wristwatch Kah hadn't noticed before.

"Aren't you going to get your stuff?" Kah asked.

In answer, E'e tapped the wristwatch a couple times, then pressed a button next to the door, causing it to open and stairs to begin extending down to the floor of the docking bay. Kah didn't understand what E'e meant by the gesture to his watch, but was suddenly much too distracted by the cacophony that exploded through the open shuttle door to care.

E'e gave Kah a gentle nudge, pushing him out the door, down the stairs, and into noise and chaos. The docking bay was quite large, though not as large as the massive freight bay on the *Collision of Truth*. However, this one was *full*, which made it decidedly busier. There were small passenger shuttles, similar to the one he had just left, arranged into a grid of square, fifty-meter landing pads which filled the entirety of the bay, and most of the landing pads were occupied.

Small, automated cart trains whizzed to and fro, picking up and dropping off passengers throughout the bay without ever slowing or stopping. Most of the passengers on these carts were uniformed staff, typing away furiously on datapads without looking at their surroundings, but that didn't seem to slow them as they ably maneuvered through the traffic. Every Ty'gjir in sight wore a gray, unassuming uniform with gold and violet highlights in the form of epaulettes and cuffs or stripes down the legs of their pants.

One such Ty'gjir, a skinny, male Cheetah, stepped off a cart next to Kah's shuttle and stood directly in front of Kah, tapping away at his pad without looking at him, before he slapped the pad to his side, saluting smartly, and declared, "Welcome home, Captain, Sergeant. The admiral has been waiting for you. Please follow me."

Without waiting for a response, the Cheetah turned on his heel and boarded a passing cart.

Kah hesitated, then felt E'e nudge him again and, with more than a little trepidation, stepped onto the cart train, very nearly losing his balance before E'e caught and righted him and sat him on one of the passenger benches.

"Don't lose your nerve now, kid. You're almost to the starting line." E'e shot Kah a wry smile as he sat down next to him.

"Why'd that Cheetah call me a sergeant?" Kah asked, still looking around, as if there was a sergeant hidden behind him.

E'e shrugged and frowned. "Guess you must be a sergeant. The porters don't make mistakes. That's a good first thing to learn." He clapped Kah on the shoulder again. "Congratulations on the promotion, Sergeant."

"Th-thanks, I guess." Kah did not like this idea. He thought he would start at the bottom and would work his way up, earning responsibility as he rose through the ranks. Starting at sergeant was — he began mentally counting ranks in the hierarchy of the fleet's ground forces — six ranks from the bottom. That meant he would begin his military career in command of other Ty'gjir. He wasn't ready to take charge of others' lives. *He* knew that. What was the *admiral* thinking, making a cub responsible for soldiers?

Kah's palms began to sweat and he fidgeted in his seat. He couldn't think like that. He needed to be prepared for any responsibility he might be given. He needed the admiral to trust him to take on any challenge. This was just another hurdle to be cleared, and, like the rest, he would clear it. For now, he just needed to think about something else.

He scanned the hangar as his cart swept by. The uniformed Ty'gjir who buzzed about, whom Kah now knew to be porters, never seemed to stop moving. He tracked one as she made her way to five separate shuttles, pausing and taking notes at each, but only speaking to two disembarking crews. What could she be writing about? What sort of information did they hold on their datapads that the Cheetah had instantly recognized him and E'e, and knew information about them which they themselves did not yet know?

Kah's imagination began to wander before he made another observation — almost none of the shuttles matched. They were of widely varying size, make, and model. He did note with some pride, however, that the shuttle on which he arrived appeared to be the nicest. But if this were the United Fleet of the Dal Territory, shouldn't there be some level of uniformity among its craft, beyond some stripes of violet and gold? He did not have much more time to wonder, however, as he felt E'e nudging him again.

"This is our stop, Kah'riss," the Bay said as he indicated the Cheetah, several carts up, stepping off the train and moving toward a large set of automatic doors.

E'e stood up and, without apparent effort or concern, stepped off the moving train, turning to wait for Kah to do the same. Kah, in turn, grabbed his bag and attempted to mimic E'e's actions, taking a deep breath and confidently stepping from the train, planting his foot perhaps too hard on the floor and sending minor shocks up his leg. He did not, however, fall over and look like a fool. Success.

E'e must have followed Kah's thought process, because he gave the young Jaguar a slightly patronizing grin and a chuckle which could hardly be heard over the bustle of the hangar and beckoned for him to keep up.

Kah trotted behind E'e as the two wound their way through the crowds to keep up with the fast-walking Cheetah, who had just reached the double doors and stopped to wait, thank the gods. Not letting the opportunity go to waste, the pair managed to close the distance to the Cheetah, who looked decidedly displeased.

"Please, keep up," he snapped, before turning and resuming his rapid pace through the doors and into well-lit, stark white hallways.

The hall was markedly less crowded than the hangar, which made keeping pace with the porter much easier, and also made it easier to take in their surroundings, though there was much less to see in the largely empty halls. The walls and ceiling of the halls were plain, luminescent white, but the floor was a shiny black which reflected Kah's likeness as he looked down at his feet. There were evenly spaced doors every ten or so meters, but every door was closed and not one was labelled, leaving Kah to wonder what secrets they kept—except, perhaps, the washrooms, which were prominently branded.

A bathroom's importance was universal, Kah supposed.

As the trio left the hangar further and further behind, twisting and turning through the labyrinthine halls, the populations of the hallways disappeared entirely, leaving them in awkward silence, aside from the clicking of the porter's heels and the loud squeaking of Kah's shoes on the floor. Kah became so focused on silencing his footsteps that he lost track of the distance they had walked until, suddenly, the blank walls on either side of the hall gave way to transparent glass. Outside his tunnel, stretching endlessly to the left and right, innumerable glass corridors ran parallel to his own. He blinked a few times, trying to decide if this was merely reflection or if the ship was, in fact, lined with glass tubes, like his home. He soon received his answer as, to his left, mag-trams flew between the corridors at intervals and a tram pulled to a stop outside the wall to his right.

A door slid open, allowing access to the tram, and the Cheetah darted aboard. Kah and E'e followed suit, joining the porter onboard and sitting down on the relatively comfortable passenger seats. The Cheetah, however, stood, grasping an overhead rail the instant before the tram pulled away from the station. It was remarkably quiet inside, other than a sort of pulsing hum which seemed linked to the tram's approach of each station, even when it did not stop.

That is, it was remarkably quiet until E'e sniffed loudly and cleared his throat, looking toward Kah and bobbing his head from side to side, apparently to a tune playing in his head. Kah grinned, reminded of E'e's rhythmic bouncing while he cooked. He wondered if lots of Ty'gjir from the wider Empire also idly bounced, or if it was just one of the many peculiarities of the Bay.

The tram slowed and pulled to a smooth stop at a station which, to Kah, looked identical to all the previous ones they'd passed. Despite the similarity, the Cheetah moved to stand beside the unopened tram doors, prompting Kah and E'e to do the same and, as the doors opened, they all proceeded through. Kah expected that, after the trio had wordlessly speed-walked off the tram platform, they would have a distance of blank white halls to traverse, as well. Instead, the glass corridors opened into a large, circular chamber. This one saw significantly more activity than any of the halls, with Ty'gjir boarding and disembarking from what appeared to be a broad selection of elevators arranged along the outer walls of the chamber.

For the first time, Kah perceived an instant of indecision in the porter as he seemed to debate which lift would see them to their destination in the timeliest manner. As Kah drew level with the porter, he watched the Cheetah's eyes scan over the crowds and doors before he darted ahead toward one of the groups. It didn't look to Kah like a promising elevator or crowd. He suspected the porter just didn't like that his wards had caught up. However, by the time the trio reached the lift, most of its crowd had dispersed, either off to their respective destinations, or had given up and moved to a different elevator.

The door opened with a cheerful ding, much higher pitched and more pleasant than those back on Pinto'Neth, and, with the diminished crowd, everyone waiting was able to squeeze aboard. Kah stuck close to E'e, but ended up closer than he had hoped as more Ty'gjir elbowed their way in, cramping the already packed elevator even further. The lift began to move but, according to Kah's positional sense, didn't only move up or down. It seemed to follow diagonal tracks, zig-zagging its way through the bowels of the ship, but, after several stops, maintained a consistent, upward path.

Forced into the tight space, Kah had no choice but to assess the scents of everyone aboard. E'e still smelled thinly of sapser, though, as muted as it was, it took on a sweet, almost honey-like scent. The remainder of the Ty'gjir on board, however, smelled almost uniformly of antiseptic. Kah wondered how long he would have to live here until he, too, lost his scent. Soon, Kah heard the elevator door ding open and felt E'e begin to sidle his way out of the throng, so, as politely as he could, Kah pushed his way through the mass of uniformed, sterile-smelling soldiers and out into a rather intimidating sight.

Before him stretched a long, dimly lit, and gently downward-sloping room lined with screens, projections, and monitors. While it wasn't nearly as crowded as the lift had been, nearly every monitor was occupied by severe-looking Ty'gjir. The entirety of the room was ringed by paneled windows, providing a view out into the star-studded void, with much of the view occupied by the bright blues and whites of Aurum.

The center of the room was dominated by a large table, which appeared to double as a projector and was currently displaying a star map of the Rae'gal Arm of the galaxy. Various stars were highlighted, and tiny figures of ships moved in rapid, straight lines throughout the territories, some blinking out, while others grew in size upon reaching their destinations. On the far side of the table stood a female Ty'gjir with tall, tufted ears — a Caracal — whose face was lit from below as she gestured at various points on the map, a small group of onlookers hanging on her every word.

"Captain E'e and Sergeant Kah'riss have arrived on the bridge!" The porter's outburst startled Kah and he flinched despite himself. When Kah turned to look back at the Cheetah, however, he had stepped back aboard the elevator, which closed and thrummed away somewhere into the ship.

With the porter gone, Kah returned to the central map and found the female Ty'gjir's hard gray eyes locked on him. She swept out from behind the table, leaving her entourage to wait for her as she and E'e strode towards each other, Kah following meekly behind. At about two meters apart, they stopped and E'e offered her a very formal salute, the first time Kah had seen him make such a gesture. Kah echoed it. She nodded and gave a quick tap to her left shoulder in reply before the corners of her mouth flicked up in a tiny smile.

"Welcome home, Captain."

E'e grinned back at her and answered, "It's good to be home, Admiral."

"And you, Kah'riss. It's good to finally, formally meet you. I am Admiral Achaera'fra. Welcome to your new home, the *Litany of Ash.*"

Kah had waited to hear the gentle, low rasp of her voice for days now, but wasn't sure if he was supposed to or allowed to respond, so just gulped and nodded. Achaera'fra's eyebrows rose a little at Kah's lack of a verbal response, but her tiny smile didn't change as she looked down at him. Kah, meanwhile, took the chance to get a good look at the person to whom he had entrusted his future.

The admiral was tall, with perfect, rigid posture. While she had worn only a gray, unassuming uniform at his exams, here, she wore an elaborate ensemble of violets and golds which radiated authority — more like a prince than an admiral, Kah thought. From the distance, Kah could also see the silvering of the fur around her muzzle and gray eyes. With E'e's revelation of his age, Kah could scarcely guess at how old that made her. After her salute, her left arm bent, raising her hand to approximately the level of her chin, and she idly clicked her claws. Pulse after echoing pulse washed from her claws across her face, searing a map of her features into Kah's brain.

"Follow me. You are the last onboard, but we will not be last to the briefing, and I am eager to get started."

With that, she waved a gesture over her shoulder and one of the members of her entourage at the maps took up the presentation where she'd left off. Marching away, past the elevators behind them and into another hallway, Achaera'fra's zeal lent speed to her steps. Despite his nerves, Kah, too, was eager to get started on . . . whatever it was he would be doing, and trotted to keep up. While they traveled the halls, every passing fleet member stopped to salute the admiral and waited for acknowledgement from her before carrying on with their duties. She, however, never broke stride, confidently leading E'e and Kah through dim halls, speaking to her two companions all the while.

"I hope your journey here was pleasant." She did not wait for a response before continuing. "The *Grace* has been my personal shuttle for many years. A home away from home, if you will, with all the creature comforts I can stand. We are somewhat slim on long-distance shuttles, with our military craft traveling to retrieve people like you from all the corners of the Dal territory. Hence, the luxury and comfort of your trip. Perhaps it was a nice departure from your usual fare. The *Litany*, however, is a wholly different story.

"There isn't another dreadnought like him in the Dal fleet or, as far as we know, in the whole of the empire. He is ruthless, efficient, and entirely self-sustaining. This self-sufficiency requires increased rationing of resources, of course, but the results are more than worth it. While most dreadnoughts fly with escorts of multiple cruisers and smaller craft, the *Litany* is designed to go it alone, wielding the firepower necessary to hold off an armada, a fleet's worth of fighter craft to engage in space combat, and the systems to lay siege to entire worlds for an eternity. It is with this in mind that you were chosen. You'll learn more at the briefing, of course. Speaking of classified matters outside a secure room is ill-advised, even if I do command the loyalty of every Ty'gjir aboard."

Kah listened intently to the admiral's speech, looking with awe at the vessel around him as she sang its praises. Another perfect machine, precisely tuned for war. He, however, was only growing more confused as to how he could be of use aboard such a ship. E'e's face was unreadable. Kah had, during their trek through the *Litany*, decided he would be seeing much more of E'e than he had initially thought. He wasn't simply a pilot, certainly, and he was likely not a typical captain, either. He was an agent for the admiral—a rather important one, Kah suspected, given their familiar rapport.

The trip was relatively short, lasting only moments longer than the admiral's speech before she stopped at a large, matte black door. She looked into a panel next to the door for a moment before there was a beep and a hiss as the barrier slid open. The room within was dark, lit only by the pale blue of a projection which ran the length of a long table and split the room in two. It was, by Kah's estimation, a simple conference room. Rather anticlimactic, he thought, until he saw the group of Ty'gjir who stood to attention at the admiral's arrival.

Spread throughout the room were just shy of twenty soldiers, each rising with a salute as the admiral entered. Each bore the clear marks of battle, with plenty of scars and bionic augmentations to replace damaged or missing structures. These Ty'gjir, unlike everyone else he and E'e had passed on the ship, were fully kitted for combat, wearing armor and weapons as if they were ready for battle to break out at a moment's notice.

"Who is still missing, Colonel?" barked the admiral as she entered.

In response, a large Lion with a sparse, burn-scarred mane and a patch over one eye stepped forward and saluted. "As of your arrival with Captain E'e and Sergeant Kah'riss, we are only missing Captain Sorna'li and her two wards."

"How soon can we expect them?"

"Momentarily, Admiral. We thought they would arrive before you had the time to step away from the bridge." The Lion finished his statement with a small smirk, earning a withering stare from Admiral Achaera'fra. Kah liked the sound of his voice. It was deep and rumbly, reminding him, in a way, of his father's.

"I told you I would not be the last. I haven't ever led you astray before, have I, Colonel?"

"No, ma'am."

"We will wait for the remainder to arrive before we begin." Yet no sooner had she finished the declaration than a door on the opposite side of the room hissed and slid open, revealing three Ty'gjir, who entered and promptly saluted.

At the lead was a short female, shaped like a Leopard, but with long, stretched rosettes that turned almost to stripes—a Clouded Leopard, if Kah wasn't mistaken. Behind her were two spindly Servals, both male, and almost perfectly identical, down to their facial patterns and the flicking of their absurdly large ears. The instant the door closed behind them, Admiral Achaera'fra slapped a large button on the table and, after a moment, a calm, neutral, male voice toned overhead.

"This room is now secure."

At that, the admiral slammed her fist on the table, bringing all other noise to a standstill. She smiled, the corners of her mouth just rising, but her teeth showing as if she were giving an open-lipped grin. It was a very off-putting expression, which Kah thought perhaps might be due to her not having much occasion to practice. As her eyes flitted through the assembly, Kah followed her inspection.

Every person in the room looked to be a seasoned warrior, with the exception of himself and the two Servals. He also noted that, once again, he was visibly the youngest Ty'gjir in the room, though the Servals only looked slightly older than himself. This was not a proud, or comforting notion. He expected that, whatever dealings he would have with this group, he would have to prove himself to them before any would respect him.

"Welcome, soldiers. Effective this moment, the minimum rank in the room is sergeant. Congratulations on your promotions, with all the powers and duties they carry." A few heads nodded and several Ty'gjir, including Kah, saluted. "First Lieutenant Sorna'li, Second Lieutenant Rhoska'khenti, you are hereby promoted to Captain, effective immediately. Congratulations on your promotions, with all the powers and duties they carry."

The Clouded Leopard who had just arrived, as well as a stocky Cheetah with closely shaved head fur, saluted the admiral.

"With that, I hereby launch this special operations task force, codenamed Ashmaker." Grave nods and rapt attention served as answer to the admiral's words. "I have personally selected each of you due to your intelligence, proven excellence in combat, exceptional decision-making under duress, ability to act and think independently, and loyalty to our cause. It is likely that in your previous postings, you shone as the best among your fellows. That will not be the case here. All of you are examples of excellence. I expect that, as examples of excellence, you will respect the confidentiality of all aspects of your new assignment.

"For this reason, many of you have received unexpected promotions, either today, or leading up to today. These new ranks will serve to establish the chain of command among each of your squads in the likely event that your commanding officer is killed in action. They will also serve the purpose of protecting you from the prying eyes and ears of your non-Ashmaker comrades. If answers are demanded of you by a fleet member who outranks you, you will deflect and refuse to answer anything that has to do with your duties. If that fleet member insists, you will provide them with a communication code which will be given to you later in order to direct them to myself or Colonel Ons'erak, who will take care of the problem. If you do breach the Ashmaker adherence to discretion, you will be disavowed, charged as a war criminal, and likely executed."

As Kah looked around the room, eyes wide, there was more solemn nodding, but the only people who seemed even mildly perturbed by this strict insistence on secrecy were himself and the two young Servals. Kah chewed his lip, the sudden, iron tang proof of his anxiety.

The admiral continued. "I'm sure you are wondering what exactly this post entails. Allow me to provide context. Let me be the first to tell you this—we are losing this war. Despite our superior resources and experience, the enemy has vastly superior numbers, impressive technology, and many unforeseen allies which have turned the tide greatly in their favor. We have tried to fight this war in the traditional, respectable way, with military engagement and strategic point seizure. However, the favored weapons of the enemy, Prince Sol'taris, include propaganda campaigns to provoke unrest among the citizenry, as well as so-called *mercy missions* to deliver relief to worlds he has seized from the Dal territory and its allies. Of course, missions of relief would not be necessary if not for his ambition and aggressions, but the only thing the common people see is an open hand, offering succor from their troubles.

"With these weapons, the pretender is winning the support of the people of all territories, including our own—

even inciting rebellion. We have not had an effective means to combat this, as such strategy has not been employed before in our history. If we quell the rebellions, our actions fulfill Sol'taris' propaganda. If we supply our discontent worlds with more goods, it is seen as empty pandering to counter it. And we cannot appeal to our taken worlds, as we must first retake them to provide relief. These campaigns, combined with the key positioning of the enemy's seized worlds, have made effective counterattack impossible. It is for these reasons that Ashmaker was formed."

At this point, everyone in the room was leaning in, listening closely to the admiral's words. She had grown increasingly grim as the address wore on, and the situation she described sounded less than optimistic. However, everyone in the room also had clear faith that the admiral had a plan to counter this.

She took a seat at the table before continuing. "It is the mission of Ashmaker to make the enemy's planetary seizures so costly that they will not attempt to take further worlds, to make the citizenry dread Prince Sol'taris arriving on their worlds—regardless of his *mercy missions*—for fear of the fallout which will accompany his forces' arrival, and thus, choking off his support from our people. This will strangle the enemy's supply lines and ensure their advances into our territory are made without reinforcement or provisioning, severely limiting their ability to conduct any long-term operations. Our analysts believe such an initiative will cripple the enemy's offensive options, and after they have wasted significant resources attempting to overcome their limited options, allow our forces greater freedom in pushing into enemy territory. This is the broad mission of Ashmaker, but the specifics of operations will, of course, vary widely. You will bear this mission in mind while making decisions on-world. Are there any questions at this time?"

Admiral Achaera'fra scanned the faces in the room with a steely gaze, but only the one-eyed Lion stepped forth.

"Admiral!"

"Yes, Colonel Ons'erak?"

"Am I correct in assuming the task force will be arranged into four squads, each with five members and under the direct command of a captain, who themselves will act on my command?" The Lion's tone made it clear he was not asking a question, but rather answering an unasked inquiry from the lower-ranking soldiers in the room.

Admiral Achaera'fra nodded once. "That is correct, Colonel. And you will report to me, and only me. Most Ashmaker activities will operate fully under your discretion. This is now your sole duty in the fleet. During larger-scale operations, I may take a more hands-on command of the task force, but I do not anticipate this happening for some time."

The room again lapsed into silence as the admiral awaited more questions. Kah had one, though he was afraid to ask it. Why was he here? These did not sound like the kind of duties that should be given to a new recruit.

"Admiral, why am I here?"

All heads turned to the speaker. One of the young, male Servals had stepped forward with a salute before sheepishly asking his question. His voice was pleasant, high-pitched, with an odd, musical accent, though it was somewhat marred by the anxiety behind his inquiry.

The admiral, for her part, merely turned her steely eyes on him and scrutinized him before responding. "Are you questioning my judgment, *Sergeant* Nadd'ilres?"

"N-no, ma'am!" Now the Serval's nerves shone through clearly and his posture tightened, his salute lingering despite the lack of a need for it.

"Do you expect me to list all the attributes I see in you which qualified you for this task force?" Admiral Achaera'fra's voice left no doubt as to whether or not she was willing to do so.

"Th-that's not necessary, ma'am!"

"Because I am not prone to jerking off my subordinates, Sergeant. There are plenty of whores in the territory to satisfy that need." Neither her tone nor expression had changed, yet now had some invisible quality which became a dire condemnation.

"I apologize, Admiral . . . " Nadd'ilres ducked his head and took a step back next to the person Kah presumed to be his twin. Kah felt a little bit sick at the sudden tension in the air, but he was mostly glad he himself hadn't dared ask.

"Apology accepted, Sergeant. During future briefings, endeavor to keep stupid questions to a minimum, so as not to waste my time or the time of your new brothers and sisters with stupid questions — Ah, yes, that's the final point of order for now. During your operations, you will not refer to each other by your house names. You are to treat your comrades as your sisters or brothers and refer to them only by their face names. Now, unless there are any further questions, Colonel Ons'erak will escort you to your barracks aboard the *Litany*, which are permanently secured against eavesdropping, and you can become acquainted and begin preparing for your first operation. You have two months."

With that, the admiral stood and cut a sharp salute, mirrored promptly by the soldiers.

"Good luck, Ashmakers."

She slapped the button on the table, eliciting a response from the calm voice in the speakers.

"This room is no longer secure."

Admiral Achaera'fra smiled her off-putting pseudo-smile to the assembled soldiers and swept back out the way she had come in, leaving the rest in momentary silence.

"Follow me," rumbled the colonel. "We'll speak more when we've reached our quarters."

Everyone nodded and stood to attention, falling into line as the colonel left the conference room and led them out into the halls, through more of the bridge deck, and to a new set of elevators. As they walked, Kah found himself at the end of the line, behind E'e and standing shoulder to shoulder with Nadd'ilres, the Serval who had received a dressing-down from the admiral. Despite the severity of the scolding he'd received, as soon as he caught Kah's eye, the Serval flashed Kah a bright grin. Kah opened his mouth to introduce himself, but the Serval quickly put a finger to his own lips, shushing him, for the time being. A conspiratorial glance at the surroundings was all he needed to get the point across. Perhaps introductions should wait until they reached their quarters. Kah nodded to Nadd'ilres, but chanced a quick smile as they arrived at the elevators.

Unlike the lift which had borne Kah to the bridge, this set of elevators was strikingly deserted, so the Ty'gjir soon found themselves aboard a large personnel elevator which comfortably accommodated the entire group. This elevator appeared to behave as a conventional one and, after the colonel punched some numbers into a pad by the door, it plummeted toward the belly of the ship. Given the speed they were traveling, Kah estimated they must be near the ventral surface of the ship by the time they slowed to a stop and the task force disembarked. A short walk later, they arrived at another matte black door, conspicuously unmatched by any of the others they'd passed on this deck. The colonel scanned his personal datapad at a panel next to the door and, with a beep and a hiss, it opened, allowing the Ashmakers to enter.

Inside, Kah found a spacious room, the center of which was dominated by a holoprojector with cushioned seating set in the surrounding depression. To the left was a small kitchen, as well as four tables bolted to the deck, with seating at each, in addition to a door clearly marked as a med-bay. To the right was an open threshold in the wall with tiled surfaces inside — a communal bathroom, Kah suspected. The walls to his right and left rose about fifteen meters to the ceiling and had walkways which overlooked the common room. Through an open door on one of these balconies, Kah saw a bed, so suspected the rest matched. Straight across the room, however, was a large, glass wall which ran floor to ceiling. Beyond it, the space widened tremendously, with rooms for a number of training exercises, including a combat ring and a firing range, as well as a lonely door set into a nondescript, windowless wall.

As the common area filled with Ty'gjir, the door closed behind them and a quiet voice intoned from a panel next to the door, "*This room is now secure.*"

After the voice fell silent and the Ashmakers filtered in to stand at ease, the colonel took up position before them all. "As you have probably gathered, I am Colonel Ons'erak. According to our orders, you are to address me as Ons, or Colonel, or Colonel Ons. I will be heading this task force in all its operations. This area will be our designated quarters to use as we see fit, including recreation, as well as training, practice, cooking, washing, and sleeping. However, as this room and its contents, like the rest of our resources, are classified, that also means we will have to clean up after ourselves. I expect that this will not be a problem." Ons scanned the group with his remaining eye, daring dissent.

"You are to share sleeping quarters with your squad mates. However, your squads have yet to be formalized. The admiral has provided me with a dossier on each of you, detailing your abilities and history, as well as her own judgment of you. However, I would like to assess you all for myself before I split you into your squads. I imagine you are tired of such assessment, but I do not care. If this task force is to operate as the admiral has planned, you will all need to assume the roles which best fit your capabilities. So, get comfortable and settle in. I will be calling you one at a time to be evaluated. The rest of you may watch or not. It makes no difference. First up, Jury. Let's go."

A thick, female Puma with a proud bearing and a prosthetic arm stepped out from the group and followed Ons as he walked through a set of heretofore invisible doors in the glass wall and into the exercise area. The remainder of the group stood still for some time, watching, but couldn't hear anything through the thick glass. Abruptly, E'e, or E, Kah supposed, broke from the group and walked to the kitchen, opening the refrigerator to check its stock, then strode to the sitting area and stretched out on a couch. Seeing this, the rest of the group visibly relaxed and began to mill about, introducing themselves to each other and exploring their new quarters. Kah felt a tap on his shoulder and turned to see the same Serval grinning at him.

"Name's Nadd! Good to see my brother and I aren't the youngest here!"

Kah smiled and extended his hand to shake. "That doesn't make *me* feel better, but it's nice to meet you, Nadd. I'm, um, Kah?" Not using his full name was odd. It wasn't inconceivable that a Ty'gjir outside his family might call him by his face name alone, but it felt very strange.

Nadd took Kah's hand in both of his and shook it vigorously as his brother bounced up to them. He threw his arm around his twin's shoulders and grinned broadly. "This is my brother, Nall. He's the ugly one!"

Nall gave a wry grin and shoved Nadd aside, taking Kah's hand. A much gentler handshake. Then, Nall spoke in a voice not identical, but very similar to his brother's. "Don't mind him. He's the stupid one. That's the easiest way to tell us apart, I'm told."

"And you smell different," Kah said plainly.

Both twins cocked their heads and their large ears swiveled toward the Jaguar. He couldn't help but smile at the two. They could be reflections of one another, even in the way they moved.

"Do we?" asked Nall.

Nadd's eyes glinted with mischief. "What do we smell like?"

Kah pointed to Nall and said, "You smell like wood and like cooking, and you" — he pointed at Nadd — "smell like perfume. Like flowers."

A huge grin crept across Nall's face and he gave Nadd a gentle push, teasing, "That's 'cause Nadd here likes to dance among the daisies! A real *faer*, this one!"

"Ah, shut your face, fatty! Least I don't smell like I spend all day scouring the pantry!" Nadd shoved his brother back with a big smile on his face.

Kah didn't understand some of their insults, but the good-natured teasing woke a pang of longing in his breast and he realized how much he already missed his own brothers. His face must have shown it, too, because Nadd's arm appeared around his shoulders, and the Serval pulled Kah against his side.

"Yeah, I miss our family back home, too. Eleven brothers and sisters and three sets of twins among 'em. Can you believe it?"

Kah shook his head.

"Don't know how it is on your world, but him and me" — Nadd gestured at his brother — "had to take the fleet exams, expecting to do our four cycles of mandatory service, but now we're here, in some real thick spy shit, and both of us just wish we could go home."

Nall appeared on Kah's other side, laying an arm across his shoulders and squeezing him between the twins. "But we'll get through it, Kah, and make sure you do, too. How'd you get pulled into this mess?"

The twins looked down at Kah between them. It was evidently his turn to speak.

"I've always wanted to join the fleet to get away from my home. It's . . . bad there. My brother was stationed on our planet's orbital defense platform, but I was sent all the way out here to be an Ashmaker, I guess." Kah looked from one twin to the other. They bore strikingly different expressions. Nall appeared somewhat indignant, while Nadd looked a little sad. Kah wasn't sure what to make of either expression, but he liked Nadd's more. They kept staring at him, though, as if waiting for something more. "Where—where are you two from?"

Nadd's smile returned and he released Kah, taking a few steps away and gesturing widely with his hands. "We're from Odaial! Same place as Captain Sorna there." He nodded toward the Clouded Leopard who had first accompanied them into the conference room. "It's a small planet. Pretty much all swamps and tundra. It was warm where we lived, but the *Litany* is comfortable so far."

"So far," Nall cut in, "but we've yet to check out the food. And that's really what's most important."

"Kah! You're next."

The roar drowned all other sound in the room and Kah nearly leapt from his fur. Colonel Ons stood by the glass doors, holding his datapad while the female Puma—Jury— left the exercise area, looking cool and comfortable.

"Good luck, Kah! We'll be rooting for you!" The twins pushed Kah towards the door with matching, encouraging smiles on their faces.

Kah wove his way across the room to the door, where Colonel Ons waited, datapad in hand, and ushered Kah through, before walking him to the leftmost segment of the exercise area, which appeared to be a simple combat ring. The Lion groaned as he deposited himself in a seat at a stainless steel table just off the ring and gave Kah a thorough once-over.

"You know, when the admiral told me we were going to have a fourteen cycle-old cub in the task force, I expected you would be large for your age, but you're actually below galactic standards for your species' age bracket." Colonel Ons paused, as if waiting for an excuse or explanation.

Kah didn't have one. "Yes, Colonel Ons'er — "

"Just Ons," rumbled the colonel.

"Yes, sir, Ons, sir."

"But it also says here that you were the highest scoring examinee on Pinto'Neth during your entrance exams, despite your inability to see in the dark. Admiral Achaera'fra was particularly impressed by your scoped weapons exam and your hand-to-hand combat performance. That, on top of your insistence on remaining conscious and standing despite grievous injury, put you firmly in her sights. So, now you're in. You've already passed, so we just need to see where we should put you, what squad role fits you best."

Ons slid a peculiar pistol across the table to Kah, followed by a bandolier. "Take these and get in the ring. A number of targets will manifest and approach you from all angles. I need to see how you prioritize threats."

Kah nodded and hefted the sidearm. It was vaguely similar to the laser pistol he had used during his exams, but was much heavier, and had a strange tube attached to the end of the barrel. He checked for a battery, pulling back the slide on top of the pistol, and instead found a jacketed alloy slug loaded into the top of the firearm. After a brief inspection, he had located the firing mechanism, magazine, magazine discharge, and safety toggle. That was all he should need. Unlike the laser pistol, this weapon would have bullet drop, as well as significant recoil. He needed to remember that if he hoped to perform well.

He took a deep breath and glanced over his shoulder to the glass wall to see if anyone was watching. It looked like everyone was still mingling, except for two figures, E'e and Nadd, who were watching him through the glass. Nadd brandished a big, double thumbs-up, but E'e was, as usual, hard to read.

"Today, Kah," Ons rumbled. He sounded tired, but his voice demanded respect.

"Yes, sir!" Kah grabbed the bandolier, slung it across his chest, trotted into the ring, and stood in the center. As soon as he did so, Ons tapped something on his datapad and a floor-to-ceiling wall of ballistic glass ascended and surrounded the ring.

No sooner had the wall finished rising than a holographic model of a Ty'gjir blinked into existence ahead of him. Kah raised his pistol and fired with two, quiet *zips*. More recoil than the laser pistol, certainly, but not as much as the arc thrower with which he and his brothers practiced.

Kah also realized that the tube on the front of the pistol was a suppressor, designed to quiet the blasts of conventional firearms, which were notoriously loud. While he was thinking, another target blinked to life ahead of him. It had a sort of rifle analog in its framework hands, but it shattered as Kah quickly put two bullets into it.

No sooner had he dropped those targets than he remembered. *All* angles.

Kah spun around just as another target reached him, bringing a club shape down toward him. He darted aside and put two shots into the shape's chest. In rapid succession, targets began rising all around and above him, some holding position with their firearms, others rushing toward him with clubs, and still others with nothing in hand, taking up all kinds of positions. Kah tried to stay on top of the numbers, focusing on gun-wielding targets, followed by the nearest club-wielding targets, and, finally, the unarmed targets as soon as they began moving toward him.

He ran out of ammo after fifteen shots, so discharged the spent magazine and loaded another in a swift, fluid motion. As he spent magazine after magazine, he thought he was keeping well ahead of the threats, but they just kept coming, in greater and greater numbers. Eventually, he was surrounded, and resorted to wielding the pistol one-handed and clawing out with his other hand, trying to clear the swarm, until he was completely overcome, and a klaxon buzzed overhead, followed by Ons' voice.

"That's it, Kah. You're done. Safety on."

The targets quietly blinked out and Kah flipped the safety on his firearm, panting heavily. He tried to still his trembling hands before he returned to the colonel, but felt the adrenaline continue to pound through his veins long after the targets were gone and the ballistic glass lowered into the floor.

"Come here, Kah." Ons' expression had not changed, but he was now marking something on his datapad. Glancing around the ring, as if more assailants might spring into existence at any moment, Kah trotted back over and placed the pistol on the table, followed by the bandolier.

Ons crossed one ankle over a knee and leaned back in the chair, looking at Kah over the top of the datapad. "Your threat prioritization is very solid. However, I noticed that you treated each and every figure as a hostile, including the unarmed ones. Why is that?"

Kah blinked, confused, then answered honestly. "I didn't realize there were any non-hostile targets, sir."

"Surely you saw that some were unarmed. You shot those last for a reason, didn't you?"

"Yes, sir."

"Why?"

"I—I suppose I think an unarmed enemy is still a threat if it hasn't surrendered. All Ty'gjir have claws, sir. Those unarmed targets weren't restrained or fleeing. They weren't captured. They were standing beside the armed targets or charging me. They could try to incapacitate me or could be carrying explosives." A small cough interrupted Kah's explanation, his throat suddenly quite dry. "I guess I just didn't think there would be non-hostiles in this exercise, sir."

Ons grunted once in response, typing on his datapad.

"All right, let's move on." The Lion stood from his seat with a drawn-out grunt and began walking to the next segment of the exercise area with Kah in tow.

Kah knew he had failed. He might already be in the task force, but was it possible to fail so hard that he was removed? He was certain he had just done so.

As they drew up to the unassuming, blank wall Kah had seen earlier, he was tempted to keep walking and leave through the glass doors, but E'e was standing out there, watching. Instead, he stuck close to the colonel as he situated himself at another bare table and opened his data pad.

"This next test will assess your stealth. Your goal is to make it through the course as fast as possible without being seen by the cameras. I will be watching the feeds."

"Yes, sir." Kah's ears burned with disappointment in himself. Ons was simply humoring him after he'd failed the first test, surely, but Kah could at least try to make a good showing here. However, his only experience with *stealth* was trying to keep his footsteps silent to stop their noise from interfering with his sound maps. As he stepped up to the door in the unassuming wall, he did not have high hopes.

"You can start whenever you're ready."

Clutching the handle of the door, Kah swung it inward. Inside was a broad, open space dotted with numerous, low walls jutting out of the floor at odd angles. Across the way was a sizable, plasteel structure, a building comfortably contained within the confines of the course, complete with multiple stories of windows, balconies, and doors. Given that, Kah decided this strange first room was meant to simulate the exterior of a building, with natural terrain leading up to it.

Now, to find the cameras. Kah looked about, but there was no camera in evidence. Luckily, the room was silent. He clicked his claws, as the admiral had done while she spoke, and painted the room in echoes. To his ears, everything appeared largely as it seemed to his eyes, except one spot on the façade of the building, a tiny point where the sound reflected as if off a convex, rounded surface on an otherwise flat wall. A camera lens.

Kah grinned and fixed his eyes on the spot. Sure enough, there was a tiny, reflective speck on the exterior of the building which he would almost certainly have missed had he searched with his eyes alone. If they were all like this, the test would be easy.

Keeping his footsteps as silent as possible, Kah darted across the yard to the front of the building, staying well clear of the sightline of the camera, and, clicking his teeth the while, making sure he didn't pick up a different lens from his new angles. He eyed the front door of the building. There would, of course, be a camera positioned to surveil the interior of the front door, so he would pursue a different option. He stepped back and looked up. If all he had to do was reach the other side of this building, why not just go over it?

So, he did. Digging his claws into the pliant plasteel to find purchase, Kah scaled the exterior of the structure, springing off balconies and windows for extra speed, and found himself approaching the roof in relatively short order. There was barely enough clearance between the roof of the building and the ceiling for him to squeeze through.

For anyone larger than him, it would be impossible, but he could fit. A few clicks informed him there was no camera atop the structure, and he calmly wormed across the roof.

He suspected this was outside the course's bounds, but nobody had *told* him as much. He would make it to the other side, and no cameras would detect him. The building was deep, and it took a fair amount of time to reach the other side, though certainly less than it would have were he inside, dodging cameras and winding through halls. But reach the other side he did, locating the cameras on a few balconies and avoiding those as he climbed down to the ground level, weaving his way across the terrain to the button which would sound his victory.

A few moments later, Kah rang the buzzer, and Ons' voice sounded overhead. "All right, Kah, you may come out now."

Kah grinned and began making his way toward the entrance, this time, walking through the building. It did indeed have bizarre, circuitous architecture inside, and it took Kah some time to navigate through it and back to Ons, waiting outside, drumming his fingers on the tabletop.

He glanced up at Kah and rumbled. "Interesting."

"What is, sir?"

"Since this course was installed, nobody has completed it so quickly. On top of that, not only did you go unseen by any of the cameras, but you also did not set off any motion alerts. You must be some sort of ghost." Ons' tone was flat as he stared piercingly at Kah with his one eye. "Would you care to explain yourself?"

"I climbed over the building, sir." Kah saw no reason to lie and figured he would be found out even if he had.

"You climbed over the building. Climbed a twenty-meter wall using only your claws, crawled across the roof, which doesn't have enough clearance for my fist, and dropped down the other side."

"Yes, sir."

Ons looked hard at Kah for a moment before concluding, "A viable solution. Good use of your natural abilities to find a way around the problem, Kah. You might find that trickier in your next test, however." Ons tapped away at his datapad for a few moments. "You're going back in. Your objective this time is to eliminate the fifteen targets inside the building, again without being seen by the cameras. Get to it."

He tossed Kah a sheathed knife and tapped on his datapad with an air of finality before leveling his one-eyed stare at the young Jaguar, which was enough to send him scurrying off.

Minutes later, Kah was back inside the building. He had resolved to clear the site floor by floor, starting with the uppermost and working his way down. There were plenty of cameras to spot him, but, leading mostly with quiet clicking, he navigated safely around them. The targets inside were more holographic Ty'gjir, projected from tiny, mobile bases, which whizzed in choreographed circuits throughout the building. This did not add much to the challenge, however, as the mobile projectors were loud enough to Kah to announce their presence from anywhere on each floor, and he simply had to wait until the targets were outside the view of a camera before sticking them with his knife.

In a matter of minutes, Kah was back outside, standing at attention before Colonel Ons, who was characteristically dour.

"Tell me, Kah. How did you avoid the cameras entirely without ever seeing one?"

"I could hear them, sir."

"You could *hear* the cameras?" Ons looked supremely dubious.

"I could. It's — It's something I've been doing for years." Kah had never spoken to anyone outside his brothers and Sala about his odd talent. When he said it aloud, it sounded kind of stupid.

"What is? Spit it out, Kah. There are plenty of Ashmakers waiting in line." Ons drummed his fingers on the tabletop again.

"Since I spent my whole life without the use of my eyes, I learned to listen as clearly as other people can see. So now, when I hear a noise, it sort of makes a picture for me." By the end of his description, Kah's voice had trailed into a meek whisper.

"What you're describing is echolocation. Jaguars cannot echolocate." Despite the doubt in his words, Ons leaned forward, clearly interested.

"I can, sir," Kah said matter-of-factly, somewhat indignant that he was being called a liar.

"Prove it, Ashmaker. How many fingers am I holding up?" Ons held one arm behind his back, apparently extending a number of fingers which were obscured to Kah's view.

Kah clicked his claws once, painting a portrait of sound as the sharp click echoed off the stark durasteel of the walls. "One, sir."

"And now?"

Click.

"Four."

Click.

"One."

Click.

"Two."

Click.

"Two."

Click.

"Five."

A smile split Ons' scarred face and he stood from his seat, tucking his datapad away. "Well now. That is interesting. I have a good idea of where to place you, Kah. The rest of the day is yours to do what you will. Get to know your brothers and sisters some. Relax. Don't forget to stop at the mess hall." Ons led Kah to the sliding glass door, opening it and ushering him out. "Your marksmanship still leaves much to be desired. We'll start work on that tomorrow. You are dismissed."

"Yes, sir!" Kah smiled, happy that the colonel was happy and saw a use for him.

Pulling out his datapad, Ons checked it momentarily before roaring, "Heks!"

A thin, white Tiger with black stripes stood from the couch and loped to the door, where Ons beckoned him within before shutting the sliding glass doors. As soon as the door slid closed behind him, Kah felt a clap on his shoulder and turned to see E, Nadd, and Nall grinning at him.

"How'd it go in there?" E asked, pushing the twins aside.

Kah smiled meekly. "I think it went well. Ons seemed pleased with me, anyway."

"Gotta admit, I'm glad I watched you go first," Nadd chimed. "Now I know that I can expect to get swarmed in that first test. Woulda freaked me out a bit if I didn't have any warning." He emphasized the point with an exaggerated expression of fear. "But you" — Nadd began pushing Kah towards a crowd — "have to catch up on meeting people. You've fallen behind!"

X

"Before we go any further, why are you divulging this information about Ashmaker?"

It doesn't matter.

"But surely, given its classified nature, you should not let it go so easily as that?"

It doesn't matter anymore.

"Please, do not be upset. We would not want you to get in trouble for telling us too much."

Something tells me it's all right to tell you.

"We are glad you have faith in us. We will not betray you. We will not do anything to hurt you."

Thank you.

"You can keep going, but only if you feel comfortable doing so."

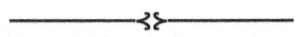

Over the next two hours, Kah was introduced to most of his Ashmaker sisters and brothers as they all funneled in turns into the exercise area to be assessed by the colonel. They were an exceptionally colorful group, with wildly varying life experience. There were twenty Ashmakers, plus Colonel Ons, which, to Kah, seemed like much too small a group to effect the kind of change the admiral had mentioned. Each member of the task force, however—except Kah himself—radiated self-assuredness, and seemed confident they would be able to overcome any challenge thrown at them.

The four captains were, perhaps, the most interesting of the group, with more years behind them than anyone else in the room. Kah already knew E, though didn't know his combat experience, or specialty, or if he'd ever even seen battle.

E, however, was more interested in introducing Kah to Captain Sorna, the Clouded Leopard. Without any real preamble, he dragged Kah bodily to where she was speaking with a number of other Ashmakers and pushed him toward her.

"Here she is, Kah! What did I tell you?"

E held Kah by both shoulders as the young Jaguar stared, confused, at Sorna. What *had* E told him? Kah scanned her thoroughly, looking for some clue as to what E told him about her. She was short, almost as short as Kah himself, and was pale golden-furred with long, stretched rosettes and stripes. Most of her long, black head fur was bound in a tight, efficient bun, but a pair of stray locks fell to frame her face. Her face was slim, with numerous scars and large, dark blue eyes with markings running down from their corners in tear-like black lines. And she was staring at him—waiting. The blood quickened in Kah's veins as his brain made a frantic, futile search for the information E wanted and Captain Sorna was waiting to hear, to no avail.

"See? So pretty you're dumbstruck at the sight of her!" A wistful sigh brought E's chin to rest on top of Kah's head.

Sorna rolled her eyes impressively, scoffing, before she grabbed E by the face and pushed him off Kah's head. "You're a creep, Captain. Glad to see you've brought another creep aboard." She spoke with the same musical accent as Nadd and Nall, though her voice was decidedly huskier, yet more feminine than theirs. It was also decidedly unamused.

A sudden burn rushed to Kah's cheeks as he remembered what E had told him about her on the shuttle. Kah ducked his head and closed his eyes tightly, squeezing his hands together in apology and sputtering, "I'm sorry I didn't recognize you, Captain Sorna! You *are* the prettiest lady in the galaxy!"

He felt a flick on the tip of his nose and blinked, wrinkling his nose, cross-eyed, at the assault. Sorna glared at him, leaning in close.

"I'm also your superior officer, Sergeant, and if you repeat anything else this reprobate tells you to say, I will personally throw you out an airlock," she threatened, then pushed him backwards into E and stormed away.

E caught Kah against his chest and squeezed him, sighing longingly again. "Was I right, or was I right, kid? Sexy and feisty! Makes your heart pound, doesn't she?"

Kah wasn't exactly sure what he was supposed, or even *allowed* to say, so simply swallowed the nerves that had stopped up his throat and nodded, before Nall grabbed him and tore him away from the captain with a smug grin.

"Not so great with women, huh? Worry not, my friend. I will show you the way."

Nadd stepped in and pushed his brother away. "Says the dweeb who's never had a girlfriend."

"Shut up! Neither have you!" retorted Nall.

"Yeah, but I have an excuse." Nadd looked about as smug as any person Kah had ever seen until E stepped in and separated them all, providing Kah an avenue to escape the commotion.

Freed from the center of attention, Kah fled to find a safe, comfortable wall to hide behind. He liked every Ashmaker he'd met, but he was still unused to how fast and loud non-Pintoth Ty'gjir seemed to be, and he could already use a break. And a snack. Luckily, everyone else was far too focused on their conversations to notice Kah go missing, and he subtly made his way over to the refrigerator in the kitchen area.

Opening the door released a puff of cold and revealed a magnificent variety of packaged foodstuffs lining the shelves. There was more food here than he'd ever seen in one place, and it was all *different*. E hadn't exaggerated when he said Kah was missing out by having only eaten food bars. With such a variety in front of him and little culinary experience, however, Kah had no idea what he was looking at and, after a brief, frustrating scan for anything familiar, moaned, defeated. The refrigerator door swung closed and exposed a new Ty'gjir behind it, watching him. Flinching despite himself, Kah settled his nerves and looked the Ashmaker over.

He was male, tall, and largely unremarkable in appearance. His fur was a uniform, pale brown, as were his eyes. His face, though, seemed elongated, with a long, narrow muzzle and tall, thin ears, as well as small eyes that glared out from above sharp cheekbones. Meeting his eyes forced a shiver up Kah's spine and left him with the distinct impression of something *off*.

"What are you doing?" The voice hissed out from behind sharp teeth, like fine cloth being dragged across rough stone. It was less a question than an accusation.

The intensity of the Ty'gjir's glare caught Kah off-guard. He wasn't doing anything wrong. Was he? Attempting an uncertain, disarming grin, Kah straightened up and answered, "I was hungry, so I thought I'd find a snack. But if that's not allowed. . ."

As Kah let his voice trail off, the Ty'gjir before him was pointedly unaffected by the feigned innocence, boring into him with an unforgiving gaze. "That's what the mess hall is for, cub. Find your way there."

"A fine suggestion, Captain Gray." Kah heard E's voice from just behind him as, once again, his shoulder found itself a perch for the taller Ty'gjir's paw. "I was just about to take some of our youngest comrades to the mess hall for some dinner. Would you care to join us?"

Captain Gray's eyes didn't move from Kah, despite E's sudden appearance. "I'll pass," he hissed, before slinking away.

Kah felt E's grip on his shoulder tighten as the pair watched Captain Gray stalk away and into the crowd before E relaxed.

"Thanks for the rescue. I appreciate it," Kah sighed.

"No problem, kiddo. But don't mind Gray. He's an okay guy, just—eh, a bit of a prick. Very, *very* good at his job, though." E looked down and gave Kah a grin. "But I wasn't lying to save you. We're hungry. Wanna go grab some grub with me and the loudmouth twins?"

Kah followed E's gesture as he jerked his thumb over a shoulder at Nadd and Nall, arguing about something to do with girls and being unable to "win" them. Regardless, Kah grinned and nodded.

"Good. Let's hop to. I'm starving." E began marching to the center of the room with Kah in tow. They grabbed the twins and, together, the four left the secure task force barracks and made their way through the cold, durasteel corridors to the aft mess hall.

As they marched through the hallways, chatting warmly to pass the trip, Kah reflected on his new home. The stark lights of the bare corridors and constant dull humming of the dreadnought in motion were already beginning to fade from Kah's attention. The clean, antiseptic smell, too, was receding to a sort of default. It felt unsafe to allow any of the new sensations aboard the *Litany* to become his new standard, but at least it was easy to pick out sights, sounds, and smells that didn't belong. He didn't think about the fact that, as he became lost in thought, he was allowing the idle chatter and jesting of E and the twins to become background noise, as well.

In his head, Kah revisited the slew of new people he'd met — those he would have to come to rely on, and who would rely on him. Already, he had realized his role in the group — socially, at least — was to be dragged to and fro by his larger, more extroverted companions. Although, honestly, he didn't mind at all. He was more than happy to ask an occasional question and trigger an avalanche of answers from those more forthcoming. He didn't feel that he had much to contribute to most conversations and, regardless, was much more interested in listening than he was in speaking. He was comfortable with the arrangement. It reminded him of home, and his brothers.

Soon, Kah realized they'd all fallen silent, and his three friends were staring at him, as if waiting for something. "Uh, sorry, what?"

"We asked what kind of food you're in the mood for. You've got plenty of options." Nadd spread his arms, as if to encompass the entirety of the wide room in which they'd just arrived. The majority of the room was occupied by rows of long tables to seat hundreds of hungry soldiers, and built into the walls were small alcoves, all of which housed a storefront, counter, and a kitchen which receded further into the depths of the ship.

Then, the smells hit him. A dizzying array of scents suddenly assaulted his nose, all of them just as good as E's cooking aboard the shuttle. Much to his embarrassment, Kah's mouth began to water, but his three companions laughed good-naturedly.

"There! That brought him out of his coma!" E chuckled.

"Good to know that if I can't get him to pay attention, I just need to light the stove," Nadd said with a nudge and a wink.

Kah looked around, counting thirty different food counters, each with a distinct scent. It was a bit too much for his nose to make sense of, and he swallowed, somewhat dismayed. "I don't really know where to start."

E's teasing voice nearly cut him off. "While you were sleepwalking, I told them that you'd only ever eaten fuckin' nutrient paste brick things and some steak and potatoes on the shuttle. Told them you didn't realize any food other than that existed. They didn't believe me. So, now it's your job to act impressed by stuff from every duchy in the territory. I myself am going to stick to the food from home."

With that said, E walked off, making a beeline through the tables to a counter on the far side of the room, leaving Kah with the twins, but not for long. After scanning the room, Nall followed closely behind E toward his counter of choice, leaving Kah alone with his brother.

Before Kah could follow along, Nadd threw his arm around Kah's shoulders and started walking him in a circuit around the opposite side of the room, chiming, "If it's true that you've never had real food, then you've probably never had *real* food."

Kah cocked his head and glanced up at the signs over the food counters, trying to decipher the words through all their strange, hard-to-read fonts, wondering which were real. "What do you mean?"

Pulling a face of mock offense, Nadd declared, "The only food worth eating, of course! Food from Odaial."

He pointed proudly to a sign at the end of the row of counters which read, in large, childish lettering, *Odie's 'Ome-cooked Eatables.* Leaning on the letters was a depiction of some kind of winged reptile-like creature with large eyes and an apron stretched over its strange, rounded anatomy.

Kah was dubious. "What's it like?" A few, tentative sniffs of the air drew him closer to the counter.

"The best! You'll love it, I promise!" Locking an arm perhaps too tightly around Kah's neck, Nadd hurried him the remainder of the distance to join the queue.

Loosening the Serval's grip just enough to breathe, Kah was nonetheless trapped under Nadd's gangly arm and couldn't help but take in his floral scent as he bounced in place. For the smell alone, it was vastly preferable to being crushed in Calan's armpit, but that wasn't the only difference between the Serval and Kah or his brothers. His ear pressed against Nadd's ribcage, Kah heard the high, fevered patter of the Serval's heart, beating at a rate nearly twice his own, doubtless to keep pace with the ceaseless fidgeting which seemed to possess every inch of Nadd's body. Kah glanced up in momentary alarm, but if the Serval felt any discomfort, his face didn't show it. Alight with a sharp-fanged smile, Nadd glowed with anticipation, his green eyes sparkling above sharp cheekbones dusted with tiny, black spots.

Swept up in the Serval's excitement to share a taste of his home, Kah grinned in the friendly headlock — a grin which faltered only slightly when he noticed Nadd's refusal to make eye contact. When it was their turn, Nadd nudged Kah to the counter where a large, round, male Lion was waiting to take their order.

"Welcome to Odie's. What can we 'ome cook for you today?" The Lion had a large smile on his face as he spoke, but there was a crushing lack of enthusiasm in his voice.

Kah did not trust this person, or Odie. Regardless, he stared up at the overhead menu, with its vast array of options — its *dizzying* array. Feeling impatience mounting both in the Lion and the line of Ty'gjir behind him, Kah abandoned the menu, looked at the cashier, attempted a polite smile, and said, "Meat, please."

The Lion answered with a blank stare. A stare Kah mirrored, until Nadd cut in.

"We'll have two number fours, please! With one medium drink and one extra-large drink." Nadd offered a huge, charming smile to the Lion, who breathed a sigh of relief as he punched something into a panel in front of him, shaking his head.

A short wait later, Nadd and Kah carried large trays of food to their table, made easily visible by E and Nall waving their arms above their heads. Approaching them, Kah looked down at the container of food on his tray. It was a shallow dish with four cuts of fibrous, white meat swimming in an orange, pulpy liquid. It didn't look terribly appetizing, but it smelled amazing, like pure sweetness and warmth. Nadd had a matching dish on his tray, and carried a reasonably sized cup of some transparent, bubbly liquid as accompaniment, while Kah maneuvered a massive cup of the same, which threatened to spill with every step he took.

As they sat down, Nall looked at the tray in front of Kah and glared at his brother, but with the tiniest smile playing on his lips. "You're a jerk, Nadd."

Nadd looked offended. "I'm giving him a taste of home. Besides, that's why he has an extra-large." He looked to Kah and grinned winningly. "Don't pay any attention to him. You'll love it. Really."

It did smell good, and it clearly wasn't poison. Or liquor. Besides, Nadd got the same thing, so how bad could it be? Just to be sure, Kah waited until Nadd sliced a piece of the meat, dipped it in the orange liquid, and popped it into his mouth. Yes, clearly not poison, and Nadd looked very pleased with it. Fine. Kah wasn't one to let food go to waste. He, too, cut a cube off the white, stringy meat, dipped it in the orange liquid, and apprehensively placed it in his mouth, chewing once.

It tasted very much like it smelled. The meat was rich, tender, and juicy, both naturally, and from the liquid in which it was served. But there was also a slight tartness, like the orange liquid was trying very hard to be sour but couldn't quite overcome its own sweetness. Kah liked it! He swallowed the piece and cut more, making a conscious effort to savor the food, unlike his first meal on the shuttle.

Across the table, Nall was grimacing slightly, waiting for Kah's verdict, and E had both eyebrows raised, impressed by something. Nadd, however, carried a wide, sharp-toothed grin, which grew more and more sinister by the moment. Kah still didn't know why. The food tasted good. Better than anything he was used to, anyw —

It hit him. Tiny beads of sweat began to accumulate on his forehead, and breathing was suddenly a little hard. No, it wasn't hard to breathe, but every time he took a breath, it *burned*. It burned his whole throat and mouth. But the food wasn't scalding. Or was it? It definitely felt hot now. Maybe it was so hot it burned off his nerve endings. Could that happen? Maybe Nadd just couldn't feel with his mouth anymore. Kah couldn't even get to the pain to staunch it, and blowing on it certainly didn't help. Sweat and tears running freely down his face, Kah grabbed his drink and took a hefty draught. The bubbles stung a bit, but not nearly as badly as the food, and the cold was more than welcome.

He heard Nadd snort next to him and Kah glanced over, now hanging his mouth open to let the heat escape. Fully turned in his seat and watching Kah's reaction to the meal, Nadd himself was entirely unaffected.

"Why does it hurt?" Kah panted, pouring the drink into his mouth. "Why does it hurt so bad?" What was wrong with it? With him?

Nadd broke into full-on laughter, a funny, chirping sound, but Kah was much too concerned with survival to care about the peculiarities of his companion's laughter.

"Try to breathe through your nose, Kah. Keep drinking. It'll pass after a while," said Nall, sitting across the table with his face in his hands, trying not to watch.

The feeling did pass, but not before Kah had finished his extra-large drink, as well as the drinks of his three companions, and also put a heavy dent in the communal supply of napkins, lost to his running nose and watering eyes. Despite how good it tasted, food from Odaial was not worth the pain. Nall seemed to anticipate this conclusion, and, sometime during Kah's suffering, had exchanged their trays, leaving Kah with a dish from Sozen, which, as Kah had already discovered, was harmless.

After they finished their meals, Nadd brought Kah a new dish—a cold treat made of frozen cream and sugar. Once Nadd finally convinced him it was safe to eat, an assessment corroborated by E and Nall, Kah tucked in ravenously. Near-instantly, Kah had a new favorite food, mostly for the taste, but also because it killed the lingering burn in his mouth. With full bellies, cool mouths, and apologies accepted, the four trekked back through the ship to the Ashmaker quarters.

Arriving, Kah excused himself from his friends to take an extended visit to the bathroom, discovering that there were roughly twenty enclosed private stalls to accommodate the task force. A shower was necessary, he decided. The *spicy* food, as the twins had called it, had about drenched his coveralls in sweat, and he was eager to be clean, so he helped himself to one of the private booths which matched the toilet stalls. Finishing his ablutions, Kah felt much improved, and wandered back out to the common area, where, it appeared, Ons had just called everyone to attention.

"Ashmakers, gather 'round," the colonel rumbled. "I have assessed each of you and will now assign you your squad and specialty. These may change at the discretion of your squad captain, but I do not anticipate or encourage this. Captains, please step forward."

Ons unholstered his datapad as the four captains strode to the fore, standing at attention abreast the colonel. Kah scanned the line. All the captains looked capable, but he most wanted to be placed with E, and certainly didn't like the idea of being assigned to Captain Gray's squad. Kah felt nerves beginning to jostle his already-quavering stomach. Ons sniffed once before rumbling out names and assignments. Most were familiar to Kah at this point, but there were still some unfamiliar names and faces.

"First squad, commanded by Captain Gray," Ons began. The evil-looking Ty'gjir stepped up.

"Heks, designated marksman." A thin, male white Tiger took his place beside Captain Gray. He looked just as severe as the captain.

"Spring, demolitions," rumbled the colonel. A muscular female Ocelot stepped forward on a bionic leg and, as she turned at attention, Kah saw she had a dimly glowing bionic eye and a prosthetic arm to match.

"Nall, medic." Nadd's twin brother rushed up, nearly tripping as he darted through the assembled Ty'gjir.

"Sind, infiltrator." Finally, a thin, female, calico Domestic sprang forward in a sinuous motion. She was much taller than Kah, though he couldn't discern her age.

"Ashmakers, please salute first squad! Hail, first squad!" Ons roared with a proud salute. The room echoed his roar and salute. "First squad, dismissed!" Without further ceremony, the first official Ashmaker squadron dispersed back into the crowd. Ons checked his datapad again and rumbled, "Second squad, commanded by Captain E: Nadd, designated marksman; Pol, demolitions; Jury, medic; Kah, infiltrator."

When Kah's name was called, he nearly leapt from his spot to join E but just managed to control himself. Instead, he marched stiffly to the front of the room, standing beside Nadd, as well as a tiny, wiry, male Ty'gjir with a bushy, ringed tail, presumably Pol, and Jury, the proud-looking female Puma with the prosthetic arm who had been the first Ashmaker to be assessed by Ons.

"Ashmakers, please salute second squad! Hail, second squad!"

There was a thunder of salutes as hands struck shoulders, followed by a roar of, "Hail, second squad!" Kah looked out at his brethren, each full of pride and respect and, for the first time, felt like he imagined it would feel to be a soldier.

"Second squad, dismissed!"

Kah and the rest of his squad trotted back into the group, standing together. E gave him a friendly nudge in the shoulder and smiled down at him. This was exactly what Kah wanted. Captain E made him feel safe, and when Kah was safe, he was confident. If he were going to accomplish his goals with the Ashmakers, he knew it would be with E at his side.

"Third squad, commanded by Captain Sorna . . . " Ons began.

As five more Ashmakers were called to the front of the room, Kah planned. Until he had in some way proven himself, he was unlikely to earn Ons' ear, let alone the admiral's. He would need to learn as much as possible, as quickly as possible, to become stronger, faster — more useful to his superiors. There could be no slip-ups. Every single moment had to be spent as productively as possible so that his merit would shine on Ashmaker's first mission. With hard work and dedication, he would be a hero for his people.

It didn't occur to Kah that he might not survive.

"Ashmakers, please salute third squad! Hail, third squad!" The shout brought Kah out of his thoughts and, together, the room roared with the colonel, welcoming their brothers and sisters to the fold.

Ons cleared his throat and dismissed third squad back to the group, once again checking his datapad.

"And last, fourth squad, commanded by Captain Rhoska . . . "

Kah glanced over at Nadd, whose eyes were fixed on his brother, standing apart from them with the rest of first squad. Nadd ground his teeth and fretted in place. Kah hadn't seen the Serval behave like this, but understood how he felt. He wanted to be with his brothers, too, and not being able to protect them weighed heavily on him. But if common Ty'gjir beliefs held true, the connection between twins would be even stronger.

Trying not to draw any attention, Kah reached out to the Serval and clasped his hand, hopefully in a comforting gesture of solidarity. Unfortunately, it seemed to startle Nadd a little, and he flinched fairly dramatically, though his expression quickly changed to pleased surprise when he saw the source of the grasp, and a charming grin soon replaced his alarm.

"Hail, fourth squad!"

"Fourth squad, dismissed!" thundered Colonel Ons. "Ashmakers, your squad is your new family. You will eat together, sleep together, work together, fight together, and, gods willing, win this war together. Specialized training will begin for each squad role tomorrow. I encourage you all to sleep soon and well; we start early. Dismissed!"

With the ceremony and dignity of a noble's blade, Ons sheathed his datapad in its holster and marched up the stairs on the left side of the room to the topmost level, entered his own room, and closed the door behind him.

"Ashmakers," E called out from beside Kah, gesturing at numbers on the walls over the raised walkways, "each squad has designated sleeping quarters with three rooms each, one for the squad captain and two for pairs of squad members. You may select your bunkmate only from the members of your squad. Choose well. There will be no switching. Now, get some rest."

As soon as E mentioned pairs of squad members, Nadd pulled Kah firmly against him. Nadd would have been Kah's first choice, too, since he couldn't room with E. He liked the Serval a lot and felt at ease with him—in spite of his spicy food.

With much conversation, all the Ashmakers gathered their belongings, which had, until now, remained slung against the wall of the quarters. Everybody conferred closely with their squad mates, trying to decide rooms. It seemed most people had already had a good idea of whom they would choose as a bunkmate but were split into different squads than expected.

Kah wondered how Nall would do. He had likely anticipated rooming with his brother. Indeed, when Kah looked for him, he saw the typically extroverted Serval standing outside a group of obvious veterans, nervous and alone. That is, until the calico Domestic, Sind, grabbed him without a word and dragged him to a first squad room. Kah smirked and shot Nall a wave. Now *he* knew how it felt to be dragged about.

"Well, roomie"—Nadd started pulling Kah toward the right side of the room, where the second squad quarters were located—"what say we get settled in? I have a ton to unpack, so we have to decide how we're splitting up wall space."

After a brisk trot up the stairs, they arrived at their third-floor room. It was a modest affair, with a bunkbed, two chests of drawers, and two desks with matching stools. It reminded Kah very much of his own room back on Pinto'Neth, which made unpacking easy for him. He selected a dresser and organized his few clothes into it, then placed his few trinkets on top of the dresser. A sharp, shiny piece of obsidian Thurv had carved for him into a claw shape, an interestingly shaped green-blue chunk of nordium which he had worried glossy, the locket containing the picture of his family. These were the few things Kah had of his own, and they were all he thought anyone might want.

Then, Nadd unpacked his things. He had brought lots of practical clothing, but also some more . . . recreational-looking garb. Unlike Kah's one picture, Nadd had numerous photos of people and places from Odaial — many more, Kah thought, than one Ty'gjir might need. When Kah voiced his thoughts, Nadd took it as an invitation, and began to regale Kah with stories of the Ilres family and their home while he continued digging through his bags, tossing Kah several large, rolled-up sheets. Curiosity rendering his fingers clumsy, Kah unfurled one of the sheets and found it to be another picture, though there was no way it was a member of Nadd's family.

Covered in text and exciting, often violent images, this and several of the others, were what Nadd called posters, and each represented a holonet show or film he liked. Kah, with his limited holonet access, had never seen one, and was interested to hear about them, finding Nadd only too happy to oblige. Some of the pictures, however, didn't seem to serve the same purpose. Colorful fields of abstract shapes, as well as striking views of Ty'gjir figures in dramatic poses, Nadd called art, which appeared to be the product of a profession devoted solely to creating interesting-looking objects or images. To each his own.

At some point during Nadd's animated discussion of art and film, however, Kah unwittingly drifted off to sleep, smiling at his new friend and his amusing, if questionable tales.

The next day, and, indeed, the following month, was spent in intense training, while the *Litany of Ash* began its journey through the Dal territory. Each Ashmaker was separated into training specific to their specialty. The designated marksmen were placed under Captain E, who took them to the firing range to familiarize and practice with a variety of firearms, as well as undergo threat identification and target-spotting training. The medics joined Captain Rhoska for study and practice of different lifesaving and battlefield medical techniques, as well as familiarization with some military grade medical gear. The demolitions training was conducted in a special area Kah never saw and was supervised by Captain Sorna. Kah enviously imagined this training was very exciting, if loud. Kah's own training, the infiltrator training, was overseen by Captain Gray and took place almost entirely within the building segment of the exercise area.

Captain Gray described the role of the infiltrator as a silent vanguard for the squad, scouting ahead, quietly removing hostiles, and accessing that which the enemy did not want accessed. To this end, the infiltrators practiced avoiding a variety of detection methods and devices which Captain Gray had installed, as well as the other infiltrators acting as mock patrols. Anything closed and secured counted among the obstacles an infiltrator was tasked with removing, so mechanical lock-picking and digital code-slicing were a large part of the training.

Finally, they drilled specialized close-quarters firearm and hand-to-hand combat, to which Kah paid special attention. Having been blasted by concussion rifles during his fleet entrance exams, he had little desire to be shot again, and didn't enjoy the notion that an amateur with a firearm could defeat an expert in hand-to-hand combat with the pull of a trigger. It seemed unfair. So, any technique Captain Gray could show him which might level the playing field between Kah and an opponent armed with a gun, Kah furiously strove to commit to memory.

Kah *was* behind the rest of the Ashmakers. There was no denying it. Even with his special talents, his skills were raw and unhoned. He simply lacked the real experience that the rest of the Ashmakers had, and that Gray was eager to remind him he did not. His training was brutal, unforgiving. Each minor improvement to Kah's form, his technique, was earned with bruises and blood, both of which Captain Gray was hungry to see spent in droves. But pain, Kah could endure, and if that's what was necessary to gain ground on his comrades, he would.

A week in, exhaustion was already a constant companion, but so, too, was pride. Kah had found that he had a solid knack for every aspect of the infiltrator training, and finally began to feel like he was capable of contributing something to the Ashmaker cause. His evenings, Kah spent getting to know his squad mates. Nadd was a font of interesting tales, some of them highly dubious, but all entertaining, though Kah still felt that, while he liked Nadd a great deal, he didn't know him very well. E, he knew *quite* well. This left Jury, the one-armed Puma, and Pol, the tiny, bushy Ty'gjir.

Intimidated at first, Kah thought upon first seeing her that Jury would be terse and difficult to get to know, but it appeared he was mistaken. She was very friendly and reminded him a bit of Sala, not just because they shared an accent, but because of their stern, caring, demeanor. She told him she had grown up on Aurum, Sala's home and the capital planet of Kah's home duchy, but had left when she discovered her talents for medicine went underused on the planet's healthy, affluent population.

Jury joined the house fleet of Duke Aur'kura in her late twenties and soon distinguished herself for her exceptional battlefield medical skills and heroism, including an instance in which she and her commanding officer were caught in an explosion and she carried him to safety, despite having had her arm destroyed by the blast. Kah was awed. With Jury's permission, Kah investigated her prosthesis, which was markedly more advanced and flexible than the relatively cheap and common protheses back on his homeworld. The tale of her injury sounded like something out of one of Nadd's films.

Kah felt much safer knowing Jury was in his squad.

Pol was an entirely different story. He was a Kodkod, he said, and had a voice which matched his attitude. Skeevy and sneering, he proudly spit stories of his life before the military on his homeworld of Chiod, which housed a global metropolis. He and two other Ashmakers, Mits and Hundery, were part of a criminal gang which specialized in high-end heists with high body counts. When the gang was captured, rather than execute its members or send them to prison, the authorities sentenced them to compulsory military service, and they would serve that sentence for the rest of their lives.

Kah had already met Mits and Hundery. They were distant, but seemed pleasant enough and resolved to their service, whether in penance or out of a simple desire to survive, Kah couldn't say, but serve they did, and without complaint. Pol, however, seemed determined to advertise and cling to his criminal past, vocally railing against his sentence and pledging to escape it, despite having already been active duty in the fleet for twelve cycles. E claimed Pol was all bluster and had been talking this way for years, but that didn't help Kah to trust him.

On the evening of his thirtieth day aboard the *Litany*, Kah and the Ashmakers were ordered to clean their quarters in preparation for more intensive exercises the following day. Kah was among those assigned to collect spent shell casings and batteries from the firing range. He and four other Ashmakers swept up the firing range with only the lonely sounds of metal tinkling across the floor to accompany them.

Dressed in the sleeveless training uniform he had brought home from his examinations, he carried a durable plastic bag to and fro, dragging it along the ground as he collected kilograms of spent ammunition the other Ashmakers had swept into piles. He didn't know any of these Ashmakers terribly well, so, while he was not fully comfortable in the silence, he was also not confident enough to start conversation. When it was time to carry the bags out to the recycling chute, it came as a massive relief, especially when he saw Nadd cleaning up the kitchen.

The Serval was playing loud, upbeat music over a radio while he bounced around the galley, thoroughly scrubbing up every iota of food waste he was able to locate, all while wearing an incongruous, floral-patterned apron over his loose-fitting clothing. Much like he had with E on the shuttle, Kah found the rhythmic movements somewhat hypnotic, and kept his eyes glued to Nadd as, grinning, he dragged the bags across the room to the recycling chute. When he had finished depositing the bags, Kah caught Nadd's eye. The Serval had stopped for a breather and was bent over, wiping sweat from his brow. Kah waved and sidled over to him, leaning against the counter beside him.

"What are you doing?" Kah shouted over the colorful din of the music.

Nadd smiled, narrowed eyes marking his suspicion, as if Kah might be luring him into a trap. "What do you mean? I'm cleaning!"

Kah tried to imitate Nadd's rhythmic bouncing but didn't have much of a talent for it, though his attempt managed to draw a few bright, chirping laughs from the Serval.

"Dancing!" Nadd explained, shaking his hips. "It helps the work go by faster!"

Kah instinctively cocked his head at the new word, his obvious confusion painting Nadd's face first with a smirk, then, slowly, with horror.

"Don't they have dancing where you're from?" Nadd asked.

The Jaguar shook his head. "What's dancing?"

Nadd broke from Kah and paced away, running a frustrated hand through his head fur and muttering something that was lost in the music. Pausing before the younger male, the Serval worked his jaw, his face conflicted. At last, he held up a finger and abandoned Kah for the radio, pushing a button several times to change the tune to something smoother — less thumping, but still upbeat. Returning to the Jaguar, Nadd offered a hand, waiting for a moment while Kah cocked his head again. Seeing he wasn't making progress, he took Kah by the paw and pulled them together, provoking a tiny squeak of alarm.

Positioning Kah's right hand on his shoulder, Nadd placed his own on Kah's waist, but kept the fingers of their left hands entwined. Leaning close to Kah's ear, the tall, lithe Serval whispered, "*This* is dancing."

Maneuvering the small Jaguar by his waist, Nadd began to twist and twirl with Kah around the kitchen. Instantly on guard, Kah kept his eyes on his feet while Nadd spun them, trying to ensure that he wouldn't trip and ruin things. At the speed they were going, a fall could be catastrophic, and Kah didn't want to embarrass himself in front of his friend.

"You're thinking too hard," Nadd chided, only audible for the proximity. "Just breathe."

A deep breath brought Kah's eyes back to Nadd's. The Serval was all smiles as he led them around and around, and his brazen joy was infectious. Within moments, Kah found himself beaming as well, and tried to stop thinking, to simply enjoy the movement and the music. As Nadd's dance broke the bounds of the dining area, hurling the pair into the common room, a quick turn brought the far wall into view, where two Ty'gjir leaned, watching. Kah felt his face flush with heat as he saw E nudge Nall, pointing to he and Nadd, though he wasn't quite certain why he should be embarrassed. While Kah ducked his head, Nadd only laughed and gave Kah's waist a comforting squeeze, managing to quell his anxieties and revive his grin.

Kah finally understood why everyone felt compelled to dance to music. He was having *fun*, even as he barely avoided stumbling and bringing them both to the floor. Nadd, on the other hand, was perfectly deliberate in all his movements, and not even Kah's clumsy steps, it seemed, could mar his dance. He was smooth and graceful and practiced. His movements were like a ritual—a physical prayer. For a moment, Kah was happy simply to share in his friend's excellence.

Soon, however, the song came to an end and, breathless, the pair slowed to a stop. Nadd hugged Kah against himself, somehow finding the wind to laugh. Crushed against Nadd's chest and listening to the furious drumming of his heart, Kah had less success. Eventually, as Nadd's grip loosened and his own breathing slowed, the Serval's scent slipped within Kah's nose, and Kah was delighted to find that Nadd still smelled like flowers, despite his month on the *Litany*.

Remembering something Nall had said when they first met, Kah pulled back from Nadd, still smiling as he held him at arm's length, and asked, "Why are you a *faer*?"

Nadd's smile disappeared.

Trembling, the Serval blinked a few times before a profound hurt made itself known in the shining of his eyes, but it was quickly lost to a snarl. The embrace broken, Nadd planted a hand on Kah's chest and shoved, sending him tumbling down into the central dip of the common room, stopping only when he cracked his head against the large projector. Kah hissed in pain and clutched the back of his head with both hands, his eyes wide with fear and confusion as he searched through the bursting stars for his friend.

Above him, a thousand condemnations were playing across Nadd's face, drowning any concern he might have felt for Kah's fall. His mouth twisting with the beginnings of a dozen curses, the Serval instead landed on something quieter.

"I thought you were better, Kah." His voice caught as he hissed Kah's name and, as he stormed away and up the stairs to their shared bedroom, Kah could swear he saw tears in the Serval's eyes. The slam of the door shaking him from his stupor, Kah checked his hands for blood and, sure enough, found a not-insignificant quantity staining his fingers as E rushed over and knelt beside him.

"You okay?" The captain set about applying pressure to Kah's head wound as he looked into Kah's eyes, checking that his pupils were equal, round, and reactive to light and accommodation.

"Yeah, I think I'm fine." Hoping to confirm his words, Kah gingerly patted his injury a few times, feeling the warm, sticky blood catch on his finger pads.

"What happened? You looked like you were having a great time," the captain said lowly, his eyes narrowed.

Kah shook his head, still confused. "I don't know. I thought we were. We danced, then I asked him what a *faer* is."

E glowered. "Why would you ask him that?"

"Because he still smells like flowers, and Nall said he dances in daisies because he's a *faer*, or something like that."

"Mmkay, well that was fucking dumb, but you get a pass from me this time, because you apparently don't know why it was fucking dumb." E heaved a sigh and sat down next to Kah, leaning his back against the projector. "This would be easier if you weren't so weird. It's hard to know what you know and what you don't. I'm not sure I'm really equipped to have this conversation with you, kiddo. I could tell you all about *my* life and childhood, but this just wasn't part of my experience."

Kah looked quizzically at E. "You've never danced? But I've *seen* you dancing."

"No, dumbass. I've never — Listen, Sozen was a really good place for all kinds of Ty'gjir, but there are places that aren't. I'm not going to tell you what kind of Ty'gjir Nadd is. That's a conversation for the two of you, but I kind of thought you'd realized."

Kah still didn't understand — maybe it was the rapidly growing lump on his head — but it was clear E wasn't comfortable talking about it. He would have to speak with Nadd, and the sooner, the better. Kah rose to his feet and started for the stairs.

"Whoa, whoa, whoa," E stopped him with a firm hand on the shoulder. "Not so fast, kid. He needs to cool down, and we need to get your nog' taken care of. Come with me."

Dragging Kah to the med bay, E planted him in a seat before he tramped over to the glass door separating the exercise area from the remainder of the quarters. "Jury, we need you!" he shouted, opening the doors.

Characteristically alert, Jury arrived in short order, apparently anticipating why she was needed, because she toted a first aid kit at her side. The Puma looked at Kah, staunching the blood with a towel, and sighed.

"What happened here?" Jury asked, the high, bright voice still a surprise coming from her muscular frame.

"Two of the kids got in a bit of a spat. Nothing serious, but this one hit his head pretty good," E answered.

"Well, let's see what we're working with." Without another word, Jury opened the med kit on the table and brought out a few tools. The first looked much like a stylus with a square lens on one end and, as she brought it up to Kah's head, she began to explain what she was going to do to him.

"Step one — we remove the fur around the area so we can get a good look at the injury," she muttered, holding the stylus up to his scalp. Kah heard a quiet beep and caught the distinct smell of smoldering fur as, he assumed, the fur around the wound was burned away. "Hmm. Pretty good one, honestly. Hit your head on" — her eyes scanned the common room for the culprit — "the projector? Right on a corner, it looks like. No skull damage or deformity, but you cut deep into the soft tissue."

Kah was silent. This was not his first time being treated for such injuries. He was just waiting on the antibiotic cream and staples.

"You're a healthy, young male, and the room is clean, but we're going to disinfect the area anyway." She pulled a small can off the table and held it to his wound. There was a quiet hiss, and Kah hissed back as something painful sprayed onto the wound. Next, she produced a syringe and a small bottle from the kit, drawing a small amount of the bottle's contents into the needle and levelling it with his head. "This is going to reduce the inflammation so the spray-flesh sets properly."

Kah winced a little as he felt the needle sink into his scalp a few times, followed by the rush of cold as Jury emptied the contents into his skin.

"Now the spray-flesh —" Jury retrieved another can, this one much larger, and gave it a good shake before spraying its contents onto Kah's head with a thick, heavy sucking sound. His scalp began to tingle and itch. This was *very new* to him, and he found himself wondering what exactly was happening back there.

"One more step and you're finished." Finally, she produced a tube and squeezed a small amount of a white, granular cream onto the tip of her gloved, prosthetic finger, before applying it in slow, gentle circles to Kah's wound. The itching intensified enormously, and it took all Kah had to not scratch at himself.

"You're all done, Kah." Jury packed everything back into the med kit before standing and bending at the waist to pinch Kah's cheek, saying with a smirk, "You were so brave."

Kah gently batted her hand away, but couldn't suppress a small smile. "Thanks, Jury."

"No problem. Let's make sure this is the last time I have to treat you, okay, infiltrator?" She gave him a final pat before heading back to the exercise area. The entire affair took, perhaps, ten minutes. Walking with her to the door, E gave Kah the opportunity to investigate his wound.

Prodding at it, Kah found no evidence of the wound at all, aside from a patch of hot, smooth flesh where once there was a tear. As he ran his fingers over the area, he began to feel the scratch of new fur growing under his fingertips. This was much better than getting shaved and stapled or stitched. If it kept healing at this pace, he probably wouldn't even be able to find the site of his injury tomorrow.

Soon, E returned, watching Kah feel his own head in wonder. "Fleet medics get the best stuff, right?" He smirked down at Kah and helped the Jaguar to his feet. "Now, as your captain, I clear you to go talk with Nadd. But don't fuck it up, kiddo. Squad exercises begin tomorrow, and I expect you boys to be friends again by then. Hop to." With that said, E sauntered through the glass doors and into the exercise area to continue his own assigned task.

Kah stood still for a moment, chewing his lip to steel his nerves, before he marched across the room and up the two flights of stairs to his room. He arrived just as Nall exited, closing the door behind him.

Nall's face was a mask of disappointment as he said, "I don't think he wants to talk, Kah."

"I don't care." The hostility in Kah's own voice surprised him. "It's my room and I can go in when I want, especially if I need to talk to my squad mate. Get out of my way." He must be more upset than he had thought. Kah made a mental note to tone it down during his conversation with Nadd.

Caught off-guard by Kah's aggression, Nall stepped aside, ceding the entryway. But he also made quite clear he would not be leaving his brother undefended, and folded his arms, leaning against the wall just outside the door.

Kah confidently stepped into the room and clicked the door closed behind him. Inside, the overhead lights were switched off, but this posed minimal challenge. Despite deliberate attempts to quiet himself, the sniffling from Nadd's bunk painted a sad, sketchy image of the Serval, curled into a tight ball in bed around his pillow. The room was otherwise silent, until Kah sat on the bottom bunk with a quiet squeal of bedsprings.

"So," Kah began, not quite sure what to say, his confidence quickly evaporating. "Um, what *is* a *faer*?"

There was a derisive snort from the top bunk. "Fucking really, man?"

"I understand that it upsets you, but I don't know why. Or why your brother would call you one if it hurts your feelings so badly." Kah lay on his back, staring into the darkness at the underside of the bed where his friend was curled.

There were a few sniffles before Nadd responded, "We can call each other whatever we like because we know we don't mean it. It's just teasing. But you're . . . new. You're not family."

The words were obviously true, but still, after Kah had worked so hard to strike up a friendship, they stung deeply. Despite his reflexive wince, Kah tried to keep himself calm and his voice level.

"I'm sorry. I didn't even know I was insulting you. I wouldn't have said anything if I knew. I didn't want to insult you. I liked dancing with you. I like you." Kah tried to speak simply and honestly. Whenever Kah and his brothers were upset with each other, pride took a backseat to making peace. It didn't matter that Kah hadn't *meant* to call Nadd a *faer*; it was only important that Nadd had been hurt by the word.

There was a very long pause. No sniffles, no sighs. Just the occasional squeak as Kah shifted position on the bed.

"I like you, too." Now, Kah heard Nadd draw a deep, ragged breath before he continued. "A *faer* is a creature of myth. Do you know what myths are?"

"Yeah, I know what myths are."

"That's one thing, at least," Nadd snorted bitterly. "A *faer* is, like, a tiny, delicate person with wings that lives in nature and makes plants grow. They play tricks on people. They're selfish and do whatever they want without regard for anybody else."

Kah pictured the description — a small, dancing, winged feline — and compared it to Nadd. He did smell like flowers, and he was a prankster. That connection was apparent, but Kah didn't understand why it would be quite so hurtful.

"Odaial's not like other worlds in the empire," Nadd continued. "Ty'gjir weren't the first ones there. The swamps that cover the planet are full of massive predators. The skies are dark with Odaith dragons. Even the plants are dangerous, and the fruit can be *lethal*. Most Odaith settlements were originally built in huge trees to shelter from the dangers, and the oldest and largest are still hidden in the branches. Local customs are built around survival of the race at all costs, even though modern tech keeps the average Odaith safe from all the planet's natural dangers."

Kah had no idea where Nadd was going with this.

The Serval took a deep breath. "Because the *population* is so important, proliferating is vital, at least according to tradition. Hence, the eleven siblings." He chuckled wryly. "But if, for some reason, you *don't* reproduce, or don't *want* to have children, you're seen, not just as a freak, but as someone who doesn't care at all about his family, his people — anyone but himself."

Kah began to connect some less-apparent dots. "So, people like that are called *faer*, because they're selfish?"

"Yeah. They're publicly shunned and spit on."

"Do you not want to have children?"

"Not really, no." Nadd's voice started to catch again.

"But why would anyone know that about you?" Kah could tell they were approaching the heart of the matter but wanted to do so gently.

There was another long pause. "Because, I'm gay."

"What's that?"

"For Day's sake, Kah!" Nadd heaved an impressively exasperated groan and rolled off the bed, landing softly on his paws. Kah had a very clear echo picture of Nadd as the Serval felt his way to Kah's bunk and searched for Kah's head with his hands. Out of courtesy, Kah shifted his position to put his face in the way of Nadd's exploring fingers. Finding him, Nadd gripped the sides of Kah's face, brought his muzzle close, and pressed his lips aggressively against Kah's.

What was going on? Why was Nadd kissing him? His face burning and ears ringing, Kah's map of the room, drawn only by his pounding heart, became an indistinct blur that faded past the Serval's face. And while Kah froze in blind, wide-eyed panic, Nadd's own eyes were closed, his large ears folded back over his head. Kah had seen Thurv and Sala behave the same way when kissing, but— but they were married. Nad was— Kah was—

He was beginning to understand.

Eventually, Nadd withdrew, blinked a few times, and quietly shifted to the edge of the bed, staring in silence at the darkness veiling the far wall. His shoulders were hunched, his ears pinned back, and his hands tucked in his lap. Despite the boldness of his actions just moments before, Nadd now reeked of fear, souring his flower scent.

Kah, for his part, lay in stunned silence for several moments before he regained control of his faculties. "Why did you kiss me?"

Nadd's shoulders shuddered. "Because I'm a guy who's attracted to men. I'm gay, Kah."

"Okay, but why did you kiss *me*?" Kah insisted.

Nadd turned a little, the barest shred of hope glistening in the wells of his eyes. "Because . . . I don't know. I like you. A lot. You're cute, even if you don't know anything about anything."

Kah growled and pushed Nadd out of bed with a foot, sending him to the floor with a dull *thump.* Crawling to the edge of the bunk, Kah's face assumed a soft smile as he looked down at Nadd, who stared back, squinting in the dark.

"Why are you smiling?" he asked.

"You complimented me. You like me enough to kiss me." Kah sat up on the edge of the bunk, still grinning down at Nadd. "That's pretty neat."

"But do you . . . like me . . . the same way?" Nadd asked, his eyes huge, full of hope and apprehension.

Kah paused for a moment, then shrugged, just barely cocking his head. "I don't know. I don't think I've ever liked anyone that way. I definitely like you. You're the best friend I've ever had, other than my brothers. I don't think Pintoth are supposed to feel one way or another about, you know, gay . . . stuff, but I've never known a gay Ty'gjir until now."

Nadd deflated, ducking his head, but tried to put a smile on his face. "I guess that would have been a lot to hope for." He stood from the floor, dusting off his shorts and avoiding Kah's eyes, and said, "But I hope you can see why I was upset. I'm sorry I pushed you." He paused. "Both ways."

Sighing, Nadd started to climb back up into his bunk, but Kah grabbed his shirt, taking hold of his attention, as well.

"Don't—I don't know," he said. "Don't give up hope. It's a new idea for me. I never knew this was an option, so I think I need to think about it."

Nadd smiled at him, though his smile was now sadder than before, for some reason Kah didn't understand. E made girlfriends sound much easier. After Nadd returned to his bunk, Kah left the room, giving Nall a nominal smile and a thumbs up as he passed, though he didn't know if he'd made things better or worse.

While his hands idly finished his duties for the day, Kah again and again revisited his conversation with Nadd—the scent of his fear when Nadd confessed, the pain he felt when he thought Kah rejected him. He wondered what growing up on Odaial must have been like for Nadd—if he'd lived his whole life in fear of his community, or if he'd had a safe haven in his family, like Kah had. Finally, as he scrubbed the day's labors from his fur in the shower, he wondered what the future might hold for himself, now that girlfriends *and* boyfriends were possible.

Yeah . . . Kah supposed he could see himself with Nadd. They got along well enough. Nadd made him laugh. He was nice to look at. But if they were to reach any sort of future together, they had to survive.

XI

"How sweet."

Don't mock me.

"We are not mocking you. What did you think of Nadd'ilres' confession?"

I realized injustice exists everywhere, not just on Pinto'Neth.

"Good. Did it also occur to you that such injustices may shape others into those you call enemies?"

Yes.

"And what do you think of that?"

It doesn't make a difference.

"No?"

No. If my enemy is someone just like me, who has experienced the same struggles but has chosen to pursue their goals as my enemy, I know there is nothing I could do to change their convictions, so I would have to treat them as any other enemy.

"Interesting."

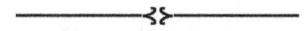

The following month passed in a blur of competitive, squad-based training exercises designed to prepare the Ashmakers for working together with their squadmates against highly trained foes. Kah came to rely on his squad as his family and knew they would always be where they were needed. Soon, the *Litany of Ash* was poised to strike its first target, and Ashmaker was ready to begin its first operation. The night before the *Litany* was to drop into position, Ons gathered the Ashmakers in the common room to brief them on the operation.

The roar of the one-eyed Lion silenced the hushed murmurs in the common room as the colonel addressed the company, pacing slowly in front of them. "Tomorrow, we begin. While Caraby's orbital defense platform is attached to its tether for provisioning, the *Litany* will drop out of hyperspace outside the interdiction field and take position on the opposite side of the planet. The *Litany* will generate its own interdiction field and deploy its stifle, choking off all communication on the planet. All but these—" Ons brandished a tiny earpiece which, when worn, would be all but invisible. "Through these earpieces, you will be able to communicate at virtually any range with your squadmates and with me. I will coordinate all squad movements from the *Wildfire*," he said, referencing the Ashmaker mobile operations gunship.

"Your captains have the details of each squad's mission on-world, and they will tell you what you need to know. They know the plan and have backups for all contingencies. We have received new intelligence, however, which suggests the occupying hostiles are disguised as civilians. They have eschewed their house colors in order to deter retaliation for their occupation. Don't let this slow you. Bear in mind that every armed individual at the tether and on the ODP is an enemy, regardless of their uniform or lack thereof." Ons stopped pacing and stood before the task force, his one eye scanning every face. "I wish we had had more time to prepare you, but having watched you for the past two months, I am confident in your abilities, and could not be more proud of all of you. Captains, please brief your squads on the details of their role in the coming operation. Then, everybody, get some rest. The admiral's eye will be on us tomorrow. Dismissed!"

Not one for fraternization, Ons dipped his chin in a solitary nod and retreated to his office.

E wasted no time, turning to his squad and pulling them to one side of the common area, away from the others. Over the next two hours, E laid out, in exhaustive detail, second squad's objectives during the coming operation, fielding all questions and answering them comprehensively. Kah's squad had what appeared to be a relatively simple role to play and would head the assault on the tether. As they discussed the strategy, Kah realized that much of this past month's training was conducted specifically with this operation in mind. Good. That meant their intelligence was reliable and that circumstances on Caraby had not changed.

After E finished his briefing, second squad retired to their quarters, eager to rest in preparation for the coming day, but, hours later, Kah and Nadd lay in the dark, each knowing that, despite his best efforts, the other hadn't yet fallen asleep. Quiet, carefully measured breaths were the only sounds in their cozy quarters, a harsh contrast from Nadd's usual snoring, until he broke the silence, whispering from his top bunk.

"Kah?"

"Yeah?"

"How are you holding up?"

Kah furrowed his brow at the top bunk. "I'm fine. Why?"

There was a long silence, then, "Have you ever killed anyone?"

Kah briefly considered lying but decided that wouldn't serve much purpose. "No. Not yet. Have you?"

There were a few quiet squeals of the bedsprings as Nadd shook his head. "I've hunted lots of animals, but never killed anything intelligent. Do you — do you think it's any different?"

"Yes," Kah answered, mulling over his response. "Animals don't use guns."

"Very helpful," Nadd scoffed. Kah could hear a tiny smile begin to form on his lips. "I mean, do you think it will feel different?"

"Yes. I think it will be . . . harder, knowing that they have families like yours and think like you do. But I think knowing that they'll kill you if you don't kill them will help." Kah fidgeted in his bed, clicking his claws together while he thought. "And" — the words sounded much more juvenile than he had hoped — "they started it."

"I guess that's true. And it'll help knowing that I'm watching out for you guys, protecting you from trouble." Nadd sounded about as uncertain as Kah.

Kah said nothing, now wracking his brain, trying to suppress his nerves. This was all to help his people. All of it. Even killing others. Rest did not come easy to the young, frightened Ty'gjir. Eventually, however, merciful sleep quieted their troubled minds, carrying them gently toward a new day.

"Go!"

The voice blared over the *Wildfire*'s intercom scarcely a moment before Ons catapulted the gunship out of the docking bay and into space. The sleek, triangular craft screamed away from the *Litany of Ash*, treating the Ashmakers within to an exceptionally uncomfortable flight. From the windows of the *Wildfire*, however, they had a remarkable vantage point from which to watch the *Litany* deploy its stifle, a massive, sail-like apparatus which swung out from the flanks of the dreadnought in a great web, attempting to embrace the world below as the sails erupted in yellow light, ostensibly killing all communications devices on the planet. With the orbital defense platform safely tethered on the opposite side of Caraby, and with no communications to alert it to the presence of the dreadnought, the *Litany of Ash* should be safe from the ODP for long enough for the Ashmakers to complete their mission.

The *Wildfire* dove toward the planet's atmosphere at terrifying speed, aiming to ride the mid-atmosphere across the planet to the tether, safely out of range of the ODP, but high enough to avoid visual detection. Specially designed to confound radar and functionally invisible to the vast majority of scanning equipment, the gunship was the perfect platform from which to oversee the Ashmakers' clandestine operations.

As it quaked violently around them, Ons called out, "We're now entering the atmosphere! Twenty minutes until drop-in, third squad!"

Kah looked around the dim, red-lit bay where the Ashmakers were strapped into seats with their squad mates. Third squad, led by Captain Sorna, was fully equipped for aquatic infiltration, in tight wetsuits with tighter, flexible armor underneath, as well as facemasks, rebreathers, and waterproof armaments. She calmly spoke with her squad, inaudible to Kah, but clear to her team via their communicators. They would also be infiltrating the tether, but by means of a river. Kah knew nothing else about their mission. True to Ons' word, in roughly twenty minutes, they unstrapped from their seats and ducked into a series of slim, heavily cushioned pods, large enough only for one occupant each.

After they were situated in their drop pods, Ons set the gunship to autopilot and came to see them off. His rumbling, roaring voice could be heard and felt even over the noise of the flight.

"Third squad, remember your mission. You are prepared for this, and I expect, after you are successful, I will see each and every one of you at the exfiltration point." He was met with solemn nods. "All-Father watch over you all. Third squad, away!"

Ons walked down the line of pods, slapping a button outside each, triggering the doors to snap shut and the pods to drop from the *Wildfire* with a harsh, sucking sound.

"Five minutes, second squad!" Ons called out.

Kah clenched his teeth and gripped his locket tightly. Suddenly, the operation—his new life—was very real. A quarter of the Ashmakers were already gone, and his squad would deploy next. He felt a hand on his shoulder and looked over to see E giving him an easy grin. The Bay, like the rest of his squad, was dressed in a loose-fitting dropsuit, designed to fall behind enemy lines less conspicuously than a paratrooper. Then, he spoke, his voice sounding through the earpiece as clearly as if they were in a silent room.

"Jury, Pol, Kah, Nadd. You know the plan. It's a simple in-and-out. The only trick is that we don't leave anyone or anything behind us. Just make sure you drop in with the rest of the squad, okay? We don't want to waste time searching for anyone." E gave the squad a thumbs-up, but his yellow eyes rested firmly on Kah. "Relax! It'll be easy."

Replying with a faltering smile, Kah tried to control his pounding heart, running over the plan in his head.

"Second squad, prepare for drop-in!" Ons' voice appeared in Kah's ear and, as one, the squad unstrapped from their seats and stood up, walking toward the rear of the gunship where a heavy blast door awaited them. E gave the door a solid knock, then popped a smart salute toward the front of the shuttle, where Ons stood sentinel. In response, the door hissed loudly and slid open, revealing an empty bay waiting for second squad to enter. And, as soon as the final member of the squad stepped inside, the door slid shut again.

E walked in front of the team, offering each member a nod and a thumbs-up and demanding one in return before moving to the next. Then, his voice cut through the noise again. "Second squad, ready to roll."

A light flashed overhead, followed immediately by the opening of a great door at the rear of the shuttle, revealing the light of day outside.

Ons' voice appeared again in Kah's ear. "Second squad, you are clear to drop. I'll see you on the other side."

Turning to give his squad another casual smirk, E strapped a pair of goggles over his eyes, then leapt out the rear of the *Wildfire*. A moment later, Jury, then Nadd, then Pol followed. Kah's heart was beating so rapidly it felt like it would burst, but, with a deep breath, he steeled himself and ran out the back of the ship, into the open sky.

It was bright. *Really* bright. And as the *Wildfire* screamed away toward the horizon, Kah was left alone but for the fiery plumes of the clouds catching the morning sunlight. The air rushed past him as he plummeted toward their shining peaks. Would it hurt? What would they feel like? How far below them was the planet? Then, he saw the specks that were his squad mates disappear into the cloud cover. He was thinking too hard again. He knew what to do.

As he had been taught, Kah tucked his arms and legs together and dove, hurtling down to give chase. Just before hitting the clouds, he took a deep breath and screwed his eyes shut. Where he expected an impact, however, he received only a soft, persistent breath of cold moisture. Kah peeked an eye open and blinked in surprise at the sudden, encapsulating darkness. Relief flooded his breast. In darkness, there was safety, even plummeting, alone, through the shadows and toward the ground. Unfortunately, it was not to last, and as quickly as he'd reached the darkness, he was thrust once more into a vibrant world of harsh, unforgiving light.

Stretching as far as Kah's eyes could see in every direction, Caraby was cloaked in verdant forests veined by rivers which mirrored the bright blue of the sky. The air was so clear that even his untrained sight challenged the horizon, an impossibly great distance away, and he could see vast forests, thousands of meters below, blanketing most of that space. He'd never seen anything so wide, so open . . . so *exposed*.

Up here, anyone could see him. They already did. He could tell. The occupying hostiles already had him in their sights. He tried some evasive maneuvers, rolling and spinning through the air as he dropped through the atmosphere, but even if they missed him with their shots, they'd still know he was here. The mission had failed before they'd even touched the ground.

He'd killed them all.

"Kah, are you all right?" Colonel Ons' voice rumbled in his ear, breaking through his panic. "You're hyperventilating and your heart rate is elevated. You need to calm down."

The young Jaguar tried to take a slow, deep breath. Everything was fine. Nothing had gone wrong, yet. Like Nadd said, he just had to breathe. Just. Breathe.

He closed his eyes, muttering the prayer Sala had given him, inaudible over the rushing air, even to his own ears. *"Oh Lord of Veils and Keeper of Secrets, cloak me in darkness. Hide me from the eyes of mine foes, that I may return home unscathed and unafraid."*

After a few recitations, the ritual calmed his heart rate and he felt he had enough control to open his eyes again, repeating the prayer in his head as he scanned the surroundings. In the distance, he could see among the trees the muted grays of a large city, made miniscule by his altitude. His eyes followed one of the bare roads which cut through the trees from the city, tracing it behind his field of view until it opened into a broad, bare swatch of ground, split by a river and razed of its trees to make room for a large, fortified ziggurat. From the apex of that ziggurat, a massive structure of durasteel and cable thrust skyward, breaking through the clouds beyond the reach of Kah's eyes.

The tether.

Below him, a circle of green appeared as the dropsuit of one of his squad mates deployed. He focused in and aimed his body toward that target as a low alarm began to sound from his suit, alerting him that it would soon automatically deploy. As three more green circles appeared, he tried to position himself over them and over the clearing for which they were aiming. A final countdown began to play in his earpiece.

Kah splayed out his arms and legs and, as the countdown ended, loose membranes deployed in the spaces between his limbs, massively slowing his descent as he became a living parachute. Kah simply had to let the dropsuit do its work. As he drew nearer the ground, the membrane between his legs automatically retracted its own slack, dropping Kah's lower half below the rest of his body, and, with only minor discomfort, the dropsuit engaged its reverse thrusters and he landed softly on his boots.

"Touchdown, second squad." E's voice filled his ear the moment Kah's feet touched the ground and, as Kah began to shed the dropsuit, the captain trotted over, grasping him by his shoulders. "You okay, kiddo?"

Kah nodded, drawing rapid breaths of relief. "Yeah, yeah. It just felt really, um, *apparent*. I panicked a little, but I'm okay now."

Graver than Kah had ever heard him, E said, "Good. We all need you to be at your best right now. There's no room for mistakes on the ground, Kah."

Kah finished doffing his dropsuit, nodded, and swallowed. As he did, E collected the discarded dropsuit, rolled it up, and, in a peculiar motion, tucked the large bundle of fabric into the impossibly small space of his wristwatch, until the suit had disappeared entirely. As E gathered the remainder of the dropsuits into his watch, Kah looked around the small clearing at the rest of his squad mates. Each wore a nondescript set of workman's coveralls, except Nadd, who was decked out in woodland camouflage from his paws to the tips of his radar-dish ears.

Gathering what now appeared to be a motley work crew together in the high grass of the clearing, E addressed them all. "You're in the fight now. If any of you had second thoughts, it's too late to turn back. The only way off this planet for us is the *Wildfire* or a body bag. Remember your orders and your oaths. Protect your squad mates and yourself. The enemy will not hesitate." E never looked at Kah while he was speaking, but Kah felt the words were meant specifically for him. Everyone, however, joined the solemn nod. Seemingly satisfied, the Bay gave a quick nod and said, "Second squad, moving to rendezvous with transport."

"Copy, second squad," rumbled Ons' answer.

After receiving the go-ahead, E turned the face of his watch and, in a grotesque echo of stowing the dropsuits, reached inside an invisible space, his hand warping to fit, and drew out three rifles, which he passed to Jury, Pol, and himself, then a long, silenced sniper rifle for Nadd. Finally, he produced a suppressor and passed it to Kah. Everyone checked and loaded their weapons, and Kah attached the suppressor to the sidearm belted under his coveralls alongside an excess of knives. Satisfied, the squad began moving through the tall grass and into the forest.

Stepping out of the sunlight and into the shadow of the canopy, Kah was surprised by the instantaneous drop in temperature. If the planet was bathed in light all the time, shouldn't it be uniformly warm? Or was the atmosphere here not meant to trap and evenly distribute heat? Probably a design flaw. More important than the heat, however, were the massive plants surrounding them. The trees *were* as tall as buildings, and there were so many of them, with enough branches to completely blot out the sun. Kah ran his hand over the trunk of one and furrowed his brow. It wasn't smooth or shiny or soft, like the wood aboard the *Grace and Fanfare*. Instead, it was rough and abrasive, but chipped away remarkably easily. *Cheap* wood, he guessed.

His ears twitched, picking up the faintest crunching sound from somewhere on the other side of the tree.

"Hold up!" Kah fervently whispered. The squad halted its advance, and everyone dropped into whatever cover they could find, waiting.

After a tense, silent moment, E murmured, "What is it, Kah?"

"There's something over there. I can't see it, but I can hear it." Kah peered around the trunk of the tree, trying to pinpoint the indistinct sound.

"Move in. We'll cover you," E said, aiming his rifle toward the vicinity Kah had indicated.

Creeping through the undergrowth as silently as possible, Kah scanned the area, but couldn't make out anything useful. The sound was coming from a thick tangle of bushes, but there was no vantage point from which he could see into them. The bushes were more than large enough to conceal a fully-grown Ty'gjir, perhaps even two, so Kah recognized the danger in approaching. He kept his pistol fixed on the dense greenery, darting from shadow to shadow around it in a circle. If he had been seen by whoever was in the bushes, surely, they had lost him by now. He just needed to get them out.

As he considered his options, however, the bushes shook violently and a section of them rose from the ground, dropping clumps of dirt and foliage as thin roots snapped. Then, it quivered, dropping much of the remaining soil and revealing eyes, a neck, legs. Drawing itself to its full, three-meter height, stood a strange creature on six, stilt-like legs. It was covered in scales which looked and rustled in an impressive imitation of leaves and were colored in greens and browns on its back, but stark white on its belly and the underside of its long neck and thin head. It looked in Kah's direction with wide, black eyes, dappled as if with stars, and shook itself again, flaring out more leaf scales which covered the bush-like, webbing antlers which crowned its head.

"Stand down. It's just a kudar. Good catch, though, Kah. Keep sharp." E's voice whispered into Kah's ear, but he wasn't paying attention, instead hypnotized by the bizarre, alien thing before him. The kudar locked its deep, infinite eyes with Kah's as if searching for ill intent, then slowly, blithely loped away between the trees.

Jury nudged Kah from behind, scolding him in a hushed tone. "Sightseeing can wait. Come on!"

Kah's ears flushed with heat and he reassumed his tactical advance, crouching low and moving with the squad in quick, soft, short steps. They had no way of knowing how many hostiles would be in the area and their intelligence did not provide information on patrol routes outside the tether, so movement even this far out was a tense, quiet affair, and remained so for the following hour, as second squad stalked through the woods to the rendezvous point, where a transport awaited them.

When the forest opened up in front of them, it was to a dirt road which wound through the woods and out of sight to the left and right. Waiting beside the road was a dusty, wheeled vehicle with a covered storage bed. E approached cautiously, sweeping his rifle to the right while Pol mirrored him to the left and the rest of the squad scanned the surrounding trees for anyone who may be watching. Apparently content, E closed the distance to the transport and reached up under one of the wheel wells, retrieving a set of keys with numerous hanging charms and bangles.

"Pol, Kah, sweep the ride," E ordered.

As the rest of the group took up guard, Kah set about searching the underside of the vehicle for anything out of place. Any trackers, bugs, or explosives had no place aboard. This was to be a standard, unaltered transport. It was, however, well-used, which made searching for anything unusual fairly simple. Anything not caked in a thick layer of rust would be new and most likely did not belong. Luckily, there were no such objects hidden on the underside or in the engine compartment of the transport and, as Kah finished up, now covered in a fine coat of dust, Pol exited the vehicle and popped a thumbs-up. E gave the signal and the group piled in, with he and Pol sitting in the cab up front and everyone else seated under the dark, tenting cover of the storage bed, hidden among various power tools and construction equipment.

The transport creaked to life and bumped its way down the road, barely visible through the canvas flap at the rear of the storage bed. For several minutes, the shaking of the transport around Jury, Kah, and Nadd provided the only distraction from anticipation. The uncharacteristic silence was not lost on Jury, who cast a concerned glance over Kah and Nadd, their ears pinned back as they anxiously fiddled with their weapons in the dilapidated vehicle.

"Are you guys okay?" Already, the muscular Puma's voice had taken on the cool, soothing flavor she used when medically treating them during squad exercises.

Kah grimaced a flat smile and nodded.

Nadd, on the other hand, was honest. "Yeah, I'm kinda freaking out," he said, despite a toothy, chattering grin.

Jury offered him a sympathetic smile and nudged him from the crate which served as her seat. "What do you have to freak out about? You'll be far away from all the action."

"But what if I miss? What if you guys need me and I screw up?" Nadd's smile broke, and he looked as nervous as he felt.

"I haven't seen you miss yet," Kah cut in. "Why would you now, when there's more on the line?"

Nadd did not look reassured.

Indignant his encouragement did not produce the desired results, Kah furrowed his brow, glaring at the

Serval. "What? You think we can't take care of ourselves? That if you miss once, we're all going to die?"

"What? No, I don't think that!"

Jury picked up where Kah left off, teasing Nadd in mock offense. "You know, we are a team of very capable soldiers. The success of the mission isn't riding on you alone, you conceited little jerk. Despite what you may think, we can hold our own pretty well."

"Come on. You know I didn't mean that." Nadd pursed his lips and glared at his squad mates.

"Well, good! Because I'll take you on any day. You and your spicy food." Kah gently slapped Nadd's thigh, finally drawing a small smile from his friend.

"Okay, point taken, sorry! I'll just hide in my tree and you guys will be fine without any help from me." Nadd raised his hands in surrender and slyly smirked at his teammates.

"Well, we didn't say that," Jury coughed. "Just, you know, don't go getting a big head."

Nadd's large ears fanned up and forward as he assumed an earnest smile, teasing, "It's far too late for that."

As the transport sputtered to a stop, Kah gently squeezed Nadd's knee and looked up into his large, green eyes. Nadd simply grinned and clapped a hand on top of Kah's.

"I think this is where I get off," he chirped. "Wish me luck! I'll be watching over you."

The canvas flap at the back of the transport pulled open, revealing E, beckoning to Nadd. "Let's go. This is your stop, Nadd. Remember our rendezvous point and the backup should that one fail."

The Serval ducked out of the back of the transport, hopping down to the ground, and shot E a salute. He turned and flashed Kah a final smile, then hefted the rifle across his back and walked into the forest and out of sight.

"Kah, I'm taking your place back here. You and Pol are up front. Let's move," E barked. His voice carried none of the mirth or teasing tone on which Kah had grown to rely.

Kah ducked out of the back and proceeded to the passenger seat of the transport, hoisting himself up to the door and taking a seat beside Pol, who gave him a weather stare as he entered. Kah had never spent any time alone with the Kodkod. He didn't particularly like the Kodkod. Somehow, the mere prospect of being alone with him made Kah wish the impending conflict would come more swiftly. Regardless, Kah strapped in and nodded in greeting, unwittingly signaling Pol to hit the gas, sending the transport careening down the bumpy, unpaved road.

After several minutes of awkward silence, with no end in sight, Pol spoke up, his thin, whining voice pulling Kah from his thoughts. "Why are you here?"

Kah slowly turned and looked at him. "Pardon?"

"What are you doing here? You're a kid. You don't belong in the military," Pol sneered, shooting a dismissive look in Kah's direction.

Kah bristled, his pride somewhat bruised. "You know I'm as capable a soldier as any Ashmaker."

"Yeah, very impressive. But why would a kid join the military?"

Kah's shoulders fell. "My da wanted my brothers and me to get off world. The military was the best way."

Without passing Kah a glance, Pol raised his brows and snorted. "The *best* way? You'll be off Pinto'Neth, sure, but you'll never settle anywhere else." The Jaguar cocked his head quizzically as Pol continued. "Especially not a kid like you. You're going to do your prince proud, carrying out his will for your entire life. You'll probably die in battle, and your family, if any of them are left, will get a shiny, twenty-credit ribbon to remember you by. But at least they'll have that, because, after not seeing you for decades, they won't remember much else about you."

"Why would you say that?" The question snapped out of Kah before he could stop himself. Pol didn't know him. He couldn't hope to understand, yet his words cut Kah to the bone.

"Somebody has to tell you the truth," the Kodkod scoffed. "Have you heard E or the colonel talk about their families? No, because they don't have families. We don't get to get married, and we certainly don't get to have kids. All you get is what you started with, but after serving for twenty years with no contact from your brother, sister, mother, are they even family anymore?" He shrugged in answer to his own question.

An incredulous, widening smile took root on Kah's face while Pol complained. Why should he believe someone whose only service to others came on pain of death? And why did his words make Kah *so* angry?

Before he could stop himself, Kah snapped, "Maybe you don't get the chance to have a family because this is a sentence for you, not a job. I'm proud to do what I can to help my sector. *My* family is proud that I'm fighting for them. Maybe *yours* went no-contact because they were ashamed to have a murderer counted among them."

If Pol's short laugh was any indication, Kah's words hadn't hurt him as badly as he'd wanted. "Didn't figure you for one of the zealots, cub. I thought you were innocent. Stupid, but innocent. Maybe this is the right life for you."

Shortly thereafter, the trees opened into the multi-kilometer expanse which had been razed flat to make room for the tether. The road wound its way up the hill on which the tether was perched, stopping at a gate in the high, reinforced concrete wall which surrounded the facility. From the road, with no surrounding cover, Kah could easily spy a small booth before the gate, inside which stood two Ty'gjir, as well as another in the gatehouse atop the wall, and several more patrolling the battlements. Approaching on foot would have been suicide. Approaching *undisguised* would have been suicide.

E's voice buzzed inside his ear. "Second squad, moments from hostile contact."

"Copy, second squad. You are clear to proceed," Ons' voice calmly replied. Here, on the field of battle, the colonel sounded more relaxed than Kah had ever heard him aboard the *Litany*.

As the transport approached the gate, the two Ty'gjir stepped out of the booth and into the road, holding up their hands as a signal to stop, and Pol complied. The Ty'gjir, an Ocelot and a Wild, approached both sides of the transport, their claws hovering near the triggers of their laser rifles as they inspected Kah and Pol. In addition to their laser rifles, they both wore conventional armor vests, as well as unmarked, civilian clothing, as Ashmaker intelligence had suggested.

The male Wild approached Pol's window and eyed him warily. "What's your business?" he demanded in a thick, drawling accent.

In a perfect impression of the guard, Pol responded, "We got a runner out in the city this morning, said comms are down up here and y'all need 'em fixed."

"Who's the kid?"

Pol reached across the seat and slapped Kah in the chest. "This here's my apprentice. Hard worker. Sweet as honey, dumb as rocks."

Kah shot a glare at the little Kodkod but nodded to the soldiers, drawing a derisive chuckle from the Wild.

"*New* apprentice, from the look of it," the guard teased.

Pol grinned. "No, sir! Just a real slow learner."

The other guard, a female Ocelot, spoke up. "And what's in the back there?"

"Tools of the trade, ma'am. Everything we need for the job to go off without a hitch."

"Fine, fine. But you know how it is. Would y'all mind stepping out of the transport and walking us around to the back so we can give that a look?"

Pol shrugged, passing an easy nod to Kah, and both unhurriedly unstrapped themselves and opened their doors, not chancing any sudden movements, lest they test the reactivity of the soldiers' trigger fingers. As if to drive home the necessity of their caution, the guards aimed their rifles at the disguised Ashmakers, who raised their arms and slowly circled to the rear of the vehicle.

As she marched behind Kah, her rifle fixed on his back, the female guard asked, "What outfit did you say you were from?"

Without missing a beat, Pol called, "I didn't, ma'am, but we're from Simple Solution. 'For the most complicated problems, there's just one Simple Solution!'"

Pol was very quick. Kah wondered if he'd been given a script or if he was improvising.

"Don't think I've heard of it," the male guard said, shrugging. "Where's your shop?"

"Oh, way" — Pol waved a hand vaguely — "*way* downtown. It's a new location, near the old armory."

"Ah, I think I know the spot, sure."

Reaching the rear of the transport, the Kodkod walked directly to the canvas flap concealing E and Jury while Kah stood off to the side, each watched by one of the guards. But as Pol began to reach for it, the guard watching him chuckled grimly.

"See, the thing is, we already got a work crew out here an hour ago. Can't imagine why we'd need two."

Pol's tiny hand froze in midair for a moment, then he dropped both hands to his hips and turned around to face the guard, tapping his foot. "Are you telling me, boy, that you asked more than one crew to come out here?"

The guard flinched and aimed down his sights as Pol turned toward him, but the little Kodkod spit on the ground and shook his head, his wiry fur bristling, hardly acknowledging the guard or his rifle as he complained.

"We canceled a day of jobs for this rush order, and it was all for nothing?" He shot Kah an exasperated look. "You know who's going to be pissed about this? Cousin Nadd."

Pol's front was suddenly painted crimson as the Wild's head burst in a shower of bone and gore. The Ocelot jumped, startled at the horrid sound, and reeled around to see what had happened. In an instant, Kah was on her, a karambit sliding free of his sleeve as he pounced and drove the claw-like blade up and into the base of her skull, dropping her instantly. He breathed out once, hard, trying to rid himself of the tension, and wrenched the blade free of her skull. As he rose, her body settled, eyes to the sky — wide, frozen in an expression of terror, even as they reddened from the internal wound.

Kah stared, paralyzed, as the life fled her eyes, caught on the thread of destiny he had severed.

"Clear."

Pol's declaration ripped Kah out of his trance, and he looked over to see the Kodkod flicking his wrists, trying to shake off any loose guard. In a moment, the canvas flap on the back of the transport flew aside as E and Jury leapt out. E looked at the guards on the ground, then up to the gatehouse, where a tiny hole broken in the window was barely visible.

His large eyes darting around the area, assessing the situation, E muttered, "Good shooting, Nadd. Is the wall clear?"

"Yes, sir! The southwest wall is entirely clear of hostiles, as far as I can see," Nadd chirped through the earpiece. Kah knew his voice well. Its cheer was deliberate and strained.

E nodded, and, coldly, passed down his verdict. "Begin eliminating hostiles at your discretion. Ashmakers do not take prisoners and we do not leave survivors."

The cheer all but died in Nadd's voice, and Kah felt his pain as if it were his own. "Y-yes, sir."

"Second squad, armor up. Kah, we need this gate open. Get up there and make it happen." E jerked his chin up toward the gatehouse. Kah stepped out of his coveralls, revealing the black, close-fitting, flexible infiltrator armor he had been issued, while his squad mates donned heavier, less specialized battle gear which E had produced from his wristwatch.

Stepping forth, Kah examined the ten-meter-tall concrete walls. Once fine and smooth, they were now riddled with the pockmarks of small arms fire, likely from the recent assault by the current occupiers. That would certainly make the climbing easier.

"Kah," E murmured from behind him, thrusting a slender, black, enclosed helmet into the Jaguar's hands. "Don't forget this, and keep your head down up there." With nothing more to offer him, E gave Kah a somber nod and firm squeeze of the shoulder. "Get infiltrating, kiddo."

Drawing a deep breath, Kah pulled the helmet down over his head, attaching it with several snaps to the armor around his neck. It fit extremely well and, to his delight, he found could hear exactly as well with it on as he could without. Thank goodness. Despite his recent introduction to full-fledged sight, Kah remained highly dependent on his ears, and didn't want a helmet to deafen him to his surroundings.

Without a word, Kah pressed a switch on his wrist and, from the toes of his armored shoes, climbing spikes extended, mimicking his natural claws. The claws of his hands were already free and exposed, protruding from his gauntlets, and, with great haste, Kah scaled the damaged wall, using bullet holes as handholds, and slipped noiselessly over the ramparts. Not wasting any time, he ducked into the gatehouse, where more carnage awaited him.

Another of Nadd's targets, unrecognizable in its current state, was strewn across the rear walls of the room. Kah gritted his teeth and dug through the pockets of the creature, looking for the key which would allow him to open the gate. He growled in frustration as his initial search yielded no results but as he turned the body over, he found the key attached to a lanyard wrapped around the corpse's finger. Kah cut the lanyard with a claw and brought the key to the gatehouse control panel, inserting the key in the appropriate slot, then paused.

"Everybody ready?" he whispered to the empty room.

"We're good to go, Kah. Open her up," came E's response.

Turning the key, Kah was rewarded with a loud, low-pitched groan as the steel doors of the gate below began to slide open. He peeked out the front window, watching the doors inch apart. It would be a slow process. Hopefully Nadd had them covered. With that thought in mind, Kah rushed to the interior window of the gatehouse, looking over the complex.

The area inside the wall was mostly bare, open ground, like the terrain surrounding the outer walls, with the exception of a large, fully occupied airfield. The only other structure was the base of the tether, a great, tiered ziggurat with guards patrolling every level. Or, at least, they had been. As Kah watched, the patrolling occupiers soundlessly fell, the walls behind them blooming with red. Nadd was busy.

"We're through, Kah. Close the gate."

Snatching the key from the console to trigger the gate's close, Kah rushed down the gatehouse's interior stairwell, finding himself outside and beside his squad's transport. Jury beckoned him from the covered bed and he hopped aboard, ready to continue on to the tether. Instead of traveling directly to the ziggurat, however, the squad first wove its way to the airfield, where numerous freighters and shuttles stood idle.

From his seat in the back of the transport, Kah could barely make out the quiet whirring of moving parts and peeked out from under the cover, watching numerous tiny spheres drop from the vehicle and roll across the tarmac. He recognized the spheres as remotely controlled charges and, as they split up, each perfectly diverting course to a different craft, Kah knew Pol was at the helm. The Kodkod was a master at maneuvering the tiny, destructive devices. As each charge neared its target, it leapt up and magnetically secured itself to the aircraft, waiting only on Pol's command to detonate.

That objective accomplished, the transport rumbled away from the airfield and back toward the main entrance of the ziggurat, where two soldiers stood guard. As the transport pulled up, the sentries approached the vehicle, guns trained on the cab. Before giving them the chance to speak, Jury and Kah leaned their weapons outside the storage bed and fired several, quiet shots into the unsuspecting foe and bringing them down, the Ashmakers' silent rounds easily splitting their armor. Pol put the vehicle in reverse, parked it facing toward the gate, and second squad poured out, ready to breach the base itself.

Looking over one of the outer walls and into the distance, E asked, "What's the situation look like from there, Nadd?"

Nadd's answer came quickly, again in a false, chipper tone. "Everything looks good from here, Captain. I don't see any more hostiles on the exterior of the facility."

"Good job. Keep an eye on the tether to make sure nobody escapes. Kah, get that door open."

E nodded toward the ziggurat's entrance, secured, it appeared, by a local control panel. Trotting over, Kah examined the panel closely. No card readers or mechanical keys. This was locked purely by code. He could pull the panel and open the door by tampering with the electronics, but that might set off an alarm. So, for the sake of subtlety, Kah retrieved the slicer from his kit and went to work, attempting to digitally retrieve the passcode. Apparently an older lock with no scrambler, the door almost immediately surrendered a sequence of numbers — the last to have been entered, and the correct code. With a welcoming chime, the door began to open. Kah stepped aside as E raised his rifle, firing three, quick, quiet shots into the relative darkness of the base's interior, earning a muffled cry from the shadows.

Glancing at the rest of the team, the captain crept forward into the base, whispering, "Second squad, entering the complex. Let's move."

XII

"How did that make you feel?"

Killing people?

"Yes."

For a moment, sad.

"And then?"

Then, nothing.

"And how did you feel about that?"

About feeling nothing? I felt . . . it was appropriate. To help my people, those ones had to die. I couldn't be crippled by emotion.

"Why are your people more worthy of life than those Ty'gjir?"

Because those Ty'gjir were my enemies.

"We think you are hiding behind that answer."

If I am, you won't find me.

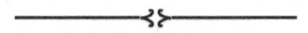

Kah darted down the empty, slate-tiled hallway far ahead of his squad, the soft soles of his infiltrator boots barely making a sound on the floor of the tether base. Approaching yet another closed door, he pressed the side of his helmet against it. Inside, two voices could be heard, chatting idly and painting a clear image of the room for Kah's now-honed echolocation.

"Thirty meters ahead of your position, closed door on the left, three hostiles inside," he whispered. "None on alert, two armed."

E's voice hummed in his other ear, "Copy. Keep moving toward the center."

Kah cast a glance down the hall to check the squad's progress. Behind him, E, Jury, and Pol swept through the rooms he had declared occupied, cleansing them of any hostile presence. The mission was to reach the central lift of the tether, planting charges along the way and clearing the structure of any enemies who may pose a threat to their safe withdrawal. Kah's stealth training and extremely acute senses had earned him the task of scouting ahead, warning the squad of any danger and marking occupied rooms for neutralization.

Silently padding up the hall toward a small alcove on the right, Kah paused to listen before entering. Nothing. Closing his eyes, Kah focused on the sound. A few light taps with his claws against the concrete wall was enough. Twelve separate stalls, one occupied. Twelve washbasins. A bathroom.

"Thirty-five meters ahead, bathroom on the right, no door. One occupant in the furthest stall," Kah murmured, paying closer heed to the rest of his surroundings, as well.

"Copy. We're falling behind. Clear any —" There were two quiet rips as E fired his suppressed laser rifle. "Clear any rooms with only one hostile yourself, but do not take unnecessary risks."

Just breathe. As long as Kah followed his orders, it would be over soon.

Checking his karambit and suppressed pistol, Kah silently crept into the bathroom and to the far end of the aisle of stalls, where his target sat alone and unsuspecting. Standing a distance back, he took aim at the door of the stall, but paused before pulling the trigger. The door was wood and the walls of the bathroom were tile. Despite his weapon's suppressor, gunfire in this room would be *very* loud. Resigned, Kah holstered the pistol and ducked into another stall, waiting for the occupant to finish their business and to emerge within reach of Kah's knife.

The flush of a toilet signaled the end of Kah's wait, and the stall door swung outward. Its occupant, a young, male Wild, strode lazily toward the sinks without a glance at his surroundings, unaware that Kah was already behind him, reaching for him. The Wild ran his hands under the faucet and looked up into the mirror, his eyes widening in shock as Kah whipped the karambit around his neck and tore the blade across his throat, cutting off the Wild's scream before it could leave his lips. Instead, he released a quiet, agonized gurgle and grasped at himself before he fell, writhing, to the tile floor, leaving Kah face to face with the mirror.

Covered head-to-toe in his infiltrator gear, he no longer recognized his reflection. The Kah in the mirror had changed. Sleek, high-tech armor concealed his black rosettes, hugging his body more tightly than any clothing he'd *choose* to wear, a trait allowed by the self-aligning micro-plates which were woven into the fiber of the armor. The bodysuit was equipped with numerous belts and straps to carry equipment, as well as hardpoints which locked into place over the inflexible parts of Kah's anatomy. The vaguely feline-shaped helmet completely enclosed his head, and his face was masked with a matte black ballistic shield, opaque from the outside, but translucent from within — perfect, but for a single drop of blood striping his vision crimson.

His eyes falling from the mirror, Kah looked down at the Wild and stepped back before the pool of Ty'gjir blood touched his boots. Wordlessly returning to the hall, he saw that second squad had nearly caught up to him, leaving a trail of open doors and discarded batteries in their wake. E greeted Kah with a nod as the Jaguar skulked out of the bathroom, then ducked into the room Kah had previously indicated, leaving him alone in the hall once more. Back to it.

An intersection lay ahead, and Kah checked all directions before advancing toward the tether's core. A few empty rooms. A few more with one, poor, lonely, doomed soul within. Over the next several minutes, Kah expended much of his ammunition as he silently emptied the facility of life, granting his squad the time they needed to catch up. There was no time for hesitation. As long as he followed his orders, this would be over soon. Hopefully.

He estimated they were close to the center of the facility now, but the way forward was barred by a large, reinforced door beyond another intersection. Spotting an access panel on the wall next to the door, Kah holstered his pistol, retrieved the slicer from his pocket, and proceeded forward to open it. As he approached the intersection, however, two Ty'gjir turned the corner, stopping as they caught sight of him. A beat. Kah blinked. How did he miss them? But his body was already moving. Sprinting to close the distance, he dropped the slicer to the ground and, as one of the hostiles raised his weapon, Kah launched himself from below, leading with both hands.

Catching the sentry's outstretched wrist, Kah twisted it back, then dragged the karambit in his right hand down the arm and ripped it through the crook of the guard's elbow, rendering the limb useless. Spinning around the disarmed guard without freeing his wrist, Kah aimed a hooking kick at the head of his next target, slapping his own wrist as his foot connected. At the moment of impact, the climbing spikes on his boots extended, burying themselves several centimeters into his enemy's skull before dragging that target to the floor with the Jaguar's momentum. Finally, Kah slashed across the back of the disarmed guard's neck and his head dropped limply forward, still cradling his useless arm, even in death.

Leaping back, adrenaline pounding through his veins, Kah waited for either enemy to rise, or retaliate. But as their blood spread across the floor, running in rivulets between the tiles, Kah realized that neither Ty'gjir would ever move again.

Despite himself, Kah felt his breast swell with pride. He'd overcome people who were actively trying to kill him. Retracting the climbing spikes, Kah turned to retrieve the dropped slicer, locking eyes with E as the captain exited a room. Seeing the corpses in the hall, E took on a grim smile before he and the other two continued up the hallway toward Kah, meeting him at the intersection as Kah inspected the slicer for damage. Jury and Pol peeked around the corners and signaled the all-clear, waving Kah across the juncture to the security panel and covering the halls while he worked.

The heavy door was significantly more resistant to incursion than the outer door, and Kah spent several minutes exploiting security vulnerabilities before it finally surrendered. Sliding open, it revealed a large, busy room, broken up by six columns arranged around its center, which was itself a large freight elevator. The columns contained smaller, personnel lifts and also acted as the rails on which the freight elevator rose all the way up the tether to the ODP. Arranged in concentric rings around the lifts was a legion of control consoles, nearly all of which were occupied, but few gave the opening door a passing glance.

Before any could sound the alarm, however, E nodded and second squad raised their weapons. In a storm of muffled hisses and light, they unloaded into the room, first picking off the clearly armed combatants before moving on to the fleeing or hiding hostiles. In under a minute, and with scant few returned shots, the large room lay smoking and empty of life.

Apparently satisfied that they were alone, E barked out, "Pol, get to work. Kah, Jury, secure the room and cover Pol while he sets the charges."

Before the smoke had settled, the squad had all but confirmed that everyone involved in the gunfight was eliminated. However, as Kah made to return to E and Pol at the freight elevator, his sensitive ears picked up a tiny intake of breath. Slowly, cautiously, he followed the sound to a terminal whose front panel had been removed, exposing bundles of wiring and mechanisms inside. Kah prowled around the terminal, looking for some sort of hatch but, sure enough, the only way inside was the removed front panel.

Even Kah would have some difficulty squeezing into the space. He considered his choices, but opted for the direct approach, giving the terminal a few knocks with the grip of his pistol and barking, as authoritatively as he could manage, "Come out. Now."

A firmer knock produced a small voice, saturated in fear. "Okay! Please don't shoot!" it said and, slowly, a pair of empty hands, followed by a thin set of orange-furred arms emerged from the terminal.

Keeping his pistol trained on the Ty'gjir as he disentangled himself from the bundles of wires inside the terminal, Kah saw dusty coveralls and realized, with growing dread, that this was one of the workers who had come from the nearby city to fix the tether's comms. He was a child, barely filling his oversized coveralls, tears trailing black down a dirty, frightened face. No, he wasn't a child. He was Kah's age. Maybe even a cycle or two older. But his eyes were innocent, bright—undarkened by the weight of a planet's worth of suffering.

His attention trained on the boy, Kah turned his head and shouted, "Capt—"

Rip!

Kah's eyes came to rest on the barrel of E's pistol, gently smoking, glowing with recent discharge as it aimed just over his shoulder. Kah followed its sightline back to the young Ty'gjir workman, who stared with a confused expression at his own smoking chest for a moment before he folded to the ground, clutching feebly at the blackened crater in his body. Through the lazy smoke, Kah saw E's eyes narrowed, his teeth bared against the reality of his own actions. He drifted to Kah and, for an instant, Kah thanked the gods for the inscrutable visor concealing his face, because he had no idea which expression his body chose to make its horror known.

Ashmakers don't take prisoners.

The boy looked to him with his brows steepled and his mouth hanging in an unspoken question, but Kah didn't know what to do. What was a mercy to someone so close to his end? Kneeling beside the dying boy, Kah placed a hand on his arm, if only to act as silent escort to the other side of the Veil. After an eternity, the boy's dry, popping wheezes stopped and, as he fell still, so, too, did the chamber, a peace broken only by the occasional curse from Pol, hard at work at the freight elevator.

"Kah?" He pulled his gaze from the boy, noticing Jury for the first time despite her nearness. Her bionic hand landed with unexpected tenderness on his shoulder as she looked sadly into his visor. "We need you at the elevator controls. Are you ready?"

Swallowing the lump in his throat, Kah nodded and stood up, leaving his sorrow in a smoking heap in his wake. At the console, he assumed control of the lifts, which Pol had loaded high with stacks of charges—just like the training exercises. The young Jaguar shot a thumbs-up in E's direction, unable to look at him, but couldn't escape the voice in his earpiece.

"Charges are set, second squad is awaiting the go-ahead to send up the payload."

"Copy, second squad," answered Ons. "First and third squad are clear. You are clear to deliver the payload."

E gestured to Pol, who flipped a toggle on a handheld remote and glanced over to Kah with his small, beady eyes.

"Kid, you're clear to send up the freight whenever. One minute later, send up the personnel elevators. Then, you've got two minutes to follow us out. We'll clear the way for you." Pol's tone was *gentle*. Despite his abrasiveness, it seemed, he did have some semblance of decency.

Offering his team a weak, invisible smile, Kah pointed to the door. "Get moving. I'll be right behind you."

Lingering behind the others, his lips still drawn into a pained sneer, E would not leave. But reasserting his pointed finger, Kah shooed him out and, wordlessly, second squad left their infiltrator behind. The instant they were out the door, Kah activated the freight elevator, sending it and its explosive payload up the tether to the ODP, crowded with unwary Ty'gjir — enemies, he reminded himself.

He was thinking too hard. He didn't want to think right now. He wanted to be back aboard the *Litany* and far away from here. As long as he followed his orders, he didn't have to think about anything, and it would be over soon. *Please*.

When the freight elevator loudly shrieked up the umbilical structure to the defense platform, one of the several reinforced doors leading into the chamber began to slide open and, through the narrow aperture, a fist-sized device tumbled into the room. Kah squinted at the thing for an instant before he recognized it as a flashbang grenade and dove behind the nearest console. He managed to avoid the flash entirely, but the impossibly loud bang focused what felt like all the sound in the universe to a single, high-pitched ringing which drowned Kah's senses, and he instinctively slapped his hands to the sides of his helmet, attempting to block out the debilitating noise.

After a few moments, Kah remembered that enemies would most likely follow the grenade, and he peeked out from behind his console, catching a glimpse of several armored hostiles examining the stack of charges on one of the elevators, before one caught sight of him and pointed, noiselessly shouting to his companions as they raised their weapons and began to fire, filling the air around Kah with flashes of silent red light. The infiltrator frantically attempted to unholster his pistol, blindly slapping the terminal in an attempt to send up the personnel elevators. It had been close enough to a minute. Probably.

A switch depressed and Kah watched as the lifts began to rocket up the tether. Now, he could go.

Peering around the console again, Kah caught one of the hostiles in the open and put a pair of shots in his chest, felling him. The rest ducked into cover and, seizing the opportunity, Kah sprinted for the door, followed closely by a hail of laser fire. Colliding with consoles and stumbling over downed bodies, Kah tripped his way to the exit, unable to properly orient himself without the use of his ears.

A great, shuddering groan tore through the facility, nearly throwing Kah to his knees in his stupor. Some of the bombs had detonated. Clenching his jaw, he struggled to his feet and started tearing wildly down the straight, coverless hallway, refusing to slow even as he fired a few shots over his shoulder, hopefully suppressing his foes to some extent. Then, something struck his shoulder, knocking him forward and onto the ground, while other laser rounds shredded the area all around him, ripping up tiles and concrete in bursts of razor-edged stone.

Desperately scrambling upright, he renewed the mad dash down the firing lane to the speck of light at the end of the tunnel. A muted buzz in his ear alerted him to some attempted communication from his squad but, still deafened, he couldn't make out the words. It could wait. It had to. Instead, he ducked, bobbed, and weaved, remembering the *crack* of concussion bolts exploding around him when he faced down his first enemy.

Another splash of heat across his lower back, but he remained standing, gritting his fangs against the pain. One shot exploded just ahead of him, destroying a series of light fixtures and bathing a stretch of the hallway in blessed shadow. Safety.

Through desperate breaths, Kah prayed. "*Oh Lord of Veils*" — a sudden burst of heat across the back of his neck — "*and Keeper of Secrets*" — a bolt skated across his arm — "*cloak me in darkness.*" He plunged into the area of shadow. The only light was the open doorway ahead and the red of lethal fire. "*Hide me from the eyes of mine foes*" — a beam shot by, just over his left shoulder, and he drove the last of his strength into his legs, tearing on with speed fueled by delirium — "*that I may return home unscathed and unafraid!*"

Kah dove through the open door, directly for a covered bed loaded with tools. He was only dimly aware of a disturbance in the air as a slug ripped past him and into the darkness of the base. Stretched horizontally, he flew between E and Jury, crashing none-too-gently into a trio of crates stacked in the back of the vehicle. Immediately interposing himself between Kah and the open door, E fired his rifle into the darkness, his mouth open wide, shouting something drowned by the ringing in Kah's ears.

Churning headlong from the base, the transport abandoned the dirt roads in favor of grass and bare fields, making directly for the outer walls and salvation just beyond. As E fired out the rear of the moving vehicle, Jury rushed to Kah, examining his back, shoulder, and arms. Apparently satisfied, she mouthed something to him, patted his armor down, and returned to the open canvas flap to crouch alongside E, providing covering fire for the exfiltration. Deaf to her ministrations, Kah's eyes followed her as she took aim, opening wide the canvas and offering him a clear view outside. A flash in the sky seized the Puma's attention and, eyes wide, she grabbed E, hurling him to the bed of the truck beside Kah, just as an enormous, flaming mass impacted the world outside.

Displaced air exploded over the vehicle, carrying with it dust, stone, and steel, as well as the titanic blast of the collision. Carried by the force of the shockwave, the transport's rear wheels leapt off the ground and, after an instant of serene weightlessness, the vehicle found the outer gate, dashing its inhabitants against each other and the equipment in the back. Blind as a cub and shaken from his senses, Kah felt a feeble slapping against his helmet and pawed back, his claws catching only the billowing tatters of all that remained of the canvas canopy which used to shade the truck's bed.

A face eclipsed the burgeoning view — E, who grabbed Kah by the shoulders and shook him roughly, shouting, " — and open the gate!"

Addled by the surrounding cataclysm, Kah cocked his head, earning a firmer slap across the helmet.

"Come on, kiddo! Get up there and open the gate!" E pointed somewhere behind Kah's head. The gatehouse.

"Yes — yes, sir!" Struggling to his feet, Kah limped for the entrance to the gatehouse while E dug through the rubble, trying to free Jury's pinned right side. Pol was invisible, trapped in the entombed cab, but the captain would see to him. Kah put on a burst of speed as he entered the gatehouse and mounted the stairs three at a time until he stood, once again, at the control terminal. He turned the key to open the gate and chanced a look out the window to check the tether, but was frozen by the spectacle before him.

The sky was on fire.

The bright blue of the early afternoon had been replaced by harsh, bloody reds and oranges as untold numbers of blazing masses streaked down around the collapsing tether to ignite Caraby's great forests. The terrain around the ziggurat had split asunder as if cracked by the hand of an angry god, with more ruptures rapidly appearing, burning craters joining with each other in a sea of flames, hungry for ever more world-bound debris.

They needed to leave. Now.

Kah virtually threw himself down the stairway on his way back to the vehicle. E had taken the wheel while Pol sat in the rear, nursing a gruesome head wound and staring back toward the tether through a curtain of his own blood. An unnaturally twisted prosthetic hanging limply at her side and dribbling a gray foam marked the only indication that Jury had felt the explosion, her head cool and eyes scalpel-sharp as she dressed Pol's injuries, one-handed.

Kah leapt into the cab of the vehicle next to E and stamped his foot on the steel, shouting, "Go, E! Get us out of here!"

In a final, heroic effort, the abused transport spluttered to life on protesting wheels and groaned its way out the gate while E answered, his voice clear to Kah's recovering ears, "Second squad, three minutes from extraction point. Prepare for immediate departure."

Colonel Ons' voice rumbled through what remained of the ringing. "Copy, second squad, we are here and eager to see your smiling faces. Quite a show you've put on."

"We have a flair for the dramatic, sir," came E's humorless reply.

In spite of the thunderous crackling of wildfire around them and the occasional bit of falling conflagration, the bumpy drive was strangely peaceful—the world and all its troubles receding away from the cab of the jostling truck. More for some than others it seemed, as, after a minute of Kah's terse company, E yanked the earpiece out of his small, round ear, shooting a glance at the Jaguar.

Shaking his head, he released a wracking, tattered breath. "I couldn't let you to make that choice, Kah."

Kah only stared, sidelong, at his captain, his mentor. His friend.

"The kid in there. He was going to die. He *had* to die. That's our mission. Ashmakers don't take prisoners and we don't leave survivors." E's tone sounded more like he was trying to convince himself than he was Kah. "We couldn't let him go and *you*—" The captain stopped himself, his mouth closing in a hard line. "You can't disregard orders. So, I took the choice from you. Easy. There was nothing you could have done to stop me," he continued, arguing with nobody. "At least this way he didn't suffer long."

"Yes, sir." Kah's mumble could barely be heard over the sputtering engine.

"I've shouldered my fair share of guilt and I'm sure I'm due for more, but I won't be guilty of that," the Bay sighed. "I won't believe your blood's that cold. Not just yet. If I'm sacrificing my soul to stay ignorant, so be it, but . . . but I needed to save *somebody* today."

The conspiratorial whispering of the fire filled the cab as Kah carefully chose his words. "Then, thank you for saving me. I hope I . . . I *won't* disappoint you."

As he replaced his earpiece, E pulled the truck off the road, rushing through forest which hadn't yet been caught in the blaze and out into a clearing. He managed a tired version of his signature smirk, saying, "See that you don't, kiddo. I don't want to have to kick your ass."

There, in the tall grass, waited a slim, camouflaged figure with radar-dish ears, waving his arms excitedly. Nadd had beaten them here, thank Day.

Pulling the transport to a stop, E yelled, "Second squad! Pile out! Let's get out of here!"

On cue, five cables dropped from an unseen point above. At the end of each cable was an ascender and, in mere moments, the members of second squad hooked themselves in and raced skyward through the smoke and heat to where the *Wildfire* lay in wait, hovering among the clouds. As they arrived aboard the gunship, Captains Sorna and Gray unhooked each of them from their ascenders, ushering them into the interior of the craft. Soot-stained and exhausted, second squad gathered in the troop bay of the gunship as it screamed through the atmosphere and away from the disintegrating tether.

But before they were out of sight, Pol gave a grim chuckle through his curtain of blood, drew a remote from his bandolier, and flipped a switch. In answer, numerous vast bubbles of white and blue light expanded from within the ziggurat, joining together as they touched into one, massive sphere. Then, without a sound, the sphere collapsed on itself, crushing everything it had contained into a single, tiny point. Where the ziggurat had once stood, there was now only a massive, perfectly circular crater. If anything in or around the tether had survived the falling sky, it certainly hadn't survived whatever that was.

He was certain he would be impressed if he weren't so tired, but Kah's eyes were shockingly heavy, his head hurt, and all he wanted was to sleep. No sooner had he entertained the thought than, held securely by his straps and tucked safely between his comrades, Kah's consciousness began to drift into the ether.

XIII

"Are you aware of how reports portrayed these events in the months following the operation?"

Yes.

"And what do say to that? Kah?"

The reports were probably truer than they realized. Or I realized.

"And, despite this, your sights were still set on saving your homeworld?"

Correct.

"How many people would have to die to satisfy your delusions?"

My delusions?

"This absurd notion that you could be some kind of he — Forgive us. Try to ignore that."

Very well.

"Why don't we move on?"

"Kah . . . Wake up, lazy!"

Kah cracked open his eyes, a hazy silhouette taking the welcome shape of Jury, leaning very close to him. Drawing a ragged breath, he found that the effort produced a strange hiss, prompting him to open his eyes wide, and saw that he had a plastic mask strapped over the end of his muzzle, funneling oxygen directly into his nose and mouth.

"What happened?" he groaned, his voice a cracking whisper.

Checking various readouts on her datapad, Jury shot him a sympathetic smile. "You passed out on the *Wildfire*. We didn't notice until the colonel's debrief on the way home. Nadd said you weren't quite as talkative as usual." She gave him a wry smile. "It looks like your armor's filter was damaged during the operation, and you were stuck breathing discharge for a while. Luckily, he noticed before anything too serious happened, and we purged it from your system. You should be back to normal, right as rain, in just a couple hours."

Trying to clear his vision, Kah blinked, and saw that he was covered by a thin sheet on a medical cot. He was safe at last, he thought, sinking into the bed. But a niggling thought soon wormed its way into his brain and his eyes snapped open before he wrenched the sheet off his body.

"Oh, thank the gods," he sighed in relief. Jury's eyes widened at the curious display and he gestured at himself, dressed only in his underclothes after his armor had been removed. "No catheter!"

She snorted, laughing into a plain, purely functional prosthetic hand—a replacement for the one she usually wore. "Uh, no. You've been out, oh, forty minutes. I didn't feel a catheter was medically indicated," she teased, cautiously manipulating his neck. "Besides the smoke inhalation, you did take a few gunshots. Luckily, our armor is pretty solid, so you came out of it with nothing but a few burns that won't even leave scars. The blisters will be pretty annoying for a while."

Kah gingerly prodded his shoulder with a small wince. The fur seemed to be undamaged, as far as he could tell, but he had obvious bubbling of the scorched flesh beneath. Scowling, he asked, "So, when am I allowed to move?"

She shrugged, turning away as she checked other readouts. "Now, if you feel up to it. Your oxygen saturation is good. Your toxin levels are low. If you want to move about on your own, I certainly won't stop you."

Permission granted, Kah sat up and removed the uncomfortable mask from his muzzle, working his jaw a bit. He made a mental note to avoid wearing masks in the future before he flung his legs over the edge of the bed and hopped down to the cool tile floor. Approaching the medic from behind, he threw his arms around her, hugging her tightly.

"Thanks, Jury, for saving me," he muttered, smiling.

Jury flinched at the sudden embrace and looked under her arm at Kah. A tiny chuckle slipped her lips.

"I didn't peg you as a hugger, Sergeant," she teased, but brought her prosthetic arm down and around him, squeezing the young Jaguar against her side. "But I'm busy. Lots of clerical work. Get out of here," she ordered, still grinning.

Popping a grateful salute, Kah padded across the floor to the medical bay's exit. As he opened the door, a dull roar of conversation burst through the threshold, welcoming him to the Ashmaker common room. Most of the Ashmakers were present and enjoying a state of rare informality, even for the bizarre assembly, lounging around the seating area wearing only underwear or civilian garb, raising their drinks to each other in a train of unceasing toasts.

One of his comrades from another squad, a Lion called Kraer, noticed Kah enter and raised his drink, calling, "'Eyyy!"

The rest of the Ashmakers quickly took up the cry, raising their drinks and echoing him as any hope of a subtle entrance vanished. Kah felt himself blush at the uniform attention and flashed what he hoped was a nonchalant wave, before Nall tripped up to him, grinning from ear to ear, and thrust a bottle into his hand.

"Good morning, shunshine! E and Nadd've been telling us all about what an ass-kickin' ass-kicker you are! Who would've guessed?" Nall said, his words slurred by an atypical slowness.

Briefly concerned that Nall might have suffered a head injury, the Jaguar soon detected the sharp perfume of liquor on his breath. Rolling his eyes, Kah gently pushed Nall out of smelling range, but E caught the stumbling Serval against himself, relieving Kah of the bottle.

"None of that for you, kiddo. We know how you get." With an easy wink, E replaced the bottle he had taken with an aluminum canister of the same bubbly beverage Kah had used to temper the spicy Odaith food on his first night aboard the *Litany*.

The Jaguar smiled and opened the can, nodding his thanks. "Where's everyone else?" he asked, his voice low. "It looks like we're missing a few."

To his surprise, E's teasing smirk bloomed into a wide and relieved grin as he answered, "It's not what you think. Jury and the other medics are finishing some paperwork. Some of the others, like Pol, are in surgery for their injuries, but nothing too serious. Everyone made it home. Oh, and Ons is talking to the admiral. They should be here soon."

Kah slumped his shoulders with a deep sigh, freeing tension he hadn't realized he still carried, and joined his comrades, sitting between Nadd and Nall as everyone swapped exciting stories of their missions. It seemed no other squad could quite match the thrill of fleeing the falling tether, however, which bolstered Kah's ego. He wondered, though—had the kudar escaped the inferno? As that small, sour thought wriggled into Kah's skull, the door to the Ashmaker quarters opened and Ons ducked in, followed by Admiral Achaera'fra.

The colonel snapped to attention and roared, "Admiral on deck!" bringing all conversation to an abrupt end as the Ashmakers leapt to mimic the colonel's posture.

"This room is now secure," remarked the automated alert from overhead as Admiral Achaera'fra approached the task force. She paced up and down the line of soldiers several times, a bemused half-smile playing on her lips as she assessed them.

"Ashmaker." Her low, rasping voice filled the room, commanding reverence. "Today, together, we have struck the first blow of retaliation against our enemy, the traitor prince, Sol'taris. Each of you performed above and beyond the call of duty and faithfully carried out your mission. I am grateful to all of you for your faith and for your loyalty to our cause. What you have done here today will be felt for the rest of the war." She halted, allowing the silence to lend gravity to her words. "You have reduced Caraby, a major resupply point for the enemy navy and a thorn in our side since it was claimed by their fleet, to an indefensible, tactically worthless rock. No more will the traitor princes use our own worlds to recuperate before they dig their treacherous hooks deeper into Dal territory. By choking off this supply point, you have effectively trimmed Prince Sol'taris' claws, rendering the resources he poured into Caraby completely wasted."

A ripple of pride swept through the Ashmaker ranks, shoulders squaring and chests swelling as the admiral celebrated their triumph, idly clicking her raised claws together.

"The interior worlds of the Dal territory will rest easier with heroes like you protecting them, though they may never know who you are or what exactly you have done for them. You may never attain the kind of glory or celebrity that some shall, but know that High Command, myself among them, deeply honors you for your actions and sacrifices. I am proud of you all. Celebrate and sleep well tonight. Your comrades will take care of the rest. Thank you, Ashmaker!"

A proud salute crashed her right fist to her left epaulette, and, with a chorus of thuds, the Ashmakers echoed her motion, crying in unison, "Thank you, Admiral!"

"Dismissed!"

The majority of the Ashmakers returned to their revelry with a renewed fervor. Kah, however, quietly slipped from his spot between the twins and edged closer to the admiral, now speaking privately with Ons and turned away from the group. She was happy. He had performed well. This seemed the perfect opportunity to speak with her about his homeworld. He attempted to wait casually but, as his superior officers' conversation stretched into minutes, his confidence in his initial estimation withered, and he nervously bounced in place, chewing his lip, trying to be close enough to be noticed, but not so close that he appeared insistent. It was a delicate balance. He didn't know for certain, but it felt like he failed spectacularly in the effort, an impression further cemented when he heard the admiral breathe a deep sigh before turning to look directly at him.

"Yes, Sergeant?"

Kah saluted, taking a long step to close the distance between them, stammering, "Admiral, Colonel, I—"

"Colonel Ons'erak told me that you were instrumental in the destruction of the tether and the orbital defense platform, Sergeant. You've done me, your family, and your world proud. It would appear my judgment of you was well-founded." She smiled—*triumphantly*. A triumph directed largely at the frowning colonel.

Heat rushed to Kah's ears and he saluted again, stammering, "Th-thank you, ma'am! It is my honor to serve!"

"It pleases me to hear that," she began. "But I suspect you are not here to tell me as much. What can I do for you?"

Working up his nerve, he took another step forward. Why was he still only in his underwear? "Admiral, uh, ma'am. I'm glad you mentioned my—my homeworld. That's what I want to talk to you about."

"Yes, Pinto'Neth," she cut in. "I admit I don't know much about the place, aside from its nordium export. Say what's on your mind."

"Admiral, I had hoped that, if I performed my duties well enough, perhaps I might earn your favor, and I could ask you for help . . ." Kah's voice trailed off. This was harder than he expected, and the piercing gazes of the admiral and the colonel made it no easier.

"For help? What help? Spit it out, Ashmaker," the colonel demanded.

Kah steeled himself and declared, perhaps too loudly, "Admiral, Colonel, everyone who lives on Pinto'Neth is dying. All we do is mine nordium to export to the territory, and we don't have proper safety equipment to do it. All the miners get sick. We don't have enough medicine to treat the miners alone, let alone the members of their families who catch it. We don't have food. We don't have sports. We don't even have *light*."

Admiral Achaera'fra scowled, glancing at Ons, but the dam on Kah's tongue had broken and his words spilled forth, uncontrolled.

"*Everything* there is poisonous. Our schools only teach us how to keep our heads down and be better miners. They're not even allowed to tell us they're sending us to *die*. The instructors know it's wrong, but the ones who complain don't last long. The best they can do is tell us to join the baron's fleet, to run away from our families and our home." Pointing around the room at the wide-eyed onlookers, Kah's eyes filled with tears. "The oldest people I've ever known are standing in this room—*decades* older than my da was when he was bedridden for the last time.

It's like they don't want us living long enough to know better. But now I'm an Ashmaker, and I know better. I know what food should be. I know that I should know my gran and granda. I know what I look like. I know how Ty'gjir *should* live, and I know that *nobody* on Pinto'Neth lives that way!"

Realizing he was shouting in an otherwise quiet room, Kah dropped his hands to his sides, embarrassed, and stared at the floor, watching drops fall from his face to spatter against the tile. "Please, help us . . ."

There was a long period of quiet.

"Colonel, what do you know about this?" the admiral asked.

Ons shook his head, his one eye wide, and answered, "He's never said anything about this to me. I don't think I've ever heard him say this much about anything."

Kah tried to swallow the lump in his throat and sniffed, raising his eyes. Before he could, however, a hand appeared on his shoulder. It belonged to the admiral, who looked at him sternly, her mouth set.

"I confess my ignorance to your plight. I will have to look into it further, but, if what you say is true, I'll do what I can to help you and your people. *Our* people."

Achaera'fra's unyielding gaze demanded his, pouring her steely surety into him, and Kah knew, in that moment, that he was on the right path. With a crisp salute, the admiral smirked and turned on her heel, never entertaining a backward glance as she declared. "Rest now, Sergeant. You've done good work today. *I* have an invasion to oversee, but you may celebrate the first of our many victories together."

With that, Admiral Achaera'fra swept out of the Ashmaker quarters, leaving Kah and his comrades to follow her command and to spend the remainder of the evening in relaxation and celebration. A few of the more curious Ashmakers interrogated Kah about life on his home but, even as he conveyed the horrid conditions of his homeworld, he felt like a great weight was lifted from his shoulders. Admiral Achaera'fra was looking into it. She would help them.

Soon, however, the Ashmakers collectively retired as, one by one, exhaustion took them, and they returned to their bunks. Wishing Kah a fond goodnight, Nadd climbed up into his bed, leaving Kah on the bottom bunk to replay in his head the long day behind him. Everything had gone according to plan. All the Ashmakers had returned home, with no life-threatening injuries. The admiral was going to help his people when she learned the truth about his home.

He could finally rest easy.

Kah woke up. It was silent in his room. Why did that bother him? Silence was nice . . .

His eyes opened. It was never silent in his room. Nadd's hurricane of snores made sure of that. Kah clicked his claws, painting an empty bed in echoes. Checking the time, the young Jaguar sniffed and sat up, rubbing his eyes and releasing a loud yawn. As long as he'd been here, Nadd had never left their room during the night. It could be an exception brought about by an excess of festive food and drink, but something could also be wrong. Kah's mushrooming paranoia quickly convinced him there was no harm in checking.

Swinging his legs out of bed, Kah crept out of the room. Below, he could hear the sounds of a shower running in the communal bathroom. That was strange in and of itself. It was far later than his comrades usually bathed. Kah wandered down the stairs and into the lavatory, listening closely. He didn't hear any movement beyond the hiss of the falling water, but he did hear that there was nothing interrupting its flow. On tip-toe, Kah padded down the row of stalls to the showers. Still, no sound other than the running water.

He approached the single occupied booth and spoke, loudly enough to be heard over the shower. "Nadd? Are you in there?" No answer. "Are you all right?"

A quiet, uneven exhalation, but nothing more. Kah cocked his head, then knelt to peek under the curtain. Inside, he saw a gold, black-spotted shape curled up on the floor. It was Nadd.

His heart pounding, Kah squared his shoulders, grasped the curtain, and called, "I'm coming in!"

Nadd's ears shot up and, from the wet tile floor, he looked over his shoulder and glared at the intruder, covering his body. "W-what the fuck, Kah?! Get out!"

Kah immediately closed the curtain again, his ears pinning back. "Sorry, you didn't answer me! I thought you might be hurt or something."

"Well, I'm not, so go away," Nadd snapped, his voice catching.

Instinctively, Kah began to retreat, but concern mired his feet. Instead, he approached the curtain again and slowly sank to the ground, sitting with his back against the wall of the booth. He said nothing for a while, and, together, he and Nadd rested in the steam, separated only by a plastic sheet as the water tapped a rapid staccato on the tile floor.

A few minutes later, Nadd spoke up, asking, "Why are you still out there?"

Kah's answer tumbled swiftly from his muzzle. "I'm worried about you. You don't usually shower in the middle of the night. What were you doing?" Feeling foolish, Kah leaned his head against the wall. "I just didn't want you to be hurt."

"I'm not hurt. You don't have to check on me."

"I want to," Kah said. "Nobody knew I was suffocating on the way back to the *Litany*, not even me. Not until *you* checked on me."

"Would it make you feel better to see that I'm not hurt?" Nadd sighed.

"Yes."

"Oh." There was a brief pause. "Then, I guess, come in?"

Without standing, Kah opened the curtain again and scooted across the tiles into the booth alongside Nadd, who had situated himself against a wall, letting the shower water rain over him. Indeed, he did appear uninjured. That, at least, was a relief. They stewed in the quiet, the hot spray soaking their fur and running off them in small rivulets. Kah didn't mind that his nightclothes were saturated with the shower water. He could dry them later. For now, he wanted to be beside his friend.

Eventually, Kah tentatively asked, "Do you want to talk about it?"

Though the water ran down Nadd's face, it couldn't hide the unspent sorrow in his eyes. The Serval took a deep breath and muttered, "Thirty-one."

"What?"

"That's the number of people I killed today, Kah." Counterfeit mirth tainted his voice as he asked, "How about you?"

Kah considered for a moment. "I—I don't know. A bunch on the ground. More, from the bombs I sent up to the defense platform. Dozens, maybe hundreds, depending on how many people were aboard."

Nadd wrapped his arms around his knees, blankly staring ahead. "Have you thought about them much?"

If he hadn't before, Kah was certainly thinking about them now, but it didn't dull his conviction. "I don't want to think much about them. I—I knew what I needed to do. Thinking about them as obstacles instead of people helped me to, sort of, shut off." He froze. "But I couldn't help but think of that worker as . . . well, a kid. E saw that, I think, and made the choice before I had to."

"He told me. I'm glad. I don't know if I could still look at you as the same cute guy who doesn't know anything about anything if you'd killed a cub. A cub who wasn't even armed."

A wince, less from the scalding water stinging his pinned ears and more for the painful truth. "I killed a lot of people today, Nadd."

Tilting his face up to the falling water, Nadd closed his eyes. "At least some of yours got to fight back. None of mine even knew they were about to die. They were just alive one second and"—he attempted to snap his fingers, but they merely squeaked off each other in the moisture— "dead the next. Everyone else spent today feeling like a hero. I felt like a coward. You all stared down death and won. My life was never even in danger."

Placing a hand over Nadd's and entwining their fingers, Kah murmured, "I'm glad your life wasn't in danger. I felt a lot better knowing you were safe."

A pregnant silence passed between them before Nadd, at last, looked over at him and smiled sadly. "You really don't know anything about anything, do you?"

Kah blinked. "What?"

In answer, Nadd stood up, offering a hand to him. "Doesn't matter. Let's see if the mess hall is open. I could use some grub."

Pulling Kah to his feet, Nadd gave him a quick, wet hug, before he shut off the water and exited the shower, retrieving a pair of towels and bathrobes from the communal rack. The conversation came easier as they dried off and, wrapped in their robes, made their way to the mess hall. Despite the limited selection available to them at the time of night, Kah grinned and took Nadd by the hand, dragging him across the empty hall.

Seeing their destination, Nadd scoffed incredulously. "My, someone *is* feeling brave tonight!"

After a short wait for his 'ome-cooked meal, Kah stared down a dish of white, fibrous meat stewing in orange sauce. He had seen battle. He had survived an apocalypse. By the gods, he could handle some spicy food. Easily popping slices of his own dish into his mouth as he watched Kah nervously prod at his, Nadd wore an amused smile.

"Come on, brave hero. You can do it." Nadd half-lidded his large, green eyes, leaning forward on his elbows as he teased the young Jaguar.

"I-I know I can! Just gimme a second," Kah huffed, trying to decide the optimal angle of attack.

After a few more moments of Kah's strategic hesitation, Nadd whispered, "You know, I've seen Captain Gray eat two of these in one sitting."

Kah scowled as Nadd needled his pride. Spurred by the challenge, he lifted the dish high and spooned its entire contents into his mouth, trying to down it as quickly as possible.

Whistling softly, Nadd's eyes opened wide. "Man, you are going to regret that so hard," he chuckled.

Plastering a Thurv-like frown on his face, Kah tried not to let his impending discomfort show. Beads of sweat began to form on his brow and his eyes began to water, but even minutes later, with tears and sweat running down his face, he would not allow his expression to change. Apparently, it made quite a sight, because Nadd could not stop laughing at the suffering Jaguar, whose folded arms matched his stubbornly still visage, despite his feverishly tapping toes. Eventually, Nadd stood up, wiping tears of mirth from his eyes, and told Kah he would return in a few minutes to rescue him.

Through his tears, Kah stared at the smiling, returned Serval, dressed in a plush bathrobe, standing across the table and holding out a dish of blessed, merciful ice cream for him. For the first time, in that tear-blurred moment, Kah realized how beautiful Nadd was. Born onto a world that reviled him, Nadd was chosen to take life on behalf of his people and to give his in order to protect them. And somehow, he accepted his fate with a smile, growing into a man who offered levity to his comrades and laughter to his friends, who felt deep pain at the deaths of his enemies, when even his homeworld wouldn't mourn him.

Nadd was who Kah wished he could be.

Sharing in the Serval's infectious joy, Kah couldn't maintain his grimace and shoveled ice cream down his throat, beaming and laughing as the Serval playfully mocked him. With Nadd's help, Kah's suffering came to an end, but neither was yet willing to end the night. Instead, the two made their way to an aft viewport to share a glimpse of the sea of stars. When they turned the corner to the star-lounge, however, they froze in their tracks.

Spacecraft of all sizes poured out of the *Litany of Ash*, stretching in an unbroken train to Caraby's surface, where still smaller craft swarmed forth, webbing like the disembodied vasculature of a machine god across the planet's surface. The *Litany* loomed over the former site of the tether and, even now, pieces of the defense platform rained down through the atmosphere to the world below, carving through any clouds which hadn't yet fled the heat. Below, a thin, angry, orange line spread slowly outward from the site of the tether, consuming the green forests of Caraby and leaving only a massive, necrotic wound of black and gray in its wake.

Instinctively pulling himself against Nadd as the two stared, transfixed, at the raw devastation below, Kah finally realized exactly what it meant to be an Ashmaker.

———————⟨⟩———————

"Kah? Are you all right?"

Yes. I just – I have a headache.

"Well, you have had a long, difficult day. This can't be easy for you."

It isn't. I'm so . . . so tired.

"Why don't you rest now, sweetheart? We can pick up again tomorrow."

I'll do that. Thank you, Ma.

END TESTIMONY SESSION 1

— Patron Acknowledgments —

————————⟨⟩————————

https://www.patreon.com/joshswords

Thank you all for trusting me with you patronage. I hope this story gives you enough of a taste to stick around for the rest of the series!

- Ace_Wuffamute
- Alek Hagopian
- Danielle Hill
- Dion King
- Jacob Muccio
- Jamie De La Garza
- Jacob King
- Karen McHugh
- Noreen King
- SnowBlueHusky
- Tarah LP